FINALE

THOMAS MALLON

FINALE

A Novel of the Reagan Years

PANTHEON BOOKS, NEW YORK

Copyright © 2015 by Thomas Mallon

All rights reserved. Published in the United States by Pantheon Books,
a division of Penguin Random House LLC, New York, and distributed in
Canada by Random House of Canada, a division of Random House Ltd., Toronto.

Pantheon Books and colophon are registered trademarks of
Penguin Random House LLC.

A portion of the prologue first appeared in *The New Republic* as
"The Captive of San Clemente" (December 31, 2012).

Library of Congress Cataloging-in-Publication Data
Mallon, Thomas, [date]
Finale : a novel / Thomas Mallon.
pages ; cm
ISBN 978-0-307-90792-9 (hardcover : acid-free paper).
ISBN 978-0-307-90793-6 (eBook).
1. Reagan, Ronald—Fiction. 2. Presidents—United States—Fiction.
3. United States—History—20th century—Fiction. 4. Political
fiction. I. Title.
PS3563.A43157F56 2015   813'.54—dc23   2014044333

www.pantheonbooks.com

Jacket photograph by Mike Sargent / AFP / Getty Images
Jacket design by Oliver Munday

Printed in the United States of America
First Edition
2 4 6 8 9 7 5 3 1

In memory of Scott Carpenter

—and for Rene, Tom, and Kris

Blow the dust off the clock. Your watches are behind the times. Throw open the heavy curtains which are so dear to you—you do not even suspect that the day has already dawned outside.

—*Aleksandr Solzhenitsyn*

CAST OF CHARACTERS

(Those with names in quotation marks are entirely fictional.)

Antony Acland: British ambassador to the United States

Leonore ("Lee") Annenberg: first chief of protocol of the United States under President Reagan; wife of Walter Annenberg

Walter Annenberg: publisher and philanthropist; former U.S. ambassador to the United Kingdom

Marion S. Barry, Jr.: mayor of the District of Columbia

Shirley Temple Black: child film star and diplomat; chief of protocol of the United States under President Ford

Betsy Bloomingdale: widow of businessman Alfred Bloomingdale and friend of Nancy Reagan

Lindy Boggs: U.S. congresswoman (D-LA)

J. Carter Brown III: director of the National Gallery of Art

Patrick J. Buchanan: White House communications director

Pat Buckley: New York socialite and wife of William F. Buckley, Jr.

William F. Buckley, Jr.: conservative columnist and editor of *National Review*

George H. W. Bush: vice president of the United States

"Nicholas Carrollton": staff assistant, Republican National Committee

Jimmy Carter: thirty-ninth president of the United States

Rosalynn Carter: former first lady of the United States

Carl "Spitz" Channell: president, National Endowment for the Preservation of Liberty

Winston Churchill: Conservative member of Parliament; son of Pamela Harriman

"Peter Cox": former Republican state senator from Michigan; political consultant and contributor

Elaine Crispen: press secretary to Nancy Reagan

Nicholas Daniloff: correspondent for *U.S. News & World Report*

Bette Davis: film actress; performed with Ronald Reagan in *Dark Victory*

Michael Deaver: lobbyist; former White House deputy chief of staff

Terry Dolan: cofounder and chairman, National Conservative Political Action Committee (NCPAC)

Bob Dole: U.S. senator (R-KS) and Senate majority leader

"James Dugan": contributor to the National Endowment for the Preservation of Liberty

Vigdís Finnbogadóttir: fourth president of Iceland

Betty Ford: former first lady of the United States

Gerald R. Ford: thirty-eighth president of the United States

Eva Gabor: actress and television personality; businesswoman

Ellen Garwood: contributor to the National Endowment for the Preservation of Liberty

Lillian Gish: film actress

Mikhail Gorbachev: general secretary of the Communist Party of the U.S.S.R.

Raisa Gorbachev: first lady of the U.S.S.R.

Al Gore: U.S. senator (D-TN)

Tipper Gore: wife of Al Gore; cofounder, Parents Music Resource Center

Bob Graham: governor of Florida; Democratic candidate for U.S. Senate

Cary Grant: film star

Merv Griffin: television host and show-business entrepreneur

"Neal Grover": management analyst, National Security Council

Fawn Hall: secretary to Lieutenant Colonel Oliver L. North

Marvin Hamlisch: American composer and orchestra conductor

W. Averell Harriman: former governor of New York and ambassador to the U.S.S.R.

Pamela Harriman: founder and chairman of Democrats for the 80s ("PamPAC"); wife and widow of Averell Harriman

Kitty Carlisle Hart: actress; television personality; chair of the New York State Council on the Arts

Paula Hawkins: U.S. senator (R-FL)

"Jane Hazard": Michigan delegate to the 1976 and 1996 Republican national conventions

John W. Hinckley, Jr.: failed assassin and mental patient

Christopher Hitchens: journalist

Ernest F. "Fritz" Hollings: U.S. senator (D-SC)

Rita "Peatsy" Hollings: wife of Ernest Hollings

Bob Hope: entertainer

Janet Howard: assistant to Pamela Harriman; executive director, Democrats for the 80s

John Hutton: White House physician

Thomas Victor Jones: chief executive officer of Northrop Corporation

Jeane J. Kirkpatrick: former U.S. ambassador to the United Nations

Henry A. Kissinger: U.S. secretary of state under Presidents Nixon and Ford

"Sofya Kornilov": Soviet human-rights activist and political prisoner

Jim Kuhn: executive assistant to President Reagan

"Anders Little": deputy director, Defense Programs and Arms Control Division, National Security Council

"Anne Macmurray": activist against nuclear weapons; ex-wife of Peter Cox

Edwin Meese: attorney general of the United States

Walter F. Mondale: former vice president of the United States

Edmund Morris: authorized biographer of Ronald Reagan

Daniel Patrick Moynihan: U.S. senator (D-NY)

Paul Nitze: special advisor to the president and secretary of state on arms control matters

Pat Nixon: former first lady of the United States

Richard M. Nixon: thirty-seventh president of the United States

Oliver L. North: lieutenant colonel, U.S. Marines; deputy director for political-military affairs, National Security Council

Thomas P. "Tip" O'Neill, Jr.: speaker of the House of Representatives

Jacqueline Kennedy Onassis: former first lady of the United States

John M. Poindexter: vice admiral, U.S. Navy; national security advisor

"Kelly Proctor": staff assistant to Pamela Harriman at Democrats for the 80s

Joan Quigley: astrologer to Nancy Reagan

Irina Ratushinskaya: Soviet poet and dissident

Doria Reagan: daughter-in-law of the president

Maureen Reagan: daughter of the president

Nancy Reagan: first lady of the United States

Ron Reagan: son of the president

Ronald Reagan: fortieth president of the United States

Donald T. Regan: chief of staff to the president of the United States

Dennis Revell: son-in-law of the president

Rozanne Ridgway: special assistant to the secretary of state for negotiations

Nelson A. Rockefeller: forty-first vice president of the United States

Arthur M. Schlesinger, Jr.: historian; former special assistant to President Kennedy

Frank Sesno: CNN correspondent

Eduard Shevardnadze: minister of foreign affairs of the Soviet Union

George P. Shultz: U.S. secretary of state

Ann Sothern: film and television actress

Larry Speakes: deputy press secretary to the president

Robert Strauss: attorney; former chairman of the Democratic National Committee

Maurice Tempelsman: businessman; companion of Jacqueline Kennedy Onassis

Margaret Thatcher: prime minister of the United Kingdom

Sarah Vaughan: jazz singer

John Warner: U.S. senator (R-VA)

Charles Wick: director, United States Information Agency

Jane Wyman: film and television actress; first wife of Ronald Reagan

Gennadi Zakharov: Soviet physicist and spy

Jerome Zipkin: New York society "walker" and friend of Nancy Reagan

Mort Zuckerman: editor in chief, *U.S. News & World Report*

Prologue

AUGUST 19, 1976

That faint clanking sound, arriving through the open window of his home office: Was it coming from the courtyard? Was it being made with the pulley they'd attached to the house?

Christ, it couldn't be, thought Nixon, looking at his new digital watch: 6:15 p.m. No, they still had the round-the-clock nurse, and she wouldn't be letting Pat get up from her long afternoon nap for another fifteen minutes, when he'd join her for a glass of fruit juice and dinner off the TV trays.

He heard the clanking again and realized it was just the halyard slapping the flagpole. Manolo must be lowering the Stars and Stripes a little early. Nixon felt relieved to know that poor Pat wasn't once more at the exercise pulley, working it without complaint, no matter the agony, trying to regain the left-arm strength the stroke had stolen six weeks before. Thank God she could still use her right hand; he would die from the pity of it all if he had to sit there and feed her.

More of a breeze than usual was coming off the Pacific tonight. Nixon closed the window and turned up the sound on the office TV. It was prime time in Kansas City, two hours ahead of San Clemente, and Rockefeller had just taken the podium to cheers that seemed almost affectionate, nothing like the catcalls he'd gotten twelve years ago in San Francisco. *YOU LOUSY LOVER! YOU LOUSY LOVER!* Sitting on the sidelines of the Cow Palace that night, Nixon and Pat had stared ahead in disbelief, not reacting, pretending not to hear. Hell, maybe Nelson had had it coming—running off with Happy, who'd abandoned her own four kids—but Nixon would have preferred another Caracas shower of spit and stones to the shrieks of all those triumphant Goldwaterites, rushing like lemmings into Lyndon Johnson's landslide.

The Tilt-A-Whirl of the last twelve years had ended up making Nelson vice president, the unelected standby to an unelected president; and now, in a last gyration, he'd been kicked to the curb, dumped by dumb, docile Jerry in order to placate the Reagan troops, who'd damned near succeeded in nominating their own man. Christ, this was some sorry spectacle for a sitting president. Limping over the finish line with a handful more delegates than the other guy!

And now it fell to Nelson to nominate his own successor—angry Bob Dole, whom the liberals were already calling Ford's Nixon, Jerry's "hatchet man." Well, it *was* a bad choice, as he could have warned Ford, and tried to. No soap. So here was Nelson, still garrulous and not very bright—all money and dick, if truth be told—knocking himself out to be a sport:

Delegates to the convention, fellow Americans, last night in this hall the Republican Party made history. It endorsed the solid achievements of the first person ever to hold the office of president of the United States by appointment.

Christ, what's the point of bringing *that* up? Ford's biggest problem, if you didn't count the pardon, was that he owed his goddamned job to Nixon.

And I ask you, ladies and gentlemen, where else in the world would the winner go pay a call on the runner-up?

Well, what winner but Jerry would be dumb enough to go to the hotel room of the man he'd just *beaten*, barely, as if he were room service rather than the goddamned president of the United States? Same as he'd pissed away the Bicentennial, giving a half-dozen dopey speeches instead of one big memorable address. No sense of any occasion's demands and opportunities.

This could all have turned out worse, of course. The party could have decided that Nixon's replacement and pardoner was so beyond the pale that they wouldn't even think of nominating him. They could have turned to some noble son of a bitch like Richardson, just to *purify* themselves for the voters. No, he wouldn't raise his blood pressure higher than Pat's by thinking about that cocksucker, who after all was going nowhere fast. The London embassy and then secretary of commerce: What did they call it? "Downward mobility"? Christ, the bastard had done better under Nixon than Ford!

The former president was, on this summer California night, still in a jacket and tie. He never lets himself be without either when he goes to this office just yards from the house. If he starts sitting around in a Ban-Lon shirt, that'll be the end of any chance to climb back even halfway from the hell of the past two years. *Exile*, they called it. Christ, more like house arrest.

As Nelson went on, Nixon did allow himself to loosen the tie a bit, an action that tugged his gaze toward the accumulating typescript of his memoirs, piled on a cabinet near the window. He was up to 1970, and the work was getting harder all the time. Try telling the story of your administration without access to your own damned papers! Everything remained under the government's lock and key three thousand miles away, and Jerry Ford wasn't about to intercede on his predecessor's behalf for the sake of mere history.

The little, recent punishments, postscripts to the loss of the presidency, were turning out to be more inventive and sadistic than the giant axe that had fallen two years before. Only weeks ago they'd thrown him out of the New York State Bar rather than allowing him to resign: oh no, they weren't going to let him get away with *that* again—not when disbarment could be made into a miniature version of the impeachment he'd "escaped." You almost had to admire their maneuver, something worthy of Colson in his best days.

Pat, who'd never wanted to be anything more than the wife of a lawyer, had taken the disbarment especially hard—the social disgrace of it, he supposes. It had, he was sure, contributed to the worst blow of all, this stroke. If she were well, she'd be coming in here, fetching him for the short walk back to the house and dinner, scolding him when she saw he'd already fixed himself a cocktail from the little cabinet on which the typescript sat. *Put a little more water in that, pal.* His imagination could so clearly imagine her saying it, her smile untwisted and her speech unslurred.

Those sons of bitches, Bernstein and Woodward, had made her out to be a drunk. They were the main cause of this stroke, as surely as if they'd injected her with something. *The Final Days:* he'd told her not to read it, and she'd promised him she wouldn't. But she'd borrowed it from one of the two secretaries he had here each day until five o'clock—a gal who'd been skimming it, maybe for libels but probably just out of curiosity. One thing you could bet on: if Rose were still with him, she'd never have left the goddamned thing on the desk where Pat could see it. Reading the book over Fourth of July weekend is what sent the blood bursting out of her veins and brought on the heartbreak to which he now paid daily witness. To see his wild Irish rose playing with a preschooler's blocks, trying to get back the coordination in her fingers by pressing them into a little steeple!

He turned his gaze toward the huge Oriental fan mounted on the wall—something she'd been given in China, not in '72 but during their trip this past February. God, how they'd enjoyed themselves! The crowds in Canton had been as loud, as crazed with friendliness, as the ones in Cairo back in '74, two months before the end, when he still thought he might save himself by solving the whole insoluble Middle East mess.

But even in China they'd not been able to get completely away from the news back home: Goldwater—a crackpot-turned-pseudo-elder-statesman—had suggested that Nixon do everyone a favor and just stay over there. Imagine being told back in 1960 that he'd end up having more stomach for Nelson than Barry!

He returned his attention to the TV. Rockefeller was going on too long about Dole: *He has that quality of candor, of openness, of forthrightness, so needed in our times* . . . No, he doesn't. Dole is strong, but he's a shifty s.o.b. and won't play well on the tube this fall. What is picking him going to accomplish? They don't think they can carry goddamned *Kansas* without him?

Jerry, and the party, could have done a hell of a lot better, and that's why he'd been on the phone pushing Connally late last night, once Ford had eked out this pathetic victory. He'd made two separate calls to the president's hotel, but Cheney, the boy chief of staff, made sure he never got through. Well, this ticket was finished. Reagan might be going home the loser, but Ford didn't realize that the poison of the primary season would kill him in November.

Several months ago, Nixon hadn't given Reagan a chance. There'd been talk in February that his own return trip to China should be postponed—lest Ford be hurt in New Hampshire by the sudden reappearance of his evil benefactor all over the front pages. (He should still have that much influence!) Ford had managed a win up there, though not by much. The real surprise had been seeing Reagan stick it out after that, through loss after loss, until he finally started winning in the South and West, forcing Ford into the death struggle that had ended only last night.

He suspected that Reagan's wife, terrifying little Nancy, had made him stay in the race until things turned around in North Carolina— the state where things had turned *against* Nixon back in '60, when he smashed his knee on that car door and wound up in the hospital, losing days he just didn't have to Jack.

Christ, in another ten years the campaigns will all be blending together, to the point where he won't be able to tell one from the other. Well, there's no need to rush senility by getting half in the bag on a weeknight. *Put a little more water in that, pal.* He set down his drink.

Nixon's eyes found Reagan in a framed grip-and-grin photo across the room. Yes, he'd shown something like grit, staying in as long as he had, scrounging for the last uncommitted delegates, even throwing a long ball and announcing a running mate—that liberal asshole from Pennsylvania—weeks before the convention. Nixon had always considered Reagan the luckiest son of a bitch since Coolidge, though there'd been bits and pieces, here and there, that he'd admired. The students at Berkeley had never rattled Reagan—*he'd* rattled *them*—whereas the kids on campus and in the streets had driven Nixon up the wall. He didn't need his papers to remember *that* part of 1970!

Ford's people would have a hell of a time conciliating Reagan's. Agreeing to one minority platform plank was hardly going to do the job. "Morality in Foreign Policy"! Jesus, as if all Reagan's human-rights griping amounted to a damned thing. His people were trying to make Ford and Henry look like Chamberlain just because they'd agreed to whatever meaningless crap Brezhnev had wanted at Helsinki. Did Reagan really object to "nonintervention" in the Soviets' internal affairs? Well, if the world blew up, the gulags would blow with it, and the prisoners still wouldn't be free to vote or go to church; they'd only be free to be dead.

At least Ford was willing to let Kissinger remind him that the larger world was important. When Reagan heard somebody mention Canton or Cairo, he thought of Ohio and Illinois. He had no more vision than he had realism, and God knows he didn't have the wit to understand that those two things went hand in hand.

The TV cameras had just cut away from Nelson, for only a second, to show Henry taking his seat in the convention stands, next to *his* Nancy—a smart gal, even if she does smell like a tobacco barn. Now the two of them could catch the end of their old patron Rockefeller's remarks, and try to ignore the boos with which Reagan's forces had greeted their arrival.

Maybe not just Reagan's people, either. Maybe some of Ford's were booing, too, because even now Henry brought with him memories of You Know Who, the man who'd been on five of the last six tickets to come out of a goddamned Republican convention, and whose name had yet to be spoken at this one.

It was no surprise that these days he and Henry spoke as little as they did. He'd no more expected their "friendship" to endure than he had the Paris Peace Accords. All the cracks had gotten back to him ("our meatball president"), and he'd had to keep himself from puking when he first asked, last summer, for Henry's *permission* to travel to China—and been told to wait until after Ford went in the fall. Of course, once he did make the trip, Ford's people had been happy enough to have his report.

Christ, Rockefeller was still at it, quoting Truman now: *Bob Dole is a man who can pass the test once put out by that great and beloved Missourian from Independence, who said so aptly: "If you can't take the heat get out of the kitchen."*

Well, thought Nixon, I'm now the only ex-president you've got. He'd buried all the rest of them—Ike, Truman, and Johnson—during his own time in the White House. And he was still determined to make the most of his singular status, however prematurely it had been conferred. And when Ford became an ex, as he surely would five months from now, you could damn well be certain that Nixon would find a way to outshine the competition.

He looked at the pink phone messages from last night, noting one from Peter Cox. Same last name as his son-in-law, whose political career looked to have stalled out before it started. Too bad Tricia didn't have the drive of Ron's little frau! This Cox, from Dallas, was a Reagan man, he recalled; but he also took care of Connally's interests. And he must know that Nixon had done all he could in the last few days to advance John's prospects. Was it a thank-you call? Nixon fingered the pink square of paper and wondered.

Nelson had at last surrendered the microphone to some blind woman delegate from Iowa, who was assuring everyone that poor battle-mangled Bob Dole would soon be building wheelchair ramps for the disabled all over America. This was the sort of penny-ante stuff that had always bored him while he'd governed the country. NBC must be bored, too: they were cutting away from the speaker to show a film clip of Reagan, who'd yet to arrive in the hall. The footage came from earlier in the day, when Ron and Nancy had had to thank their crushed supporters.

As Nixon watched it, the usual mixture of feelings stirred in him. He could never quite make up his mind about the man. Reagan had been too smart to let Ford lure him into the cabinet; you had to give him that. But he'd always had it too easy, especially with the goddamned Republican Party in California. Usually so lazy, they'd gone all out for him in '66 and made it possible for him to do what Richard Nixon, an ex–vice president, hadn't been able to four years earlier: send Pat Brown packing from Sacramento. (Christ, Brown's kid Jerry had moved awfully fast! Now the governor at thirty-eight. Really, what the hell is wrong with Tricia's Ed?)

But this is the end of the trail for Reagan. If Carter gets in, and he will, there won't be a reasonable shot for Ron until '84—the country hadn't thrown out an elected incumbent since Hoover—and at that point Reagan will be older than Eisenhower was when *leaving* office.

In fact, Reagan is two years older than himself: and here *he* is, still only sixty-three, with his feet up on a hassock and the remote control in his hand.

All the goddamned plastic horns were getting on his nerves. He clicked off the television, just as the delegates got ready to vote for Dole. He took another look at his watch and saw it was time to steel himself for dinner with Pat. He exited the office and crossed the patio. To think that two months ago he'd still been worrying about his own slight limp, from the phlebitis! The courtyard's flowers, he could see, were neglected. Who knew if she'd ever be able to get back to gardening? But the lawns were better: the book advance and the money from selling the place in Key Biscayne had allowed them to put the groundsman on an extra day a week.

He stood still for a moment, gathering his courage into an approximation of hers. Trying not to make a noise, he tugged on the exercise pulley, wondering not how long it would take her to recover, but how long it would take *him*. He snapped on the smile he'd summoned for thirty years, ten thousand times and more, whenever he'd entered a room full of people he needed.

Onward and upward—her favorite saying.

He'd be done with dinner in fifteen minutes; then he'd go back to the office and return the call from Connally's man.

———

"What are you *looking* at?" Jane Hazard asked Anne Macmurray Cox, whose binoculars had been focused, intently and at length, on some point halfway across the Kemper Arena.

"Nothing," said Anne, lowering the lenses. "Or I should say 'good-for-nothing.'"

The two women, Michigan delegates—Anne from Owosso, and Jane from Chesaning—had met only on Sunday night here in Kansas City, just before the convention opened, but by now they had spent enough time together for Mrs. Hazard to know that "good-for-nothing" referred to Mrs. Cox's ex-husband, Peter, himself a delegate from Texas. Anne had been observing him, distant but magnified, off and on throughout each evening's proceedings, and tonight would be her last opportunity to do so. She and Peter kept in touch only about their two grown children, and he was mostly estranged from both of them, and so such occasions were few.

"He's on the phone," Anne said to Jane, after failing to resist another peek through the binoculars. Peter was using the kitchen-style wall telephone attached to the Texas delegation's stanchion, mouthing the name of whoever he was listening to, so that the person standing next to him would be duly impressed by the caller's importance—and thus by Peter's, too. Anne explained all this to Jane.

"Who is it?" asked Mrs. Hazard. "The caller, I mean."

"I wish I could read lips."

Peter would be sixty in just two years. At fifty-one, Anne had quite a bit more time before hitting that milestone, but she was annoyed, as she'd been each night this week, by how good-looking Peter remained, sort of bronze and leathery all at once, even though he was too naturally fair-skinned for what people now called the "Sunbelt." She suspected he'd had one or two "precancerous" spots removed during the last few years, as he'd already had done in the course of their seventeen-year marriage, which had ended a decade ago. The divorce had been every bit as chilly as she'd somehow always known it would be, even when he proposed to her way back in 1948. All that summer and fall in Owosso, she'd been caught between patrician Peter and, God rest his soul, Jack Riley, the local UAW man. (Man? He seemed a boy in memory.) The triangle had played itself out against the presidential election, to the amusement of the locals in what was Thomas E. Dewey's hometown. Dewey, to everyone's astonishment, had been defeated, while Peter had won both her and a seat in the state senate.

Over the next dozen years, despite his ambition and his success as a lawyer, he had never gone any further politically, and in 1960, just before Michigan went for Kennedy over Nixon, the Shiawassee County GOP decided it had had enough of Peter Cox's grating blend of the blue-blooded and smart-alecky—and picked someone else to run for his seat in the legislature.

Right now, here on the convention floor, some irreconcilable Reaganites, real crazies, were trying to put Jesse Helms's name in nomination against Bob Dole's—a futile gesture that had the Ford people, like Anne, looking at their watches.

"*Viva!*" shouted the Texas delegates, probably out of boredom.

"*Olé!*" replied the Californians.

"Oh God, not that again," said Mrs. Hazard.

Without lowering her binoculars, Anne listened to the cross-cheering from the two Reagan-heavy delegations. They'd been at it each night this week, keeping up one another's spirits in the face of defeat. And, sure enough, there was Peter, off the phone but still delighted with himself, bellowing along with his fellow Texans.

Suddenly, Jane and Anne had the same thought; both turned around to look at the skyboxes. Were Reagan and Nancy arriving to greet the faithful from their little glass house? Was *that* what the cheering signified? All week that little bitch—Anne felt no guilt using the word—had been trying to upstage the first lady with her strategic apparitions. But Mrs. Ford had managed some good moments of her own, like dancing with Tony Orlando to "Tie a Yellow Ribbon." True, the song seemed to suggest that Jerry Ford was being paroled instead of nominated—but still.

Jane, without benefit of binoculars, continued scanning the skyboxes for a sign of the Reagans. "Did you know he calls her *Mommy*?" she asked Anne, who lowered the field glasses and made a puking gesture. The sight of her index finger, pointed at her own open mouth, reminded her that she'd recently given up nail polish; she tried to see whether Jane might have as well.

It was 8:45 p.m. and, sure enough, there, at last, were Reagan and Mommy, come to hear Dole's speech and then Ford's. Up in the skybox the two figures were waving, like the king and queen of some little glass asteroid. Every person cheering them—*Viva! Olé!*—now had an unobstructed view of these devotional objects. The whole arena had been built without a single interior column, and while Anne looked toward the skybox, without cheering, she wondered how the roof stayed up. She took satisfaction in how far the actor and his little wife were from the podium that had been their goal. She and Jane proceeded to let the Reagan people, including Peter, cheer their brains out for a full six minutes. Anne had to remind herself that her side had *won*, and she made sure the lapels of her Ultrasuede jacket didn't obscure either her *E.R.A.!* button or the one that said ELECT BETTY'S HUSBAND.

The arrival at the lectern of Kansas's other senator—Pearson?—did little to calm the Reagan troops. He was there to introduce Dole, but no one was listening.

"Shouldn't they bring out Alf Landon?" asked Jane. The party's 1936 standard bearer, a twinkling near-nonagenarian, had already delivered some remarks the other night. Had the convention organizers known that the VP pick would be Dole, they might have saved Alf, another Kansan, for the task.

"He doesn't exactly spell landslide," Anne said.

"Maybe backwards," Jane conceded.

There were moments when Anne had to admit how little Jerry Ford had going for him. She didn't see how he could overcome the great crush so many Americans were developing on Carter, whose I'll-never-lie-to-you pledge seemed to one-up George Washington: Carter was making the promise without even having chopped down a cherry tree. The Republicans did seem hopelessly out of gas. Outside this arena a giant elephant balloon had failed to inflate, leaving a thousand pounds of gray latex spread across the parking lot. And inside the hall each orator had to reach back twenty years, to Eisenhower, for a GOP president whose name could be safely mentioned. Sometimes they resorted to borrowing from the other party, as Rocky had done with Truman.

Kansas City was Truman's town, of course: the bar at the Hotel Muehlebach, where Anne and Jane had last night sipped white wine until one a.m., even called itself The Haberdashery. No wonder Anne was having trouble getting her mind off Peter and '48. Now a sudden last great roar for Reagan was making her remember a Saturday night from that faraway fall: seven thousand Owossoans turning out to greet their sure-thing favorite son, who came riding down Main Street in a green convertible behind seven brass bands. Traveling in Dewey's wake had been Jerry and Betty Ford, interrupting their honeymoon with a night of campaigning for his first term in Congress.

A couple of weeks later the whole town had awakened with egg on its face. And Anne, a lonely Truman supporter, had ended up picking Peter, with whom she was forever sparring, over Jack, with whom she was forever necking. It was so long ago: one of the boys had given the other a black eye during that last tumultuous week before the election, but she could no longer remember who'd thrown the punch and who'd gotten hit.

Dole at last came out, waving his good arm. The moment had everybody up on their feet, even the Reagan people. Through the binoculars Anne could see that the vice-presidential candidate was even more damaged than today's newspaper profiles let on. He seemed hollowed out on one whole side. He was handsome in a Humphrey Bogart sort of way, but—she could tell from those newspaper pieces—too quippy and clever by half, a version of Peter without the Yale varnish. Dole wouldn't do anything to heal the still-open wounds everywhere in this arena. The vote was 1,187 to 1,070! The first real thriller of a convention since 1952, the year that Mrs. Peter Cox, wife of the state senator, had taken the marital route of least resistance and become a registered Republican.

Throwing in with the GOP had been the only way to accomplish anything worthwhile in Owosso, where Republicans ran everything from the League of Women Voters to the Board of Education. As it was, she hadn't had to compromise herself much. She'd marched for open housing and fluoridation, and there'd been no shame in ringing doorbells for George Romney, who was more liberal than many Democrats, and honest to boot.

"How does he believe all that nonsense?" she suddenly asked Jane.

"Who? What nonsense?"

"Peter. All that Reagan nonsense. The evils of détente. Cutting taxes to produce *more* revenue."

"Relax, Anne. We *won*. And the two of you are divorced, remember?"

The crowd was at last quieting down to listen to Dole. Anne put the binoculars away, determined not to look at Peter or think of him anymore. She would make herself take pleasure in her accomplishment of getting elected as a delegate. It had required nearly a year of planning and effort but had shortchanged no one. Both her children were now gone from the house—Ralph in law school out in Arizona, and Susan, having dropped out of Carleton, over on the West Coast, living with her boyfriend. Anne knew that those two were at least dabbling in drugs, and she disapproved. But good for Betty Ford for saying that a little experimentation in that realm, as well as with sex, didn't require someone's being read out of the human race.

There was nothing wrong, Anne now firmly told herself, with either of her children—or with their mother. She began making a mental list of her own recent initiatives: using her maiden name as a middle one—*Anne Macmurray Cox;* giving up golf for organic gardening. But she didn't get far with her self-congratulatory pep talk. Peter, just by being here, and bringing with him all their unhappy history, was spoiling what should have been a grand night.

His own recent history was galling. In '73 he'd married someone fifteen years younger than herself, a girl who wore a lot of turquoise and ran a "gallery" in Turtle Creek. Anne could imagine the pictures she sold—lots of clowns and big-eyed Walter Keane waifs painted on velvet.

And let us recall that hard-fought battles have never hurt our party. It was just such a contest in 1952 that gave us Dwight David Eisenhower. And President Eisenhower gave us eight years of prosperity, and President Ford will do the same!

And he *would*, thought Anne, listening to Dole, forcing herself to get caught up, if only for a moment, in the spirit of things. She wished she had one of those plastic horns. Yes, Ford would succeed in the steady old I-like-Ike way. Peter *didn't* believe all that Reagan nonsense; she was sure of it. His march to the right derived from his own little local defeat—from having been thrown aside by the party's Main Street regulars, neighbors who didn't like him, pure and simple. That was what had turned him into a full-throated Goldwater man, and sent him southward in a fit of pique. He sported his new politics the way he sported the turquoise girl and all the money he'd made in Dallas, as a badge of I-don't-need-you vulgarity that he could flash at anyone, including his ex-wife.

Dole, having quickly finished, accepted cheers without milking the crowd for more; he was already the good, subordinate running mate, willing to settle for a smaller share of everything. Only seconds after he departed, the spotlights came back on, shining down upon the lectern as if the convention managers feared that any interval in the program might allow the Reaganites to manifest their restlessness. Would Ford be hustled on right now, without any further ado?

Jane realized something else was happening. "Oh, Anne!" she exclaimed, elbowing her friend. "Look!"

It was Cary Grant, even handsomer than he'd been twenty years ago, waving to the crowd, his white hair and thick black-rimmed glasses glinting under the lights. He'd come to the platform to pay tribute to Betty Ford and introduce a little film about the first family, but the crowd— both halves of it—was too excited to let him get started. Anne and Jane smiled at each other; how nice to have a *real* star, a leading man, on *their* side; someone ten times bigger than Ronald Reagan, that supporting player who'd had to seek career salvation as a TV host and corporate pitchman.

"*I'm here,*" said Grant, "*because I've been permitted the happy privilege of introducing a remarkable woman.*"

It seemed that Mrs. Ford herself would come out before the film started.

"*Women have always been one of* my *favorite causes, too,*" Grant continued. *BETTY! BETTY! BETTY!* roared half the crowd.

Jane turned to Anne to share the moment, the feeling of celebration at last unleashed. But she saw that Anne had collapsed back, helplessly, into all the misery Peter had put her through during their years in Owosso, including all the early local versions of the turquoise girl. Not even the sudden friendly sight of Betty Ford up there on the podium—"*Mr. Grant, I accept your nomination! What woman could turn down Cary Grant?*"— would let her shake off the heavy, re-imposed weight of the past.

"Buck up," Jane whispered as the lights went down for the campaign movie. "If things had turned out differently, we'd be watching *Bedtime for Bonzo*."

As the Ford film played on—there was Jerry toasting his own English muffins, and letting an ancient Hirohito visit Disneyland—Anne felt the futility of all her recent little attempts at reinvention. She was mired in a past that Peter still governed, and she needed to convince herself that he did not somehow rule the years ahead, that the future did not belong to him and the turquoise girl, any more than it belonged to Ronald Reagan and poisonous, defeated little Nancy, up there in the skybox.

———

"Ave, my darling," said Pamela Digby Churchill Hayward Harriman, gently rousing her latest husband from his slumber in front of the television. "You asked me to wake you."

The former governor of New York and ambassador to the Soviet Union, the eighty-four-year-old scion of railroad kings and robber barons, slowly stirred. "Right," he said, trying to remember what for. "Ford."

"*Yes*," said his wife, with an encouraging smile. "He's just come on." Mrs. Harriman pointed to the television.

"He reminds me of Barkley," said her husband, after sitting up a bit.

Bishop Berkeley? Barclay's Bank? Perhaps he meant Busby Berkeley. Ave's accent sometimes sounded more English than Pamela's own.

"Truman's vice president," he said, by way of clarification.

"Yes," said his wife. "Of course." After five years at it, she still had much to learn about American history and politics.

She walked across the room to turn down the air conditioner. Americans never understood that being always-too-cold in the winter had relieved the English of any desire to be overly cool during summer. Still, it felt ridiculous to be in Washington in the middle of August when they could be in Sun Valley or at her own New York house on Croton Lake. But they *needed* to be here, before their upcoming trip to Russia, so that over the next couple of days Dick Holbrooke could give Ave a series of briefings. Her husband had secured a tiny advisory role in the Carter campaign; he would be reporting back to the Democratic candidate on whatever Brezhnev said during next month's Moscow meeting, at which Ave would explain the issues in the American election to the Soviet premier—just as he'd once explained such things to Stalin.

Pamela knew that her husband was hoping, once Carter got in, for an actual *job*. No matter that even ten years ago Johnson had worried about Ave's advancing age and deafness before giving him an assignment.

"More coffee, dear?" asked Pamela.

Ave ignored her to concentrate on the television.

Five years ago, when he'd been merely seventy-nine and a new, lonely widower, she'd been able to get his attention. As soon as Leland Hayward, Pamela's then husband, died of a stroke, she made sure Averell Harriman saw the obituary. As she'd anticipated, the news sparked old memories of their World War II flirtation, when she'd been married to the prime minister's son. Only twenty and already a mother, she'd caught the eye of attractive Mr. Harriman, who was running the American end of Lend-Lease and popping in and out of Number 10. Thirty years later, a few months after Leland's demise, Kay Graham decided to throw them back together at a dinner party. Ave was soon crowing like some *coq d'or* begging to be let down from the weather vane. She'd briefly wondered whether their twenty-nine-year age difference should be regarded as more, or less, preposterous than it had been in 1941. No matter: on September 27, 1971, six months after the appearance of Leland's obit, they'd married.

Pamela's past five years of study had really been a *return* to the interest in politics she'd maintained when married to Randolph Churchill—and, in fact, quite a bit before that. Parliaments had been loaded with Digbys from time immemorial. Political life was *natural* to her, even if she'd come back to it only because of Ave, whose ambitions had never slackened with age.

She had adopted and advanced the interests of each husband and lover she'd ever acquired. She learned about French furniture during her years with Elie de Rothschild, and a bit later, when Gianni Agnelli entered the picture, had gone so far as to read the *Encyclopaedia Britannica* article on the internal combustion engine. And between 1960 and 1971, as the fifth Mrs. Leland Hayward, she had mastered and weighed in upon all the dealings that generated a theatrical producer's box office. When Leland put on *The Sound of Music*, she gave everyone they knew a silver cigarette case that played "Edelweiss." For Ave she had even become a citizen, though she'd always felt herself to be more American than most of the actual Americans she encountered.

Her new citizenship also protected her from complaints that her electoral efforts amounted to foreign meddling in U.S. affairs. This year she and Ave had come out for Carter a bit later than they should have, so she could hardly claim that she'd *made* the Georgia governor or that he owed her and Ave much in particular. But Carter would, she suspected, come and go rather quickly, in time enough for Pamela Harriman to find, and cultivate, the *real* one, the as-yet-unknown comer whose ascendancy would be her great accomplishment.

This Georgetown residence might be too small for the operation she had in mind. It carried some nice recent legend as the house that Ave and Marie, her predecessor, had lent to Jackie and the president's children after Jack got killed, but it was cramped compared to the apartment she and Leland had had in New York, at Fifth Avenue and Eighty-third, just a couple of blocks from where Jackie eventually settled herself. Even so, Pamela was giving it her all now. During those dinner parties, she took notes on the conversation, using a cream-colored pad so tiny one could mistake it for a dollop of sauce that had splashed onto the tablecloth. She didn't *think* of herself as a hostess. She felt more as if she were working in Leland's old lines of agentry and producing.

These thoughts drifted through her mind as her watchful eye alternated its focus between Ave and the television screen, becoming truly fixed on the latter only when the camera gave a view of the skybox, where both Reagans sat with smiles firmly in place and hands firmly in their laps. A friend of Kay's had taken Pamela to the National Press Club last year for Reagan's announcement of his candidacy—all part of her continuing political education. That day, she paid particular attention to Nancy, just about her own age, with a husband ten years older, instead of twenty-nine. Even so, Reagan would now be past the point of presidential possibility.

Ave, of course, was really here to make Pamela a widow, not a wife. She had been a model of assiduous devotion these past five years, a most vigilant mother hen, and even now, on occasion, a sorceress in the bedroom. But she knew the real point of this marriage would be what derived from it once Ave was gone, the life she would make from the last fortune and surname to come her way. Leland, alas, had *not* been made for widowing; he had left her with too many debts and too little purpose. Still, marriage was always more rewarding than mistressing—a truth she had not grasped until she'd been set aside by both Rothschild and Agnelli. She suspected that Nancy Reagan had intuited the lesson early.

"Hello, Mummy," said Winston Churchill. "Hello, Ave."

"Hello, darling," Pamela responded to her son, who had just entered the room. Ave added a muffled, friendly grunt to the greeting.

Winston, at thirty-five, was now the Conservative MP for Stretford, as well as a trustee of the National Benevolent Fund for the Aged. He was here in Washington this week on a visit to some American counterpart of the charity—Pamela had forgotten its name. She did not mind being a grandmother, but was less keen on this particular job of Winston's. His choice of a philanthropy somehow suggested that *she* had caught the disease of age, and that he might be pursuing its cure or relief in the way that other afflictions, cancer and so forth, inspired children of the sufferer to spearhead charities.

But at least Winston was *loyal*. One didn't have to fear some poisonous book coming from his pen, the way she feared the one supposedly in the works from Leland's daughter, Brooke. Well, *you* try being Dennis Hopper's stepmother-in-law. That was no easy ride; some missteps had been inevitable, and she wouldn't think of them now.

"You met him, darling, didn't you?" Mrs. Harriman asked Winston. She pointed to Reagan, before he disappeared from the screen.

"Yes, Mummy. A year ago last spring."

"With that awful woman."

"Yes, Mummy. The Milk Snatcher. The Grocer's Daughter."

Pamela saw little likelihood that Mrs. Thatcher, the new leader of the Conservative opposition, would get any closer to Number 10 than Reagan had gotten to the White House.

"Remind me, Winston. What did the two of them discuss?"

"It was a sort of *tour d'horizon*." His face darkened as he used the diplomat's phrase. Anything French reminded him of his neglected childhood, when his mother, finished with Randolph, had decamped for Paris and Rothschild. "It was mostly foreign policy, I seem to recall. And I do remember—" He suddenly smiled, leaving the sentence unfinished.

"What is it you remember, dear?"

"What Mrs. T. said to me afterwards."

"And what was that?"

Winston hesitated a moment, and grinned. "'Poor dear, there's really nothing between his ears.' But she liked him nonetheless." Mrs. Thatcher, like his mother, was a man's woman, flutteringly susceptible in the midst of all her drive to the simplest sort of boyish charm.

"Go into the bathroom, dear."

"I beg your pardon?" It was as if he were once again a little boy, weekending at Chequers and being told to have a pee before going in for his audience with the Old Man.

"Look above the toilet," Pamela said.

Ave, annoyed by the chatter, motioned for Winston to turn the volume up, which the young man did before obediently heading into the little half-bathroom off the den they were in. Once there, he found what his mother had intended for him to see: a framed poster for *Mr. President,* the Irving Berlin musical that Leland had produced in the early sixties. Pamela's son was mystified as to why she would be urging him to look at this instead of, say, the two Matisses in the hallway. He walked back into the den.

"They actually thought of Ronald Reagan for the lead," his mother explained. "Leland had heard that he was a passable singer. He and Josh Logan seriously considered hiring him."

Winston could think of nothing to say.

"I'm afraid Reagan couldn't have made the show any worse," Pamela reflected. Robert Ryan had turned out to be as awful as Irving Berlin's senescent songs. And no one wanted to look at Nanette Fabray playing a first lady when they could see Jackie Kennedy, the real thing, on their TV screens.

"Come sit next to me, dear, and let's listen to this speech with Ave."

The camera took a final shot of Reagan. The losing candidate cocked an eyebrow. What did the gesture mean? Was it a sign of Reagan's sudden, if momentary, engagement? Was it acting, or an indication that he'd just *stopped* acting? Pamela was not able to tell.

While Ford cleared his throat, the camera swept from skybox to podium, briefly catching the winsome, clapping presence of Shirley Temple Black, who, the anchorman explained, was now the nation's chief of protocol.

Now *that* would be a fine job for Jimmy Carter to give Pamela Harriman. She looked over at Ave. Was it too late for him to buy it for her, with a great boxcarful of Union Pacific cash?

———

With his right hand, Christopher Hitchens paddled the little white ball against the wall. With his left, he reached for a glass of whiskey resting on the Ping-Pong table. He was alone, at three a.m., in the basement of the *New Statesman*'s offices in Great Turnstile, having come down here after getting bored correcting the final proofs of his latest article.

Three years shy of thirty, and a half dozen out of Oxford, Hitchens was becoming, in truth, a bit bored with himself, no matter that he was now climbing the masthead of his youthful dreams, laying down column inches inside the same London weekly through which Shaw and Orwell had spoken up against capitalism and cant. Over the last eight months, the *New Statesman* had dispatched him to Spain's nascent and unpromising half-democracy; to a pro-PLO conference in Colonel Qadaffi's Tripoli; and to the Baghdad of Saddam Hussein, *who has sprung from being an underground revolutionary gunman to perhaps the first visionary Arab statesman since Nasser . . . Make a note of the name*, he'd written.

Quoting himself came naturally, and why not? Hitchens made and won arguments with a style as crisp and springy as this Ping-Pong ball, in a voice that belonged untransferably to its owner. Whether deployed in Lisbon or Milan or Jerusalem, it worked with a devastatingly quiet self-assurance. As he had learned never to turn up the volume in conversation, so had he mastered the art of never resorting to italics on the page.

For all his recent foreign travel, it was domestic affairs that now called him back upstairs. Until his friend Fenton returned from holiday, Hitchens was charged with writing the "Spotlight on Politics" column. In Saturday's issue, once he fully sharpened this recalcitrant proof, he would be bringing readers news of how Mrs. Thatcher's "brittle schoolmarmish accent" was, half against her will, being marinated into something more plummy by a team of media coaches. If they succeeded, the results might help grease the lady's path from mere opposition to Number 10.

During the past few weeks he'd done so well with Fenton's column that there was talk of sending him to the fall party conferences—Labour in Blackpool and the Tories in Brighton. But the mere thought of those two vacation locales gave him, the son of a naval officer, a feeling of seaside-sickness, not from any undulation of the ocean, but from the second-rate twirling of all the tiny Ferris wheels and carousels. Even now, when it came to amusements, his countrymen seemed to do it up beige instead of brown. Larkin may have been mildly encouraged when British "sexual intercourse began in 1963," but thirteen years on, there were still times when one could scarcely notice, let alone get, any. People here seemed continually to detumesce amidst the browned-out and guttering GNP, whereas in distant New York, which had eschewed austerity for gaudy, flat-out bankruptcy, the orange shag carpets were alive with all things venereal and inviting.

He envied Cockburn, who at this minute was over in the States covering Gerald Ford's convention. A bland enough affair to be sure, but enlivened—he now learned from a perusal of his colleague's just-arrived copy—by a measure of Barnum-like spectacle: John Dean, erstwhile snitch and newly appointed correspondent for *Rolling Stone*, was dodging Republican fists in Kansas City; and Miss Elizabeth Ray, the congressional secretary famously unable to type, was on the scene to offer the nonstenographic services she'd once reserved for a Democratic committee chairman.

Ronald Reagan, it seemed, had "at least offered the politics of the conservative imagination." That was Cockburn's gentle *envoi* to the patent-leather loser, and more than he deserved, thought Hitchens. Reverend Carter—a toothier, disco version of the Jazz Age Coolidge—would of course be the one to end up ruling the Day-Glo republic.

A part of Hitchens wished to be there instead of, well, here—where at 3:25 a.m. the radio, instead of being alive with paranoiac Yanks calling in on one subject or another, was broadcasting music so lugubrious it might be announcing the death of an East Bloc leader. Let anyone dare toss him the Johnsonian chestnut about how a man tired of London was tired of life and he'd toss it right back: he was tired of London because he was *ready* for life, of a louder sort than seemed available here. (*Thinking* in italics *was* permitted.)

Amis and McEwan would be showing up nine or ten hours from now for the usual Friday lunch. And since he himself was in the midst of a dry spell—with no woman waiting to throw her three-a.m. arms around the torso of the Hitch—he might as well, he decided, sleep here. It was a pity the basement offered only the hard apparatus of Ping-Pong instead of the soft baize playing field of a billiards table, but he seemed to remember a decent enough couch in the conference room upstairs.

Still, improvising the arrangement made him realize he should be making a more strenuous effort to find, as he often put it to friends, his first wife. Was she somewhere in America tonight? Or perhaps the *second* one was over there?

———

Ford's speech, thought Nancy Reagan, had been about as weighty as the balloons that dropped at its close—the promise of "a safer and saner world" thanks to "dependable arms agreements"—but he had surprised everyone with what seemed to be a spontaneous invitation from the podium to the skybox: *I would like, I would be honored on your behalf, to ask my good friend Governor Reagan to come down and say a few words at this time.*

What choice had that left her and Ronnie? None, except now to make this underground race to the rostrum, which was so far away it might as well be in another time zone. The concrete tunnel they were in amplified the click of Nancy's heels, and her mind went to the film vaults under Hollywood: she'd recently gotten a letter asking if she'd lend her name to some preservation group trying to halt the decay of all the old nitrate and acetate reels. She'd sent them fifty dollars and hoped they wouldn't include *Crash Landing*, her own last movie, in their plans.

"What'll I say?" asked Ronnie, who had his hand on her lower back. He was pushing her, however gently, to move even faster and catch up with Mike Deaver, ten strides ahead of them.

Irritated at the pace, not to mention the long distance between them and their destination—all this to do a favor for Jerry Ford!—she wondered how Mike, the aide who usually anticipated everything, had failed to have something prepared for *this*.

"I don't know," she replied at last to her husband. "Go with 'shining city on a hill.'"

"Maybe," he responded. She could tell, even as the two of them scurried in the half-dark, that he'd just cocked his head to the left.

Another voice, belonging to one of the Secret Service men who'd be quitting them tomorrow, said, "This way, Mrs. Reagan." The agent pointed to a cement staircase up ahead. It was bathed in a shaft of light from above, and two balloons had fallen onto one of its steps. Down it came the sound of the convention orchestra playing "Everything's Up to Date in Kansas City" for the umpteenth time this week. And so, for the umpteenth time, she banished from her mind the thought of Alfred Drake, with whom she'd had the briefest affair when he was doing *Oklahoma!* on Broadway.

The stairs, it turned out, led directly to the podium. She and Ronnie and the agent climbed them quickly. The noise from the arena grew louder as they surfaced, and then came the roar of recognition. Her eyes found Mike, already up near the microphone; he was gesturing for her and Ronnie to come forward.

She refused to look toward the Fords. As Ronnie walked ahead of her, bathed in the cheers and screams, she looked up at the dozens of klieg lights, a whole little constellation of them, and thought about what Joan

Quigley, her astrologer, and Merv's, had told her more than a year ago: an "adverse configuration of Saturn" would doom any presidential run by Ronald Reagan in 1976.

Standing in place as the plastic horns blared and the crowd continued its yelling—louder than anything the nominee had received—Nancy congratulated herself on having avoided kissing Betty, who stood on the other side of the lectern under her ten-years-out-of-date helmet of hair. She wouldn't kiss her when this evening ended, either. Not after that interview a few months back. *When Nancy met Ronnie that was it as far as her own life was concerned. She just fell apart at the seams.* And they called *her* a bitch! Everyone who knew anything about those long-ago days knew that Ronnie, shredded to pieces by Jane Wyman, had been the one falling apart.

As he now got ready to speak, she looked at him with what the press called The Gaze, locking it in place like a seat belt before takeoff. People wondered how she never appeared bored listening to the same speech for the fiftieth time. It was simple: she never listened to it. As she persisted in The Gaze, her mind in fact became especially active, diverting itself to dozens of matters requiring thought and worry. But her eyes were so large and attentive—they'd been perfect for the little bit of film acting she'd gotten to do—people couldn't believe she wasn't genuinely enchanted.

At this moment there was plenty to worry about, not just the absence of a prepared text. The lights were harsh and Ronnie wasn't made up, things that Mike might have done something about in advance, if he'd figured on their being up here. But it was too late for that—and for everything else.

It could all have been so different. If there'd been a snowstorm in New Hampshire on the day of the primary, *their* passionate voters would have turned out and Jerry's tepid ones would have stayed home. Ronnie would have stopped him then and there, assumed a look of inevitability, and made a straight march to the nomination. In the end, exhausted, they'd run out of time, and her weather wishes had grown more extreme. If a tornado had only lifted off the roof of this arena several nights ago, the sign would have been clear, and the delegates would have reconvened somewhere else, shocked into doing the right thing.

Not yet able to make himself heard, Ronnie tried to tamp down the crowd, patting the air with his hands, as if it were a piano keyboard. The delay was so long that The Gaze actually faltered, and Nancy noticed Stu Spencer, *their* aide before he'd deserted to Ford's side and come up with the nastiest ad of the whole six-month struggle: *When you vote Tuesday, remember: Governor Reagan couldn't start a war. President Reagan could.* It was one thing for Lew Wasserman to represent both Ronald Reagan and Jane Wyman after the divorce. But what Stu had done was atrocious, and he had joined the long list of people she would never forgive. Jane, curiously enough, was not on it: she had shut up throughout the campaign, as she had during the previous ones, resisting the press's attempts to get her to throw a zinger in the direction of her ex.

The orchestra stopped, and so at last did the cheers. She could barely get The Gaze locked back into place. Her heart was in her mouth: What would he find to say? She looked at her shoes, fearing that he might settle for that ancient ballad—*I am sore wounded but not slain. / I will lay me down and bleed a while / And then rise up to fight again.* The press would scorn him for it, say it was sore-loserish and all wrong for the occasion. But aside from all that, it was simply too sad; just playing the words in her head right now was bringing her to the verge of tears. She knew that this defeat had bled them to death, that there would be no fighting again. The past weeks of scavenging for delegates had done her in. Pretending to know the names of the wives and children of the men she was dialing; charming them, cajoling them, phonying it up—all of it harder work than the table-hopping and self-introducing she'd once done in the commissary after getting her MGM contract.

She was terrified, at this moment, that the podium was the precipice of a huge embarrassment. There had been too many farewells already: her agonized toast to Ronnie last night at dinner; this morning's tear-filled goodbye to their volunteers. Enough!

Thank you very much, Mr. President, Mrs. Ford, Mr. Vice President, Mr. Vice President to-be . . .

She knew what the politicians on the platform were thinking: how calm he was; not a quaver in his voice; as if he were just getting ready to give the Panama Canal speech inside one more VFW hall in North Carolina rather than saying goodbye to twenty thousand people under these lights, these badly aligned pseudo-stars, here in this vast, weirdly unbuttressed arena. But this was nothing. How many times had she heard him tell the story of that night in 1940, in South Bend, when he'd stood up and talked, in person, to *two hundred thousand* people at the *Knute Rockne* premiere, the whole thing going out over Kate Smith's radio show to more listeners than had tuned into Jerry Ford tonight.

I believe the Republican Party has a platform that is a banner of bold, unmistakable colors, with no pale pastel shades.

She'd joke about this line with Ted Graber, her decorator, when she next saw him. But come to think of it—yes, here was her inexhaustible ability to worry about anything—the line seemed to have something wrong with it. Was it too close to that one about Goldwater's '64 platform? *A choice, not an echo.* She broke The Gaze, imperceptibly, to steal a glance at Barry, whom she would also never forgive. Sticking with Jerry Ford, after all Ronnie had done for him in '64! Merv tells her she's the *real* Irishman in the family. "You know what Irish senility is?" he'd asked her at lunch a few weeks back. "You only remember the grudges."

She feared, without note cards from Mike Deaver, that Ronnie would "go up," forget whatever words he'd decided to speak. She can see the cameras, not just broadcasting this moment but recording what will be the last important film clip of Ronnie's career, and she doesn't want him to fade or fumble his way through it.

He *is* fading—lately, in some hard-to-define way; he's harder for anyone to connect with. Not her, of course, but he's been baffling many of the others who've been clustered around them in all the hotels they've been moving between. She has no idea what's next for the two of them: he's already turned down the chance to become Sevareid's split-screened opposite on the *CBS Evening News.* "People will get tired of me on TV." Even now he prefers radio.

She would get through the next moments by concentrating on the plus side: no more harrowing landings in the Flying Banana, that prop plane they'd made do with while Mr. and Mrs. Grand Rapids swanned around on Air Force One. And no more worrying that Patti would suddenly pose nude or marry one of the Eagles just in time to make the Tuesday-morning papers on the day of a primary.

If he could just bring this *speech* in for a landing, they could go home, and she'd be willing to spend a whole month at the horrible flea-ridden ranch he loved, without a single trip back to Pacific Palisades.

If I could take just a moment; I had an assignment the other day. Someone asked me to write a letter for a time capsule that is going to be opened in Los Angeles a hundred years from now, on our Tricentennial.

She has no recollection of this. And that adds to her nervousness. She can imagine what the liberal cartoonists will do—show Ronnie burying himself as some smiling has-been artifact of the twentieth century. But there is no turning back from this last moment.

His words spread through the arena and out over the television air-waves:

It sounded like an easy assignment. They suggested I write something about the problems and issues of the day. I set out to do so, riding down the Coast in an automobile . . .

Who, several thousand listeners were thinking, still says "automobile," as if it were something new?

Then as I tried to write—well, let your own minds turn to that task. You are going to write for people a hundred years from now, who know all about us. We know nothing about them. We don't know what kind of a world they will be living in.

What, Nancy wondered, will they know about *him*? What will it all have amounted to? Wouldn't this video clip, the one now being created, just crumble to dust along with the reels of *Crash Landing*?

And suddenly I thought to myself, if I write of the problems, they will be the domestic problems of which the president spoke here tonight; the challenges confronting us, the erosion of freedom that has taken place under Democrat rule in this country . . .

Anne Macmurray Cox ground her teeth at this McCarthyite reference to a suffix-less "Democrat" party, but she listened politely to the litany of conservative complaint:

. . . the invasion of private rights, the controls and restrictions on the vitality of the great free economy that we enjoy. These are the challenges that we must meet . . .

Then, through her binoculars, she took what would be a last look, for a long time, at her ex-husband. Peter Cox was watching the proceedings with an intentness that he had never displayed in their pew at Christ Episcopal back in Owosso. The magnified sight disturbed her. Had her analysis been wrong? *Was* Peter actually a true believer in this glossy false god whose hair was dyed darker than her own? She made a mental note to rejoin the Presbyterian Church, yet another affiliation she'd exchanged for Peter's.

And suddenly it dawned on me: those who would read this letter a hundred years from now will know whether those missiles were fired. They will know whether we met our challenge. Whether they have the freedoms that we have known up until now will depend on what we do here.

"Well, of *course* they'll know!" exclaimed Pamela Harriman. "Dear God, if there *is* anything between his ears, it's straw."

Her son shooshed her and pointed to Ave, who was sleeping.

Will they look back with appreciation and say, "Thank God for those people in 1976 who headed off that loss of freedom, who kept us, now one hundred years later, free, who kept our world from nuclear destruction"?

Richard Nixon, having returned to his office following supper, relieved to know that Pat was again, already, sleeping, wondered if these people Reagan was talking about would ever appreciate *Nixon*, the first man to have *done* something about limiting those missiles, whose locations and throw weights Reagan didn't have the slightest goddamned idea of.

And if we failed, they probably won't get to read the letter at all because it spoke of individual freedom, and they won't be allowed to talk of that or read of it.

"Can you follow this?" Anne Cox asked Jane Hazard. "Are these future people supposed to be vaporized or just in prison?"

"He lost me driving down the Pacific Highway," Jane answered.

This is our challenge . . .

Nancy Reagan, whose nervousness about this improvised speech had trumped The Gaze and made her actually listen, could recognize the sound of a peroration coming on. They would soon be out of here. The benediction, she imagined, would be short and unfervent—the country's Holy Rollers had already gone over to Carter.

. . . we have got to quit talking to each other and about each other and go out and communicate to the world that we may be fewer in numbers than we have ever been, but we carry the message they are waiting for.

We must go forth from here united, determined that what a great general said a few years ago is true: There is no substitute for victory, Mr. President.

Applause that had been pent up by reverence, and by the riddle-like nature of Reagan's remarks, finally let itself go. The orchestra returned to life and played "California, Here I Come," a tune the Ford delegates could now sing as an order for Reagan to scram, once and for all.

On the platform the party elders buzzed with gabby relief. Unity! A microphone picked up Rockefeller's words of congratulation to Reagan— "Beautiful! Just beautiful!"—and Nixon heard them in San Clemente. A network floor reporter, one hand to his ear, shielding it against the din, declared with professional courtesy to the defeated that "nothing in Ronald Reagan's political life became him like the leaving of it." Richard Nixon, named like his brothers for English kings, vaguely recognized the quotation as being from Shakespeare. He also suddenly recognized what no one else seemed to: that this blankly genial, overappreciated son of a bitch, two years older than himself, was heading not for a pasture but a short stretch of wilderness, on the other side of which lay something vast.

Part One

AUGUST 19–OCTOBER 6, 1986

AUGUST 19, 1986

Through the open window Nancy heard five revs of the chain saw, his signature warm-up. Even before the tool could bite into the madrone's trunk, she knew that it had to be Ronnie—not Barney Barnett, out there with him—who was felling this particular dead tree. In no time at all he would clear three or four more from the property. Chopping them down remained his favorite form of exercise here at the ranch.

She liked the sound of the saw, found it as soothing as Ronnie found the company of Barney, the California highway patrolman who'd been his driver during their years in Sacramento. The neatened-up grounds always pleased her, the way the saw left the healthy trees standing, just as Dr. Davis, her neurosurgeon father, would leave the sound matter intact after removing the bad.

Today's *Washington Post* had already arrived, brought up the mountain by the government car that delivered the documents and the letters from ordinary people, a sampling of which Ronnie, still the softest touch, insisted upon seeing, even while here on vacation. The newspaper now rests, with a stack of others, atop a pool table not far from the couch she's sitting on. The house is so small there isn't even a proper rack for magazines. When visitors see how modest the space is—nothing but two little fireplaces to heat it—they always express surprise, intending a compliment (*It's so down-to-earth!*) that somehow comes out as an insult, as if they're really saying *I didn't imagine a spoiled bitch like you would put up with anything this primitive.*

In fact the house *is* too small and rustic. After all this time it remains Ronnie's idea of escape, not hers. She's *not* Marie Antoinette, the way people claim, but at the ranch she can never fully shake the sense that she's wearing that shepherdess's outfit the queen would don in order to go play in a little hut behind Versailles. She tries to remind herself that Ronnie and Barney have made a lot of improvements to the property, however rough it might still feel. The mission-tile roof they've put on never leaks, which is more than you could say for the ceiling of that arena in Kansas City a decade ago. Collapsed! Just a few years after they'd all been standing under it.

Ronnie's laughter, softer than Barney's, now came in on the breeze. It was always hard to tell if he was in an especially good mood, since his disposition was generally so good to begin with. But this summer, more than half a decade into his presidency, things have been going along in a way that's pleased—if not calmed—even her. George Shultz, to everyone's relief, has decided to stay on, so there's no danger of having to replace him with someone who might turn out to be like his predecessor, the preening, excitable Al Haig. And there's supposedly technical progress being made on SDI, though she herself cares more about making sure there's a follow-up to last year's meeting with Gorbachev and Raisa. If they're ever going to name a bridge or an airport after Ronnie, it'll be because he's signed a treaty, not because he's thrown some light beams into the sky, like Jack Warner staging a premiere in the parking lot at Grauman's.

There's been more good news besides. The tax-reform bill would probably get through the Senate in another month or so. She might not know much about its contents, but if even the liberals were calling it a "reform" bill, then it would be good for Ronnie politically—and postpresidentially, if that was a word. More and more that had become her focus—the "legacy"—and she didn't care how many concessions they made to Gorbachev, not if that's what it took to get Ronnie cast as a peacemaker. She'd sit here if need be, part of a cozy summit by one of the two fireplaces, listening to that dame lecture her on Marxist whatever-it-is—a small price to pay, like the hour spent on the Fourth of July standing beside that waxen philanderer, Mitterrand, when they all rechristened the Statue of Liberty and created the most spectacular photos of Ronnie's presidency, the heaven-sent backdrop beyond anything even Mike Deaver had been able to arrange during the first term.

Mike's current troubles, a small black cloud above the generally sunny landscape, were something she wouldn't think about now.

Of course, Ronnie's fine mood came mostly from the fact that they were *here*, at the ranch, although the *amount* of time he was spending here had just become a new source of worry to the first lady. She would have to banish that thought as well. In fact, before she even skimmed the *Post* she would call Mother, still slowly dying in Phoenix.

But as she reached for it, the telephone began ringing. The Signal Corps operator came on the line: "Mrs. Reagan? Mr. Regan."

The names were so close—except for her long "a" versus the chief of staff's long "e"—that the four words always sounded silly, the way each morning's phone call between Queen Elizabeth and *her* mother would begin, she'd been told, with the operator saying, "Your Majesty? Her Majesty."

She detested Don Regan. Mike's biggest mistake had been allowing Ronnie to let the treasury secretary and Jim Baker switch jobs at the beginning of last year. She'd had almost nothing to do with Don when he was in the cabinet, but as chief of staff he presented her with constant irritations. Each of them was unable to disguise dislike of the other, and the only way for her to handle a call from him was to plunge in as if *she'd* been the one to place it.

"Don," she began. "You need to take care of this little ranch problem before it gets out of hand."

"What 'little ranch problem' is that?"

She could picture him in his suite at the Biltmore over in Santa Barbara—big Mr. Merrill Lynch stuck in the same hotel as the traveling press corps. And she could tell from his voice that she'd knocked him off guard—good!—as if she were summoning him to come fix a broken latch in the hay barn.

She explained the problem: "I saw something in the *Herald Examiner* yesterday—I hope you did, too—about how by this time next year Ronald Reagan will have spent a year of his presidency in California."

Some reporter had done the math: at the current rate, Ronnie would accumulate three hundred days at the ranch, plus another seventy-five or so at the Annenbergs' and the Century Plaza in L.A. "They ran the story with a sort of favorite-son pride. But that's not how it'll play in the rest of the country if anyone picks it up. It will make Ronnie sound lazy." She paused for a few seconds. "What are your plans for dealing with it?"

Regan, his Irish already up, responded in the voice he'd inherited from his father, a Boston cop: "I don't know. Suggest that you spend more time in Washington?"

His tone froze her for only a moment. "Well, since that's not an option," she declared, "you need to come up with something else, and you need to do it soon."

The injustice of the reporter's statistics seemed self-evident to her. Didn't the work of the presidency always go on right here in the Santa Ynez Mountains? Her husband had signed bills on the house's patio; they'd entertained the queen and Prince Philip in this very room. And this morning, before Barney arrived, Ronnie had put in a good half hour on a third draft of his latest letter to Gorbachev. Cap Weinberger and that ridiculous new national security advisor with the pipe, Poindexter, had so overstuffed him with contradictory arms-control facts that the letter was all bollixed up.

"I was actually calling *about* something," Regan said.

She remained silent. She was already angry enough with him that that slight stammer might come into her voice, and if it did she would lose the game, or at least this inning of it. She counted to ten, until one would have thought the line had gone dead.

The chief of staff blinked first: "We've got to get the president to Alabama and New Orleans in mid-September."

The first lady said nothing, though she knew how crucial the midterm elections were. If the Republicans were to hold the Senate, they needed to get Ronnie out campaigning one last time.

"So how would September eighteenth be?" Regan asked. "Would that be a *good* day? A *bad* one?"

The sarcasm in his voice earned him further silence.

"Maybe an *in-between* one?" he persisted.

"I'll have to get back to you," Nancy said at last.

"Well, maybe you can tell your 'friend' that we need her to be quick with the forecast."

They both knew—how she wished she'd been able to keep him in the dark!—that the friend in question was her astrologer. The "forecast" was Joan Quigley's reading of Ronnie's prospects on days when the White House staff wanted him to travel.

"I'm not wild about October first," said Nancy, shifting the subject in a way guaranteed to further exasperate the chief of staff.

"That can't be changed," Regan said crisply.

"Hmmm," said Nancy.

Regan, as usual, had reached a fast boil. "The president cannot fail to be present at the dedication of his predecessor's library." After six years of traveling the Third World and hammering together those houses for the poor, all of it accompanied by relentless criticism of Ronnie, Jimmy Carter was finally going to cut the ribbon on the building in which scholars could now go to research his miserable four years in the White House.

"Hmmm," was all Nancy said, again.

"Well," said Regan, "get back to me as soon as possible about September eighteenth. Enjoy your day." He hung up the phone.

It was unclear to her which of them had won. Maybe neither. But she tried to sit herself back on the couch with a nonchalance that would make her feel and *look* like the winner, if only to herself. Opening up the Style section of the *Post*, she went right to page 7 for Ronnie's horoscope, which she always read before her own:

AQUARIUS (Jan. 20–Feb. 18): Following initial delay, money will be received. You'll locate needed material, pieces will fall into place. Refine techniques, streamline procedures. You are going places! Pisces, Virgo persons play roles.

She never much liked Sydney Omarr's forecasts—she needed Joan's customized charts for anything important—and this one annoyed her by failing to deliver the instant feeling of applicability that made you say

Of course. "Money"? After "initial delay"? Maybe that had something to do with the vote on the tax bill, but the ambiguity peeved Nancy; as did the absence of a Cancer, her own sign, from the list of persons who'd be playing a role in Ronnie's life today.

And yet, Gorbachev—March 2—was a Pisces. The recollection of this fact prompted her to reread the short paragraph. It still didn't add up to much. But if Ronnie wanted to "streamline procedures," he should find a new chief of staff and replace the odious man she'd just spoken to. The only thing she liked about Don Regan was his marriage. He and his wife were almost as close to each other as the Reagans, though the protective balance with them was reversed in a way that Nancy secretly envied. Don Regan organized much of his own life around his wife's terrible arthritis, always making sure that Ann wasn't overburdened. It would be nice, Nancy imagined, to have someone doing that for her, instead of her always having to do it for Ronnie. But that's how things were, she thought, without regret, as she regarded the dried lavender in a nearby vase. The flowers in here were always dried, because freshly cut ones made Ronnie sneeze.

She would spend much of today on the telephone, the way she did in the White House. No one there had been so glued to a receiver since Lyndon Johnson had occupied the place like some caged stallion. It had recently occurred to her how much LBJ would have liked the new cordless phones. Right now the one on the couch cushion was ringing again.

"Mrs. Reagan, I have Mr. Griffin on the line."

"Oh, good!" Merv was always fun.

"How are you, Merv?" she asked, as if she'd just sat down on his talk-show couch.

"Thrilled," he replied, in that familiar, excitable purr. "Now that I'm talking to my favorite first lady."

"Aw, you're sweet. I heard that you just taped your last program."

"It airs September fifth," said Merv. "I didn't *dare* ask you to come on, you're so busy."

"Oh, I would have!" said Nancy. Don Regan, or one of the young men who worked for him—known around the White House as "the mice"—should have been smart enough to arrange it.

"*No!*" said Merv, conveying what sounded like real disbelief. "Oh, well. The whole show—forty-eight hundred episodes!—is beginning to fade from my mind. I'm buying hotels!" he announced, like a retiree who'd just discovered tennis or bridge. Only months ago he'd sold his production company to Coca-Cola for a quarter of a billion dollars.

"The Two Hundred and Fifty Million Dollar Man!" enthused Nancy, with the surprisingly personable giggle that sometimes managed to bubble up through all her anger and anxiety. "You know, I've been meaning to call you. We're planning a Gershwin evening at the White House this fall." Joan had already okayed October 26, though there was little to fear, since Ronnie wouldn't be leaving the grounds for the event.

"Ooh," said Merv. "*Great* idea."

"We've got Marvin Hamlisch putting it together."

"*Super* talent."

"And Kitty Carlisle." She pronounced the name with the slightest hesitation, hoping he'd hear it and reassure her. "I haven't seen her in years, and I know she's a very active Democrat."

"She'll be *fine*," Merv purred. "You know, she even dated Tom Dewey before he croaked. He wanted to *marry* her."

"No!" said Nancy, giggling again, this time with relief. But seconds later she thought she should do a little more checking.

"Sarah Vaughan?" *She won't make any kind of Lena Horne or Eartha Kitt trouble, will she?*

She didn't have to be specific. Merv could always tell what she was after: "No problem there, either."

She again felt better. Merv really did know everybody, and his judgment was excellent. She ought to ask him about Just Say No—it was running out of steam and could use some fresh celebrities—but a glance at the clock told her that she needed to get ready for her afternoon ride with Ronnie. The chain saws had stopped, and she bet he was already on his way to get the saddles from the tack barn.

"Did I tell you my fella's gotten me a new horse?" she asked Merv. "'No Strings.'"

"Ooh," he replied. "Great *name*."

Nancy chuckled. "Nothing comes without strings."

Merv laughed. She could picture the way his tongue would now be pressing up against his front teeth.

"Any chance of lunch?" he asked. "Before we lose you again to Washington?"

"You bet," said Nancy. "Though right now I'd better scoot. Thanks for cheering me up, Mervyn."

She lingered on the couch for just a moment, reluctantly skimming a *Post* article on the death of Way Bandy, who'd done her makeup for the Scavullo shoot only three months ago. AIDS. She shivered just thinking about it. If he'd made one bad poke with the tweezers, my God, she could have . . . She dismissed the fear, telling herself she couldn't be in any worse danger than Barbra Streisand and all his other clients. After all, Doris Day had actually *hugged* Rock, right up until the end.

She folded the paper, put it back on the pool table, and got up to get her straw hat. She never truly looked forward to riding; she'd only learned to do it to please him. She nodded to the agent, just beyond the open front door, to let him know she hadn't forgotten the time. Through the doorway came the sound of the dogs, barking at some stray cats who'd joined the ranch's menagerie only the other day. Eventually, they'd be buried with all the other dogs and horses and cats, under the patch of land that Ronnie called Boot Hill; each got a little grave marker that he carved himself. This was the man that the "activists"—the nuclear-freeze types, the AIDS protesters—called heartless!

She looked out the window toward the riding trails, wishing they could be paved over for golf carts instead of horses, the way Nixon had done with so many of the ones at Camp David. A second Secret Service man, carrying the nuclear football, came into view several paces behind Ronnie, who'd already said goodbye to Barney and was on his way, sure enough, to the tack barn.

Scarcely an hour ago, when he kissed her goodbye, she'd tenderly brushed two spots on his face that were scabbed over from the other day's liquid-nitrogen procedure. Just the routine removal of a couple of brown spots from a handsome man who'd spent a little too much of his life in the sun: nothing to worry about. And yet, as she touched the half-healed punctures, she had winced, suddenly imagining them as bullet holes, the way even now, five years later, every slammed door or dropped fork still sounded like a shot.

———

Across the country, through a barred set of fourth-floor windows, John Hinckley looked down on the St. Elizabeths graveyard. A few of the headstones, he reasoned, were probably for people who'd died right here in the maximum-security ward of the hospital's Howard Pavilion.

There was no way *he* would die here, unless he got shot escaping, which remained a possibility, if he could get his girlfriend in Chicago, or his other girlfriend, the one right here in St. Elizabeths, to aid and abet him. He would need, of course, a gun; his current lack of one still felt somehow curious, like the absence of an apostrophe in the hospital's name.

But he did not believe he would have to shoot his way out of here. He had decided that he would *talk* his way out, gradually, incrementally, through the voices of his lawyers and, whenever Judge Parker permitted, by means of his own voice, addressed directly to the court. Twice a year he was allowed to petition for his release, but he'd never done that, because he knew what the outcome would be. He had adopted, instead, his slow-and-steady strategy, wearing his clip-on tie to court every several months and motioning for the next carefully calibrated expansion of his privileges: the right to walk on the hospital grounds; permission to speak with the news media. This latter request has been denied, despite the logic of his argument that such interviews would be helpful in building up his "self-respect and dignity." Judge Parker's refusal is a setback, but it does not refute the basic wisdom of his own long-term plan. His remorseful letters to the *Washington Post* are definitely shifting public opinion in his direction. And you have to consider this: he is able to write them only because the hospital no longer monitors his incoming or outgoing mail—itself a tribute to his increasing sanity.

Behind him the noise in the day room grew louder. Three angry residents of the ward, ignored by several more listless ones, were arguing over the choice of a TV channel. This afternoon there seemed to be nothing but soap operas and *Love Connection*, and the fruitless search for an action movie or sports event was raising tempers already inflamed by the District of Columbia's August heat, which the pavilion's air conditioning did little to alleviate.

Then a cry of delight changed the room's mood. *"Damn!"* shouted the patient closest to the television. "Gonna get me some motherfuckin' *kaboom!*"

Hinckley turned to look at the screen. A rocket was launching, and everyone knew how its brief journey would end. They had seen CNN's *Challenger* clip so often these past seven months that it might have been playing on a loop, the means by which he'd once managed to watch *Taxi Driver* fifteen times in a row. The news channel ran the footage every chance it got, right now as the visual background for a story about a lack of progress in implementing recommendations from the commission that had investigated the Shuttle accident.

The live network anchor fell silent and allowed the sound of the January clip to take over. Yet again, less than half a minute after liftoff, one could hear: *"good roll program confirmed . . .* Challenger *now heading downrange . . . "*

Thirty-one seconds—his age, thirty-one—on the clock. The explosion would come at seventy-three, an age Reagan had now passed, because the Devastator bullet, which John Hinckley had placed near his heart, had failed to explode. The rocket, by contrast, was at this moment being destroyed by the flaw it carried within itself.

NASA's official spokesman, on the sudden fire in the sky: *"Flight controllers here looking very carefully at the situation . . . obviously a major malfunction—"*

"A major *motherfuckin'* malfunction!" shouted the patient nearest the screen. It was always "patients," never "inmates"; they were all here "by reason of insanity."

Hinckley turned back to the window, not to escape the happy shouting in the room, where a measure of good humor had been restored by the familiar cartoonish disaster, but to avoid looking at what came next, just *after* the explosion: a divergence of the smoke into two plumes that traveled in separate directions, as if trying to get away from each other. *Never the twain shall meet*, he thought, recalling a phrase he'd heard in junior high school.

He had made, in his own phrase, "the greatest love offering in the history of the world," and she had spurned it, raced away from acknowledgment of his existence as quickly as one of those plumes.

But he is over Jodie. He is ready—gradually, incrementally—to step out of here, to reinsert himself, quietly, like an explosive charge, at some well-chosen point in the vast country beyond these locked windows.

2

AUGUST 25, 1986

Thanks to a strictly kept regimen in the gym beneath his Arlington condominium, Anders Little, at thirty-eight, maintained the lean physique with which he had once competed on the Wake Forest track team. Here inside the Old Executive Office Building, he always took the stairs instead of the elevators, and during breaks in his day he would do laps of the tiled corridors. He'd make several circuits, sustaining the pace of a speed-walker, hoping to look driven instead of ridiculous. His sandy hair was thinning, but he had the tight, trim look of a career military man. One expected him to say "ma'am," and he often did—not because he'd ever been in the Army, but because his father, back in Mooresville, North Carolina, had taught him to.

Returning from lunch, Anders heard the sound of hammers coming from the direction of the vice president's big ceremonial office. The renovations to it, which promised to be long and noisy, must at last have begun. Anders, who liked quiet, paused for a moment on the second-floor landing to look up through the skylight. A plump white cloud scudded invitingly through the blue; you'd never guess that outside it was a typical August day in the District of Columbia, steamy and unbearable.

He walked into his office, room 380A. The nameplate on the door looked impressive—ASST DIR / ARMS CNTRL / NSC / MR LITTLE—until one considered that it was made of cardboard. People came and went quickly around here; it was the rare bird who stayed in one job for four years, let alone eight. The Defense Programs and Arms Control Division of the National Security Council consisted of only nine people, and in truth Anders spent his days mostly *being* directed rather than directing anyone else. Besides, much of the real action on arms control was outside the White House, over at the Pentagon or State or the ACDA, with the big brains like Perle and Adelman. Even so, Anders—a convert to Reaganism rather than an early true believer—felt delighted to be here.

He had come out of Wake Forest as a moderate Democrat in the tumultuous spring of 1970, and had managed to remain one through two years of graduate study at Fletcher and four years as a researcher at Brookings. Anders's politics, in fact, had been generally as tepid as his romances and two marriages. The first of those had occurred during the bicentennial year, when he also took a post at the U.S. Mission to the United Nations. There, over the next five years, Anders got a bellyful of the Soviets and all their lying proxies, from Czechoslovakia to Angola. He became a considerably tougher, more ideological fellow.

Early in '81 he had been assigned to a small committee charged with "facilitating the transition" from Carter's mild exiting ambassador to Reagan's fierce incoming one. Most of the career staff were horrified by the advent of Dr. Jeane Kirkpatrick, who was sulky, brooding, and brilliant, determined to use the UN as an American bully pulpit instead of an altar for penitence. But Anders had *welcomed* the arrival of this unlikely academic who compared totalitarians (chiefly the Soviets) and authoritarians (mostly our guys, often South Americans) and saw a distinction, one worth exploiting. Non-Communist dictatorships might, and occasionally did, evolve into something better; Communist ones couldn't, and didn't. They needed overthrowing.

Jeane Kirkpatrick had spotted Anders Little as a young man on a road running parallel to the longer, wider one that she had traveled. In his case, the movement was from bland belief in coexistence toward implacable opposition to the Russians. She herself had always been a Cold Warrior, but had come to realize there was no longer much room for her kind inside the Democratic Party she had fervently supported from Truman through Humphrey. If she really wanted to sweep back the Communist tide, she'd now have to get her broom from the Republican supply closet.

For a period of several weeks she talked to Anders as if he were a favorite thesis supervisee. And then, once the transition between ambassadors was complete, he'd told her he needed to go to Washington; his new, second wife, Sarah, had a job offer there. Mrs. K. had raised her eyebrows, thrust out her lips, and thought. She disliked fecklessness and confusion, and Anders could see her thinking that thirty-three, his age then, was a bit early for a second marriage. But two days later, knowing that he, too, believed in Reagan's view of the Cold War—*we win; they lose*—she'd gotten him a position on the National Security Council. The administration's arms-control policies would be, she assured him, unambiguous: *we* would attempt to control *their* arms, and to build up our own.

Mrs. Kirkpatrick was not a pretty woman, and she was almost as old as Anders's mother, but for the next few years, from his low-level vantage in Washington, he watched her performance at the UN with a starstruck ardor. Those scoldings to commissars and postcolonial despots that she'd delivered across the UN's horseshoe table from inside her shoulder-padded suits: thrilling!

Jeane Kirkpatrick might have wound up being his boss down here. At the end of Reagan's first term she'd wanted the national security advisor's job, but by now she'd been passed over for it twice, and the likelihood of its ever coming her way seemed remote. Her relationship with George Shultz was better than what she'd had with Alexander Haig, his predecessor at State, but Jeane was still stronger drink than Shultz preferred; and Reagan, who found Shultz soothing, was determined to keep him happy—no matter how much the president himself liked Mrs. Kirkpatrick. So she was now back teaching at Georgetown, when she wasn't out on the lecture circuit or writing her column. Anders saw her from time to time, and got to call her Jeane; he felt flattered when she complimented his ever-hardening views or teased him about being her "fly on the wall at the NSC."

She had brought a number of important people his way—and the sender-ID number suddenly visible on the gurgling fax machine told Anders that the most improbable of them all was now checking in:

26 FEDERAL PLAZA
212-227-8388

Sure enough, the incoming cover sheet displayed the large, legible fountain-penmanship he'd come to recognize:

Read this over and call back to discuss distribution. RN

Anders could picture the thirty-seventh president sitting just as he'd been when Mrs. K. first sent him, with a letter of introduction, to Nixon's office in downtown New York. Now, as then, the former president's jacket would be on, and his tie firmly knotted; his polished wingtip shoes would be up on the hassock, a grudging concession to comfort and phlebitis. The eraser tip of a pencil would be lightly pressing against his lower lip while he made, on a yellow legal pad, some impersonal-sounding notes meant just for himself, and perhaps posterity.

When he and Anders first met, Nixon had been not much longer acquainted with Jeane than Anders was himself. Newly back in New York from his exile in San Clemente, the former president had made it his business to meet the new UN ambassador, who had quite loathed him during all her years voting for Adlai Stevenson. But she had long since come around to—and gone past—his view of foreign affairs. Jeane Kirkpatrick respected Richard Nixon as a supreme strategist and a kind of saturnine soul mate, but she currently regarded him, thanks to détente, and with no little historical irony, as being somewhat soft on Communism.

Nixon's fax to Anders was brief and blunt, two typewritten pages, marked by its author's penchant for the seesaw syntax of antithesis:

The President must beware of Gorbachev's eagerness for a second summit, and must resist what the media claim to be the American public's appetite for one. The President's resistance to an initial summit throughout his first four years in office did him no political harm (he got re-elected with 49 states), while it did the U.S. a large amount of strategic good. Waiting for the Soviet Union's new man, the one at last in a position to do something other than die in office, signaled RR's own seriousness and strengthened the American position.

Gorbachev's current proposal—for a unilateral Soviet moratorium on *underground nuclear testing, in advance of a treaty that bans it altogether and which both countries can sign at the next summit—needs to be strongly rebuffed, however welcome it may be to the nuclear-freeze crowd and their friends in the press. The U.S. <u>needs</u> underground testing—to catch up and then to keep up. A "freeze" in this realm would be as damaging to our interests as a freeze in the production and deployment of missiles themselves. Gorbachev's proposal is not a "gesture toward peace"; it's an aggressive move.*

The President's spokesman was right to deflect it, but he allowed Gorbachev to derive a net plus just from making the offer. What is missing from our refusal is direct, persistent, in-your-face reference to Chernobyl. Without that, turning down the Soviet proposal makes the U.S. look cavalier about the possibility of nuclear accidents—at a time when <u>Soviet</u> incompetence has discharged into the atmosphere enough radioactivity to kill 40,000 people: their own citizens and Europeans.

It is vital for the U.S. to draw attention to this, but to do it in humane ways: we should flood the Soviets with well-publicized offers of medical aid and research that can improve their long-term situation—offers they cannot refuse without appearing paranoid and callous. We should extend an unlimited, no-strings invitation to medical refugees from this calamity, while pointing out, continually, how what's occurred on their soil has poisoned the environment of a whole continent. Remind our allies and the American public that the Soviets are both the perpetrators and the victims of what is, in effect, their own Hiroshima. Cement the impression that they are technologically ossified and dangerous all at once.

Any deflation of the Soviets' pride puts them in a weaker position both globally and at the negotiating table. I'm not saying that Chernobyl isn't a tragedy; I'm merely saying that it's also an opportunity. The Soviets have been shaken by this event; I saw plenty of evidence for that during my recent trip. Confidence has lessened, not increased, during Gorbachev's premiership. The man at the next summit will be less in control, not more so, than he was at the last one—so long as the Administration doesn't inadvertently contribute to the constant and deliberate buildup that Gorbachev receives in the American press.

On the subject of national pride and its effect upon the two countries'
strengths in negotiating: It is imperative that the United States relaunch the
space shuttle before the Soviets can get a version of their own into orbit—an
enterprise they do not appear to have abandoned. And in the meantime, the
Administration must resist every tendency, both subconscious and overt, to
see the Challenger *and* Chernobyl *as being somehow equivalent disasters.*
They are not: seven lives willingly put at risk by those living them do not
match the slow deaths of 40,000 people who had no inkling of what they
were in for. Chernobyl is an ongoing catastrophe on the grand scale, and the
proper "use" of it can assure that a summit takes place on the U.S. Presi-
dent's own terms and timetable.

The warning against "equivalence" sounded very much like Jeane,
who for years now had been attacking the liberal inclination to see the
Soviet and American systems as not much different morally; to view both
of them, essentially, as failed experiments in idealism. Nixon's thinking lately appeared to be moving her way, to be entertaining the possibility that his own bold attempts at rapprochement had gone further
than they needed to, because the Soviet Union, while on the march, and
still expanding, was expanding like a *gas*, a cloud sufficiently weak at its
point of origin that the larger it got, the weaker its whole existence might
be getting. This was the wildest hope in the geopolitical air, and still a
minority point of view by far, but Anders Little thought that Nixon was
beginning to pick up its scent.

Who should get this fax? Certainly Adelman and Perle. And maybe
Elliott Abrams over at State. There was no need to send it to Shultz and
Weinberger: Reagan's State and Defense secretaries had both served in
Nixon's own cabinet, and to act as if Nixon required a third party to con-
vey his postpresidential thoughts to them would be to imply, insultingly,
that he couldn't now reach out to them directly.

Anders's real quandary involved Admiral Poindexter. Nixon wanted
to be in touch with the still-new national security advisor because, having once put Henry Kissinger in that job, he continued to believe it was
where the real action and influence lay. But Poindexter, an odd, hard-

to-read figure, might think Anders had overstepped if he delivered this memo without its having been requested. And yet, that's what Nixon surely wanted, even more than direct conversation with Reagan himself. The two presidents did talk, often, and the former one was always careful to speak respectfully of the incumbent to Anders Little; but Nixon dropped hints of frustration, too, indications of uncertainty about how much of what he said really *registered* with Reagan—even about how much of it was, literally, heard.

Anders still couldn't believe he was in a position directly to aid a man for whom—with his parents back in 1960, at the age of twelve—he'd rung doorbells in Mooresville. What Nixon really wanted, even now, was to become a "back channel" for the president; a crucial, occasional, out-of-sight envoy to Moscow and Beijing. Such a position would not require confirmation by the Senate—a prospect about as likely as Gorbachev becoming the GOP's presidential nominee in '88—but it would still demand, for starters, keeping Nixon on various radar screens here, including Poindexter's. That much Anders *could* do.

Anders needed to concentrate his mind before calling Nixon back with a response to the fax, so he got up and went out into the corridor to do another couple of brisk laps around the EOB. He'd gone about a dozen yards before he ran into a pretty girl with a big *Dynasty*-style mane of blond hair. He'd seen her a few times previously but couldn't remember her name: Tawny? Dawn? Fawn?

"Hello," he said.

"Hey."

He couldn't recall whom she belonged to, so he looked up at the sign on the door she was heading toward, room 392, DEPUTY DIR / POL / MIL AFFRS. He now remembered: she was Ollie North's girl. Anders never saw much of North, and the colonel, who managed to be furtive and swaggering all at once, didn't particularly interest him. If Anders's job put him "down in the weeds"—ensnared in statistics and throw weights and warheads—North was there in a more literal way, spending his time on the survival of the Contras in the jungles of Nicaragua.

"Summer doldrums?" he asked Dawn or Fawn, hoping quickly to get through a few pleasantries and then hit his fast indoor stride.

"Maybe for *you* guys!" she said, with a big smile. She shifted a wad of gum from one side of her mouth to the other.

"Not for you?" asked Anders. "You got your money, after all." After some fierce politicking by the administration, the House had reversed itself late in June and voted $100 million in aid to the Contras.

Dawn or Fawn shook her head and its golden hair. "It's not enough. And we're still out of cash until the appropriation comes through in October. Ever hear of a bridge loan?"

"Yeah," said Anders. He and Sarah had had to take one out a couple of years ago, before they could get a mortgage on the house in Tenleytown.

"Well, we're sort of looking for one. Got any spare dough?" She flashed him another big smile.

"I've got about enough for a Diet Coke in the machine down the hall."

She laughed and headed into 392. Anders waved goodbye, did two fast circuits of the floor, then reentered his own office. He took a deep breath before dialing Nixon's direct number in New York.

"What do you think?" asked the former president, without so much as a hello.

"An excellent memo, sir."

"Who should see it?"

"Well," said Anders, "I should think Adelman, Perle, and Abrams. For a start." He paused, trying to make himself say "Poindexter." When he couldn't quite do it, he found himself adding, "And probably the VP."

"Hmm," said Nixon.

Anders suddenly remembered that Nixon could of course get it to Bush—another of his old appointees, like Weinberger and Shultz—all on his own. Now afraid that he might have given offense, he decided to take the plunge. "And probably Admiral Poindexter."

"Good idea," the ex-president said, offhandedly, disguising his enthusiasm. Still nervous, Anders changed the subject. "When did you last speak to President Reagan?"

"A month ago," said Nixon. "Before I went over to Moscow."

Nixon's information was often fresher and better than what the White House gathered on its own.

"Wait a minute," Nixon added. "I talked to him after I got back, too. I called to congratulate him on his South Africa speech. Not that it was much of one." As if concerned he might be approaching disrespect, Nixon tacked on a disclaimer: "The circumstances didn't permit a great speech, of course."

The administration was walking a fine line over Pretoria, proposing "modified" sanctions rather than the more stringent ones being advocated by European governments and protesters here at home. Don Regan had recently made things worse by saying that women sympathetic to the tougher measures would take a different view once the price of diamonds rose.

"Right," said Anders, walking a fine line himself. Ronald Reagan was his ultimate boss, and when talking to a nonappointee—even Richard M. Nixon—all of the administration's public pronouncements were to be deemed splendidly well-reasoned. So he changed the subject: "Will you have a chance to see the president at the Carter Library opening?"

"Hell, no!" answered Nixon, with a snort. "JC wants the spotlight all for himself, and he doesn't give a damn about history. Thinks of his lousy administration as the New Testament—no need to pay attention to anything that came before it. He's *got* to have Reagan there, but he figures he can get along without the exes. And God knows, without *me*."

Anders knew that, for all the phone calls and memos to and from the White House, Nixon hadn't been through its doors since '81, when Reagan and Haig had given all the ex-presidents, including Carter, a little bon voyage before sending them off to Sadat's funeral. Surely, as much as he craved becoming a back channel, Nixon desired at least one or two more chances to walk through the front door.

"Reagan needs to be *campaigning* in the South," said Nixon, with sudden energy. "Not just sitting on a platform in Atlanta, listening to Carter sermonize. If they lose the Senate in November, after having had it for six years, things will be halfway back to where they were in '80."

Curious, thought Anders, that he said "they" instead of "we" when it came to the GOP. Even before his disgrace, Nixon had lost any real taste for party-building.

"I tell you," the former president added, with a chuckle, "election night 1980 was the most enjoyable one I ever had outside of '46 and '68. Church, Bayh, McGovern, Gaylord Nelson—seeing that whole crowd go down like ten little left-wing Indians!"

Anders laughed with him, before offering the current inside view: "The political people around here think we'll hold the Senate."

"I'm not so sure," said Nixon. "The Democrats are *hungry*, and they're going to make every effort. Christ, they've got the Widow Harriman out there rattling her solid-gold cup for them. And she must have plenty of her own cash now that 'the Governor' has finally kicked off." Averell Harriman had died, at the age of ninety-four, on July 26.

"I wouldn't know about all that," said Anders, referring to wealth and society with a boyish laugh.

"Well," said Nixon, shifting into some world-weary philosophy, "you're better off for it. I never needed the Georgetown crowd when I was in the game, and now that I'm out of it I don't need to stay at the goddamned Hay-Adams when I'm back in Washington. Speaking of hotels: When was the last time you had your folks come visit? Do they like to stay on their own when they do? A lot of older couples prefer that to staying with the daughter or son-in-law. And I can tell you, the best hotel bargain you'll find is One Washington Circle over in Foggy Bottom. Not too far from the State Department, but not so close that you can smell it!"

Anders laughed, and wondered what to say. The hotel Nixon had just recommended, like some office-supply salesman who did his business travel on a budget, was also just blocks from the Watergate.

"Get ready for a test," said Nixon.

Anders started, as if the ex-president's baritone were announcing a fire drill in the EOB. But then he realized this was only one of those conversational lurches that Nixon made whenever he recognized, with a certain embarrassment, that he had let the discussion meander into small talk.

"A test?"

"It'll spring from the Zakharov thing," Nixon explained, referring to the arrest over the weekend of a Soviet spy attached to the United Nations.

Anders instantly warmed to this new subject. "When I was up at the UN, the Soviets had five hundred people in the Secretariat, and I'm telling you, Mr. President, *four* hundred of them were spies."

"They'll respond to his detention with a bullshit arrest of someone over *there*, one of *our* people, on trumped-up charges. They can't afford not to. They can keep Zakharov's arrest out of their papers at home, but all the 'representatives' of their client states will be seeing it in New York, and they can't lose face with *them*. So get ready for some kind of crap—which the administration is going to have to resist. And which means not being so overeager for a summit that we let the Russians get away with whatever the stunt turns out to be."

"An excellent point, sir."

"The U.S. goes to summits feeling hopeful; they go to achieve an advantage."

Anders copied down this latest antithesis, just as he would make a Xerox of the fax on his desk. He couldn't deny that he hoped to write a book one day.

"You know the expression *cherchez la femme*?" asked Nixon. "Well, I'll tell you the *femme* to keep in your sights."

"Raisa?" guessed Anders.

"Hell, no. *Nancy.* She's the one who's going to keep pushing Reagan back to the table. That's the big, last image she wants for him: tough man turned peacemaker. A little like myself in that regard. But she wants it for all the wrong reasons—she craves the approval of all the wrong *people*. She's more and more friendly with Kay Graham these days. Christ, she's even been sucking up to Jackie Kennedy. *They're* what she likes to see as her real crowd—not showbiz. Forget the hundred times she and Reagan have stood next to Bob Hope. Show business is what she wants to *overcome*. Even if she still sees everything in those terms. Sort of like Mrs. Harding and small-town Ohio."

Anders laughed, nervously. Criticizing the boss's wife was worse than criticizing the boss. And . . . Mrs. *Harding*? "Before my time, I'm afraid, sir."

"Before mine, too. But I've got a lot of time to read these days."

Anders ventured down the safest first-lady route he could think of: "How is Mrs. Nixon?" he asked. In the pause that followed, Anders wondered if the former president was having "thoughts that lie too deep for tears," a line he always remembered from English 350 at Wake Forest.

"She's well at the moment. Sometimes she struggles. Pulmonary problems."

He seemed to speak the more clinical word, rather than "lung," as if it would do a better job keeping his wife's afflictions in check.

"I can tell you," Nixon continued, "that *she* never felt being born in a miner's shack, or being a schoolteacher, was something she had to *over-come*. She's the same person she was the day I met her." He paused once again. "Don't know if she'd say the same thing about me."

"I'm sure that—"

"Well, let's cut out all this Barbara Walters crap."

"Should I share the fax with Mrs. Kirkpatrick?" Anders asked, as briskly as he could.

"Where is she now?" asked Nixon.

"In the South of France for a bit."

"Writing her book?"

"Well," Anders began to answer, reluctantly. All the speaking and column-writing was coming easily to Jeane. But her book was something else. She'd told him that she preferred to write about things like diplomatic strategies for dealing with Bulgaria, whereas Simon & Schuster was pressing her for "How I Unmanned Haig."

"She's going to have to make up her mind," said Nixon.

"About the book?" asked Anders, afraid he'd inadvertently spoken what he'd meant only to think.

"About politics," answered Nixon. "Whether she's going to be in or out."

"Oh, the VP talk," said Anders. "Yes." Jeane was being mentioned as a running mate for a whole series of Republican contenders in '88, including George Bush and Jack Kemp.

"God," said Nixon, "I even hear *presidential* talk." His tone indicated that he didn't take it seriously. "The Texans I speak to are crazy about her. As if she's some female Connally. The Connally of old, I mean."

Anders recalled the ex-president's infatuation with his Treasury secretary, the sleek, silver-haired assassination survivor and the biggest Democratic convert to Nixon's momentary New Majority.

"He's a sad s.o.b. these days," said the former president, with a sigh. "He's going to file for bankruptcy before the year's out. Real estate deals!" Nixon scornfully disbelieved that any man could prefer business speculation to political gambles. "He still owes eight hundred grand from 1980. That was a pretty expensive delegate!"

Anders smiled at the thought of the one convention vote Connally had managed to rustle up for all that money.

"He's got a man in his current operation, one who's sticking by him, fellow named Peter Cox, who's done me some favors. He was in the office here in New York for a drink yesterday. We were talking about *you*, incidentally—in connection with that fax I was preparing."

"Really, sir?"

"This morning he calls back and tells me how he mentioned our conversation to his wife—*ex*-wife, actually—over the telephone last night. And now she's wondering if this nice young fellow—I guess that's what I called you—could possibly show her around the West Wing and the EOB when she visits Washington in another week or two. Hang on and let me find the scrap of paper with—"

Nixon hunted for whatever note he'd made. Two hundred miles away, Anders could detect through the receiver a high degree of fuss and clumsiness. Was there no one to fetch it for him?

"She goes by *Macmurray* now," said Nixon, after returning to the line. His tone contained a hint of disdain for women's lib. "Her maiden name, I suppose. Never met her."

Anders, who like most EOB employees had given White House tours to countless classmates and cousins, said, "Of course, sir. I'd be happy to show her around."

Nixon gave him the phone number for Anne Macmurray's Washington friends.

"Well, good," said Nixon. "And how is your own wife?"

"She's fine, sir." There seemed no pressing need to admit that he'd moved out of the house and into his bachelor condo last month.

"Good. Put Poindexter in touch with me and be prepared."

"Prepared?"

"For that test I mentioned."

"Oh, yes."

"*Hasta luego*, Andy." It was his usual sign-off, jokey and almost affectionate, even if its abruptness signaled a kind of chagrin that he'd caught himself speaking to you at all.

Anders felt ready for another two or three laps of the building. He always needed to let the tension run out of him after talking to Nixon. And he'd just rattled himself with the little lie of omission about his split from Sarah.

Looking out the window of his office, beginning to stare at the building's French Empire columns, he thought, in sequence, of Cindy and Emily and Sarah, one girlfriend and two wives, as well as two or three women in between. He found himself considering a reason why his political views may have toughened as much as they had. Was it because of what the *Post*'s Style section liked to call an "inability to commit" when it came to women? Sarah had suggested as much, told him that ideology had become the only thing from which he could experience the satisfactions of fidelity. Was that it? Or was there some deeper dislocation?

Deciding that this, too, was a lot of Barbara Walters crap, he tightened his shoelaces and went out into the hall.

3

AUGUST 26, 1986

"You're late!" said Mrs. Harriman, entering her own living room with an enormous quadrangular smile.

"I wasn't told that the subway has been forbidden to . . . *penetrate* Georgetown," explained her guest, the delicately handsome, almost porcelain, Christopher Hitchens. "I had to walk the rest of the way from Foggy Bottom."

"Yes," said Mrs. Harriman, nodding in regret over her tony neighborhood's resistance to the proletarian Metro. "That *was* probably smallminded of Georgetown." Her democratic sentiments didn't extend to offering her guest a chair.

"Well, I took the opportunity to 'go postal,'" Hitchens informed her, using a phrase that had been gaining currency this week, ever since a letter carrier had slaughtered fourteen of his coworkers in Edmond, Oklahoma. "I mailed off my latest piece at the little substation over on Thirty-first Street."

"For *The Nation*," said Mrs. Harriman, taking up position in front of van Gogh's *White Roses*, which Hitchens's research had told him might now be worth $40 million. "Have I got that correct?" she added.

"You're right on the money," answered Hitchens, thinking it must be a nice relief from lying *under* it, which she'd done for so much of her life.

"This piece, however, the one that brings you here, is for Harry's wife. Have I got that right, too?" asked Mrs. Harriman.

"With complete precision," said Hitchens, out-cooing her. He only wished he could be similarly matter-of-fact about the gulf between *The Nation*'s newsprint pages and the satin sheets of *Vanity Fair*, on which Tina Brown, Mrs. Harry Evans, had asked him to have a lucrative go at

Mrs. Harriman. If all worked out, Hitchens foresaw a long and fruitful editorial commute between justice and Mammon, *The Nation* and *Vanity Fair*, the second continually subsidizing the first. What could be more agreeable?

"This isn't the only place the governor ever put you in, is it?" Hitchens asked Mrs. Harriman.

"I don't understand," she replied.

"That flat in London." He was referring to the apartment that Averell Harriman had rented her more than thirty years ago, during the war, when she was his mistress, in her early twenties and still married to Randolph Churchill.

She ignored the question. "He gave *this* house to Mrs. Kennedy to live in for a short time after the president's assassination. Before she bought a place across the street. I'm afraid she didn't stay there very much longer. New York really suited her better."

"And which suits *you* better?" Hitchens asked.

"Oh, Washington, by far!" Mrs. Harriman exclaimed, as if her ten years with Leland Hayward, the Broadway producer, had been an accidental detour before she found her true home and calling.

Hitchens appraised her tan, which he knew she'd acquired in neither of the two cities. "The sun must have been shining in Barbados," he observed.

"Yes, it was. I got back two nights ago."

"I'm recently back from sunny Jerusalem. Rabbi Kahane told me during an interview that he doesn't really want to exterminate the Arabs. He'll settle for their decimation."

He could see she didn't know the precise meaning of the last term, and that she didn't like his knowing that she didn't.

"We're off the record right now, you know," she informed him.

"Until when?"

She flashed a cold, flirtatious grin. "Until I say otherwise. Come, I'll show you our little operation."

She marched him through two or three rooms of her great Federal house before guiding him up a curved staircase with a wooden-spooled banister. They were soon passing madame's boudoir, he realized, or at least an anteroom to it, in which he could see a runner's treadmill with fancy digital controls. He couldn't imagine anyone really using such an apparatus, except perhaps the first lady of the land, his hostess's Republican counterpart across town, who no doubt threw her skeletal form onto the moving machinery each morning, as soon as Ron finally toddled off to the big Oval downstairs.

And yet, it appeared that the courtesan now leading him down another carpeted hall might indeed, in these early weeks of her widowhood, be tautening her form in preparation for one more marital safari. She seemed, to Hitchens's eye, more slender than she had several months ago, when he'd seen her across some hotel ballroom. Now, as she turned to give him an encouraging we're-almost-there smile, he noted that, while the complexion had a standard English-aristo excellence, the face had yet to be lifted. Even the teeth could use a bit further Americanization.

"Here we are," she announced, brightly. They had, he realized, actually crossed into a tinier house attached to the big one. "Kelly, say hello to Mr. Hitchens."

The younger and blonder of two assistants greeted him as he surveyed the top of her desk. A daily-schedule card for September 4, a week from today, had just come out of the Selectric: Mrs. Harriman had a hairdressing appointment in New York, with Kenneth, at 11:45 a.m.

The lady of the house now pointed to fax machines, a postage meter, and a large computer that no one yet seemed to be using. Hitchens picked up a sheet of letterhead from Kelly's desk: SENATE MAJORITY '86.

"That," Mrs. Harriman explained, "is our current project." The outfit was better known as PamPAC. Its new assertiveness and clout, under her solo direction, were the occasion for this glossy profile he'd been assigned.

"We *nearly* got the Senate in '84," she reminded him. "Despite the landslide at the top of the ticket. But we'll get it this time. With a lot of help from our donors."

"A shame," offered Hitchens, "that there can't be *public* financing of these affairs."

"Indeed," Mrs. Harriman agreed, a bit warily.

"Although I see in this morning's paper that the government has just made a generous contribution to the Socialist Workers Party." The courts had awarded that handful of American comrades a quarter-million-dollar judgment, recompense for all the FBI harassment they'd endured during the sixties and seventies.

Mrs. Harriman made a visible effort not to look impatient with such triviality. She was also, her questioner noted, staring at the much-renowned Pelt of the Hitch, the upper reaches of black chest hair exposed by his open collar. He smiled, and said, "I thought we'd lunch here."

The two assistants looked up from their desks as if to say, "The cheek!" Or, Hitchens supposed, geography being what it is, "The nerve!"

Mrs. Harriman smiled unflappably.

"Better for the *mise-en-scène*," explained Hitchens, though it was hard to forgo the still-novel privilege of being able to expense lunch—not something he could do when toiling for *The Nation*.

"Of *course* we're not going out for lunch," Mrs. Harriman said, ushering him from the office. "I'm in mourning, Mr. Hitchens."

Well, that was carrying the Jackie business a bit far. Perhaps she'd don a *mantilla*, Hitchens thought, as they headed back to the big house and then downstairs.

"And I have Ave's memorial service to organize. I've always found that if one goes out to eat lunch, lunch eats up the day. We'll have a quick meal in the garden."

"And then I'll be on my way."

"That's right."

Was the hair, he wondered, already a lighter shade? Had it turned, as Wilde would say, "gold from grief"? Word was that—with help from the oleaginous Missouri fixer Clark Clifford—she'd gotten nearly all of ninety-four-year-old Ave's $100 million.

Downstairs, as they passed through the living room, she picked up a letter that lay open on a small table near the van Gogh. "From the general secretary," she explained, with a hush. She handed it to him. He skipped to the last condoling paragraph, which, like the rest, had been thoughtfully Englished by the Soviets:

We hold in high regard Averell Harriman's active efforts for the good of
our two countries, for the sake of strengthening peace.
    Sincerely,
    M. Gorbachev

Hitchens smiled and handed it back. "While I was in Jerusalem, Natan Sharansky continued to hope for the arrival of his family. The Soviets were still holding them five months after he himself had been sprung."

Mrs. Harriman looked as if he'd sneezed onto the letter with this rude reminder of the still gagged Russian citizenry. "This should be a time for *bilateral progress*," she said, pronouncing the phrase as if she'd just studied it on a flash card.

Propelling Hitchens in the direction of the garden, she kept her eyes on his lit cigarette, clearly worried that a spark from it might land on the white carpet or, God forbid, fly up toward the van Gogh. "We can *have* that progress," she continued, "if we get rid of Mr. Reagan's Senate majority. And then of course see the back of Mr. Reagan himself."

Hitchens decided not to point out the weak spot in her logic—namely, that the kind of progress she desired appeared to be taking place, however oddly, on the watch of that selfsame wattled old fool, a man he wanted out of the White House as much as she did. He decided he'd tip her off balance by returning to the inconvenient fact he *had* pointed out. "Was the governor ever much bothered by the gulag?" he asked, as they sat themselves on some garden chairs beneath a green canvas awning. "During his ambassadorial days, or afterwards?"

"I should think," she replied, with some hesitation and care, "that you could more profitably ask me about the governor's most recent successor."

"You mean Cuomo?"

"Yes!" she said, her smile once more reaching full size. "If we *are* going to put an end to Reaganism, we're going to have to have a *candidate*."

"Is he your man for '88?" The question sounded oddly provocative, as if he were asking whether she planned to pencil in the current silver-tongued New York governor on her half-century-long dance card of assignations.

"He's very articulate and very attractive," Mrs. Harriman answered.

"More so than Senator Hart?"

"I'll try to be helpful to one or both of them."

A maid brought plates of chicken salad and green grapes. Mrs. Harriman poured Hitchens a glass of white wine and began explaining the "issues evenings" that she liked to conduct for national political figures. "We get the best minds in the party and the city—experts on both foreign and domestic policy—to come to these evenings. You'd enjoy them."

"Is that an invitation?" Hitchens asked.

"No," said Mrs. Harriman, biting down on a grape. "People have to feel they can speak *freely*, can give unvarnished analysis and advice, away from the ears of the press. I'm sure you understand."

Hitchens lit another cigarette between forkfuls of chicken salad. "Cuomo and Hart. Surely you must have a preference?"

"Governor Cuomo is, I suspect, more"—she hunted for the adjective—"*disciplined*. I could see that for myself at our '84 convention."

"Ah, yes," said Hitchens, who proceeded to quote the most memorable bit of the speech she'd given to the delegates gathered so hopelessly in San Francisco, two summers ago, to nominate Mondale: "*I am an American by choice and a Democrat by conviction.*" He paused briefly. "Not too bad a line. Who wrote it for you?"

"I was speaking from the heart. Aren't you, too, an American by choice?"

Hitchens, three years shy of forty, and five years into his own American residence, smiled. "I haven't yet made that leap." But she, not he, was the subject here. "When do you think we'll be going on the record?" he asked.

"We won't be."

He closed his Moleskine notebook and eased his glass toward Mrs. Harriman for a refill.

"Are you still a Socialist?" she asked, while looking at the Moleskine's top-of-the-line leather cover.

"A gift from an admirer," he explained. "Rather up your street, no?"

"A *female* admirer?" she asked, hoping, he realized, to land an insult by raising the possibility that the giver might be male.

"I'm a married man."

"I see."

"Time was, that wouldn't have stopped *you*," he added, taking the bottle of pinot blanc into his own hands and topping off the mere inch and a half she'd put in his glass.

"Perhaps *you* should stop," she said, a definite indication that there would be no second bottle.

"Any thoughts on the Zakharov matter?" he added. "Off the record, of course." He didn't care about her opinion; he wanted only to see the extent to which her reading had moved beyond the Style section.

"Arresting him," she answered, "will put Mr. Reagan in a difficult position if he really *does* want peace."

It was, Hitchens thought, a shallow insight, barely worthy of the term, but one couldn't say she wasn't keeping up. He decided to offer a Britannic perspective, something they could share. "It seems that Zakharov paid the school fees of the college student who actually stole the defense secrets for him. Not exactly Philby and Blunt, is it?"

"I suppose not," said Mrs. Harriman, as if conceding that treason wasn't the sort of misplaced idealism it used to be. She looked at her Piaget watch, eager to finish this ill-advised encounter.

"No, indeed," said Hitchens, in no hurry. "The Grinning Idiot, your Mr. Reagan, seems to inspire an *entrepreneurial* sort of espionage. None of that ideological quixotry our own people were so susceptible to."

She ate a last grape and pushed her plate away. Yes, thought Hitchens, she was definitely slimming. "It's a marvel, isn't it," he persisted, "how Reagan takes credit for Duvalier and Marcos being gone, after having done nothing for years but prop them up."

"I'll be seeing Mrs. Aquino at Kay Graham's next month," Mrs. Harriman couldn't resist revealing. "On the eighteenth, I think."

Zakharov aside, Hitchens decided, it was still a hostess's knowledge of the world that she had: the Security Council might as well be another mid-sized dinner party, an "issues evening" she'd yet to host. He noted, too, that her mention of the Philippines' new president and the publisher of the *Washington Post* came with no particular pleasure in their being members of her own sex. This was a woman who liked only men. Which gave him a thought. "Are you putting money into the Florida race?" he asked.

"Oh, yes!" said Mrs. Harriman. The Reaganite seeking reelection down there was a big-haired, gun-friendly woman named Paula Hawkins. "Governor Graham will make a *much* better senator. I may even make a trip to Florida to help him out."

"We shall fight them on the beaches," Hitchens murmured.

"We shall fight them where we can *win*. And we can win there." Buoyed by the thought of picking off a preposterous female Republican, Mrs. Harriman seemed ready to relent toward her guest, if only for a moment. She even leaned in to light his next cigarette. "You know," she said, woman to man, Brit to Brit, "I used to cut Winston's cigars."

He knew that she meant the Old Man, not her son.

"They say you slept with whatever general he asked you to. In order to gain information, of course," said Hitchens, nodding his thanks for the light.

"Well," said the prime minister's onetime daughter-in-law. "I certainly didn't bother with any *colonels*. I left those to Nancy Mitford."

Hitchens, whose literary tastes were the Tory opposite of his politics, knew that Waugh had liked young Pamela, called her a "tasty morsel" and given her a pass on stealing most of Randolph Churchill's furniture when the marriage collapsed. Even so, he himself couldn't jump the hurdle into being charmed. Mrs. Harriman sat before him like some gilded piece of the Andromeda Strain, joylessly efficient at colonizing and devouring.

"So you *are* married, Mr. Hitchens?"

"Yes. I'm flattered that you would try to make certain of that, though you must consider how Hayward-Harriman-Hitchens would be a bit awkward. A little too much like Hertford-Hereford-and-Hampshire."

"Or Hubert Horatio Humphrey," she answered, playing along in spite of herself, before she added, with some aggression: "*I* was *happy* with Averell, Mr. Hitchens." Her tone implied an awareness that he might be less than that in his own marriage.

"Tell me," he asked, "will young Winston be coming over for this memorial service you've got planned?"

Her resistance toward him re-expanded to its full measure. "The service will take place at the National Cathedral on the sixteenth. My son isn't yet sure he'll be able to attend, but he *was* a pallbearer for Ave at the funeral in July. Up in New York."

"Somebody can't nip over in that plane the governor bought you and bring him here for this, too?"

"The plane is really better for short hops," said Mrs. Harriman, evenly, as the maid cleared away the plates.

"Like Florida."

"Yes," she replied, almost warming back up to the subject of Paula Hawkins's possible defeat.

"Tell me," said Hitchens once again, as if they were on the record and he were asking an actual interview question, "what do you see as your reward for all these political labors?"

"The better country that will result from them is reward enough."

She'd prepared that answer before his arrival, of course, and he thought he could detect on her face a fleeting disappointment that they *weren't* on the record, at least for a moment or two.

"And if it doesn't work out?" he persisted. "Not all of your crusades succeed."

She smiled. "Yes, Mr. Hitchens. You've done your research. I know what you're referring to: I failed to marry Gianni Agnelli, isn't that it?"

"Would you have married *him*?" He gestured vaguely in the direction of downtown and could see that she understood he meant Reagan himself.

"I would point out to you," she replied, rising from the garden table, all playfulness gone, "that I married Randolph *before* his father was prime minister."

Hitchens smiled at this attempt to express her indifference to power. He was convinced that she would have made a play for the Ayatollah Khomeini had their Parisian exiles overlapped.

"Well," he said, getting up and extending his hand. "I'll look forward to seeing you at the memorial service."

"Yes," she responded. "I imagine you'll be way in the back."

4

AUGUST 27, 1986

"Oooh," said Merv. "Great *building*."

Nancy smiled and watched Ronnie humbly regard the little balsa-wood model of his future presidential library.

"It certainly is!" cried Betsy Bloomingdale, in whose enormous dining room sat the architectural miniature her guests were now admiring.

The Reagans had just made the two-minute drive to Holmby Hills from their suite at the Century Plaza, where they'd been the past few days, more or less taking a vacation from their vacation; they would return to the ranch by helicopter on Friday. Between now and then—late tomorrow afternoon in the suite—there would be a fund-raising cocktail party for big donors, potential and committed, to the library.

"The roof is just *dahling*!" cried Eva Gabor, who pointed to the model's little orange corrugations. "It look *just* like dat lovely little mission in San Looees Obispo!"

Nancy smiled, though she could do without Eva's *Green Acres* voice, which came or went according to whichever person or purpose she had in view.

Thomas Jones, the chairman of Northrop, who along with Ed Meese and Lew Wasserman would be raising a lot of the money, pointed out some of the building's features. The library would cost thirty million dollars and have an auditorium that could seat 350 people. The project would rise amidst the foothills of Palo Alto, represented in little green felt bumps at the edges of the model.

Nancy looked at this toy world with longing and fear. She wanted to be in it right now, cutting the ribbon. If she were, it would mean that the presidency was over, a movie that had been judged a hit, available for rerun but no longer vulnerable to the introduction of mistakes. And yet, to indulge this fantasy, to imagine herself walking across the model's felt lawn and through its tiny cellophane doors, was to tempt the gods—that phrase she always remembered from Smith. *Carter's* library hadn't even opened yet; and everyone knew how his last couple of years had turned out. Her husband's legacy was not yet fixed; it remained, like the nation's schoolchildren, "at risk."

Thomas Jones was explaining that Hugh Stubbins's design would command respect, the way his Citicorp Building in New York had won over even the *New York Times*. The library would become a graceful adornment to land that now, however close it might be to Stanford, got used only by a handful of farmers and joggers. Nancy looked at the little balsa-wood roof and once more imagined the arena in Kansas City, the one that could have collapsed on top of them all.

"Glenn Campbell will be doing the honors tomorrow afternoon," said Jones.

"Zee Vitchita Lineman?" asked Eva.

Jones laughed. "This is a Glenn Campbell with two n's. *W.* Glenn Campbell. The head of the Hoover Institution up at Stanford. Don't worry," he reassured Eva. "I go through the same thing all the time with that other Tom Jones."

"Oh, I know exactly who *you* are, dahling. I vas vonce married to von of your *competitors*." She meant Frank Jameson, who'd run Rockwell for ten years.

"Well," said Jones, with a courtly nod, "in some areas of life I could never compete with Frank. Or, I guess, with Merv!"

Nancy led the appreciative laughter. Eva might get on her nerves, but she liked pretending that Zsa Zsa's sister and Merv were a real couple, the way she liked pretending Ron and Doria were. Of course, these days Jones couldn't even compete in *business* with Merv, who—if you didn't count Walter Annenberg—was the wealthiest man in the room.

Annenberg himself now pointed to the model and made a suggestion: "Mr. President, we need to fill this with stuff like that old Mustang you campaigned in for governor. And maybe a piece of the emergency room at the hospital. I took this up the other day with Ed Meese. Let's have something more interesting than one more damned replica of the Oval Office!"

Nancy knew that Walter was Walter, and famously blunt, but she shot him a glance. A piece of the emergency room? We do *not* talk about March 30, 1981.

No one knew how to change a subject better than Merv, and he did that now: "Well, at least working on the library will keep Ed Meese from watching *Debbie Does Dallas*." The chubby attorney general, often called Poppin (for the Pillsbury Doughboy) behind his back, had been catching all kinds of ridicule for the report his Commission on Pornography had issued a couple of months ago, and Merv's remark got them all laughing now.

"Do you think there really could be a link?" asked Lee Annenberg as everyone took their places around Betsy's dining room table. Lee was much more tactful than her husband—she'd been Ronnie's first chief of protocol—and her question about the commission's most contentious finding, that there could be a connection between viewing pornography and committing violence, gave a momentary seriousness to the conversation. It also helped to cancel any mental image of what Ed Meese might have been doing in the dark while Debbie did Dallas.

As she unfolded a Porthault napkin, Nancy smiled warmly across the big table at her best friend. How quickly time passed: it had been five years since Betsy discovered Alfred's affair and cut off funds to his mistress; four since Alfred had died; and already three since the mistress had been beaten to death with a baseball bat by the AIDS-infected junkie she'd been reduced to living with.

"I'm sure there is," said Ronald Reagan. "A link between those two things."

His smile seemed incongruous, but Nancy knew it didn't spring from the grimy subject of pornography. He was just pleased to have heard the question. He'd been fitted with new hearing aids the other day at the Century Plaza, and though the improvement never seemed to last long, for the moment it was marked, and a pleasure to both of them.

"It happened with *That Hagen Girl*," he explained. "People see a movie and then go out and do the wrong thing. A couple of girls tried to drown themselves just the way Shirley Temple did."

That Hagen Girl was hardly pornography, but people understood what he meant and nodded. Nancy knew that he hated the film. He'd always thought it smutty—having to become the teenaged Shirley's love interest once she found out he wasn't really her father—and he'd made it when things were at their worst with Jane.

"Dat's terrible!" cried Eva, in response to the drownings.

Betsy Bloomingdale ignored her. "I'm sorry about this arrangement," she told everyone. "Lew and Edie were supposed to be here, and if we'd been thirteen, I would have done *two* tables, seven and six. As it is, we're too many for one table and too few for two!"

Everyone protested that the setup, with or without the Wassermans, was perfectly elegant. The president seemed further energized by the reference to his former agent. "Too bad about Lew. I was planning on asking him for my old job back."

Everybody laughed, and when Nancy said, "Ask him if I can have *mine* back, too!" they laughed some more.

"But didn't he put you in *That Hagen Girl*?" asked Merv, which made the whole table laugh even harder. And then, with his excellent timing—as good as Carson's, really—Merv said, to Betsy, but loud enough for everyone to hear: "I've never minded the size of the table here. I just used to be scared that when dinner was over Alfred would ask me for my Diners Club card!"

That of course was how Alfred had made his money, or at least the part of it he hadn't inherited, and it was sweet of Merv to make this little joking tribute to his memory, even if, you could bet, it would be the last mention of Alfred tonight. The postscript to the scandal—that baseball bat—remained too fresh in everyone's mind. Nancy still wondered how Betsy had gotten through it all. Maybe there really was something to Catholicism, a thought that now reminded her to say: "Ronnie, don't forget that you're supposed to call Irene Dunne this week!"

Bless Irene. Back in the SAG days, there'd been so few Republicans in the business: Irene, Bing and Bob, Stanwyck. Of course, Ronnie's success had now brought a number of others over, like Frank, but even today nothing could match the hatred of the liberals out here.

"Oh, she'll *love* that!" Betsy exclaimed.

"I'll do it before we go back on Friday. To the *ranch*," Ronnie said with a smile, so that everyone would know they weren't headed straight back to what he sometimes called the Big House, as if 1600 Pennsylvania Avenue were the set for some old Jimmy Cagney picture. While he smiled, he kept doodling on the back of the little menu card, looking up—and then over at the architect's model—every few seconds.

"Oh, eet's the *li*brary!" cried Eva, sitting beside him. She could see what was coming to life on the card.

Nancy smiled, but by now Eva was really giving her a swift pain. Before dinner was finished she would no doubt pocket the drawing, maybe to give to one of those stepchildren she'd been saddled with during that marriage to Frank Jameson. A decade from now the stepchild would get five thousand dollars for it. Nancy looked at Ronnie and marveled as he finished his penciling, spinning gold from straw like Rumpelstiltskin.

"What's 'Radiant' up to?" asked Merv, leaning forward toward Maureen Reagan, trying to make the president's daughter feel special with this use of her Secret Service name.

She brightened up at once, like a guest surprised to have found herself on Merv's talk-show couch. "I'm going back to Africa soon!"

"Mermie did a swell job for us over there a year ago." Reagan's use of Maureen's nickname made her smile even more than the code name had.

"Thank you!" she said, turning from Merv to her father and then toward the whole table. "It was Nairobi that time. An international women's conference. A UN thing."

"And Jeane Kirkpatrick said she was great," Nancy added, generously. She was making this compliment up; Jeane had already left the UN by the time of the conference, but no one at the table would remember that, and quoting praise from such a respected name would give Maureen a boost—which Maureen always seemed to need. Nancy really did make an effort as a stepmother—no one could say otherwise—and the relationship between the two of them had gotten slowly and steadily better, even as things with her own daughter, Patti, went from bad to worse.

"It'll be my third trip over there," explained Maureen. "To Botswana this time. The twentieth anniversary of their independence. Then I'm on to Mozambique."

"I met the fellow from Mozambique," said her father. "Back in Washington, not long ago. We hit it off."

"His name is Samora Machel," Maureen informed the not-very-interested table. "He and I met in April in Swaziland. And he told me just the same, that he'd hit it off with Dad. He'd be very happy with some more American investment, even though it was the Soviets who helped them with their revolution. He told me that there's an intersection of Karl Marx and Ho Chi Minh Streets in his capital, but that there *could* be one for Jefferson and Washington—or maybe even Jefferson and Reagan! He's a charmer. And he's somebody we could really make progress with."

Nancy saw that Ronnie was enjoying this, and not just because he was hearing it. She could tell that he was imagining the last shot of a feel-good picture: one set of street signs coming down, another going up.

"I met Botha at the same event," Maureen went on, "and told him that Dad was working hard to keep Congress from applying sanctions to South Africa—but that even Dad had limits, and it was past time for improvements in the racial situation there."

Enough, thought Nancy. She didn't want to get on to the blacks, or have floating through the dining room a reminder that the still-Republican Senate would probably soon override Ronnie's veto on this matter. But mostly she thought this was enough of Maureen, always a square peg, for one night. She was very pretty (Jane's nose) and quite bright, but she'd never really found her way. She'd gained a smidgen of success in TV and then another smidgen in politics, but she couldn't keep herself from overreaching (that run for the Senate nomination four years ago!), any more than she could keep from reminding audiences that she'd become a registered Republican before her father had. Yeah, yeah. And she was far too fat for a woman in her mid-forties. Strange, really, how she seemed more like Ronnie's stepdaughter than the real daughter she was, from the first, wrong wife.

Merv's talk-show instincts were kicking in. It was again time to change the subject. "How's Mama?" he asked Nancy.

She could feel her big eyes instantly glisten. "Not so great, I'm afraid. But she's holding on. And I'm still racking up my frequent-flyer miles to Phoenix." She pictured her mother wearing those little knitted gloves in hundred-plus-degrees Arizona, where the air-conditioned chill of the assisted-living place was too much for her extremities. And then all at once she had a vision of young, beautiful Edith Luckett, home for a week or two after having had a role in New York, reading stories to her— probably even "Rumpelstiltskin." How else would she have remembered that tonight?

People clucked sympathetically, and Merv tried to cheer things back up. "She could go on for a long time—just look at Mama Gabor!"

"How old is Jolie?" Ronnie asked Eva.

"Eighty-nine!"

Edie Luckett Davis was actually ninety-eight; she'd knocked eight years off her age when starting in the theater. Nancy had shaved off only two when beginning in films, though you'd think she'd committed embezzlement the way the papers loved pointing it out every July 6. But age didn't threaten her vanity these days; it simply scared her. At seventy-five, Ronnie was too old to be doing this; everybody knew it, but no one among their friends said it. And of course she would be furious if they did. But the frailty, and the never-ending maintenance—Dr. House, the ENT man, had also been to the Century Plaza yesterday—frightened her, and a glance at the people around the table was dismaying: half of them looked as if they'd come for a card game at Norma Desmond's. The only thing missing was the pet monkey.

"Ron's hosting *Good Morning America* on Monday," she announced.

"Oh, dat's *marvelous*!" cried Eva.

"Will anybody be watching?" asked Maureen. "Won't everyone be sleeping in for Labor Day?"

It wasn't any success of Ron's that Maureen resented; he was in fact still pretty feckless, what with the ballet, and then the articles for *Playboy*, and now this. What bothered Maureen, Nancy knew, was the way Ron managed to be more comfortable in his own skin, even on television, than she, his much older half-sister, would ever be.

"Any chance for him to give the message?" asked Merv.

There was no need for anyone to ask which message. He meant Just Say No, her antidrug crusade.

"Oh, I would never interfere," Nancy replied, before sighing. "It's gotten so much worse in just the last six months." Crack kept spreading and multiplying the homeless. That black college basketball star had overdosed on cocaine.

"Even O'Neill wants to push drug legislation," said Annenberg with a shake of his head, implying that the speaker of the House was a Johnny-come-lately to the first lady's signature issue.

"I guess he woke up," suggested Thomas Jones, "when he realized that the Celtics had just lost a star." He was referring to Len Bias, the basketball player Nancy had just thought of, the one who'd been drafted to play on the Boston team. Everyone started to laugh, but that stopped when they saw Nancy wince—not from a sense that they were acting in bad taste; just from a thought of that bulbous beer hound, O'Neill. What a joke that people thought he and Ronnie actually became Irish pals every day after six o'clock! The two of them detested each other, the only difference being that Ronnie had the class not to mock *him* in private. Even now he was shaking his head and smiling, as if to say, "Oh, that Tip," about a man who double-crossed him on whatever agreements they'd supposedly reached and who in the last few months had been plain vicious about Ronnie's support for the Contras, practically calling him a murderer.

"What would be in a bill that *you'd* like to see?" Jones asked her.

"Five years for five grams. First offense," Nancy answered, and everyone at the table nodded their agreement. "If you use drugs," she added, "you're an accomplice to murder. To all the murder that the trafficking involves. And that's especially true with cocaine." Everyone nodded again.

Yes, she believed that, and she'd been saying it lately, even if she wasn't certain how far you could carry the logic. Would it be the same for those who used pornography—with its connections to organized crime and all *those* murders? For a second she shut her eyes at the thought of how Alfred and that girl, the murdered mistress, were said to have *lunched* with Ed Meese, and maybe even other friends of Ronnie's out here or in Washington. She opened her eyes and looked at Betsy—a *saint*, cutting that girl off and never settling the lawsuit, no matter what dirt it dug up. People wondered why she "stuck by" Bets. Stuck *by* her? She wished she could be *like* her, could be that implacable. Her own toughness required constant improvisation, an incessant screwing up of courage. It always came out as meanness, a barely concealed panic; in truth, it wasn't really toughness at all.

The Spanish couple had cleared away the salad plates, and the beef tenderloin tips were on their way. In the meantime Ronnie was getting up to have another look at the architect's model, and Eva—oh, brother— was heading there with him.

"Does anybody know if Dick Nixon is going to Carter's dedication?" asked Jones.

"I imagine there's a 'schedule conflict,'" suggested Lee Annenberg, whose protocol euphemism generated laughter.

"I don't know why Dick or anyone else should have to be courteous to that son of a bitch," said her husband.

"You know," observed Ronnie, looking back toward the table, now seemingly able even to *over*hear things, "Dick gave me great advice before the China trip not too long ago. He told me that, at the banquets, I shouldn't ask what anything was—just pick it up with the chopsticks and swallow."

"I hope that remark wasn't brought on by my salad!" said Betsy.

"Ronnie, come back here and sit down so that we can all eat." Nancy heard the familiar maternal scolding in her voice, as if this were an ordinary night back in the early sixties and Ronnie was spending too much time showing Ron a toy train in the all-electric house GE had given them. For a lovely moment she could feel her blood pressure drop.

Ronnie returned to the table with a yes ma'am expression, pretending to be chastened. And after that, throughout the main course, the conversation revolved mostly around real estate, with talk of the office building that Twentieth Century Fox was constructing right near the Century Plaza—which led to some teasing of Merv about whether he or Armand Deutsch would be the first to buy up the hotel.

"I suspect the folks will still get comped either way," said Maureen, brightly, using that odd word she favored for her father and stepmother, the cozy amalgamation from which she was shut out. "Folks" seemed carefully chosen, intimate but still excluding, and—Nancy couldn't help but think—a little sad. To everyone else, the word conjured up only those photos of herself and Ronnie upstairs in robes and pajamas, eating off trays in front of the TV—images that surprised people who pictured them in gowns and tuxedos twenty-four hours a day.

Tonight, while Ronnie slept, she would be up and awake, looking down from the thirty-second floor at the fountains along the Avenue of the Stars. She'd be pacing and fretting about something, though she didn't yet know what it would be, maybe O'Neill's move to steal the drug bill out from under her. And when she suspended worry over that, there would be worry over something else, and then a generalized longing for it all to be finished, for herself to be tucked away inside that future library, just a mannequin in one of Jimmy Galanos's red gowns, immobile and perfect, mutely greeting visitors. The thought filled her with peace. The tourists would pass by, at last looking at her appreciatively, through glass.

When the meal ended, most of the guests moved into Betsy's enormous drawing room. Nancy remained behind at the table with Merv and Maureen. She signaled the Spanish man for a second cup of coffee, full strength; there was no point to decaf when she would be up most of the night regardless. Maureen, in a similar what's-the-use mode, reached for a second helping of the lime ice cream with shaved chocolate. "Oooh," said Merv, helping himself to a small spoonful: "Great *flavor*." Maureen playfully batted his arm away, before he asked: "So, are you going to come see Nancy give her speech to the television academy this fall? You'll get to see all of them hail the conquering heroine."

"What exactly have I conquered?" asked Nancy, widening her large eyes with what she knew was her please-reassure-me look. It would be another antidrug speech, but the audience—all those Norman Lear types sitting there, just days away from the midterm elections—might be anything but friendly.

"I'll make sure they give you a backdrop as good as what Mike Deaver arranged for the president at Normandy," Merv promised.

He didn't know that Deaver had always been a particular bane to Maureen, who couldn't understand why the "folks" wouldn't at long last let him have it. Mike's self-inflicted troubles were piling ever higher: he'd left the administration a year ago and had probably just perjured himself to the committee investigating the work he'd since done as a lobbyist for foreign governments. The White House still hadn't said a critical word about him, not even with a special prosecutor on the horizon. If it were anyone else, Nancy would have made sure he was consigned to an outer darkness beyond the one to which Betsy had sent Alfred's mistress. But it was *Mike*. He and Nancy went back forever, and he remained the only person who had ever managed to find her "off" buttons, the only one who could shut down the anxiety of the moment. Against all advice, she continued to communicate with him, from time to time, through one go-between or another.

Maureen said nothing in response to Merv's mention of Deaver, and Nancy appreciated that, truly.

"I don't think I need a great backdrop," Nancy finally replied. "What I need is a great *speech*."

"Maybe we need to postpone Miss *Noonan's* retirement," suggested Maureen, with a roll of her eyes. Nancy also disliked the peppy, self-aggrandizing speechwriter—those schoolgirl skirts!—but even so, she wished she weren't planning to depart the administration, taking her skills with her prematurely, just as Mike had.

"Don't mind me," said Maureen to Merv, who'd detected her cattiness. "I can be 'a real pain in the ass.' Don Regan's exact words to me last spring, before the Contras vote, when I thought he was screwing up and told him so."

"I never heard that," said Nancy, genuinely surprised. She turned her lambent, watery eyes toward her stepdaughter. "That dreadful man."

Maureen, a sometimes shrewd if failed politician, looked at her stepmother and said: "You know what you should do? Kill two birds with one stone: help your drug bill and help Dad with the Senate. Go down and put in an appearance for Paula Hawkins in Florida. She's strong against drugs and on missing kids and all that good stuff. Graham—the governor she's running against—isn't. Paula is in trouble and you could help her turn things around."

And lose what few allies I have? thought Nancy. Defending Ronald Reagan was one thing—her worst detractors gave her points for loyalty—but campaigning against individual Democrats was another.

"You know," said Maureen, when she failed to get a response, "I'm sure Don Regan would hate the idea."

"Oooh," said Merv, laughing as his tongue tickled his teeth. "Great *argument*. Reverse psychology."

Nancy shook her big, pretty head and looked across Betsy's dining room carpet, as green as the Stanford foothills where the library would be built. From the drawing room she could hear loud, fawning laughter over some Hollywood story Ronnie was telling.

She changed the subject for the last time tonight; pretended to be interested in what was going on with Dennis, Maureen's young, third husband. The clock said a quarter to nine and she wished it were later. She was too jittery for more conversation; she would rather be in the dark of the hotel suite, looking down at the fountains, sorting her thoughts like a solitaire deck. She rose from the table and urged Merv and Maureen to follow her into the drawing room.

". . . and I told them," Ronnie was saying, " 'That introduction was so long, I haven't had this much trouble getting on since I did a picture with Errol Flynn.' "

Eva laughed the loudest. Her magnificent wig, not anything like the cheap ones she sold through catalogues, caught the light from Betsy's teardrop chandelier.

"Think it could be time to head home?" asked Nancy.

Ronnie, for all that he might be enjoying himself, liked the idea of an early departure even better. "I think we may even have a ride," he told her.

"Mr. President," said Annenberg, "a word before you go?"

Ronnie looked surprised. But Nancy wasn't. Nixon's old ambassador to Great Britain cherished his supposed prerogatives as a member of the Foreign Intelligence Board and was forever bringing up matters he wanted to appear involved in.

"I talked to George this afternoon," said Annenberg, before pausing gravely. Everyone knew he meant Shultz, not Bush; the secretary of state was, at bottom, a trusted California businessman who could almost pass for one of their own crowd. "Casey tells him that the Soviets are all over two or three American journalists in Moscow; they're practically following them to the toilet."

"I haven't heard that yet," said Ronnie.

Annenberg looked from side to side, as if a *private* word might make more sense.

"It's okay," said the president. "We've got a lot of high officials here. Even my old chief of protocol," he said, with a wink to Lee.

"You'll have to svear *me* in as some-sing!" cried Eva.

Nancy had by now had it with her—even with Walter—but she did want to know what he was talking about.

"Shultz is sure one of the journalists is going to be picked up," Annenberg explained. "To retaliate for Zakharov."

The president nodded and pursed his lips.

"I know you'll give them a strong response," Annenberg added.

"Well," said Ronnie, moving toward the door, "it's a good thing there's no Olympics this year. That way we won't have to settle just for canceling them." This time, making his dig at Carter, he winked at Thomas Jones's wife.

"We're not going to cancel *anything*," Nancy said, with a firmness that surprised her. "You can take this up with Gorbachev at the next summit."

"You really vant more of Raisa?" asked Eva.

Nancy gave her a thin smile. Whatever Walter was talking about, she didn't want Ronnie being forced by his advisors to blow it out of proportion. Forget Walter; she would talk to George Shultz herself. She wasn't going to let Ronnie's chance of being a peacemaker evaporate just to keep one more reporter loose in the world.

The president, moving toward the door, gave the guests his what-can-I-do? look, as if *they* were reporters watching him get off the helicopter and point, apologetically, to the noisy rotors. Seeing him now, Nancy recalled the distressed look he'd had just the other day, when peering out the window of the helicopter between the ranch and Los Angeles. She'd pressed him to tell her what was the matter. He was unable, he said, to remember the name for what lay below them, no matter that he'd seen it ten thousand times. "Topanga Canyon," she'd had to answer. And both of them had been rattled for a long minute.

"Bets," he now said, giving the hostess a kiss.

Nancy brushed cheeks with Lee, Merv, and Walter: "I can't believe I may not see you until Christmastime!" she told the latter. Annenberg responded that Sunnylands, his giant desert estate, would be waiting for her and Ronnie and everybody else who always came to the long New Year's house party.

How would they get through these next four months? she suddenly wondered. The preliminary charts that Joan had done for fall, and which she'd just seen, were *not* good. They were so bad, in fact, that Nancy now wondered: Was it just a bad patch they were approaching after so much good? Or was *everything*, from world peace to Just Say No, about to fall apart under the watchful but blind eyes of Don Regan?

She had to do *something*.

She kissed Maureen last and found herself saying, truthfully, "I want to talk more about Paula Hawkins."

5

SEPTEMBER 5, 1986

"I'd recommend the navy bean soup," said Anders Little.

After an hour of nodding gratefully at everything he'd pointed out—the wallpaper in the Green Room; the Coolidge portrait hanging in the empty Oval Office—Anne Macmurray decided, here in the White House Mess, to be slightly contrary: "I think I'm going to have the chicken salad."

"Sounds good," said Anders, neutrally.

He had been amusingly house-proud when showing her the West Wing and the public rooms, and he'd certainly bent over backwards to make her feel well cared for. Taking her to lunch here was above and beyond the call of duty, even if the gesture was meant to win him additional points with Richard Nixon, the person for whom he was ultimately doing the whole favor.

But never mind Nixon. Anders Little's real focus—like that of everyone else in the building; you could feel it—remained on another man, another president, the one who hadn't been here in weeks.

"We're right underneath him, you know," said Anders. He pointed to the Oval Office above the Mess.

"But he isn't there," Anne said. *Even when he is,* she wanted to add, though politeness restrained her.

"You wouldn't hear him if he were," said Anders. "He has a famously soft footfall. They used to say he *glided* onto soundstages in Hollywood."

"Well," said Anne, who'd had enough idolatry by now. "The carpet up there is pretty thick. I imagine that down here people didn't even hear LBJ thrashing around."

Anders smiled, with a hint of surprise at the shift in her spirit. "So," he asked, as the steward took their menus, "you went to the symphony last night?"

"Yes," she answered. "Rostropovich was at the podium. Very exciting."

"A brave man," said Anders. "The press has gotten people so excited about Gorbachev's supposed liberalizations, they forget how many dissidents are still trapped there."

And of course only Reagan can free them. "Yes," said Anne. "I'm pretty sure Rostropovich got out under Peter's friend, Mr. Nixon."

"*My* friend, too, I'm happy to say," said Anders.

"I admired a lot of what Nixon did in foreign affairs. But I'm afraid Gerald Ford was the last Republican I voted for. I was even a Ford delegate at the '76 convention."

"Really?" asked Anders, brightening up unexpectedly. "I was there for the last night of that. Up in the grandstands thanks to my new job at the UN. Mrs. Black—Shirley Temple—was leading a bunch of diplomats around, and I helped."

She noted the tone to that "bunch of diplomats" and could only imagine what he would think of the political crowd she now ran with. "Things have changed a lot since then," she said, cautiously.

As the years apart from Peter lengthened, she had shaken off most of the bitterness. For a while, during the late seventies, while Jimmy Carter was installed in the room above, she had even—mostly for fun—gone back to work at Leo Abner's bookshop in Owosso, where she'd sometimes sparred with Peter during their courtship thirty years before.

"How so?" asked Anders. "What's changed for you?"

"Oh," said Anne, coming out of her moment's reverie, "grandchildren, mostly. I've now got two of them."

"Wonderful," said Anders.

"Worrisome," she replied.

"In what way?"

"Oh, I just fret about the kind of world they'll inherit. If there's any world *to* inherit."

She saw a suspicious look come over his face, different from the one old friends in Owosso, and even her son (very pro-Reagan) would sometimes give her: a look that merely asked, with a certain amusement: What's happened to *you*? But young Mr. Little looked as if he'd gone, in a split second, to DEFCON 3.

"Well," he said, stiffly, "the president believes that the best guarantee of a peaceful world is a strong defense, along with an assertive foreign policy."

Absorbing this bit of hostility, she felt less liberal than maternal. She wanted to pat the hand with which this handsome, straight arrow was holding his soup spoon, wanted to tell him to stop being so pompous, that he would live longer—nuclear war or not—if he ceased talking like a press release.

She also felt it was time to put at least a few of her cards on the table. "Right after the second grandchild was born, I went to a lecture in Ann Arbor on nuclear war, by Dr. Helen Caldicott. It really opened my eyes."

Mr. Little actually braced his shoulders; they could have been missile silos. He had raised the DEFCON level even higher and was one step away from firing. As the steward approached to refill Anne's water glass, she half expected the Secret Service to be coming up behind.

"The president," said Anders, very evenly, "met with Dr. Caldicott. In '82, I believe."

"Yes, as a favor to his daughter Patti."

"He found Dr. Caldicott—who's a pediatrician, not a physicist—unpersuasive."

"She found him ill-informed." She'd also found him frighteningly forgetful.

Having suckered Anders Little into this meeting, Anne now decided to come clean. "I joined a chapter of WAND not long after I went to that lecture. Women's Action for Nuclear Dis—"

"I know what the letters stand for."

"Good!" Her smile was sudden and genuine. "We must be making more of an impact than we thought!"

The young man smiled, too, enough to let her hope that things would remain friendly.

"I've actually moved to Washington to take a job in WAND's office," Anne confessed.

Mr. Little's smile faded. "I thought you were visiting friends."

"I fibbed."

"To President Nixon?"

"Well," said Anne, "to Peter. My ex-husband. He *still* thinks I'm just making a visit down here, and I guess that's what he told Mr. Nixon. But when I learned of your existence, and your position here, I got an idea."

"What was that?" asked Little. He was speeding through his soup.

"I'd like to interview you for *Turnabout.*"

"What's *Turnabout?*"

"A WAND publication. It's what I was hired to work on. So far we've put out only one issue. But if I could get an interview with someone on the NSC, like yourself, it would be a big help to me, and, well, I suppose, helpful to dialoguing. I hate that as a verb, but you know what I mean." As she heard herself getting flustered, she could see his expression trying, but still refusing, to soften.

"I'm afraid I wouldn't be an appropriate person for that," he replied. "I doubt that anyone around here would be."

"Why not?"

"For one thing, Dr. Caldicott routinely insults the president. And, for another, our positions are probably even farther apart than they were in '82. The two of us are proceeding from completely different premises, and—"

"Are we?" asked Anne. "Really so far apart? The president believes in a strong economy, doesn't he?"

"Of course."

She hoped she could now correctly quote what she had in mind, or at least come close: " 'Just one Soviet warhead set off two hundred and fifty miles above Kansas could cover the whole country with an electromagnetic pulse, fifty thousand volts per square yard. That would knock out all power and telephone service in the U.S.' " She had, more or less at her command, dozens of facts like this, almost all of them from books by Helen, as they all called Dr. Caldicott, even if they'd met her only once.

"*Missile Envy*," said Anders, rolling his eyes over the title. "I've skimmed it. You've noticed, I hope, that she spends ninety-five percent of her time worrying about *American* missiles. I'm surprised you could find that one little bomb of *theirs*."

"The United States has thirty thousand nuclear weapons," Anne replied, as pedagogically as she could. She didn't want to sound like an angry TV talking head.

"There's a reason we need to have more nuclear weapons than the Soviets," countered Mr. Little, his voice adopting the same patience and restraint. "*They* have an enormous advantage when it comes to conventional forces in Europe. That nuclear freeze you want so much will freeze the U.S.S.R. into a position of permanent superiority."

"Your pres—excuse me—the president also believes that with just a little pressure from us, the Soviets will collapse onto 'the ash heap of history.'"

"Yes, he said that to the British Parliament."

"It's a fantasy, Mr. Little. We'll *all* be ashes."

"Ms. Macmurray, do you see how this is getting us nowhere?"

"On the contrary! Wouldn't it be good for readers to be shown an exchange like this? And please call me Anne. May I call you Anders?"

"We're so busy with short-term crises here, we've got no time to spend on unbridgeable divides. Do you know that the Soviets have been holding an American journalist in a military prison for the past six days? Nicholas Daniloff, no more a spy than you or I."

"I do read the newspaper, Anders."

"I apologize—Anne." He spoke her first name as if it were a forced concession rather than a reciprocal privilege. "People are preoccupied and frustrated here."

Their real frustration, Anne knew, came from an awareness that they were looking a bit soft. The administration had offered to turn Zakharov, the real spy, over to the Soviets, in exchange for Daniloff, who'd been arrested for accepting some newspaper clippings and harmless photos from an old friend. Even George Will was on the president's case about the proposed swap.

Anders could see that she was pretty well informed, and after a last spoonful of navy bean he rebutted an objection she hadn't made but was no doubt thinking: "The Soviets would only get Zakharov *temporarily.* Pending his trial."

She could tell he didn't believe that any more than George Will did, but she decided to say nothing. He soon changed the subject. "Where will you be living?" he asked.

"I've found a nice apartment in Arlington. Over on Clarendon Boulevard."

He smiled and said, "I'm right nearby, on Wilson," before adding, more grimly, "since my, uh, separation."

He looked surprised to have said it, as if the personal information were another concession wrung from him over this little lunchtime negotiating table. He would be more comfortable, Anne realized, with a resumption of the statistical skirmishing.

"You know, Anders, over seventy percent of Americans say they're for a nuclear freeze."

"And the president still carried forty-nine states."

"I know," said Anne, with a sigh. "I've been depressed ever since."

Seeing her reach into her purse, he shook his head. "Your money's no good here. Literally." He waved for the check and fixed his employee number to it before signing with a flourish that seemed to restore his authority.

Then, suddenly, real excitement appeared on his face. Anne turned to see whatever had caught his eye. "Is that—?"

"Yes, it is," he said, not removing his gaze from Jeane Kirkpatrick, who'd just come in with one of the vice president's foreign-policy advisors.

"You know her, don't you?" Anne thought she could recall hearing that fact from Peter.

"Yes," said Anders, getting up. "I'll introduce you."

As soon as he made the offer his expression changed, from something masterful to something frightened. He realized what he might be letting himself in for.

"I'll behave," Anne assured him.

On their way to Dr. Kirkpatrick's table they passed two speechwriters, to whom Anders also introduced Anne.

"Working on the UN address?" he asked one of them.

"I wish," said the very young man. "I spent the morning cranking out a proclamation for National Grandparents' Day. It's this Sunday, if you guys are looking for something to celebrate."

Anders backtracked and explained to Anne: "The president will be addressing the United Nations on September twenty-second."

"I know," she answered. "We're planning to demonstrate."

He gave her a plaintive look, reminding her of her promise, as they continued on toward Jeane Kirkpatrick's table.

"*Anders*," said the former ambassador in her deep, peculiarly alluring voice. Anne was fascinated by the look of her—the heavy eyebrows, the pursed but full lips. She was a caricaturist's dream, handsome and villainous, her butchness somehow deeply feminine. Without bothering to introduce her own lunch companion, Dr. Kirkpatrick shook Anders's hand and smiled at Anne.

"This is Anne Macmurray," said Anders. "She's here from Michigan." Anne noted the slight pause within the sentence, the momentary effort he made to omit the word "visiting," so that, strictly speaking, he was still telling the truth.

"Welcome to Washington," said Dr. Kirkpatrick.

"Thank you."

Silence followed. "So," said Anders, in a jaunty panic to fill it. "How *are* you? And how, dare I ask, is the book coming?"

Dr. Kirkpatrick dismissed his second question with a wave of her hand. "*I'm* fine—or I was until about fifteen minutes ago." The eyebrows went up. "I'd be feeling better if this hijacking hadn't ended."

The remark seemed both shocking and obscure. Before entering the Mess, Anne had seen, on a CNN monitor, that the Pakistani military had subdued some Palestinian hijackers holding a plane in Karachi. About twenty passengers had been killed.

"You'll forgive my bloody-mindedness," Dr. Kirkpatrick elaborated.

"But now that that's over, the press's full attention will be back on Danil-off. That's mostly bad."

"How so?" asked Anders—reduced to being the eager student, Anne noticed.

With no visible agitation other than a forward extension of her already-pouting lips, Dr. Kirkpatrick explained: "It will return the public's full focus to a perfectly limp response to the Soviets by this administration I was once part of."

Shamefaced, Anders offered the only update about Daniloff that he had: "We've heard that they're allowing him to exercise on the prison roof."

His vividly severe mentor looked away and sipped from her water glass, before saying: "Anders, to someone who runs five miles every morn-ing, like yourself, I'm sure that that information is terribly comforting and compelling. But I'm not worried about Mr. Daniloff getting a little flabby. I'm worried about the president looking that way."

The navy steward hovered nearby with his order pad.

"I hope I'll see you soon," said Anders, extending his hand. Dr. Kirk-patrick shook it, said, "Yes, that would be nice," and ordered a *salade niçoise*.

Outside the building, after passing the Marine guard and crossing the driveway, Anders still looked crestfallen. He prepared to take leave of Anne on the steps of the EOB.

"Do you have a card?" she asked.

"Yes, of course," he said, pulling one from his wallet. "I suppose you're going to call and take another crack at me. About the interview."

"I'm not sure," Anne answered. "But I *am* going to call and say that I'm cooking you dinner. As mother figures go, I'm a lot easier than that one." She pointed back in the direction of the Mess.

———

Though he'd not had so much as a roll with his soup, Anders double-timed it up the staircase to the third floor. On the way, he passed Tawny-Dawn-or-Whatshername. She was wearing a tight business suit, a frilly blouse, and a pair of Reebok high-tops, and he could hear Bon Jovi coming out of her Walkman: "You Give Love a Bad Name."

Did *he*? Give love a bad name? He supposed his ex-wives—two of them!—and ex-girlfriends would say yes. If he did, could Anne Macmurray detect it—like some telltale condition, a kind of chronic dry skin? He almost felt that she had; he just hoped he'd been sufficiently polite. No one could blame him for getting hot under the collar over all that Helen Caldicott garbage—and then Jeane had thrown him completely off balance.

He did two fast laps of the third floor before getting stopped in front of room 368 by Neal Grover, who worked under Jack Matlock in European and Soviet Affairs. Neal was just getting back from some lunchtime errands; a yellow Tower Records bag dangled from his wrist.

"Hey, Andy Panda, how ya been?"

Anders smiled. It was the nickname he'd been given at Bud McFarlane's farewell party, when he'd made the mistake of letting it be known how much he'd love a place on the next China trip, if Reagan ever made one.

"I gave up half my morning to give somebody a tour," Anders explained.

"Tell me about it," said Neal, striking a tragic attitude. "I had two ladies from my mother's *garden club* last week. Sort of fun, actually."

"Not too different from what I had." Anders didn't mention the Nixon connection: détente remained suspect around here, and Nixon was, well, Nixon. "So," he asked, "what did I miss while I was gone?"

"Daniloff's wife got in to see him again. And so did his boss, the *U.S. News* editor. Tell me this isn't a bonanza for them. Maybe they'll get a couple of *readers* next week." Neal paused while remembering a more important development. "Somebody on Nitze's staff called. So far everything still looks hunky-dory. Karpov showed up on schedule, and they've been talking as if nothing's wrong."

Viktor Karpov, the Soviet arms negotiator, was supposed to be laying the groundwork, with his counterpart, Paul Nitze, for a meeting between the two countries' foreign ministers, Shultz and Shevardnadze, here in Washington a couple of weeks from now. Staffers called the process the "stairway to heaven": if it got built, Reagan and Gorbachev would meet again, for the first time since getting acquainted in Geneva last year.

Anders nodded. He wished he'd had the Karpov news to tell Jeane—instead of that idiotic business about Daniloff working out on the prison roof—but she no doubt already knew everything Grover did, and more.

"The Soviets are treating Shultz better than Harvard is," said Neal, a USC man. The secretary of state was up in Cambridge for the university's 350th anniversary and was being hounded by demonstrators backing both the Sandinistas and divestment from South Africa.

Anders shook his head, disgustedly. "He should show them the Princeton tiger he's got tattooed on his ass." Neal guffawed over this little-known fact about George P. Shultz. "And he should tell them to kiss it," Anders added.

"Ish," said Neal, campily.

Anders laughed. In what he soon realized was too obvious a segue, he asked, "How's Terry?"

Terry Dolan, brother of the president's chief speechwriter and still the nominal head of the National Conservative Political Action Committee, once the fiercest of all the PACs on the right, was in and out of Georgetown Hospital these days. Everyone knew why, even if nobody said. Neal was Terry's friend, but Anders now worried, on top of everything else, if he might be showing too much *interest* by asking about the sick man.

"Terry's got so few T cells—about three, I think—that I just named them for him: MX, Cruise, and Pershing."

Anders laughed, nervously. He averted his eyes from Neal's and looked instead at the Tower Records bag, knowing it more likely contained Peter Allen or Puccini than Bon Jovi. "Well, give him my best."

He had met Terry Dolan only a couple of times, one of them in Dallas during the '84 convention. There in the Fairmont Hotel he had quickly realized that he'd wandered into the "wrong" nomination-night party. But he'd gotten lit, stayed late, and enjoyed himself. He'd liked the feeling of being admired, teased, of not having to do anything himself to keep the party alive. God, could those guys drink—and there was no denying they were pretty damned funny.

Now back in room 380A, he glanced up at ubiquitous CNN before noticing, sure enough, a phone message from the Federal Plaza number. He made sure to answer it right away.

"Where the hell is Speakes on this hijack thing?" asked the former president. "Ziegler would have been out in front of the cameras already," he declared, comparing his old press secretary to Reagan's.

Anders braced himself for a short fulmination about the incumbent's excessive vacationing, and he tried to head it off by saying, "I ran into Dr. Kirkpatrick in the Mess."

"What did she have to say?"

"That there'll be more attention paid to Daniloff now. By the press."

"Well, she's right. You guys are blowing this. You can afford to put *pressure*, a lot of it, on the Soviets. If Karpov is still showing up at State"— *how did he know that?*—"it means they still want another summit. I told you there'd be a test, and so far Reagan and Poindexter are failing it. The test is *not* to determine how tough we can be without having them scrap the summit. Hell, I mined Haiphong Harbor in May of '72 and Brezhnev still showed up! The test is to gauge how Reagan will behave *at* the summit. And so far, believe me, the Soviets like what they're seeing. Anyway, what was Cox's wife like?"

Anders had to think for a moment before realizing that he meant Anne Macmurray. "Oh, she's a nice lady. And very attractive. But she didn't really want a tour. She's actually a freezenik, and she wants me for an interview. She sort of played a trick, sir."

The line was quiet for a moment, the way it would go before Nixon did his own version of laughter. "Send her one of those signed copies of *Real Peace* that I left with you. And tell her I said *Touché! Hasta luego*, Andy!"

6

SEPTEMBER 14, 1986

The first lady wished the two of them were watching *Murder, She Wrote*. They'd have their feet up on hassocks and would be nibbling at some of the rose sorbet left over from Wednesday's dinner for the Brazilian president. Instead, she and Ronnie were in front of the camera, on a couch in the upstairs residence, making the biggest Just Say No pitch ever. Ronnie, a moment ago, had begun speaking "from our family to yours."

The setting, along with the choice of Sunday night, was a good idea—worthy of Mike Deaver in his better days—but, really, who out there from sea to shining sea really believed this bit about "our family"? Anyone paying the least attention knew that she and Patti hadn't spoken in the six months since her daughter's hateful book had appeared. Even so, certain fictions had to be maintained. This morning on *Meet the Press*, in a taped teaser for this joint speech, Nancy had told Marvin Kalb that her children "tried marijuana" back "in college" and that "that was it." Oh, brother. If the red light of the camera weren't on her right now, she'd be shutting her eyes, trying to dispel a mental image of Patti snorting lines of cocaine off the coffee table of some man she'd met half an hour ago.

Whatever the political necessity of this speech, Nancy all at once felt overwhelmed by a sense of its pointlessness. She resented all the chairs that had been moved, all the cables now taped to the carpet; things would never be straightened up before it was time to go to bed. She could also see, out of the corner of her eye, a bag of microwaved popcorn that some technician had opened up near a tool box. Since last year's cancer surgery, Ronnie had been forbidden that snack, and she'd made clear that it was never to be anywhere around. Once the red light went off, if she didn't remember to stop him, Ronnie would go over to thank the crew and scoop up a handful of kernels. She was further worried that the chrysanthemums in here—more leftovers from the Brazil dinner—would set off his allergies and make him sneeze mid-speech. If that were to happen— one sneeze!—it would become the entirety of tomorrow's coverage, and all of yesterday's rehearsal at Camp David would have been for nothing.

Just Say No. Even Mike had opposed making it her signature project: drugs were too grubby, at odds with Ronnie's optimism. But the long-running initiative had given her a certain gravity, and from time to time, when she hugged the inner-city kids, it made her look and even feel maternal. When she'd started, no one could have predicted the issue's current political power; the polls now showed that nothing, with the exception of nuclear war, bothered voters more. The Democrats had gone ahead and passed their own drug bill in the House last week, and Ronnie was now telling viewers that the administration would send its proposal to the Hill tomorrow morning.

The camera captured her gaze, fixed and slightly frightened, as Ronnie described the "uncontrollable fire" now raging. Crack had made drugs an issue good enough to steal, especially in states like Florida, where she was discreetly doing what she could for Paula Hawkins, "the Senate's general in the war on drugs," as a new round of ads called the Republican incumbent. Nancy had called the head of the RNC to tell him he needed to be more aggressive down there, and she'd pledged to make a video pitch that would be shown to gatherings of the biggest donors in Sarasota and Fort Lauderdale.

Now, on the monitor, she could see her hand in Ronnie's, something everyone will notice and many will criticize. But to herself the gesture is so natural, so familiar, that she can't even feel his hand enveloping hers, not unless she concentrates and tries on locating the sensation.

Nancy has traveled over one hundred thousand miles to fifty-five cities in twenty-eight states and six foreign countries to fight school-age drug and alcohol abuse. Her personal observations and efforts have given her such dramatic insights that I wanted her to share them with you this evening.

At the sound of the numbers, her mind went not to the little statistical tribute being paid, but to a stark single digit that so often stabbed at her: as a "zero-year" president, Ronnie was almost bound to die in office, the

way all the others elected in years ending with that number had died—
one after the other, at twenty-year intervals—ever since William Henry
Harrison (1840). If she had talked Ronnie out of running for reelection
in '84, he might have been spared the curse—earned a dispensation by
humbly abdicating. But the zero-year clock was still running, into a second term, the way it had for Lincoln and FDR.

She had come around to wanting the second term, convinced herself
it was needed for Ronnie to achieve a level of greatness his library would
magnify and forever preserve. But ever since they'd finally returned
from California, the zero-year theory had had her back in its grip. This
morning's phone call to Joan from Camp David, which she'd made to
calm herself down, had had the opposite effect. Usually such a comfort—
more like a girlfriend, really, or one of those counselors she'd always been
sending Patti to during her daughter's adolescence—the astrologer had
ended up amplifying Nancy's unease into something like panic, when
she unexpectedly asked to talk about the "bigger celestial picture," to
have a conversation that extended beyond the usual attempts to schedule
Ronnie's next couple of months as favorably as possible. Today Joan had
said—literally out of the blue sky!—that she now saw Uranus and Saturn
turning "virulently" against Ronnie in 1987, less than four months away.
(Saturn! Which had doomed them in '76.) Yes, there were some bright
spots between now and January, ones that needed to be seized and maxi-
mized. But something terrible was looming, a cosmic storm.

In order to get through the peril—and who knew if it *could* be gotten through?—she would need Joan more and more. Was there enough
money to pay her? The envelopes with the invoices always came marked
with a five-digit code, which kept anyone but herself from opening them.
Every few months she would tell Betsy, over the phone, to make Joan
out a check for whatever had been billed. Bets *always* got paid back—it
was a matter of pride, to both of them—but Nancy now had to wonder
whether the financing, like the horoscope itself, would soon slide beyond
all control.

All at once she *could* feel Ronnie's hand. It was squeezing hers: a gentle cue. The moment to deliver her own paragraphs of the speech had

arrived. And so she looked into the lens and summoned the same expression she'd displayed when trying to talk Ray Milland out of committing suicide in *Night into Morning*.

Thank you. As a mother, I've always thought of September as a special month, a time when we bundled our children off to school, to the warmth of an environment in which they could fulfill the promise and hope in those restless minds . . .

———

Pamela Harriman cinched the silk belt of her bathrobe and looked out upon the rhododendrons planted by the Dutch gardener here at Willow Oaks. Nearly ten years had passed since she'd made Ave buy this Virginia estate not far from where the Kennedys used to weekend during Jack's presidency. She'd changed the place's name to Willow Oaks from Journey's End—which had seemed a little morbid for an octogenarian like Ave, and decidedly premature for herself.

It was only eight p.m., but Pamela felt ready for bed. She had a frightfully busy week ahead of her and was tired out from a day at the Devon Horse Show with her son and his wife. Winston and Minnie had decided after all to come over for Ave's memorial, and to bring three of their children. Today had been pleasant enough, though she could scarcely remember her grandchildren's names and continued to like her daughter-in-law better than her son. A psychiatrist had once told her she was unable to "bond" with him because of an overly conditioned proclivity to view every male in sexual or marital terms. The incest taboo required her to perform such strenuous, suppressive work that she had no emotional energy left for simple maternal affection toward Winston.

After making this observation, the psychiatrist had found himself dismissed faster than any gardener or cook who'd ever been in Pamela's employ.

Moving away from the window and toward her bed, she decided to sit down, just for a moment, at the Louis XV desk piled high with plans and charts for Tuesday's service. It was a brilliant stroke to be seating McNamara and Bill Fulbright together: the hawk nesting with the dove; the two of them reconciled by Ave's spirit or, more to the point, by Ave's widow. Smiling, she picked up the pages of Ted Kennedy's eulogy, sent over by whichever staffer had written it, but decided once again not to have a peek, preferring that its words fall fresh upon her ears Tuesday morning.

All the Digbys and Churchills would be at N Street for dinner tomorrow night, and on Wednesday the whole lot of them would be lunching at the British embassy as guests of the newly arrived ambassador. Antony Acland was fifty-six and a widower. She could almost imagine . . . No, those days were behind her. Her sights were now permanently fixed on this side of the Atlantic. She had embraced widowhood and did not care whether Acland had a farthing or a fortune. Still, the brief thought of his eligibility had her running one hand down the silk-robed contour of her left side, whose increasing tautness pleased her, no matter that these days the aim of her slimming was to look attractive behind the lectern instead of behind the bedroom door.

She reached over and lifted a crocodile paperweight that she'd bought to celebrate the nickname bestowed ages ago on a wily, once-formidable Ave. Underneath the ceramic reptile rested her husband's last will and testament, which she and Clark Clifford had entered at the Loudoun County Courthouse only last month: *I have intentionally refrained from making substantial provision for my beloved daughters . . .*

It was a perfectly sensible decision, made in connection with two well-fixed women older than Pamela herself. And its result? Except for one little trust here and another there, she had gotten it all, the whole hundred *million*, every house, the plane, the van Gogh. She was finally, authentically, rich, and just beginning to luxuriate in the feeling that people now wanted money, lots of it, from *her*.

After giving the paperweight an affectionate pat, she got into bed, pressing the remote control for CNN.

And there was that ghastly woman! Hand in hand with the old fool, whose wattles were looser than the ones on the wild turkeys they'd driven past this afternoon.

"Many of you," said the first lady, "may be thinking: 'Well, drugs don't concern me.' But it does concern you."

It? Isn't "drugs" a plural? Whichever the case, they concerned Pamela very much, because she, too, knew the polling data about what the public now considered big issues. She was glad the Democrats had gotten out in front of things with a House bill that was *very* severe on the enforcement side but also made at least some provision to *treat* people and not just incarcerate them. Even so, she felt relieved that Tip was leaving the speakership: the loyal opposition needed sleeker, more virile figures for the voters to focus on. Pamela was delighted that Ethel's oldest boy, Joe, would be running for Tip's seat, though every time she saw the young man she recalled his leering grandfather, the "ambassador," who one summer weekend at Chequers had rushed up to her twenty-year-old self like a jackrabbit in a homburg.

"Listen to this news account," said Nancy—*so tremulous! so actressy!*—"from a hospital in Florida, about a child born to a mother with a cocaine habit . . ."

Bloody Florida. Pamela reached across the bedspread for the *Post* and reread the story of how Bob Graham's lead down there was beginning to shrink. She fumed. The Democrats *had* to have that seat. She coveted it as she once might have another woman's ring. Well, she would just have to wrench it off the hand of this tarty Paula Hawkins, with her showgirl's hair and press-on fingernails.

The Daniloff business, further up the *Post*'s front page, might actually help. The *U.S. News* reporter had been released to the U.S. embassy in Moscow, in order to await trial, but Shultz was calling him a "hostage," a word sure to invite comparisons between Reagan and Carter. And rough-tough Ronnie had just had to release Zakharov, Daniloff's opposite number, in advance of *his* trial.

"So," said Nancy Reagan, "to my young friends out there: Life can be great, but not when you can't see it. Open your eyes to life . . ."

"Cow!" cried Pamela, before clicking off the television and shutting her own eyes.

———

Richard Nixon took his eight-year-old granddaughter by the hand. "Let's go watch TV with Ma," he proposed.

He counted it a peculiar blessing that he had always inspired his own daughters' devotion and protectiveness. Even through the worst of it, Julie and Tricia had regarded him as a kind of tender, absentminded professor ("Oh, Daddy!") rather than some Transylvanian creature of the night. And he could sense the same feelings beginning to form in this grandchild they'd gotten pretty late in the game: Julie's first daughter, Jennie; half-Nixon and half-Eisenhower; a little girl who already wanted to be in the movies or on the tube; who loved any kind of dance step or impersonation and found it hilarious that you could go into a store and buy a rubber Halloween mask with "Pa's" face on it.

The two of them headed off to the living room, where Pat would be watching *Murder, She Wrote*. He usually lasted no more than ten or fifteen minutes, but he'd shared enough of the series with Pat that one Sunday night he'd expressed the wish that he could have given her a life in Cabot Cove, the show's small-town setting, instead of the one he'd dragged her through. "Thanks, pal," she'd said, tapping his hand. "But have you considered their homicide rate?"

At least he'd gotten her out of New York, where he'd moved them from San Clemente back in '80—an almost entirely bad idea. Christ, there on the Upper East Side, *Schlesinger* had been able, literally, to look into their backyard! Something the realtor had never mentioned. For the couple of years they'd been there, Pat had been edgy and strangely wistful. Here in Jersey she was more relaxed, and his own ride to the office downtown was quick enough.

Jennie was still chattering as they entered the living room and found Pat dozing on the couch, oblivious not, as it turned out, to Angela Lansbury but to Nancy Reagan, who was relinquishing the floor to her husband.

"We better let Ma rest," Nixon told Jennie.

The girl went merrily off while he lowered the volume on the TV and ran his eyes over Pat's face and left arm. A decade after the big stroke in San Clemente, and three years after a smaller one here, he still performed these covert searches for signs of another.

In order to further implement these six goals—

The Great Communicator! thought Nixon. How exactly do you

"implement" goals? And—oh, Christ—he only now realized that *drugs* were the subject.

Well, they could blame Nixon for that, too. The goddamned "war on drugs" was the second one he never should have pursued, let alone declared. You couldn't change people's nature—they would do what they were going to do—and Ehrlichman shouldn't have jazzed up an ordinary law-enforcement issue with that crusading title. Same, really, with their "war on cancer." They'd probably been trying to give "war" a good name, attaching the word to all their worthy domestic endeavors after being called war *criminals*, year after year. Well, at least he'd never asked the damned networks for airtime to talk about drugs, which had never interested him any more than all those other domestic crusades.

This was surely Nancy's doing, which made him wonder, not for the first time: Did *anything* truly interest Reagan? Late yesterday afternoon there'd been a call from Camp David: Reagan wanting his approval of the Daniloff/Zakharov swap—which of course he'd given. What was the point of saying otherwise when the deal was already done? Object to it and the White House would start regarding him as a pain in the ass; then there would be no more calls, period. Even so, he wished they'd come to him for *advice* about things, not approval after the fact.

Neither Daniloff nor Zakharov would ever come to trial. The Soviets had gotten what they wanted: they'd retrieved their spy and acquired the confidence that they would clean Reagan's clock whenever the next summit occurred. Nixon was sure that would come soon, and that the Russians would be the ones to set it in motion. "We don't want such problems to poison the atmosphere," their Foreign Ministry was now saying about this little skirmish they'd just won.

Geneva, last year, had been a polite icebreaker. This would be something serious; fewer people around the table and more proposals on it. Nixon would resist making calls to Shultz and his new pal Poindexter during the run-up. He already sent more notes to Don Regan than he should—the effect of exile and too goddamned little to do, which made it hard not to fire off suggestions for how to handle chickenshit like the supposed "MIA issue," which no more existed than any MIAs themselves.

He needed to preserve his influence by making himself scarce. He would stay informed about any summit preparations through his friend Little—and during this period he'd publicly agree with the president whenever possible.

Nixon looked at the television. Reagan appeared incapable of believing that anyone *dis*agreed with him. The former president realized yet again that he didn't understand this guy in the least. Even now Nixon preferred an enemy he could comprehend to an ally who eluded him. Nancy he could understand just fine: she was like him, all edges, graspable in a dozen different ways. The camera had just cut back to her, sitting there in her thousand-dollar suit behind a bunch of flowers. The whole scene conveyed opulence instead of hominess. Of course, he'd done that himself toward the end, putting so many bells and whistles on the place in San Clemente when it was the Western White House. "Do we really need *that*?" he could still hear Pat saying, whenever another patio or helipad would appear.

He looked at her sleeping and thought of how little credit she'd ever gotten. Nancy might be waging her own "war" on drugs, but it was Pat who'd actually gone into a combat zone, shaking hands with the bloodied and bandaged GIs at that hospital in Long Binh. Christ, he'd turned her whole *life* into a combat zone. He glanced back at the Reagans, sitting so contentedly with each other on the plush of their televised couch, and he thought—inevitably—of the furniture onstage at the El Capitan Theatre, the night of the Checkers speech; thought of Pat, silent and agonized, managing a smile when the cameras went in for a reaction shot, while he exposed their hard-luck finances to the entire country.

He spread an afghan over her lap and clicked off the television.

———

Anne Macmurray tested the new plantation shutters in her fourteenth-floor apartment. What an odd city, she thought, looking eastward from Arlington toward Washington. It was more like a stadium: the suburbs, with their newly sprouted office towers and condominia, were growing taller than the actual District of Columbia, whose buildings stayed respectfully lower than the Capitol dome.

She had the TV on inside the still mostly bare apartment. Ronald Reagan was inveighing against "those who are killing America and terrorizing it with slow but sure chemical destruction." He sounded a bit like Helen when she moved off nuclear weapons and got on to the environment. But unlike Dr. Caldicott's, Reagan's voice perpetually soothed, even when he spoke of "this cancer of drugs" and compared it to the gulag and the Holocaust. Rhetorically, he and Nancy were doing nothing by halves tonight.

Whereas Anne herself was still splitting the difference. Telling herself there would be no takers for it, she had not tried selling the house back in Owosso. Lovely as the town remained, the Rust Belt did remain weary and recessed, no matter what anyone said about the "Reagan Recovery." So her old house stood empty—and seemed to be awaiting her return. If she did go back, could she call it anything but failure?

She looked through the shutters' wooden slats toward Wilson Boulevard, wondering which tower might contain Anders Little. If she didn't soon succeed in getting him here for dinner, the meal she served, thanks to the new tax act, would be only eighty-percent deductible instead of a hundred. (This new rate, she thought, was surely the biggest blow Reagan's true believers would ever suffer at his hands.) But was she really seeking just an interview with Mr. Little? Exactly what interest *did* she have in this tightly wound old young man? Certainly not a romantic one: he was more than two decades her junior, and she was *not* protesting too much when she told herself that the thought was absurd. Even so, was there something of Peter in him that perversely appealed to her? No, she decided. However nettlesome he might be, Mr. Little was, at least on the surface, polite. Peter had never even pretended to be. *You're not going to be here long if you're with me,* he'd told her on one of their first dates in 1948—a warning against becoming overly fond of Owosso, where she had still been a new arrival. He was, he assured her daily, going places, and the town, like the state senate, would be just a stepping stone.

Of course it had worked out otherwise. Owosso had been the only venue of their marriage, just as Lansing had proved the end point of his political career. She imagined Peter as he must look tonight, in his own glassy aerie above Dallas, the turquoise-festooned second wife long gone. The man she'd left, fifteen years after he'd left Anne, was trying to stay in the game as a semi-big contributor, even to the point of subsidizing John Connally, his bankrupt former patron.

Reagan was now telling everyone not to let down the World War II vets by allowing their grandchildren to get high. He was coming to a close, so that Nancy might have the last word: "Won't you join us in this great, new national crusade?" asked the first lady.

"Whatever," said Anne, who had once worried a great deal about drugs, but whose daughter seemed to have moved past all that by now. It was probably not too early to begin thinking about her grandchildren when it came to this subject, but how could she think of anything but herself and her ex-husband right now while she watched the dissolving sight of *those two*, hand in hand, onscreen? Was it disgustingly possible that she envied this overlabeled, overcoiffed, brittle little woman, just because she had a man who (desperately) needed her?

Anne walked across the room, which echoed with the clap of her flat shoes on the parquet. She fished from her purse the business card she'd been given by Anders Little. She would leave a message on his office machine—another way, this one useful and modern, of splitting the difference. She would hang up the phone, having comfortably dispatched the ball of whatever game they were playing into Mr. Little's court.

If they'd had technology like this back in '48, how much better might she have controlled her romance with Peter!

———

"JUST SAY NO!"

The cry went up from several men at the bar as Hitchens entered Annie's Steakhouse. The patrons of the mostly gay establishment had turned tonight's spousal White House broadcast into a drinking game. The shout and swallow that greeted each new customer only added to a boisterous opening-night feeling that had pervaded the restaurant for the past couple of weeks. Annie's had just moved to its new location, ceding its old corner a few hundred yards down Seventeenth Street to a new gay bar called J.R.'s.

It didn't take Hitchens long to find the man he was looking for, though he'd met him only once, two years ago, at Reagan's last convention—the Gipper's Dallas jubilee. There he was, at a back corner table, perhaps two stone lighter, tapping his emaciated fingers on a checkered tablecloth to the juke-boxed tune of "Private Dancer." Where did he get the strength? Hitchens wondered. The man was still handsome enough; the Village People mustache had thinned less than the hair atop his head. Still, the flannel shirt he wore, during what was still a Washington summer, had been chosen not to complete the already somewhat retro clone look but to keep him warm against the chills of infection and whatever useless medicine he was taking.

"Nice to see you again, Dolan."

"Nice to see *you*, Chris!"

Dolan managed to get to his feet while Hitchens exhibited the slightly curled lip that awaited anyone who used the verboten "Chris" instead of "Christopher" or "Hitch." They both then took their seats beneath a wall poster announcing a high-heeled drag race to be run at midnight on Halloween along the block and a half between the new J.R.'s and the relocated Annie's.

Dolan saw Hitchens reading the poster. "Well, I won't be doing *that*!" he said.

"How are you getting on?" Hitchens asked.

"I'm out of Georgetown Hospital on a quick furlough. I'm sure I'll be back in soon enough, coughing and throwing up. But for now I'm two pounds up! And breathing pretty well," he added. He slid a copy of the book he'd cowritten across the table: *Reagan: A President Succeeds.*

"How very thoughtful," said Hitchens. "Succeeds at what, exactly? Besides perhaps employing your brother." Anthony Dolan, though not the author of tonight's drug address, remained Reagan's chief speechwriter.

Terry Dolan laughed good-humoredly. "Reagan's *achievements*? Where to start? Take the Contras. You—"

"Gangsters."

"A freedom movement!"

"Is that so?" asked Hitchens. "Name one other in history that had no manifesto."

"You need to consider the excesses of the Sandinistas since they've come to power—"

"Reagan and company were against the Sandinistas *before* they came to power," said Hitchens, as softly as he said everything else. "Their real excess was their opposition to Somoza."

"Chris, I didn't interrupt you."

"Manners aside, Dolan, would you be fast enough to do that?"

He felt pity for this poor, mentally forked creature. There was no joy in dispatching an opponent not at the top of his game. So Hitchens paused, allowing the man across from him to get, first, his breath and then a word in.

"It's nice to be home," said Dolan, looking around the restaurant. "Back in the neighborhood. Did you have far to come?" He asked the question as if he and not Hitchens had been the one to request their meeting.

"My place is a bit off Capitol Hill," Hitchens answered. "I was running a little late, so I hopped a cab. The Ethiopian driver was happy enough to bring me here, but I rather doubt he'd be equally pleased to run me home. Too many of his own dark brethren in the neighborhood. Amazing how quickly the new arrivals assimilate the native racism."

Dolan laughed. "But you seem to like it here! Are you going to stay? Come on, tell me *one thing* you think America's doing right."

"Over here libel lawyers can't descend upon me for each understated hyperbole."

"Got it. So what did you want to see me about?" asked Dolan, who all at once seemed worried his energy might give out before they reached the point of the conversation.

"Well, it wasn't my intention, but now that I've gotten a look at you, I feel the inclination to ask: What do you think of Mr. Reagan's AIDS policy?"

"Well, they do need to speed up the AZT approval process. Get it out of the FDA bureaucracy."

"Ah, yes," said Hitchens, "the libertarian view. Let's assume that AZT proves a bit more effective than, say, laetrile did against cancer. And let's assume that it's made available to all. How do 'all' then afford it?"

"Oh, the market will work that out."

"I thought it might. You know, it would be a welcome spectacle to see people on their deathbeds crying for socialism instead of God. Tell me, Dolan: you're expressing this faith in the market as someone who does not *have* AIDS?"

"That's right."

"What *do* you have?"

"Anemia," answered Dolan. "Complicated by diabetes."

"Type 1? Type 2?"

"Not sure."

"Really? How about whether or not you're a homosexual? Sure of that?"

"I'm not. A homosexual, that is. But I have nothing against people who are."

"Did you have nothing against them when you approved that pitch for Congressman Crane in '82?"

"I never really approved that. But I apologized for it anyway."

"Before or after Larry Kramer threw a drink in your face?"

Dolan laughed, as if the incident were an ordinary political war story, one now tamed into anecdote by both sides, each now fond of the other. Of course, thought Hitchens, were Kramer to come in the door tonight, he'd dump a whole pitcher of queer beer on Dolan. Which would only add to this fellow's wishy-washiness. If there were a real *tension* in Dolan, the sort of intellectual or moral conflict that can make hypocrisy heroic, that would be one thing. Weak-willed muddle was another. A few years ago Dolan's libertarian side had allowed him to add his name to the letterhead of something called CAIR—Concerned Americans for Individual Rights—a GOP-style issues group urging that the boys be decriminalized, though not much beyond that. And then he'd failed to show up for their first meeting.

"How come you didn't propose that we rendezvous at, say, Afterwords?" asked Hitchens, naming a sexually neutral bookstore-café a couple of blocks away.

"Oh, I love this place," Dolan answered.

"I thought you might," said Hitchens, who took a look at all the preppy-handbook Hill Rats, young men who did their best to ignore the older, more furtive cottaging types he remembered from his youth—men who'd gotten used to not running from the law just in time to start running from the plague. A tense gloom underlay the jollity here, and in the mix of types he could imagine a few gentlemen quite a bit worse than Dolan, ones who still derived their greatest sense of psychological safety from oppressing their own.

"What made you the way you are?" Hitchens asked Dolan. "Politically, I mean."

"Oh, it was Nixon! All those liberal domestic policies of his when I was in college."

"And what keeps you that way even now?"

A predictable recitation of Evil Empire threats and laissez-faire miracles followed. Hitchens tuned out most of it before asking: "Ever miss the game? The old NCPAC hijinx?"

Dolan smiled, laughed, and coughed. "Well, I'm not *entirely* out of it!"

"Oh?"

"I still dabble in what's left of the PAC. When I'm up to it."

"Actually, that's what I came here to discuss."

"Really?" asked Dolan.

The winsome eagerness was dreadful. It would have been so in the pre-plague days, too, but now of course it was worse, the genial manner managing to sustain itself as the body from which it emanated shrank to nothing and denial expanded to include most of reality. Perhaps this was what the Christians called grace—instead of sociopathy.

"I'm doing a story about how the competition has quite overtaken you. Mrs. Harriman, specifically."

"Oh, Lady Pamela!"

Hitchens noticed the big smile and wondered if he'd just given Dolan the idea to dress up as La Churchill for Halloween, while watching the drag race from a frail distance.

"Any thoughts on her operation?" asked Hitchens.

"Oh, it's smooth enough," said Dolan, with the first touch of wariness he'd shown, as if he were still playing the electoral game at his peak. "What are you trying to figure out?"

"Mostly whether she's like your man Reagan: an ancient, pretty face, propped up by others, entirely dependent on cue cards."

Hitchens realized that Mrs. Harriman's *opposite* could probably be located in Dolan himself: a sharklike natural when it came to direct-mail politics, but—no matter the two visible lesions on his face—almost certainly still a naïf when it came to sex and men.

"She's not so smart that she can't be tripped up," said Dolan, after some consideration.

"Who's going to do that?"

"Us!"

The smile was now so bright that Hitchens feared the meds might be talking.

"Watch where she spends her PAC funds in Florida," Dolan said, more soberly.

"On Sadie Hawkins, presumably."

"Keep track of all the different pots the cash gets funneled into."

"Yes," said Hitchens, trying to hide a certain boredom. "Very Woodward and Bernstein. 'Follow the money' and all that. But I don't see us meeting in underground car parks. For one thing, I don't drive, and for another I doubt you could withstand the fumes."

Dolan laughed. "'Car parks'! So British. I love it! But you won't need to follow the money. I'll lead you to it—as soon as Mrs. H. has blundered and put it in the wrong place."

"Why do me such a favor?"

"Two birds with one stone. Short-term and long-term gain. What I do will drain a little cash from Graham's campaign; and what you write will put a dent in Lady Pamela's reputation."

"I'm rather surprised you still even think in the long term."

"Good one, Chris!" said Dolan.

"Of course 'end-times' may be coming for us all. The Reverend Robertson will be at Constitution Hall Wednesday night, revving up the faithful for his run to succeed the golden Hollywood calf."

Dolan smiled yet again. "I wouldn't put any money on him."

"How about putting money *in* his campaign? Would you? If your own PAC were still flush? Maybe just enough to keep the base tickled?"

"That I might do."

"So: *in* him but not *on* him? Isn't it supposed to be the other way round?" Hitchens pointed to the safe-sex slogan on a poster near the one advertising the Halloween race: *ON ME, NOT IN ME*.

"Good one!" said Dolan, a second time. "Chris, I hope we can get together again, once I'm able to tell you where Mrs. Harriman has put her money."

"Well," said Hitchens, "let's hope our next meeting isn't in hospital." He looked around for a waiter. "Tell me, Dolan. Whom does one have to fuck to get a drink around here?"

———

"Great *speech*," said Merv.

"Ronnie did all the work," Nancy replied, managing a laugh over the phone. Her husband was still down the hall, chatting with one of the crew and, she hoped, not eating popcorn.

"Well, he was great, *too*," said Merv, always so supportive. Had she ever thanked him for keeping Patti off his talk show—and, from what she'd heard, a few other shows, too—when her daughter had been hawking that awful book?

"I heard you cut a rug the other night with Paul Anka," said Merv.

"Yes," she said, with a laugh. "The Brazilians loved it."

Aside from being supportive, Merv was also intuitive, and when he didn't say anything else for a moment, she knew he was sensing the enormous degree of her current unease.

"Merv," she brought herself to ask, "how long is it since you introduced me to Joan?"

"Rivers?"

"No. Quigley."

"Oh, about a dozen years, I guess."

"I'm not"—Nancy could hear the hesitation in her own voice—"really sure how well I know her."

"What do you mean?" asked Merv.

"Can I trust her?"

"Joan? Oh, I think so. You already trust her with the schedule, don't you?"

"Yes, but I've never really brought her into anything else—anything bigger. Honest."

"What could be bigger than the comings and goings of Ronald Reagan?" asked Merv.

Could she confide to him—or Bets? or maybe even Mermie?—the idea that had formed in her mind as she sat there on the couch tonight with Ronnie, while he talked and her hand went ice-cold inside his? No, she decided, she couldn't; not yet. "Will you be here for the Gershwin thing?" she asked, hoping he somehow wouldn't notice the change of subject. "It's October twenty-sixth."

"Wouldn't miss it!"

"Wonderful! Or, *'s wonderful*, I guess I should say. You just made my day. And it's been a long one." It was better just to sign off. "I'll tell that fellow of mine you thought he did well. Night, Merv."

Ronnie needed to resign by New Year's. Or, at the very latest, by his birthday on February 6. Her mind was racing: he'd be turning seventy-six and they could bring back Mike to do a big "Spirit of '76" sendoff. They'd invent some medical reason, but however they did it, they needed to be gone from here by then, before Uranus and Saturn, casting their double-shadow of doom, fully caught up with him. If things could somehow hold between now and then, he would go out on top, with a seventy-percent approval rating and a new tax law that cemented the prosperity he'd brought. But between now and then there would be so much else to do. The approaching planets needed to be—and *could* be, with some partial success, as she understood it—resisted. Ronnie had to retain the Senate in November, and he *had* to make a big breakthrough with Gorbachev. Both of those things absolutely needed to happen, and to be frozen in place as a bulwark against those distant spheres, which she now saw coming toward them like cannonballs fired at a castle. Ronnie had to be out of here by the time they struck.

She put on her nightgown and took a Dalmane to conquer the sleep-lessness she'd otherwise be experiencing tonight. Her mind turned again to Patti, who always pointed out, so predictably, that prescription drugs were "really no different" from the stuff people bought on the street. Her daughter had recently reversed the tubal ligation she'd undergone years ago after some crushing romantic experience—a bad idea (the reversal, that is), which Nancy had learned about only secondhand. The ligation *itself* had been a bad idea—"Does he know?" Nancy would always ask Patti when she started dating someone—but over time she had grown accustomed to the thought that Patti, the only one of the children likely to give Ronald Reagan a biological grandchild, wouldn't be doing that. There was an odd comfort—similar to what she felt when imagining herself as a glass-protected mannequin in the Reagan Library—in the thought that Ronald Reagan's DNA would not keep projecting itself into the future.

He had just come back in, given her a peck on the cheek, and gone into the bathroom to wash his face. Within a few seconds she heard the water running, and she stood still, fixed to this spot on the carpet, waiting for the moment when he would close the tap and the flow would stop.

7

SEPTEMBER 16, 1986

Pamela Harriman walked up the aisle of the National Cathedral to an almost jaunty recessional version of "Jesu, Joy of Man's Desiring." She nodded and smiled to those in attendance on each side of the church, feeling unfamiliarly like a bride without a groom.

Which was not to say she lacked for suitors: of the eight hundred people seated in the nave, fully one percent were likely aspirants to the Democratic presidential nomination for 1988, and each of them craved the help of PamPAC—no matter that Arthur Schlesinger's eulogy for Ave had just deplored, with a certain sibilant spritz, the current age's "hustle and opportunism."

Mario Cuomo, Pamela's current favorite among The Eight, sat closest to the front, ennobled by his attainment of Ave's old position as governor of New York. And since he was sitting on the aisle, he could respond to Mrs. Harriman's nod with a quick kiss.

She ignored those in the row in front of him: George Shultz with his plump wife; and Barbara Bush, the equally plump wife of the absent vice president. Pamela had been miffed when the Number Two's regrets had arrived by mail last week, but decided the slight wasn't worth making into a grudge. One of The Eight, whoever it turned out to be, would make mincemeat of Bush in two short years. But first the Democrats had to get the Senate.

Invigorated by Cuomo's kiss, Pamela glanced down the row in which he sat: Lady Bird was there, along with the elder baby Bird, Lynda, and her husband, the former governor of Virginia. Pamela didn't want him becoming Number Nine—rumors about a taste for beauty queens and drugs had reached her. She nodded at Chuck Robb and continued on her way, smiling at the whole array of Bidens and Gephardts, Dunders and Blitzens. She felt eager for the next phase of the proceedings; they would now all come to her at the tip of a receiving line she had asked be set up at the back of the church.

But her pleasure collapsed into annoyance when she noticed the poisonous Mr. Hitchens sitting on the aisle, not even halfway to the rear of the cathedral.

Hitchens nodded solemnly as she passed.

Confusing the usher and scoring this choice seat had been child's play, no harder than switching place cards at a dinner party, a maneuver he was sure the adventuress now sweeping past had performed any number of times.

Hitchens had had a call the other night from Italy. Gore Vidal—never one to mind the long-distance *lire* when telling a choice story—had informed him that the late Averell Harriman wasn't in fact reposing beside his previous wife, Marie, beneath the patch of ground into which mourners had seen him lowered last July. Once the graveside crowd dispersed, Harriman had been resurrected and placed into a "receiving vault" to await conveyance toward his final destination: a bosky little dell fully three miles away on the family estate, where he could be joined by Pamela, perhaps two or three decades from now, once she was good and ready to begin her own eternal rest. As the Maestro had explained over the excellent transatlantic connection, the bishop who interred Ave had recently conceded to a friend of a friend that the ancient ambassador had been buried "liturgically, not physically." It sounded like one more halfway measure—*on me, not in me*—something like consubstantiation, the Protestants' lite-beer version of the Catholics' mad Eucharist.

Hitchens's eyes, along with everyone else's, followed the widow up the aisle. The Cold Warriors gathered here were basking in the old Anglo-American Special Relationship, which they'd created. Reagan and Mrs. Thatcher had almost sexually rejuvenated it into something more special than ever, but today's spoken tributes had been to a more antique version of the old romance, with those stories of how Ave had been with Churchill on the day of Pearl Harbor. (Was there, Hitchens suddenly wondered, a whiff of conspiracy to that? He should ask his pal Blumen-thal, whose mind liked to gambol over history's grassy knolls.)

He realized, while watching her golden helmet of hair recede up the aisle, that he felt a certain envy of Pamela: *she* had made her irreversible leap to the New World, whereas he, like some consubstantiated Communion wafer, remained betwixt and between. He had not come to the States in specific search of an American spouse—or to flee a British one. After a half decade of marriage he remained attached, unsatisfactorily, to his Cypriot wife—the thought of whom made him remember the sweet two-year-old boy also at home, and the pleasant obligation to bring him back some little present from today's outing: Was there perhaps a tiny plastic gargoyle available for purchase in the vestibule?

There was this larger question to be answered, too: Would little Alexander—British father, Cypriot mother, American residence—end up even further sliced and diced than himself? Trifurcated instead of merely split?

As always, short-term thinking now performed its merciful banishment of the longer-range kind. Hitchens began looking forward to Florida, where he had decided to do some chasing after the principals and operatives in the Graham-Hawkins race. It would be useful to witness some stumbling by Mrs. Harriman—he could see a headline: PamSPLAT!—though at the moment his glossy profiling of her engaged him less than a few other murky tributaries down which his Sunday-night conversation with Dolan seemed to be sending him. Nonetheless, his divided self felt somehow ready for the full Florida yahoo: the reddest necks and the biggest hair; the chance to tempt himself with a full-immersion expat baptism.

He watched Senator Edward Moore Kennedy, alarmingly fat and mottled of complexion, waddle past the pew. The bootlegger's youngest child had spoken of the warm relations between Ave and the Kennedy family, no matter that they'd never given Ave the secretary of state's job he craved: "He gave his help and his heart in our happiest days and hard-est hours." Pity anyone near Teddy's Cutty-Sarked breath during the delivery of all those aspirated aitches.

Hitchens now ventured out into the aisle, jumping the queue, as it were, since many of those in the pews just ahead had yet to release themselves. He could not forgo the opportunity presenting itself in the form of Dr. Jeane Kirkpatrick, Madonna (old sense) of the Contras. He felt a surge of interest. Mrs. K. seemed to be present as a twofer: not only a representative of Reaganism and its absent Ronnie, but also an avatar of those Cold War Democrats who, unlike the gang here, had bolted to the dark side instead of turning supine toward the Commies.

She was, Hitchens noticed, accompanied by an absurdly fit man about his own age; the sight of him made Hitchens want to light a cigarette. An astronaut perhaps? As he fell in behind, he heard the word "Shevardnadze"—the name of the Soviets' foreign minister—pass between them. The verbal mode seemed interrogative, but Hitchens was unable to catch the full drift. So he thrust himself forward, closer to the nubby suit and messy curls of Dr. Kirkpatrick, and found that proximity brought with it the same submissive sexual twinge he had once felt during an encounter with the pre-prime-ministerial Mrs. Thatcher, who had actually swatted him on the bum with a sheaf of papers.

"Was the president unable to attend?" he now asked the former UN ambassador, over her shoulder.

Anders Little turned around, as if he were a security agent. "It's Hispanic Heritage Week," he explained, crisply. "He has an event in the Rose Garden."

"Ah. Perhaps he can turn it into a Victory Garden for Enrique Bermudez," said Hitchens, naming the most thuggish of the Contras. "He can still send vegetables even if the law now prohibits him from sending guns."

Traffic had stalled in the nave. Dr. Kirkpatrick, turning around, looked at Hitchens and pointed to her companion, saying, "This is Anders Little," less an introduction than a hand-off, as if Hitchens were a dog to be walked or a ticking package to be disposed of. Little reflexively gave him a business card embossed with the seal of the National Security Council.

"Christopher Hitchens," announced the nuisance itself, extending his hand not to Little but to Kirkpatrick, even though Little's name was now ringing a faint bell from the booziest part of Sunday night's conversation with Dolan. Before the meds had made him shake like some flannel-shirted Giacometti, at which point Hitchens put him into a cab, Dolan had let slip something interestingly indiscreet. The dialogue reentered Hitchens's head as the congregants recommenced their shuffling through the cathedral:

—*They're pretty much everywhere, from the East Wing to the NSC.*

—*The NSC, you say.*

—*Sure. A couple of them. There's my friend Grover, and then there's the Nordic dreamboat. Let's just say no one's sure about him.*

You had to love that "they're."

Was Anders Little, against whose sinewy neck Hitchens's face now almost pressed, the Nordic vessel in question? And was he "oriented" in that direction? After having made a few unenthusiastic hops across the sexual median, during his school and university days, Hitchens himself had become a "confirmed mulierast," to borrow the Wilde circle's phrase for the heterosexual male. Where Anders Little was concerned, perhaps Dolan and Grover were guilty of wishful thinking? Maybe; but now that the line had begun moving faster, Mr. Little could be observed shepherding La K with a finesse worthy of any walker proud to be protecting Mommy Reagan from the lunchtime crowd at Le Pavillon.

As more pews emptied, Hitchens fell behind and became separated from his new focus of interest. Forced to drag his feet with the superannuated and senescent, he felt an impatience like that being experienced by the minority of comers and go-getters stuck behind with him, those eager to get back into the artificial light of their offices on K Street and the Hill—after, of course, a word with Lady Bountiful. Exasperated, he at last saw an opening through two sets of padded shoulders and barged through it, managing to regain his position directly behind Dr. Kirkpatrick and her Hyperborean escort. But the din of murmuring made it hard to pick up every word.

". . . can see why you took me here . . . ," said Little. ". . . so grateful . . . a real education . . ."

"Yes," said the pouting neoconservative, vexed by the crush. ". . . would say the seminar's a little overenrolled."

Dr. Kirkpatrick's history with the administration might be judged, Hitchens thought, more a rhetorical triumph than a practical success.

The lady had much work to do in the world, and there was even talk that the most moneyed and crazy of Ronnie's bombardiers might push for her to succeed him in '88.

"... does Shevardnadze arrive?" Hitchens caught these three additional words from Kirkpatrick to Little.

"... Friday ... if nothing goes wrong."

"It already has."

Her remark appeared to stop Little in his verbal tracks. Did she mean that Reagan's men had blown the Daniloff affair?

"... really bringing the letter?" she continued, before once more going out of range. "... when ... know?"

"Maybe not until he lands," said Little, unaware of Hitchens's renewed nearness. "But sources seem to ... yes."

What red letter were they speaking of? Hitchens wondered. And what was its importance? If he were a deadline reporter, he supposed he'd be rushing back to his bureau. But here he was, still wavering between *Vanity Fair*'s heated pool and *The Nation*'s sea of red ink—just as he couldn't make up his mind between the mother country and her still-juvenile-delinquent spawn, America.

Just when it seemed that reaching the Widow would take all morning, the line began a steady, quick movement: Pamela had begun her hand-shaking work with dispatch. Hitchens soon found himself face to face with Janet, the more senior of the two assistants he'd met on N Street. The other one held Mrs. Harriman's handbag.

"Hello," she said. "Mr. Hickey?"

"Hitchens."

"Oh, I am sorry."

"Not at all. You've such a large mailing list."

She smiled, but was already trying to move him along.

"I hear that Graham has a new ad up in Florida," he informed her. "Did you pay for it?" The challenger's latest TV spot accused Senator Hawkins, Ms. Drug Interdiction, of trying to defund the Coast Guard, if only accidentally, during some procedural vote.

Janet smiled. "I'm not sure this is the place or time."

"Why not?" Hitchens responded, looking around. "Aren't we in Heaven's waiting room? Rather like Florida itself."

Kelly, the blonder, junior assistant, laughed. Hitchens noted the supportive gesture, even as he persisted with Janet: "Hawkins is gaining on Graham. And you won't be able to out-narc her. She's making her own *staff* take drug tests."

Janet adjusted her smile to something more severe and urged him toward Mrs. Harriman with a look that said, unmistakably, *no questions*.

"Thank you for coming," Pamela said to him, with no smile at all. She quickly turned her head and beckoned the approaching Lynda Bird.

"I'm so glad the governor is with God," said Hitchens, giving Mrs. Harriman's hand a quick squeeze. "Seeing as he can't be with Marie."

8

SEPTEMBER 22, 1986

Anne Macmurray stood against the curved wall of tiny Ralph Bunche Park, across from the United Nations. THEY SHALL BEAT THEIR SWORDS INTO PLOWSHARES read the biblical inscription above her head. The park wasn't much more than a half-moon encroachment upon the grounds of the old Tudor City apartments, which could be reached from the sidewalk by a flight of steps that ran along the inscribed wall.

This morning the space contained about fifty people, almost all it could hold. Most were women, listening on someone's radio to the words that President Reagan was speaking in the General Assembly Building across First Avenue:

When the United States began work on technology to make offensive nuclear weapons someday obsolete, the Soviets tried to make that the main issue—as if the main danger to strategic stability was a defense against missiles that is still on the drawing boards rather than the menacing ballistic missiles themselves . . .

A chant went up, and Anne joined in: "*Star PUPILS! Not Star WARS!*"

To Anne's way of thinking, the maddest of all the mad Catch-22s governing the arms race was the probability that Reagan's missile-defense fantasy would now prevent a reduction in all the *offensive* weaponry with which he'd made Western Europe bristle: the Pershings, the cruise missiles, and all the rest. "*Star PUPILS! Not Star WARS!*" she shouted even louder, before venturing onto the sidewalk, as far as the policeman would allow, to take some pictures with her little Olympus. If they came out well, she'd run a couple of them in the next issue of *Turnabout*.

Looking through the viewfinder, she tried to convince herself that

the damp, cloudy weather was to blame for the low turnout of demonstrators. But she knew this was wishful thinking. The whole antinuclear
movement seemed to be running out of steam, to be aging as surely as
Reagan himself. This little rally badly needed the absent Helen Caldicott's energy and charisma, but even she appeared to be shrinking. There
were rumors that her marriage was crumbling, and that she might for-
sake the U.S. for her native Australia—just give up and get ready to live
out the last apocalyptic pages of *On the Beach*.

If she left, WAND would probably collapse, and what would that mean
for Anne? It might be a selfish consideration in the face of civilization's
life or death, but if she lost this little job, she would probably have to take
more alimony from Peter, when she already hated taking as much as she
did, all these years after the divorce. Her son, Ralph, the father of her
newest grandchild, was now successfully practicing law in Phoenix, and
he'd offered to put her on an *allowance*, a mortifying idea she had nipped
in the bud, reminding him that not so many years had passed since *she*
had given *him* a raise from three dollars a week to four.

*The United States continues to respect the antiballistic missile treaty—in
spite of clear evidence that the Soviets are violating it.*

With Armageddon on his mind, Reagan still managed to sound consoling before the General Assembly; Anne wished that the woman with
the radio would just turn him off. No one was truly listening to him, and
he couldn't hear their chanting—even if he were suddenly to appear on
the sidewalk, stroll right past them, feigning deafness, the way he did
with the newspeople each Sunday night when he disembarked from the
helicopter on the South Lawn. He got away with it every week, allowing
the dog, that pretentious little King Charles spaniel, to drag him back
into his gilded cage, as if he were helpless to do anything else.

Anne had come up from Washington last night with two women she
didn't really know, and the lady she'd just met beneath the Isaiah quotation seemed more interested in protesting Israel than in decrying the
arms race. But she wouldn't worry about all this now. She had a *job*, as she
sometimes needed to remind herself. So she checked the camera to see
how many pictures she had left, facing the closest thing she could find to

a patch of sunlight. She shot the last frames on the roll of twenty-four.

Once she heard the camera rewinding itself—what would they think of next?—she looked up and suddenly recognized Anders Little. It was almost as if Reagan himself had walked into view. The young man had just bounded up the park's curved staircase and was showing a policeman the laminated pass that had allowed him to walk down this stretch of First Avenue.

Anne stared hard in order to be sure. Yes, it was Anders. Above the little park, he was looking back across the street at the great green glass domino of the Secretariat building, an imposing miracle of calm, what the UN's founders must have imagined the world could be brought to when they erected the structure. Now she could see him looking down at the little knot of demonstrators, no doubt pleased there were so few. For a split second he met her gaze.

He had never responded to her phone message. And so she wondered whether she should wave, or glare, or just pretend she hadn't seen him. She could almost hear her daughter saying, "You can't charm *everyone*, Mother." Which was true. She would look away. She put the camera back into her PBS tote bag and reassumed her place beneath Isaiah 2:4.

"*HEY, HEY! HO, HO! ICBMs HAVE GOT TO GO!*" She joined in the chant, which sounded like a cheer from Ralph's old football games at Owosso High.

She would not let herself get discouraged. When things finished up here, she would enjoy her walk back to the San Carlos Hotel, where she'd arranged for a late checkout time, and on her way there she would stop in Elsner's bookshop, where, according to the neighborhood sightseeing pamphlet she'd read this morning, there was a thousand-to-one chance of running into Greta Garbo—better odds than she might ever have again.

I don't vant to be alone.

———

Anders Little couldn't place her for a second. But once he did, he remembered—*oh, shit*—that he'd never returned her call. Did he still have that skittish, cheerful message on his machine? If she'd just spotted him pretending not to see her, did that mean he no longer *could* return the call—or did it mean he was now truly obligated to?

He turned his back on the Secretariat building, whose shiny green glass was the algae on an institution Ed Koch—his kind of Democrat, and Jeane Kirkpatrick's—had dubbed a "cesspool." Walking west through Tudor City, Anders increased his always faster-than-normal pace. He had twenty minutes to get to Park and Thirty-eighth before checkout time arrived at the Doral, the sort of fancy hotel you could book your way into for a surprisingly low price if you knew how to use your government per diem right. He'd gotten a late start after his workout this morning, unable to resist extra time in the hotel's excellent gym before heading over to the U.S. Mission to the UN, his old place of work, at First and Forty-fifth, a block up from Ms. Macmurray's little demonstration. He got detailed there for about twenty-four hours each year, tasked with helping to coordinate the president's UN visit.

A free trip to New York was nothing to sneeze at, but Anders could hardly be said to enjoy the annual assignment. At thirty-eight, he resented having to feel like an advance man, and few things brought less prestige to someone on the Reagan NSC than the reason he was always picked for this gig: a UN background—his long stint there in the years *before* Jeane Kirkpatrick had arrived to shake the place up.

He'd come up from Washington yesterday morning, in time to catch *Me and My Girl*, a hot ticket but easy enough to obtain when you were talking about a Sunday matinee for a party of one. Right now, passing the Third Avenue apartment he'd once shared with his first wife, he realized that he felt no regrets, only an emptiness that had nothing to do with her and that he refused to subject to even his own scrutiny and interpretation, let alone anyone else's.

He reached the hotel room at ten minutes to twelve, and threw the last of his things into an overnight case not much bigger than his gym bag. Then the phone rang.

"Little," he answered.

"Big?" responded whoever was on the line, as if playing a game of Password. Anders recognized the caller as Neal Grover.

"Hey, Neal," he heard himself saying. For all his rush to beat the clock, he felt a fleeting wonder about just when "Hey" had replaced "Hi," no matter whom you talked to.

"I couldn't track you down at the United Nothing," explained Grover. "But Connie here said she knew you'd be staying at the Doral. Good for *you*."

Anders laughed. "It won't be much of a bargain if I get charged for another day."

"Okay," said Grover. "Got your calendar with you?"

Anders extracted his Filofax from the overnight bag. "Got it. What's up?"

"Ever meet Spitz Channell?"

"I've heard the name." It was a peculiar one; it sounded like the Danzig Corridor or some other place that had been fought over during World War II.

"He works for Ollie North now and then," Grover explained. "He gives presentations to supporters of the administration. *Generous* supporters."

"'Presentations'?"

Grover laughed. "That's our word, and we're stickin' to it. 'Educational seminars.'"

"What do they want with me?"

"Spitz has heard good things about you. He'd like you to talk Soviet affairs with a group he's got coming on October seventh. That's a Tuesday. Five o'clock at the Hay-Adams. Can you do it?"

Looking at the clock instead of his calendar, Anders said, "Sure."

"Good. And don't worry about the Hay-Adams being a cut above even the Doral. One of Spitz's guests will pick up the tab. Believe me."

"Okay, got to run," said Anders. But since he still had four minutes, he allowed himself to ask one more question. "Anything going on in the office I should know about?"

"Nah," answered Grover. "Everybody's idling until Shultzie and Shevardnadze can settle this thing."

The Daniloff negotiations were expected to reach a climax here in New York, maybe even this afternoon. The secretary of state had alternately played good cop and bad cop during his weekend meetings with the Soviet foreign minister. Twenty-one Soviet UN personnel had been expelled yesterday—given the heave-ho on an Aeroflot flight out of Kennedy—though it hardly mattered: everybody knew that when it came to the real business of exchanging Zakharov for Daniloff, it was the Americans, not the Soviets, who had already blinked.

"Our side has decided to 'move on,'" said Grover, giving a sarcastic emphasis to the new term of art for the last gasp of any scandal or stumble. "All the talk is about *the letter.*"

Reagan had mentioned it half an hour ago in his speech:

Just a few days ago I received a reply from General Secretary Gorbachev to my communication of July twenty-fifth. And for the moment, let me say simply that we are giving his letter serious and careful consideration.

"I haven't seen it," said Grover. "So far they're keeping it pretty far up the food chain. But I'll tell you what I *have* seen: a copy of a cue card that one of the mice in Don Regan's office slipped me. Want to hear the first talking point for the president's meeting with Pérez de Cuéllar this morning?"

Anders laughed. "Sure."

"'MEETING WITH THE SECRETARY GENERAL,'" Grover recited. "'GLAD YOU HAVE RECOVERED, YOU ARE LOOKING WELL.' Jesus, things are getting a little *basic*, wouldn't you say?"

Anders laughed again, more nervously this time. Joking about the boss always made him feel disloyal, guilty of playing into the hands of their oh-so-smart liberal enemies, the ones who'd gone to Harvard instead of Eureka—or, for that matter, Wake Forest. He also had the unpleasant sensation that Mommy—which they all should *stop* calling the first lady—could somehow hear him.

There was never any stopping Neal, of course. Anders's eye went back to the clock as his colleague offered some gossip about how the letter had been delivered to the White House on Friday: "Shevardnadze was already in front of the fireplace with Reagan and Shultzie when he realized he'd left the damned thing at the Soviet embassy. So they had to send a Russian staffer back up Connecticut Avenue to fetch it. And when he returned with it, they wouldn't let him hand it to his boss in the Oval Office. Somebody got the idea he might be KGB. I mean, what was he going to *do*? Install a listening device while Reagan and Shultz *watched*? They finally allowed the guy to pass the letter through the door without actually stepping over the threshold."

Anders knew what Neal was driving at, even before he made the moral of the story explicit. "You know, Andy, in my heart I think of us as the defenders of the Alamo. But my head tells me we sometimes look like the guys in fucking *Police Academy*."

"I hear you," said Anders. "But now I've *really* got to run."

"Okay," said Grover. "Don't forget about the seventh. It's a big deal, believe it or not. Look your handsomest!"

Anders laughed with a different sort of nervousness and said good-bye, glad that Neal at least hadn't said *prettiest*, which he was more than capable of doing.

Grabbing the overnight bag, Anders patted his breast pocket, knowing it contained a Xerox of the letter that Neal hadn't seen and Reagan hadn't elaborated on in his speech. A hand-delivery of this copy, which Anders was about to perform, would be, he knew, the only significant work he did today.

———

Nixon pushed away the remains of his cottage-cheese-and-ketchup lunch and continued watching the C-SPAN repeat of Reagan's UN speech. They'd finally gotten cable here in the Federal Plaza office, and he was paying for it himself—not that he'd get any more credit for *that* than he got when he gave up Secret Service protection. Christ, *Lady Bird* still had agents guarding her on the government dime! Were they afraid that somebody down in Texas might pelt her with wildflowers?

The United States is proud of its record of nuclear safety and intends to maintain it.

Good, Nixon thought, listening to the president get in a dig against Chernobyl. An awfully small one, but a dig nonetheless. Maybe *something* got through to him, once in a great while, from all the memos Nixon sent. Only yesterday Reagan had called yet again about Daniloff, from Camp David, once more seeking praise and reassurance for a course of action that already had been set. Nixon hated having to give pseudo-advice twice in less than two weeks, but as he'd done a week before, he swallowed his annoyance and slathered on the compliments.

You couldn't argue with Reagan's delivery—it was excellent, as always—but watching the tube today Nixon had been more impressed with the younger, even more improbable figures who'd mounted the UN's dubious podium, especially Juan Carlos. The idea that Franco's little prince—same as the Pope in Rome—should turn out to be a bulwark of democracy!

"Mr. President, Mr. Little is here."

"Thanks, Ro—." He caught himself. After all these years, he sometimes still said "Rose" instead of the right name for whatever secretary sat outside. "Uh, send him in."

As soon as Anders entered, Nixon pointed to the television and said, "Well, he's doubling down on SDI."

People always thought the ex-president's *in medias res* openers were designed to project an all-business air of command, but Anders had come to realize that Nixon started conversations this way out of shyness, a desire to avoid the agonies of chitchat.

"Yes, sir, he is."

"It's interesting," said Nixon, who didn't take his eyes off the TV. "Sit down, Andy."

"Thank you, sir," said Anders, finding a place on the couch. He knew that Nixon walked a fine line when it came to the Strategic Defense Initiative, which could only be fully developed by scrapping the old antiballistic missile treaty—an agreement that Nixon, a believer in the deterring power of "mutually assured destruction," had negotiated himself. But times had changed, and if Reagan's cold-warring came with a belief in the mystical possibility of smashing nuclear missiles as they flew through the sky, the former president wasn't going to mock it; he would point Reagan toward the proper strategic use of such a fantasy.

"This 'sharing' business is nonsense, of course," said Nixon, referring to Reagan's standing offer to give the Soviets any knowledge yielded by the U.S.'s own SDI research. "It will never come to that. But it's a good rhetorical gambit."

"I think you're right," said Anders, who wondered whether he should give Nixon his present right away or hold off for a bit.

"How were the protesters up in midtown?"

"Pretty tame, Mr. President. Not many at all, in fact."

"The 'freeze' has come and gone," Nixon declared. "Reagan's going to Geneva helped. But at some point he's going to have to bring home an agreement, or else the left will be back on his case as badly as they were in '82 and '83."

"I agree," said Anders. "You know, I actually saw Anne Macmurray at the demonstration, small as it was."

"Macmurray?"

"She was married to your Texas friend."

"Oh, yeah. Cox," said Nixon, assuming a grim expression. "Strange fellow. And I suppose if *I'm* saying that, you can take it to the bank!" He paused, as if deciding how much more he should say. "The guy seems to be giving away all his money these days."

"Oh?"

"To a lot of different causes. A couple of them mainstream, a few of them crazy. Texas will do that to you. What he'd really like to put his money into is a presidential run by somebody like Jeane. Is anybody throwing together a committee for her?"

"I don't think so. At least not yet. I saw her last week; she took me to the Harriman memorial."

"I saw *that* on C-SPAN too!" Nixon pointed to the television, now on half-mute with Reagan still speaking. "I'm living my life through that thing these days."

Anders couldn't tell whether he was amused or rueful. But the old man didn't elaborate on this theme of vicariousness. He instead allowed his memories and resentments to pivot in the late Averell Harriman's direction. "The *Crocodile*," Nixon harrumphed. "Can't say I ever saw any evidence of teeth." His baleful expression was undercut by the cheerful grandchild's drawing that hung a foot away from him.

The replay of Reagan's speech was coming to a close, with a shot of Shevardnadze conspicuously withholding his applause.

"Boorish," said Anders.

"Hell," Nixon responded. "Are you old enough to remember when they banged shoes? God, the gang around Khrushchev! Thugs and peasants; you could practically smell the manure on some of them." He paused and repositioned himself, as he always eventually did, toward the future. "Gorbachev is certainly something different. And Christ—*Raisa*!" He spoke of the Soviets' first couple as if they were the "Harvard types" he so often complained about to Anders's receptive non–Ivy League ears.

"Well, sir," said the younger man. "Speaking of Gorbachev . . ." He reached into his pocket and extracted *the letter* with a bit of a flourish. "The official translation," he explained, handing it to Nixon.

"Poindexter okay with this?" asked the former president, trying to mask his evident excitement with an offhand tone.

"He won't object," Anders took it upon himself to say.

What Nixon held had been copied, with permission, from Jeane Kirkpatrick's copy of this letter, whose rumored dispatch she'd mentioned last week in the cathedral. Anders didn't know from whom she'd obtained the letter, but she'd sounded no cautionary note about it the other day when he told her he was soon to see Nixon in New York.

After putting on his glasses—and assuming an alarming resemblance to the way he had looked on the morning of his resignation—Nixon began reading, a fast skim until he got to the last paragraph, which Anders by now had almost by heart: *An idea has come to my mind to suggest to you, Mr. President, that, in the very near future and setting aside all other matters, we have a quick one-on-one meeting, let us say in Iceland or in London, maybe just for one day, to engage in a strictly confidential, private and frank discussion (possibly with only our foreign ministers present). The discussion— which would not be a detailed one, for its purpose and significance would be to demonstrate political will—would result in instructions to our respective agencies to draft agreements on two or three very specific questions, which you and I could sign during my subsequent visit to the United States.*

Looking up from the page, Nixon displayed a grim face. "They're going to do this right away? Where's the time to prepare? And, believe me, whatever they call it, it's still a summit and it'll raise plenty of expectations. Christ," he added, after a pause, "even if he has Shultz sitting next to him . . ." He gave in to exasperation: "I was on the phone with Reagan yesterday. He spent more time talking about the squirrel on his windowsill than he did about Daniloff."

It was a little like listening to Neal Grover, thought Anders. But he knew better than to assent to Nixon's criticism of his successor-thrice-removed. If Anders knocked Reagan, then Nixon would start wondering whether Anders Little, outside this room, might be knocking *him*.

"This is *very* big," Nixon declared. "This is the real thing, and Gorbachev is trying to trick Reagan into thinking it's another exhibition game." The former president took another grave pause. "Well, I appreciate your bringing me this, Andy."

Anders could tell that Nixon wanted him to leave, so that he could start running various summit scenarios in his head.

"You're very welcome, sir."

"London or Iceland?" asked Nixon. "Which is it going to be?"

"I don't think they'll know that for another day or two."

"They need to pick Iceland. Otherwise Thatcher will be hovering in the background. Her presence will make people wish *she* were doing the negotiating. Reagan will look better by himself."

Anders could already imagine the fax on this subject that would be coming to Don Regan or Poindexter.

"Noted," he responded. "You should pass that on, sir."

"What time do you go back?" asked Nixon.

"The four-o'clock shuttle," Anders answered. "I hope I don't run into Cox's wife!" He was surprised to hear himself say it. "And, you know, whichever other freezeniks she traveled up with."

Nixon snorted, and Anders braced himself for a mini-tirade against left-wingers or, worse, the Jews.

But the president seemed suddenly more mournful than vicious. "You know," he said, "when Dean talked about that 'cancer on the presidency,' I wasn't fazed in the least. Cancer never frightened me. But if he'd said *tuberculosis*, well . . ." His voice trailed off.

"I don't follow, sir." Was he launching into a story about the brothers he'd lost to the latter disease?

"It's Cox," said Nixon. "The woman's ex-husband. He's got liver cancer. That's what's put it in my mind."

"Oh."

"And that's why he's gone off on this political spending spree. Trying to make some sort of splash before he checks out. He says he's told no one else that he's dying, and I think that's likely the truth."

"But then why would he tell *you?*"

"Probably wanted to hear my you-can-survive-anything speech. I've given it more times than I unfurled 'peace abroad and prosperity without inflation at home.' You'd be surprised at how many people ask me to buck them up. I don't suppose you associate me with *hopefulness*, do you?"

Anders guessed that he was supposed to laugh. But he was preoccupied by this sudden new knowledge about Peter Cox, a peculiar thing with which to be burdened when Anne Macmurray presumably didn't know it herself. Would *his* knowing it make him more likely, or less, to finally return her call?

"Well, sir, maybe—"

"It's a good little pep talk for individual listeners—people afraid of whatever's just hit them. All that deepest valley/highest mountain stuff. How you can't appreciate the second without having been through the first." Nixon clicked off the television. "Doesn't make it true, of course."

9

OCTOBER 1, 1986

"This has given us a lot of ideas for *ours*," said a smiling Ronald Reagan to an unsmiling Rosalynn Carter, as the incumbent president concluded a quick tour of his predecessor's new library.

"Yes," agreed Nancy, who was thinking: ideas for what *not* to do. All these kitsch displays: the "Peanut Brigade" banner from '76; the kids' letters—"Please stop people from killing the whales"—and worse, Carter's replies to them, signed "Jimmy."

"Good," said Rosalynn, without adding any words or warmth.

The two presidential couples filed out into the sunshine, toward the speakers' platform, as the Fort McPherson army band played "Hail to the Chief." Nancy looked over the four circular pavilions that had just been constructed on this hillside and thought they looked like a monotonous world's fair.

Still, as much as she tried, it was hard for her to dislike the Carters themselves. No matter how prudish and pickle-pussed the two of them might be, there was no getting away from how much they had done for her and Ronnie—first, by defeating the Fords, whom she had no trouble at all disliking; and then, once in the White House, by screwing up so badly they seemed to have spent their whole four years rolling out a red carpet for the Reagans. Someone on Mike Deaver's staff used to refer to the thirty-ninth president as "the Mastermind," insisting that Jimmy Carter was the greatest Republican strategist of all time.

Nancy looked back at the building they'd just exited, as if to pay the design a compliment with some extra attention. She was actually trying to take comfort in the thought of how Carter's papers were now neatly stored in towering rows of banker's boxes that ran along a huge curving wall. Even failure could be made to look like accomplishment; something settled, *achieved*. So maybe there was hope for her and Ronnie if things really did fall apart.

No, things could fall to such smithereens that even an illusion became impossible to construct. Nixon's library still wasn't built, and from what she heard it would be a penny arcade of cheap statues and props, while the documents it ought to house remained far away under the government's lock and key, serving the prison term that Nixon had avoided.

She and Ronnie, along with the Carters, reached the platform. Applause—and jeers—could be heard from the crowd of spectators on the hillside. Nancy for a moment couldn't tell if the disapproval related to the Sandinistas or South Africa—probably the latter, given that most of Atlanta's black establishment was here for the dedication. She looked over at Carter, who had just taken his seat; today was the first time she'd seen him in five years, since the night Ronnie had sent all the ex-presidents off to Sadat's funeral. She regarded his pursed preacherly lips and thought of the handwritten notes to Sadat and Begin now on display in the library behind them, signed "JC," as if they were memos from Christ himself, ordering the tribes in his Holy Land to make peace.

Well, she thought, it was decent of him to pout over the disrespect the protesters were showing Ronnie. But after a few more seconds she realized the reason for his sour expression: *he* was being protested, too! She strained to make out the chant that had gone up:

YOU TAKE THE HIGH ROAD! WE'LL TAKE THE NO ROAD!

On the flight down, one of the advance men had told her that a lot of locals opposed the four-lane highway being built to bring people here; the courts had actually halted construction for a while. These boos must be putting a bit of a damper on JC's sixty-second birthday—not that his successor's unavoidable presence hadn't already cast a pall over it. Ninety percent of the news cameras here would be leaving halfway through the program, as soon as Ronnie finished his speech.

She waved hello to Carter's little strawberry-blond granddaughter, who would cut the ribbon. The girl looked just the way awful little Amy, who'd grown up into more of a slob than Patti, had looked during JC's White House days. His deciding to quote her on "nuclear proliferation," as if she were some Quiz Kid, during the '80 debate! Another gift from the gods.

In one way it was good that she and Ronnie hadn't gotten to the White House sooner than they did. Had that happened, Patti, who actually did talk about nuclear proliferation, might have been living with them, as the world's most impossible college student, foisting people even worse than that horrible Caldicott woman on her soft touch of a father.

Nancy looked at her tiny platinum wristwatch.

———

"I often get invited to library dedications," spoke the president. "There aren't that many people still around who knew Andrew Carnegie."

Jimmy Carter displayed his large, recently whitened teeth to the crowd, imitating amusement while he stole a glance at Mondale, the other person here who'd had the experience of playing straight man to this dunce on a national debate stage. Carter noticed, to his dismay, that Fritz's stomach, larger than when he'd last seen it, was shaking agreeably. His own vice president was actually *enjoying* this.

I can think of no other country on Earth where two political leaders could disagree so widely yet come together in mutual respect.

The old actor was *sounding* generous while really paying himself a compliment, letting the audience trick itself into thinking that the thirty-ninth president had a peanut shell's worth of respect for the fortieth. This business of pretending that we're "all Americans" just trivially separated by party labels was the domestic version of the "moral equivalence" that Reagan and his kind—chief among them Jeane Kirkpatrick, former Democrat—were always deploring on the international plane.

Reagan was now praising Carter's mother, "Miss Lillian," as well as his sister, Ruth, recently swallowed by the pancreatic cancer that stalked the family—and was likely to get them all before long. He himself was expecting a short ex-presidency, and he was determined to do something different and redemptive with it.

Jimmy Carter spoke these words in his inaugural address as governor of Georgia: "I say to you quite frankly that the time for racial discrimination is over."

The man being quoted adjusted his smile to something grave and appreciative; he avoided meeting Coretta King's gaze, so as not to appear to be fishing for additional compliments. But a part of him longed to have a lapel microphone into which he could say to Reagan: "Yes, and *you* started your 1980 campaign against me talking about states' rights in Philadelphia, Mississippi." The thought of that murderous hamlet, with three civil rights workers buried in an earthen dam, left him righteous—and ever so slightly uneasy. He had come a long way in his ideological life, as far forward as Reagan had gone backward, but he still hoped the papers from this gubernatorial campaign Reagan was referencing would remain unprocessed a while longer, lest some zealous researcher become intrigued by a few leaflets that might suggest why Jimmy Carter had actually gotten only five percent of the black Georgia vote in 1970.

. . . using his gifts—in particular, his superb intelligence . . .

Reagan made intelligence sound like a handicap, the way his aides had mocked his predecessor for actually reading the Air Force budget instead of just approving it. Looking out into the audience, Carter observed Sam Nunn, the sort of conservative Democrat on his way to extinction and thus, like a liberal Republican, highly respected. He knew that Nunn considered Reagan's supposed toughness to be the proper antidote to Jimmy Carter's own now-legendary weakness, and his jaw jutted forward at the thought of the false comparison. If *he'd* made a deal for Daniloff like the one announced yesterday, there'd have been a dozen cartoons in the papers this morning depicting him as a frightened bunny rabbit. Eight years ago, on *his* watch, two Russian spies had gotten fifty years in jail apiece, whereas Zakharov had just been allowed to leave the U.S. with a plea of *nolo contendere*—and been given permission to come back in five years! That was Reagan's *toughness.*

. . . your countrymen still have vivid memories of your time in the White House . . .

He could see two aides smirking, as if to say "Do they ever," and then realized that one of them wasn't even Reagan's but a guy who'd worked for *him*!

. . . repairing to a quiet place to receive the latest word on the hostages you did so much to free, or studying in your hideaway office for the meeting at Camp David . . .

It was as if the class football hero had been ordered to pay tribute to the class grind.

And there's only one thing left to say. From the fortieth president to the thirty-ninth, happy birthday. And, Mr. President, if I could give you one word of advice: Life begins at seventy!

As everyone laughed—including Fritz, with god-awful gusto—the former president realized that this was the line that would play on the evening news. There *you* go again, you son of a bitch. He had to trump him, or at least come up with something sufficiently gracious to guarantee a few words of his own on tonight's broadcasts. So at the top of his typewritten remarks, he quickly penciled in a new lead:

Having heard you speak, Mr. President, I finally, for the first time, understand why you won and I lost.

It was the sort of lie he'd once promised never to tell the American people. The truth was he'd come to understand this long ago.

———

Nancy watched as the Air Force One operator tried, and failed, to get through to one senator after another, while the president leafed through a folder of papers, and any chance of quashing the Senate rebellion against the administration's South Africa policy slipped away. The vote to override Ronnie's veto of sanctions was tomorrow! And losing it would be terrible. Senator Zorinsky of Nebraska? Not there. Senator Boren of Oklahoma? Can't be located. It was a waste of Ronnie's time, and the umpteenth example of Don Regan's mismanagement. Why not *schedule* the calls? Or why not have invited a few of those on the call-list to take a spin on Air Force One? (Assuming they could stand seeing Jimmy Carter again.)

And why make yesterday's announcement of Daniloff's release at that campaign stop in Missouri? As if it were an *accomplishment*! Why not just sneak out a low-key written statement after six p.m., by which time it would have been too late for Rather and Brokaw? Don Regan had wound up putting this dubious bargain on an equal footing with yesterday's big news, the *good* news: the summit that had been agreed to—two days in Iceland, next week.

Nancy went back to her book, the one by Paula Hawkins that Maureen had given her the other night. *Children at Risk: My Fight Against Child Abuse—A Personal Story and a Public Plea.* This whole suddenly discussed subject was getting a little overblown, but at least the author's idea of abuse was forced sex and kidnapping, and not a bunch of nonsense like Patti's boo-hoo memories of getting slapped by her mother in the car.

She couldn't make up her mind about this gal, this "general in the war on drugs." The hair was way too big, but she did have energy and oomph; and it didn't hurt to remember that there were people who still thought Nancy Reagan was too flashy. No matter how much she tried pleasing the Georgetown Cave Dwellers like Kay Graham, she couldn't shake off the lacquer and sunshine of Pacific Palisades. It had *killed* her the other day to hear Lucky Roosevelt, Lee Annenberg's successor in the protocol job, say that there were too many old pinky-ringed crooners doing the entertainment at state dinners. Well! Nancy Reagan might have a desire to emulate Jackie Onassis every so often, but not to the point where she was going to make Ronnie suffer through some long-haired cellist after coffee and dessert.

Her food chain of worries was, as always, running in reverse—the small fish devouring the bigger ones. She'd been focused a minute ago on the survival of Ronnie's reputation, the drive to hold the Senate, and now she was fretting over some crack Lucky had made about Paul Anka.

She struggled to picture the biggest two fish of all: Saturn and Uranus, setting their merciless sail through the heavens.

From where she'd tucked it inside the book, she took out the one-page script for the video she would make just before supper, the tape that would be shown to potential Florida donors. She eyeballed it once more and asked Ronnie: "Why don't you call Paula Hawkins?"

He looked at her as if to say: That's an interesting idea, but what have I got to tell her?

"You could let her know I'm making this video once we get back. That it was Maureen's idea and I thought it a good one."

After looking at some underlined phrases in the script, the president signaled for an aide to set up the call. Senator Hawkins was on the line in what seemed an instant; she must have broken a heel running for the receiver, thought Nancy.

"Well," said the president, "we were sort of in the neighborhood." The plane was still over North Carolina. "So I thought I'd call 'the Senate's general in the war on drugs'—and turn you over to that war's commander in chief."

"Oh, Mr. President!"

"Hi, Paula," said Nancy.

"Hello, Mrs. Reagan! I've already heard—from Maureen—about the help you're providing, and I can't tell you how thrilled I am to have it! We're going to show that video at *three* big dinners—in Fort Myers, Naples, and Sarasota."

"We'll be shooting it late this afternoon."

"I bet that'll be a day at the beach for *you*!" said Senator Hawkins, sounding a little too much like that awful woman evangelist with the eyelashes. Nancy found herself feeling miffed and falling silent. You didn't bring up the Hollywood past with her. With Ronnie, yes; but not with her.

The senator seemed to catch herself. "I mean, you did such a marvelous job with that drugs broadcast a couple of Sundays back."

"Thank you," said Nancy. "We're a little concerned about your polls."

"They're moving back up!" replied Senator Hawkins, as quickly as she could.

"Well, if they go a little higher, we might be able to do a little more. We might be able to come down there." She deliberately left it unclear whether the "we" was royal or included Ronnie. But the senator got her drift. The first lady was offering her a kind of challenge grant, as if polling percentages were dollars that could generate matching funds. Make it worth Nancy's while and she would make it worth the candidate's. Fully incentivized, Paula Hawkins cried "Wonderful!" The word came in loud and clear at twenty thousand feet.

"Are U.S.-Soviet relations back on track now that Mr. Daniloff is free?"

The president, hoping as always that the Rose Garden wouldn't make him sneeze, replied to the reporter: "Well, we'll find out in about ten days."

"Why'd you let them pick the date and place for the summit?"

"And why did you cave on Zakharov, Mr. President?"

"Didn't you in effect let Mr. Gorbachev call you a liar? When he wouldn't accept your word that Mr. Daniloff isn't a spy?"

Reagan gently shook his head. An exhausted Nicholas Daniloff, whose freedom he had secured, appeared almost protective of the older man, no matter that the press were Daniloff's colleagues and that he himself was still experiencing a prisoner's fears. The president gestured for his guest and family to head on into the White House for a proper welcome home. "The fellow's jet-lagged," Reagan told the reporters with a smile, as if he weren't the only one being harassed.

"Now that you're back," came the last shouted question, *"what do you really think of Jimmy Carter?"*

Even Nancy laughed at that one, as she helped usher Daniloff into the Oval Office. Finally, she thought, having observed his courteous behavior toward Ronnie: Somebody who knows how to behave. She didn't like his teenaged son's FREE NICK DANILOFF T-shirt, but she blamed the mother, not the boy, for that.

The conversation with Paula Hawkins had left her feeling focused and fierce. She now helped to arrange everyone on the white couches, making sure Daniloff was on her husband's left, though she hoped Ronnie had remembered to turn *both* hearing aids back up after leaving the hum of Air Force One. The blanks fired by that prop gun fifty years ago had done more lasting damage to him than John Hinckley's bullet.

With everyone soon in place—the Daniloffs and their children; George Bush; the woman from State; and Mort Zuckerman, the freed reporter's boss at *U.S. News*—Ronnie launched into one of those jokes that Soviet citizens told about their own sad system. It was as if he, and not Daniloff, had just returned from Moscow.

" 'Pick up the car ten years from this Thursday? Can't do it—the plumber's coming that afternoon!' "

She laughed at the familiar punch line. Daniloff, a bit flummoxed, smiled and repeated his gratitude for the "personal interest" the president had taken in his plight.

To avoid an awkward pause, Nancy asked the first question. "Mr. Daniloff, just before you were arrested, what would you say the average Russian person was feeling about the possibilities for peace?"

Don Regan chose this moment to saunter in late, like some neighbor down the street who'd decided to drop by. She became so furious she missed most of Daniloff's answer.

Like a reporter taking a "follow-up," she asked, "And you think Mr. Gorbachev ordered your arrest?"

Bush and the woman from State exchanged surprised looks.

Daniloff's response was cautious. "I believe he probably favored it. He almost surely approved it."

She had a third question, a request for more information about Yuri Orlov, the dissident whose freedom had been added to the deal as a last-minute inducement. Mrs. Daniloff fielded that one, and then George Bush took a turn. "Nick, let me ask you to play pundit for a sec. Do you think this whole episode will be a help or a setback to things? Overall, I mean."

He was thinking, Nancy could tell, of himself, of '88. She couldn't blame him, but she still didn't like it.

"Too soon to know, Mr. Vice President," replied Daniloff.

"Well," said Mort Zuckerman, brightly, "you can go see for yourself!"

Daniloff and the rest of them looked puzzled.

"Who do you think is going to cover Reykjavik for us?" said Zuckerman.

Mrs. Daniloff broke into a sort of "Oh, no!" smile, tentatively pleased but still too overwhelmed to process anything more.

Ronnie winked at her. "We'll get him home to you in a jiffy. They tell me we leave for Iceland on a Thursday morning and that they'll have me back here in time for Sunday supper."

By five o'clock the president was headed toward the Residence, but Nancy's own day wasn't done. She kissed her husband as he stepped into the breezeway, and went off with a Secret Service agent to the West Wing lobby. Waiting for her there were a junior assistant to her press secretary and a young man from the Republican National Committee. The girl was scared of her, but the boy, cute, had all the foot-in-the-door push of an old Fuller Brush salesman.

"Mrs. Reagan," he said, "it's awesome to meet you!" His name was Nick Carrollton. "We're so grateful you're doing this! It could make a big difference!"

Well, she thought, sizing him up: overdoing things beat *underdoing* them.

"I used to work with Terry Dolan over at NCPAC," the young man explained, a little breathlessly. "The Hawkins race was such a triumph for them six years ago. I'd hate to see us lose the seat at such a crucial point in the president's second term!"

"How is Terry?" asked the first lady, softly. Word of his illness had reached her through his brother and the speechwriting staff. Everyone knew what it was, of course, but even Mike had been afraid to ask around for details.

"As well as can be expected," said Nick Carrollton, who had a way of making even solemnity sound exuberant.

The girl finally spoke. "There'll be hair and makeup in the EOB, Mrs. Reagan."

"I had a touch-up on the plane," said the first lady. "But thanks for arranging that."

Regulations prohibited filming a political ad in the White House, but the EOB had a fourth-floor studio designed to look like the mansion's library, and when Nancy arrived she was relieved to see that the late afternoon's soft sunshine would be allowed to do some of the work of lighting her. Trying not to think about Way Bandy, she submitted to a fast fluff from the boy with the comb. The script was in place on the teleprompter, and she was all ready to go when, to her surprise, Maureen bustled in.

"I'm *so* glad you're doing this," said her stepdaughter, in the course of a big hug and air kiss. It was evident that Nancy wanted to be quick about things, but Maureen couldn't resist asking: "How was Carter?"

"Jimmy who?" answered Nancy, uttering the familiar cry from early in '76. Their own primary campaign that year had left her feeling genuinely close to Maureen for the first time. Another thing to thank Carter for.

She fixed herself in the faux Louis XV chair, widened her eyes, and began to read. Off against the far wall, the young man from the RNC looked at her with a touching fervor.

She was able to do things in one take, with only a single stumble that she dealt with by just starting the sentence over and trusting the splicer to get it right:

My husband has been able to keep the peace thanks to a strong military that he's helped to rebuild. But even a first lady needs officers in the field. When it comes to the war on drugs and our successful Just Say No program, my general in the U.S. Senate is Paula Hawkins.

The rest of the script threw in the missing-children business; a sentence about education ("We're still a nation at risk"); and a veiled reference to the slickness of the challenger, Bob Graham. Then came the simple closing: *I need Paula Hawkins; Ronald Reagan needs Paula Hawkins; and the people of Florida need her more than ever.*

"Super!" cried Nick Carrollton, who applauded as if she'd just done three hours of *A Streetcar Named Desire.* Then, of course, everyone else in the room, except for the Secret Service man, had to clap, too. "Well," said Nancy, pointing to him, "at least *this* agent doesn't take ten percent." Everyone laughed, but she instantly regretted making a Hollywood joke.

She posed for a few pictures and made a point of letting people hear her tell Maureen how much she looked forward to dinner with her and Dennis next week.

Some gawkers were at the door, EOB staffers she didn't recognize. She

said hello to them, and goodbye to young Mr. Carrollton, who was holding the videocassette of what had just been shot as if it were the nuclear
football.

"Neal Grover!" she heard him shout to one of the gawkers, after she
started down the hall. "Terry's gonna *love* this!"

10

OCTOBER 3, 1986

"Some more?" Anders Little asked Anne Macmurray. He held up a second bottle of pinot grigio.

He was eager for the chance to top up his own glass, too. He had begun to enjoy himself and could see that she was pleased with that. She'd been anxious—so had he—over a cocktail, and then during his fast, athletic march through the salad. But he'd relaxed a little over the vegetarian lasagna she'd made.

Both were still pretending they hadn't glimpsed each other in New York, and that Anders had at last simply gotten around to calling Anne back, with no special prompting by embarrassment or guilt. Even now, after he'd loosened his tie and leaned back in his chair, Anders was avoiding plenty of subjects, both personal (Peter Cox's illness) and political (the enormous blow the administration had suffered in the Senate yesterday). The overriding of Reagan's South Africa veto was still hard to believe—a major foreign-policy rebuke on the eve of a summit! And yet, if he and Anne *could* allow themselves that topic—she was also obviously restraining herself—Anders would tell her that he actually agreed with the thirty-one Republican senators who went against the president. Yes, in the short run the vote would weaken Reagan in Reykjavik; but in the long one you could only be successful with the Soviets by operating from the moral high ground.

The summit itself was the biggest elephant in the room. The moment he'd arrived, Anders had noticed today's *Post* open on a table near Anne's little Ikea couch. A PROVOCATION? REELING TOWARD REYKYAVIK was the headline over George Will's column, which mercilessly drummed the new conservative line that the administration's cave-in over Daniloff showed an embarrassingly desperate desire to make a deal on much bigger matters. The president—Ronald Reagan!—had felt compelled to say, "It'll be a cold day in Hades when I go soft on Communism."

But tonight's conversation remained light and local. Anne told Anders how she'd gotten most of the ingredients for the lasagna at the venerable Eastern Market on Capitol Hill, and he'd gently urged her not to stray much further south or east than that when she continued her explorations of Washington. She assured him, despite whatever impressions he may have formed, that she was *not* going to become involved in a local councilwoman's efforts to ban even *toy* guns from the District—a watercooler topic around the city today.

Anne was warm and self-mocking in a way he often wished he could be himself. But whenever he tried that kind of humor, his self-criticisms came out stiff and serious instead of charming, and he wound up taking them, depressingly, to heart. It had always been like this for him, even as a boy in Mooresville, a place he now told Anne about in exchange for her stories of Owosso. She had, he learned, come there from Darien, Connecticut, via the University of Michigan, and had speedily absorbed its upper-midwestern mores, the way some people discover among their in-laws the family that should have been theirs all along.

Skipping coffee, they brought the wine bottle over to the couch, where Anne, who now knew about both his marriages, dared to offer Anders a fix-up with a girl she'd met, a community-college teacher who volunteered weekends in the WAND office.

"I can guess what you're thinking," she said. "But, honest, she's hardly political *at all*."

Anders knew what this meant: the girl had an uninformed, sentimental aversion to nuclear weapons, a reflexive desire to make the world a better place without first thinking things through. But he wasn't annoyed in the least. He was practically giggling when he held up his hands—"Stop, please!"—to ward off his hostess's good intentions.

"What's her name?" he asked.

"Lisa." Anne smiled with an unexpected sense of accomplishment.

"So, tell me, Ms. Macmurray, do you think Lisa's ever considered how much the defense budget would have to rise if we got *rid* of nuclear weapons? It would go up by hundreds of billions of dollars. Otherwise the Soviets would roll over Europe, and eventually us, with their superior conventional forces. And then?" he added, laughing at his reversion to type, "what would happen to all the money for community colleges and the rest? Poof! Gone! Our Lisa would be out of a job."

"You must have had a *very* intense week," said Anne, patting his knee, pretending she wouldn't be drawn into this.

"I'm sorry, I swear!" he declared. "You're right: no more, or we'll be off to the races."

She might as well be tickling him. All at once she found herself thinking, preposterously: *Oh, my God, he's adorable.*

"It *has* been an intense week," said Anders, still smiling, but straightening up a bit, as if pledging to behave.

"Does a 'pre-summit'—a 'personal session'—really require so much preparation?" asked Anne. She was teasing him with phrases the administration had been using to keep the public's expectations low. "I'm not badgering, honest. I'm just wondering if you're finding any time to do all your running." *Jesus*, she thought, *am I ogling him?* It was her turn to sit up straighter.

"I'm really not very crucial," he replied. "This week or any other. I mean, my parking space is on the *Ellipse*, Anne. I've mostly been adding a lot of arcane detail to the 'talking points' of the guys going on this Sunday's shows. It's my job to make them hard to follow."

She could see the curious effects of his self-disparagement. He'd intended to offer it playfully. But the smile was gone and he looked strangely flimsy, genuinely displeased with himself.

It seemed smarter to stay in political waters, at least for the moment, than to coax anything private from him: "Doesn't everyone in the White House 'speak from the same page'?" she asked.

"Oh, the disarray I could tell you about!"

This minor, unspecific indiscretion had Anders looking somewhat shocked with himself. And Anne, instead of feeling like a proud Mata Hari, finally getting somewhere, felt the way she used to at her parties back home, more than twenty years ago, when one of the males would come out to the kitchen and start telling her more than she ought to know about his marriage.

Anders was thinking of all the interoffice arguments that had involved even the release of Yuri Orlov. Some thought the springing of any dissident was a feather in the president's cap; others found it grotesque to thank the Soviets for releasing one man while ten thousand others stayed locked up. Recovering some of his smile, Anders settled for saying, "My lips are sealed, Ms. M. And so, I'm afraid, are everybody else's. There's going to be a news blackout during the summit."

"You just said 'summit,' not 'pre-summit.'"

"*Touché.*"

"Well, I'll tell *you* something," said Anne. "If Ronald Reagan comes back from Iceland with a good agreement, I'll contribute to the Republican Senate candidates in Michigan *and* Virginia."

"I'll tell the RNC that," said Anders, whose smile got bigger once he realized he'd been had. "Wait a minute! There are no Senate races in *either* of those this year."

"*Touché,*" said Anne. "Say it again."

Anders was worried that the Senate elections might make Reagan—and Shultz—go even easier on Gorbachev than the two of them had these past few weeks. But at this moment, in this apartment, he wanted to think with his right brain, or was it his left? Whichever was the "feelings" one.

"What does your friend Mr. Nixon think of what's happening?" asked Anne. "On NPR Dr. Kissinger said he was 'veddy drubbled' by the sudden speed of everything."

Anders was on the verge of giggling again. In fact, he *wanted* to: he was happy to be here! He poured himself more wine. He was drawn to the genuineness and merriment of this woman. He also had the sense that he was *seeking* something from her. But what? Did he actually—no, that was too ridiculous; she was, what, *sixty*?

"I don't mean to unseal your lips," said Anne.

"About Nixon?" He shook his head and smiled. He had gotten a skeptical earful from the Old Man just yesterday, over the phone, though Nixon wasn't saying anything public about the summit. And he himself shouldn't be saying anything here.

"Really, I'm not going to press you," said Anne. "But I might point out that I'm almost certainly the only member of WAND who voted for Richard Nixon *three times*."

He could see her trying to read him, trying to figure out the fast alternations between gaiety and anxiousness that he couldn't figure out himself. She took another sip of wine.

"The first time, in 1960, I suppose it was still Peter pulling me along. But after that I have only myself to blame."

Watching her expression as she made this casual mention of Peter Cox, Anders realized, with a horrible sense of confirmation: *She really doesn't know.*

"Peter—" he started to say.

"Yes, Peter," said Anne, laughing. "A man who seems to regard Richard Nixon as his moral compass!"

"He's dying," said Anders.

"Nixon?" asked Anne, so startled she put her wineglass down.

"No. Peter."

She shook her head crisply, as if correcting him on a matter of simple, provable fact; reestablishing, say, that she lived on the fourteenth floor and not the tenth. "My children would have told me."

"*I* shouldn't have," said Anders, who was in a sudden emotional panic. What had possessed him to say something?

"What's wrong with Peter?" asked Anne, whose face had swiftly shed its denial. Her gaze was steady.

"Liver cancer. That's all I know. Nixon told me. Your reference to him just now made me—"

"Why would Nixon bring it up?" She asked the question with an intense focus, like a spouse seeking crucial information from a doctor.

It took Anders a moment to remember. "Because I had mentioned you to *him*. To Nixon."

"Why would you do that?"

This time her question sounded confused, even childlike. Why? For the same reason, he guessed, that he had finally returned her call. She had gotten under his skin, weeks ago, the first day they met.

"I saw you in New York," he confessed. "At that little demonstration near the UN. Before I saw Nixon. So you were on my mind that afternoon. I should have said hello or waved. But—"

He looked at her imploringly, then bounded up from the couch. "I should clear the table."

Anne reached out, grabbed his wrist and made him sit back down.

"I'm so sorry," said Anders. "I've had too much to drink. It wasn't my place—"

She brushed his cheek, very gently, undramatically, as if she were only patting his forearm. "My children may *not* know, I now realize. Or they may know and not want to tell me. Peter grew into a very stubborn, secretive man, and there's more of him than me in Ralph and Susan."

It was strange, thought Anders, that this terrible revelation had somehow put her even more fully in charge of the conversation. Here he was, maladroit and confused, while she, after only a moment's hesitation, was crossing over—guided by some instinct—into the next phase of her life.

She poured them what was left of the wine.

"You know," she said, "I was at Peter's side in five little local campaigns, all winning ones, for the state senate. Going to pancake breakfasts at the Lions Club; stapling flyers to phone poles. Every other year, a few nights before Election Day, I used to pass out Halloween candy inside orange-and-black wrappers that said 'TRICK OR PETE!' Pat Nixon had nothing on me. Peter and I were always pictured in the *Argus-Press*—the Owosso paper—holding hands as we entered the polling place. And you know what? I never once voted for him."

"Really?"

She laughed. "I disapproved of almost everything about Peter—intellectually, personally. Falling in love with him was a *terrible* idea; I knew that from the day we met. But I thought it must be *real* love if it had no basis in reason. And voting for the other man seemed to keep it pure."

"I still don't understand what made me tell you."

"I do," said Anne, her smile now soft and composed. "You realized I didn't know. And that made me look vulnerable and foolish. It hurt you to see that, and you know why?"

"No."

"Because you like me," she said, quoting the speech from last year's Oscars that everyone still made fun of. *"You really like me!"*

Anders smiled, looked downward, and put his arm around her.

What he really wanted was her arm around him—to protect him from what, he didn't yet know.

11

OCTOBER 5, 1986

Pamela Harriman had so few women friends that she regarded Kitty Hart as the best thing to have come out of her marriage to Leland Hayward. Even now she stayed with Kitty on East Sixty-fourth Street whenever she came to New York, knowing she would find her still as wonderfully soothing as she was groomed. Greatly sensible and a respecter of privacy, Kitty, in her unending prime, was like some lovely black-bristled, silver hairbrush come to life—a perfect, confidence-inspiring implement with which to start or end, or just touch up, the day.

Standing with her on this Sunday afternoon inside the Metropolitan Museum, in front of Matisse's *The Conversation*, Pamela felt both energized and calm.

"Kitty, do you realize that, if you'd agreed to marry Tom Dewey, we would *both* now be the widows of governors of New York?"

"Well, of *ex*-governors, I suppose."

"You're right," said Pamela. "I guess neither of us rates an oil painting up in Albany."

"Besides," said Kitty, pointing to Matisse's relaxed married couple, "I can assure you that I never saw Tom Dewey in his pajamas."

"Really?" asked Pamela, who had always loved buying that particular item for her suitors.

"We never got that far," explained Kitty. "A surprisingly nice man, but a little dull."

Pamela had come up to New York on Friday; lunched with Schlesinger; gotten her hair colored by Kenneth; and then, at the last minute, canceled a consultation with Dr. Aston, who supposedly could give anyone a face-lift to equal the Duchess of Windsor's, the best anyone had ever seen, no matter how poisonous its possessor. Yes, she knew it was past time for her to join the ranks of the surgically assisted, but a surprising squeamishness seemed to be stopping her. The pounds had been coming off in the months since Ave's departure, and all that should remain was to find a couple of weeks in which she could have the operation and then disappear for a convalescence. But she wasn't ready. Maybe next year, between capturing the Senate and then firing the starter pistol for her preferred presidential candidate.

She felt disappointed not to see Mario Cuomo here today. But John Carter Brown, across the gallery, looking at Cézanne's *Woman in Blue*, had thrown together this little party on a last-minute whim. When he'd heard that Pamela would be in town, he'd persuaded the Met to do a small closing reception for "Impressionist to Early Modern Paintings from the U.S.S.R." The show was a result of last year's Geneva summit— the Soviets had had to give Reagan *something*, Pamela knew, just to be polite—and it had started its American travels on the walls of Carter Brown's own domain, the National Gallery in Washington.

Fourteen years younger than herself—and not yet *quite* separated from his second wife—Brown had been attentive to Pamela, a member of his Trustees' Council, in the months since Ave's death. He of course had his cap set for her van Gogh, just as surely as her future Democratic senators and presidents had their eyes on the PamPAC purse. No matter. Carter was a genteel escort to have; a useful and mostly pleasant chap, and the closest one could find on these shores to a genuine aristocrat: a Brown, of Rhode Island. Not that anyone's pedigree had ever especially interested Pamela. *I am an American by choice and a Democrat by conviction.* She was probably *more* American than Carter Brown. If he had as healthy a respect for money as he did for art, he would never have allowed himself to be divorced from his first wife, a Mellon.

"Just under two hundred thousand people saw the show in Washington," he was telling Jayne Wrightsman. "Without having to pay a penny."

Two canvases away, the Soviet ambassador—a new one, not nearly as nice as Dobrynin had been—was complaining rather too loudly, to

Ronald Lauder, about Lauder's complaints against Russian treatment of the Jews.

"Perhaps I should break this up," said Kitty Hart.

She was such a good sort, thought Pamela—a born diplomat, and a Jew to boot; splendidly useful at a moment like this. Really, Kitty was *wasted* on that state arts council, the thought of which reconfirmed Pamela's determination not to settle for something so paltry once the Democrats' ship came in.

And there, having arrived at the last minute, was Jackie, who now appeared to be counting the goldfish in another of the Matisses, flashing that huge smile so unfortunately compromised by her smoker's teeth. Why didn't she take care of them? It was like looking at some spectacular Cecil Beaton set through a scrim.

Pamela caught the eye of Maurice Tempelsman, who came over, kissed her hand, and walked her back toward Jackie. As they went, Pamela tried to remember whether Tempelsman *owned* diamonds or just sold them. He'd been generous, moderately so, to the Democrats, but God knew it was a most curious arrangement that he and Jackie had. She herself had been involved with plenty of married men, but none of them had ever lived with her instead of the wife.

She embraced Jackie in front of the goldfish and asked, "How is Caroline enjoying married life?"

"Three months of it!" Jackie replied, with cryptic exuberance. While the former first lady grinned, the contours of her face rose, and Pamela quickly appraised what might be another example of Dr. Aston's work. No question; it was excellent.

"They're *all* so grown up now!" Jackie mused. "Bobby's son Joe is running for Congress in Massachusetts—and Kathleen is running in Maryland!"

"Oh, I know," said Pamela. "Kick would be so proud of her namesake." The original Kathleen—Jack's sister, long since killed in a plane crash— had been Pamela's real friend among the Kennedys, but surely Jackie didn't think that this would result in the dispatch of any PamPAC money in young Kathleen's direction—for a mere House seat when the whole

Senate was at stake? No, Ethel could pay for that with whatever she had left. Pamela allowed a few seconds of smiling silence to settle the matter, and Jackie turned back to Matisse's goldfish bowl.

Cy Vance was approaching, while a photographer, who'd just missed the shot he wanted of Mrs. Harriman and Jackie, remained positioned nearby. Pamela smiled at the former secretary of state, who was a friend, but moved away; too much of Jimmy Carter and failure clung to him, and she could do without a picture. She pointed to her watch by way of excuse and made Carter Brown see the gesture, too. He'd proposed that they make a day of it—fly back to Washington together for a little supper right at the Gallery, where he'd walk Pamela through a show of early American furniture that was opening next week.

She hadn't bothered with Ave's plane on Friday, and it was in fact time to catch the shuttle. So she mothered Carter out the door of his own party and down the Met's front steps, at the bottom of which waited a town car and a handful of AIDS demonstrators who'd gotten wind of the little afternoon bash: HEALTH FIRST, ART LATER read their placards. Pamela looked past them and across the street to the apartment she had once shared with Leland.

The car got them quickly to LaGuardia and the Eastern shuttle's VIP lounge. Once aloft and on her way home, Pamela regarded a spreadsheet of recent polls prepared by Janet. Included were some numbers for the Graham-Hawkins race, which showed the challenger ahead but not by much. It was hard to believe that he was actually Kay Graham's half brother-in-law. At a dinner Pamela had given for him back in February he'd seemed reasonably adroit and appropriately oleaginous for a popular southern governor, but she continued to wonder about his instincts and judgment. (Never forget that the brother had committed suicide.) Down in Florida, Bob Graham had scheduled the kickoff of his Senate campaign for the morning when the *Challenger* would be "launched"—get it?—and everyone knew how well that had turned out. And then there were these *diaries* of his that Pamela kept hearing about: an obsessively voluminous record of the man's every breakfast and sneeze.

She had agreed to travel down there in a couple of weeks to raise last-

minute funds. Word had reached her, from a semitrustworthy source at
the RNC, that Nancy Reagan had the other day recorded a commercial
to air during the final days of the campaign. (So stupid to think one had
to bug the opposition's phones in order to get this sort of information.
Just have somebody find the right low-level person and pay him a little
attention—that's all it usually took.)

She looked across the aisle at Carter Brown, who was dozing over a
book on Bonnard. She knew, with a vague sort of disappointment, that he
would be quite indifferent to any of the statistics on her own lap. What
a strange, brave new world she'd entered—wishing that a man would
acquire *her* interests! She put the spreadsheet into the empty seat beside
her and absently began playing with a bracelet that had once belonged
to her great-grandaunt Jane Digby, who'd had everyone from Balzac to a
Syrian sheik. Pamela saw that the late-afternoon sun had started to fade;
her reflection was becoming more visible in the plasticky glass of the air-
plane's little window. The low resolution of what she saw was flattering,
and the image became yet more so when she pushed up her right cheek,
just a bit, giving herself a further sense of what she might look like if she
gave herself over to Dr. Aston.

———

*I retired the other night wondering, for the first time, if the President's
sureness of touch had begun to desert him; to have been outmaneuvered by
the Senate and the Soviets all in one week seemed suspiciously like careless-
ness . . .*

Christopher Hitchens regarded the short article he was still typing
on this early Sunday evening. He wondered, here beside a full ashtray in
his empty house on a deserted Capitol Hill, whether readers of the piece
would hear its allusion to Lady Bracknell. And he fretted, for the briefest
moment, over his always-errant punctuation:

*If Reagan wants to return from the frozen north, with something that will
keep his team in control he will need more than the snapshots and anecdotes
that he brought home from Geneva last year.*

The most doubtful matter right now was where he would find a bloody fax machine after six o'clock on a Sunday night. His best chance was probably some drugstore out in the suburbs; once again he found himself making the usual irresolute resolution to obtain a driver's license before he reached forty.

He took a sip of cabernet, a fine, full-bodied substitute for solid food on a night his wife and little boy were both away. He imagined the former up in Philadelphia, drinking her own glass of wine (white) and pouring out her discontent to the old girlfriend across the table. He could not blame her. They had gone on for five years now, and he didn't imagine either of them would wait another two before scratching the itch that was supposed to arrive only after seven.

The telephone rang.

"Mr. Hitchens, if you'd like to see her, you'd better hurry."

The voice was familiar. "If you'll identify 'her,'" he responded, "perhaps I'll be able to identify *you*."

"The 'her' is Mrs. Harriman."

"Ah," said Hitchens. "Give me your own first initial and I bet I'll come up with it."

"This is Kelly."

"Of course," he replied, recalling the girl from the N Street office and cathedral. "Assistant to Janet. Janet operating as Mrs. Harriman's artificial intelligence—in the same capacity that, say, Secretary Shultz serves Mr. Reagan."

Kelly laughed, without the slightest trace of caution.

"Where and when?" asked Hitchens.

"The National Gallery, at seven o'clock. Go inside to the free concert. I'll find you there and get you into the private party Mr. Brown is throwing."

"Is there a reason you're providing me with such assistance?"

Another laugh, lower this time, pleasingly throaty and conspiratorial.

"Has she been beastly to you, my dear?" Hitchens asked.

"No more than usual," Kelly answered.

"Then you should have called sooner."

"Either way," said Kelly, "was I running the risk of having the phone answered by a wife?" Hitchens could hear the tinkle of ice cubes on the other end of the line: Kelly was fortifying herself for a crucial piece of information.

"The terrorist is away," he heard himself saying, with a touch of fondness.

"Is she that bad?" Kelly asked, disappointed at a wife's evident existence, but encouraged by the description.

"I use the term in a political, not marital, sense. She's a rather strenuous Greek Cypriot. We met in exciting geopolitical circumstances."

"You'll need to explain more when we have time," said Kelly.

"Patience and courage. I'll be there in twenty."

———

As it turned out, Carter Brown had tonight arranged for the second room of the National Gallery's American furniture show to hold not just a table for two but a whole dinner party. Several small tables would seat about fifteen guests. "Surprise!" they now called out to Pamela. They were all, he was sure, the sort she would like. Bob Strauss, the old DNC chairman, was the first to come over to her, with his wife, Helen. "Looks just like your livin' room, darlin'!" It looked like nothing of the kind, but Pamela agreed with the Texan wholeheartedly. "And the next time we're all in *that* room," Strauss added, "there'll be no more cryin'!" On election night '84, as Mondale sank, Ed Muskie had actually wept.

Pamela smiled and listened to the pleasantly muted music coming from the Gallery's free concert several rooms away. She went up to Antony Acland and thanked him once more for the family luncheon he'd hosted at the British embassy after Ave's memorial. He was talking with Susan Mary Alsop, who Pamela knew would be thinking the same thing that had just crossed her own mind: about how, during Pam Churchill's most disreputable decade, the British ambassador to France had refused to invite her to lunch when the queen passed through Paris.

Throughout the room, the spoken conversations were entirely political. This was, after all, Washington. Circulating with particular relish was the news that Raisa Gorbachev had just changed her mind and decided to go to Iceland with her husband after all—leaving Nancy Reagan flummoxed and flat-footed.

On the subject of the Soviets' first lady, Dick Holbrooke now said to Pamela, "When she finally comes here, *you* should have her to tea."

"Exactly right," Bob Strauss concurred. "After all, when old Ave saw Andropov he made sure Pam was right in the room with him."

Pamela smiled at the compliment (Ave had scarcely known where he was) but broke away from the two men to go greet Senator John Warner. "My favorite man from the other side of the aisle!"

Four years after his second divorce, from Elizabeth Taylor, Warner replied, "My only trouble comes when I go *down* the aisle."

Pamela was enjoying herself, but became slightly nervous when she noticed Adnan Khashoggi and the latest wife he'd converted to Islam. She wasn't sure even Jane Digby had gone that far, but this ludicrously rich arms dealer had performed the trick twice, the first time turning someone named Sandra into Soraya—before the girl went off and had an affair with Pamela's son, Winston. Right now she could see Susan Mary Alsop whispering to Carter Brown, no doubt pointing out this slight faux pas with the evening's invitations.

Brown shrugged his thin frame and rolled his eyes, saying with an exasperation louder than he probably imagined, "Well, what can you expect? My *mother* was a character witness for Claus von Bülow!"

Pamela rather shuddered at the name. Claus had been a not-unattractive man back when he was working for Getty, and she herself had very nearly— This unpleasant train of thought was fortunately interrupted when she heard the accents of her native land coming up behind her.

"Don't mean to *needle* you," said Christopher Hitchens.

She turned around and saw that this attractive young man, without a necktie and bold as brass, had been not only eavesdropping but actually *taking notes*.

"How did you get—"

"Don't be unduly fearful. I won't be staying for dinner. Just this one flute of champagne." He held it in the same hand as his notepad.

"I'd forgotten about your article," Pamela lied.

"I forget about it, too. Intermittently. But as you can see, I do find moments for it here and there. Ambient chatter can be awfully useful in setting a tone." He looked down at his notes. "One of your friends was saying that Khashoggi is worth four hundred times what the governor died with. My arithmetic isn't always good, but I'm imagining that makes forty billion, Khashoggi-wise. Of course, little overheard bits like this take the writer only so far. There's really nothing like a full, on-the-record interview."

Carter Brown, looking over, seemed aware of trouble. He appeared almost ready to signal for a guard, as if Pamela were a *fauteuil* being vandalized. But she indicated with a shake of her head that everything was all right.

"You cannot," she whispered to Hitchens, "continue stalking me as you would a deer."

Hitchens smiled in the direction of Carter Brown. "I should think I'm only one of many hounds in pursuit of the fox. So how about it?" he asked. "A proper interview? As the American poetess said, 'Candor is the only wile.'"

If he'd managed to find out she was going to be here, thought Pamela, there was no telling what else he might know. "All right," she said. "When?"

"It requires the proper setting," Hitchens instructed. He recalled his conversation with Dolan, and an earlier one with the lady herself. *I may even make a trip to Florida to help him out.* "The Sunshine State?"

"Yes, I am planning a trip there. Orlando, as it turns out. I'll have Kelly Proctor call you."

"Always happy to hear from Kelly. In the meantime I'll go off and purchase some sunblock." He made a little bow in retreat, setting his glass of champagne—world's most overrated beverage—atop a sideboard behind a velvet rope. On his way out he nodded pacifically at Carter Brown and stopped to introduce himself to Ambassador Acland, who despite all the chatter about the summit was looking distinctly bored, perhaps because the political subtext of the conversation was entirely domestic rather than international. Was Ronnie finally sinking? everyone wanted to know.

"Oh, yes. Hitchens," said the ambassador. "Have we lost you for good? To these shores, I mean."

"Hard to say. But an apostatical nature assures that one will always return home—if only so one can leave again. In fact I'm right now trying to *send* something home." He extracted from his breast pocket the three typescript pages of his pre-summit musings. "I don't suppose Mr. Brown has a fax machine inside one of these federalist credenzas."

"You can come along with me," said Acland. "I'm booked here only through cocktails. I'll run you up to the embassy and we can dispatch it from there."

"Thoroughly decent of you."

"Your brother's stuff is usually more in my line," the ambassador confessed.

At this mention of Peter Hitchens—his more conservative, less flamboyant sibling—*the* Hitch's right eyebrow raised itself an annoyed millimeter.

The writer and the diplomat made their way out of the exhibition rooms and into a corridor, where the sounds of the concert swelled. Nearby, Kelly Proctor stood, regarding a still life from the Gallery's permanent collections.

"Half a second?" Hitchens asked the ambassador.

"No trouble at all," answered Acland, who used the extra moment to greet a latecomer.

"Get everything you want?" Kelly asked Hitchens.

He looked her up and down. "Hardly *everything*."

"Well," she said, "not *yet*."

"I'm afraid I've got to run up to the embassy with my new friend, the ambassador. He's letting me use their fax. But tell me: Do you still expect to be in Mrs. Harriman's employment by the time she goes to Florida?"

"At the end of the month? Probably not."

"I was rather hoping she'd take you along," said Hitchens.

"*You* can take me instead."

Hitchens smiled. "I scarcely know who you are, Ms. Proctor."

"Then I'll have to make sure you get a copy of my résumé. I've just redone it." She cocked her head in the direction of Ambassador Acland, who was now standing by himself. "You'd better 'carry on,'" she said with a smile.

"Will do." He realized, as he said it, that he'd almost stuttered on the "d." The return of this small childhood affliction was a sure sign of attraction.

As they drove away from the Gallery, the ambassador began working the limousine's inconsequential-looking phone. The whole car was, in fact, decidedly modest for such an important emissary of Mrs. Thatcher. Hitchens couldn't find so much as a can of soda, let alone a "wet bar," in the backseat.

Passing the embassies along Massachusetts Avenue, he considered them as little semisovereign outposts, yet more in-between places. *On me, not in me.* Reykjavik was another: an island nation; part of the Western world, but also, sitting by itself in the middle of the Atlantic, a piece of the polar one. His mind returned to the typescript in his pocket—he took it out—and to the supposedly internationalist conversation back at the Gallery.

"Dreadfully sorry," said Acland, hanging up the phone.

"Tell me, Your Excellency—off the record, deepest background and all that—is it true that the prime minister has developed some reservations about the *headlong* nature of this summit? One hears that she would rather have Mr. Reagan not go at all. I don't suppose you'll let me know whether there's anything to that?"

Looking at the ambassador's right profile in the dim light of the limousine, Hitchens thought he could detect a confirming twitch, the barest movement in some little ganglion of diplomatic anxiety.

"Is that part of this piece?' asked Acland, pointing to the typescript on Hitchens's lap.

"Perhaps part of the next one."

The ambassador said nothing further. Hitchens looked out the car window as they passed Thirtieth Street and entered the embassy compound, cheek by jowl with the Naval Observatory, beside whose dome George Herbert Walker Bush would rest his head tonight, dreaming of ascendance to Reagan's bedroom on Pennsylvania Avenue.

"Hello, Bronson," the ambassador said to a young clerk not far from the embassy's main entrance. "Perhaps you'll help my friend here. He's got a fax that needs sending. Where's it going, Hitchens?"

"To the *Spectator.*"

Acland seemed surprised by the article's Tory destination.

"I do occasionally write for them," Hitchens explained. "I'm one of the vipers they hold to their bosom."

"Big of them," said Acland. "Anyway, I'll be in the library. Bronson can point you to it if you'd like a bit of a snack once you're through. And after that we can get somebody to run you home."

"Awfully kind of you," said Hitchens, as he scribbled out a cover sheet for the fax. Bronson explained that things would take a minute. The machine had just become engaged by an incoming transmission.

Hitchens used the brief delay to take a last look at the piece, which he decided was too speculative and generally unsatisfying. He would prefer to focus on the implications of what actually *was* happening, not simply on what *might* transpire. His mind returned to the ambassador's nearly imperceptible twitch in the limousine. Was that the *real* story? Was Western Europe in danger of being ignored, or even pushed aside, after it had spent the last three years coddling American missiles?

And if that *were* the case, shouldn't he himself be buying earmuffs as well as sunblock? Wasn't Reykjavik about to become the center of the action? True, there was rather a lot on his plate right now: his impending jaunt with Mrs. Harriman plus Dolan's murmurings about a sort of Homintern inside the National Security Council. It was all rather a lot to chase in the same month. And yet, what better way to get a glimpse of the NSC than to watch its boys scramble up the Icelandic summit?

It was, he had always believed, one world; perhaps this would turn out to be all one story.

He put a note to Charles Moore, the *Spectator*'s editor, at the bottom of the cover sheet: *Too late to spring for a ticket? C.H.*

"Oh, Mr. Hitchens," said Bronson, bright with surprise as he reached for the incoming fax. "It's for you!" He stapled the two pages and handed them to his guest:

RÉSUMÉ OF KELLY PROCTOR
Born July 10, 1962

12

OCTOBER 6, 1986

"Anders Little!" cried Carl "Spitz" Channell, rising from a banquette in the Hay-Adams's restaurant. The heartiness of the greeting seemed designed, Anders immediately felt, to give Channell's several guests, who were in the middle of cocktails, the impression that he knew Anders Little better than he did.

Shaking Channell's hand, Anders thought that he looked like a healthier version of Terry Dolan: slightly built; sporting a thin mustache; about forty and more or less handsome. A few additional facts—that he'd once worked for NCPAC; was in and out of North's office; and was pals with Neal Grover—made up nearly the rest of what Anders knew about him.

"Mr. Little is going to talk to you about Soviet affairs," Channell explained to the four people seated, two of them on the banquette with their host and the other two in Chippendale-style chairs on the other side of the table. Two were elderly women: one a Mrs. Garwood from Texas, the wife of a judge; and the other, whose name Anders never caught, the head of a foundation supporting family values and representational art. One of the men was called Pete and the other James Dugan; the latter somehow seemed to know quite a few things about Anders and to have been waiting for him with some eagerness. Dugan's blondness appeared to have been helped along by a hair colorist, and his tan to have come from a sunlamp. Even the muscles, visible beneath his expensive suit, somehow looked as if they'd been purchased instead of honestly acquired at a gym. Pete, whom Anders judged to be in his late sixties, was a more authentically attractive man, a sort of handsome ruin, tall and stooped, who would occasionally muffle a cough.

"I'm going to sit you next to James," Channell told Anders, settling the group, now at full strength, back into their seats.

Mrs. Garwood seemed particularly full of beans, wearing on her loudly colored blouse a big button that said *NEPL:* NATIONAL ENDOWMENT FOR THE PRESERVATION OF LIBERTY—the outfit Spitz Channell had been running since '84.

"See what you get for a million dollars?" joked Spitz, pointing to the button. After some all-for-one laughter from those assembled, he explained to Anders: "Most of the people here have been working with Ollie North on and off for the past year."

"Oh, call Ollie 'Mr. Green,'" said the representational-arts lady, provoking chuckles from the others. "Green" appeared to be North's not-very-secret code name.

"We've had quite a day," said Channell. "We got to listen to the president, who came by the EOB for about twenty minutes."

"He was *wonderful*," said Mrs. Garwood.

"He was indeed," said Channell. "He assured these folks and some others who were there that when he's over in Iceland this weekend he won't be talking just about warheads. He'll be bringing up Soviet human-rights abuses; he'll be bringing up Afghanistan; and, yes, he'll be bringing up Central America."

"Hear! Hear!" said James Dugan, tapping a swizzle stick on the tablecloth. He signaled the waiter to bring a second round for everyone. Anders ordered a vodka tonic.

"And after the president," Channell continued, "Ollie gave us one of his tremendous briefings."

"With *slides*," added the representational-arts woman, as if surprised by her own approval of this modern medium.

"No one can do it like Ollie," said Channell. "Or I guess I should say 'Mr. Green.' Pete was seeing him in action for the first time today, and I think he would agree."

Pete nodded, and lit another cigarette.

"I *loved* the bit about the dental floss!" exclaimed Mrs. Garwood. "Only Ollie would know that."

Channell explained to Anders: "Until New Year's, when real aid to the Contras will finally resume—I guess we should say *thanks* to this reluctant Congress down the street—our freedom fighters have had to make do with what the State Department considers 'humanitarian aid.' That's included seventeen hundred *miles* of dental floss."

Anders laughed good-naturedly, before Spitz offered a characterization of the people around the table. "These are *action-oriented* contributors—*warriors*, I'd go so far as to say."

Anders noted that Pete, who was drinking a little faster than everyone else, seemed especially pleased with this last term, though he also looked—certainly compared to James Dugan—ill at ease, as if aware he might be playing out of his league.

"As you all know," said Channell, in a lower voice than he'd been using before, "Ollie can't solicit funds; he can only tell you *needs*."

"SAM-7 missiles," said the arts lady. "Maule aircraft. I wrote it all down."

"I bought one of *those*," Mrs. Garwood said proudly. "A Maule."

Channell directed his next point to Anders: "NEPL collects money for 'education.' But that's a broad term. Education gets conducted with a lot of other equipment besides books and erasers."

The round of drinks arrived and as soon as everybody had a fresh glass in hand, James Dugan raised his tumbler and toasted: "To the president! And to Adolfo Calero!"

"And to all of you," said Spitz Channell, after lifting his own glass to Ronald Reagan and the leader of the Contras. "To the best 501(c)(3) on the books of the IRS!"

Anders's smile was thin-lipped and cautious. But Channell quickly moved the conversation away from the Contras.

"Some of you," he said, "know about other enterprises I'm involved in—nondeductible ones, I'm afraid. But I can't pass up this opportunity to make a pitch for them, too. When I was at NCPAC I always got more excited backing challengers than incumbents, since challengers are the real *future* of our movement. I like fresh faces, and one that I'd recommend to you belongs to Linda Chavez, who's running for the Senate over in Maryland against the Mikulski woman."

"*Awful* creature," said Mrs. Garwood.

Barbara Mikulski was not actually an incumbent in this race, since she was trying to rise from the House to the Senate, but she'd been around so long that she felt like one, and Channell said, "It would be great to send her packing from this town."

"Hey," interrupted James Dugan. "Just to be fair, I'd like to speak up for one incumbent—from my own state of Florida. I'm talking about Paula Hawkins, who's hanging on to her Senate seat for dear life. Any help you can give her, through Spitz or anyone else, would be grand." He patted Anders's knee near the rim of the tablecloth. "Come down to Naples or Sarasota and I'll show you what this lady can *do* when she gets in front of a crowd."

Mrs. Garwood winked at Dugan and allowed that she might have a few dollars to spare. He thanked her. "And speaking of dollars," Dugan added, "did you hear how President Reagan intends to honor his old friend Rock Hudson?"

No one seemed to know.

"Well, it appears we're finally going to be getting a three-dollar bill, and Rock is going to be on it!"

The arts lady appeared perplexed; Mrs. Garwood laughed saltily; and Spitz Channell laughed hardest of all. After a moment or two, he said, "Anders, maybe we could hear from you now, before the food arrives. We took the liberty of ordering for you, and I don't think you'll be disappointed."

Anders, feeling rather like a side dish himself—strangely incidental to this whole affair—took some note cards out of his pocket. He thought for a moment about standing up, but then decided it would look silly.

"I just thought that I would relate current Soviet efforts in Central America to what we've long seen in Mozambique and Angola—as well as, of course, for an even longer time, in Cuba. Namely: revolution supported with means just short of invasion, which we *have* had, of course, in Afghanistan.

"The Pershing missiles installed in Europe have amounted to our own sort of resistance movement against Soviet expansionism, and they represent in some respects the first real attempt we've made to fight back, aggressively, in almost two decades. The Soviets are still winning on the ground, but thanks to the president's general defense buildup, we're going to catch them. Even so, as that process goes on, we must not allow them to win in the skies."

He intended to give them some precise, cautionary information about the kinds of missile reductions that would be debated in Reykjavik— nothing classified, of course, or overly technical, but with a level of detail that would make any contributor here believe he was getting his money's worth. And yet, after only another sentence or two, Channell stopped him by saying "That's great."

"Terrific," added James Dugan, giving Anders's forearm a squeeze as the food arrived at the table.

That's it? wondered Anders, more baffled than before. What purpose was he serving here, exactly? Did Jeane Kirkpatrick know these individuals? He needed to get their names straight and ask her.

———

An hour later, the Hay-Adams's Dover sole having been fully consumed and a couple of Channell's cigars half-smoked by Pete and James Dugan, the gathering broke up. But Anders, mildly drunk and mostly curious, accepted Spitz's invitation to a nightcap at his apartment on Belmont Road.

"You did a fabulous job," Channell assured him.

"Hardly," said Anders, who couldn't remember whether he'd spoken one paragraph or two. He was now in the backseat of a chauffeured car, between Spitz and Dugan, experiencing physical discomfort on top of the other kinds the evening had already entailed. Pete was up front with the driver.

As the car pulled past the White House, Dugan gestured toward some lights in the West Wing and argued that they gave the lie to liberal grumblings about Ronald Reagan's purported indolence. In fact it was not yet nine p.m., and the window Dugan had pointed to was far from the Oval Office; but Anders said nothing. Zealotry had its place, he believed; but idol worship? He supposed he'd done a bit of that when giving Anne Macmurray her White House tour, but one of his own favorite jokes, which had made its way throughout the NSC, went: "Reagan is so lazy he's decided to replace the nuclear button with the Clapper!"

"So," asked Channell, "are you pleased?"

Anders assumed that the question pertained to the whole day's activities and was meant for Pete, who seemed to be the newest member of Spitz's network. But the query had been, it turned out, addressed to James, who said, "Oh, yes," while offering Anders's knee a light and, if need be, deniable tap.

"You can drop me off at the hotel right up here," said Pete, as the car crossed Pennsylvania and Twenty-second.

"Here?" asked Spitz, incredulously, pointing to the modest One Washington Circle.

Pete, lighting a cigarette, offered a pained smile. "I don't need the goddamned Hay-Adams," he said, with a proud note.

It was also a familiar note. Anders had heard Nixon say the same words about the humility and thrift involved in his postpresidential trips to the capital. Pete's use of the line even carried a trace of the Old Man's cadences, and as soon as he heard it, Anders realized who Pete was. *The guy seems to be giving away all his money these days. . . . To a lot of different causes. A couple of them mainstream, a few of them crazy.* Before getting out of the limo, the man passed him a business card from the front seat. Anders thanked him, and confirmed his deduction with a look at it: PETER COX/COX CONSULTANTS. A Turtle Creek address in Dallas. Anders thought for a moment of exiting the car with him. But what would he say if he did? I know your ex-wife? And I hear you're dying of cancer? He decided just to say good night and remain stuck in the backseat between Spitz and James.

Channell's apartment—a large second-floor space in a good building off Connecticut Avenue—already held nearly a dozen other guests, not one of them a woman. In fact, the only oblique sign of female presence was a painting, a Hudson River landscape given by the arts lady, Spitz explained. It was being forced to coexist with a lot of abstract works and with furnishings even more modern. The whole effect was lavish; whether it was tasteful, Anders didn't know enough to say.

"Good thing Pete isn't here for a glimpse of NEPL's 'overhead,' " said

James Dugan. He meant the remark as a joke, but Channell's silence didn't indicate it had been taken that way.

A tall, good-looking fellow named Eric came out from the kitchen and asked what the new arrivals would be drinking. He was accompanied by Neal Grover, who cried, "Hey! I do believe it's Mr. Little!"

"Glad to see you," Anders responded. It was the truth, which said something, since being around Neal usually made him less comfortable instead of more.

The two sat down in a spot not far from Spitz's home office, under a fancily framed certificate attesting to Carl Channell's attendance, for one year during the late 1960s, at the Union Theological Seminary in Richmond. Eric soon came by with their drinks, and Anders realized that he'd really begun to put it away—even more than at Anne Macmurray's the other night.

Neal pointed to Eric's retreating form: "Spitz's assistant—*and* roommate."

Sure as shooting, James Dugan now pulled up a chair on Anders's left. Anders managed to smile and say, "I really shouldn't," as he drank off an inch of the vodka tonic Eric had brought.

"Oh, go ahead," urged James. "I'm sure you'll work it off in the morning." He began to describe his own exercise regimen, which was heavy on the bench-pressing. "Play sports in school?" he asked.

"Track. Wake Forest," said Anders, who could see that the second part of the answer was a disappointment.

"I went to Yale myself. You're a country boy, like Spitz."

"Small town, anyway. Mooresville, North Carolina."

"That's right. Spitz told me," said Dugan, taking a sip of his Diet Coke. "I'll say this. You've got a great senator down there. Really holding this administration's feet to the fire."

Anders smiled. "I take it you don't mean Jim Broyhill."

"Hell, no!" said Dugan. "I'm talking about Uncle Jesse! I think he's great—and I think you're great, too."

Anders felt his discomfort turning to anger. He began wondering whether Spitz Channell often used a little pimping, along with the "briefings" and presidential handshakes, to help raise funds. "Excuse me, Dugan," he said, getting up.

"Relax," said Neal, with a calming touch to his elbow. "Let me introduce you to somebody."

"Hi!" said a bright-eyed, freckled young man, who extended his card along with his hand. "I'm Nick Carrollton, with the RNC." Anders figured he could manage a few minutes' conversation with an overeager kid before making a decent getaway.

"What are you drinking?" he asked the boy, whose glass was nearly empty.

"They told me the name, but I have no idea."

"You sure you're old enough?"

"Twenty-six!"

"How do you know Mr. Channell?"

"My first job when I got to Washington was with NCPAC. He taught me a kajillion things about direct mail and phone-banking. He's incredible at getting people to give money. Terry Dolan used to call him 'the Girl Scout cookie queen.' And he never even had to deliver any cookies; just collect the money! Spitz and Terry go all the way back to 1976."

"Are you still in touch with Terry?"

"I'm one of his 'buddies.' "

The last word seemed to Anders to be in quotation marks, though not suspicious or sarcastic ones. Nick Carrollton could see that he was perplexed, so the kid began a patient explanation, as if he were the older and wiser of the two: "I mean a volunteer 'buddy.' I help Terry out through Whitman-Walker. The clinic. I do some of his shopping, stuff like that. It can be a pain, because I live over in Arlington, but it's a great program. You should join!"

Anders didn't know what to say, and wasn't sure what assumptions were being made. He stumbled toward a reply. "I live over in Arlington, too. It sounds very nice of you to do that. For Terry Dolan, I mean." He was aware, and somewhat ashamed, that he'd just used the surname to put some distance between himself and a person he'd called "Terry" only a minute ago.

"Terry's *lucky*," said Nick. "Honest. In a lot of ways. He's got a family that loves him. Poor Spitz," he added. "Both his parents are gone."

"Spitz isn't sick, is he?"

"Oh, no," said Nick, as reassuringly as one could say such a thing these days. "He's just another one of the 'worried well.'" The phrase diminished the usual wattage of Nick's smile and made it more appealing to Anders, who could figure out the watch-and-wait meaning of 'worried well,' even as it sounded peculiarly like another of Spitz Channell's fund-raiser categories: *action-oriented contributors; warriors.*

"I'm lucky," said Nick, forthrightly. "I was a late bloomer. By the time I got started I pretty much knew how to protect myself. At least I think!"

"But you said Terry was 'lucky' too," said Anders, with a gentle, almost teasing tenderness that surprised him. He took another drink from the tray Eric was circulating. Nick declined one, though his smile was back to full size.

"I look on the bright side—of everything! And people do need to stick together. You know, Terry's still a consultant for NEPL. He can't do much, but he gets a check every month."

Anders felt drunk and bewildered; sentimental and disgusted; unable to think clearly about this layering of anti-Communism and homosexuality, like the corner of a carpet pad sticking out from beneath a rug he'd just tripped over. Spitz Channell would probably take (and skim) money from every evangelist who would laugh over James Dugan's three-dollar-bill joke—and yet, Anders's instincts told him, Channell believed in the cause to which (some of) the money was going. And this gung-ho boy in front of him, who maybe would ignore the joke instead of actually laugh at it, seemed truly to believe that it was morning in America. Christ, he *looked* like morning in America.

"You enjoying the RNC?"

"Totally!" answered Nick. "You'll never believe who I got to meet last week."

Before Nick could say "Nancy Reagan," Spitz Channell, up to now mostly absent from his own party, strode out of his office and over to James Dugan, who was soon sharing Spitz's stricken look. Dugan's tan seemed to fade beneath the track lights of the living room, and he soon bid his host a troubled good night. Anders watched all this out of the corner of his eye, while Nick Carrollton tried telling him the story of the Hawkins video.

"May I borrow Mr. Little?" asked Spitz, suddenly at Anders's elbow.

Nick looked happy, as if flattered by the thought that Anders Little might be his to loan.

Channell took Anders into a hallway dominated by another landscape from the arts lady.

"Anders, you're going to hear this on *Nightline*, so you might as well hear it from me first. I just got a call from—better not to say who. The Sandinistas announced tonight that they've shot down—with a god-damned Soviet rocket!—a supply plane on its way to our guys. Twenty-eight miles from Costa Rica, which is where we do our banking." He was rambling, panicky. "The plane was carrying fifty thousand rounds of ammunition."

"Jesus," said Anders, "what kind of plane?"

"A C-123."

Anders put his drink down on an expensive-looking table. He narrowed his eyes, unsure whether he was attempting to convey disapproval or just gain some alcohol-impaired focus on what appeared to be a crisis.

"Elliott Abrams is going on Koppel to say it's *not* a U.S. military plane—which technically it *isn't*," argued Channell. "But we've got three dead crewmen, and the Sandinistas captured the kicker."

"The kicker?"

"The guy who actually kicks supplies out of the plane during airdrops. Let's hope he doesn't have any business cards on him."

Anders thought of what was in his own pocket—PETER COX / COX CONSULTANTS—and felt a compelling urge to get out of Channell's apartment. What was he doing here? He could already hear himself having to tell someone, an investigator: *I was merely asked to speak to them, prior to the Iceland summit, about the state of U.S. and Soviet armaments . . .*

"I'd better get going," he told Channell. "They may need all hands on deck."

The host retreated into his home office as the party transformed itself into clusters of anxious conversation.

"Nice to meet you," Anders said to Nick Carrollton on his way out.

"You going already?"

"I've got a very busy week."

"Could we share a cab back to Arlington?" asked Nick.

"Sure," said Anders. "I'll take care of it." He could imagine how little this kid made at the RNC.

On their way over the Key Bridge, Anders told him why the *Post* was probably right now remaking tomorrow's front page. Nick, who wasn't dim, understood right away how this could be the start of something really bad. "Can I come up and watch *Nightline*?" he asked. He pointed to his watch, indicating that he might miss the broadcast if he stayed in the cab all the way to his own place.

Once inside the condo on Wilson Boulevard, Anders made himself one last drink while the program came on. He was worried—about this sudden situation in Nicaragua and, more generally, about himself. He shouldn't have let this kid invite himself up here. But as soon as he got over to the couch he began feeling less vulnerable; his mood turned almost protective toward the younger man who sat beside him, tie loosened, sipping a light beer.

The onscreen reporter, after throwing out a lot of what any press secretary would call "hypotheticals," was saying that "this event could raise serious legal, even constitutional, questions."

"Oh, gag me with a spoon," said Nick, before putting his head on Anders's shoulder.

After flinching, Anders realized that he was remaining put, and that his thoughts were racing even faster than his well-conditioned heart. He began to have at last some honest idea of what he might have been seeking, so haltingly and unawares, from Anne Macmurray. It was either avoidance of this moment, a last-minute diversion from it, or a sort of permission—a motherly sanction of something that had been lying in wait for him for a very long time.

The "inability to commit"; the way he'd successfully argued two wives out of having children—was all of that nothing compared to an inability to *permit* . . . he couldn't finish the unspoken sentence in his head.

And maybe he was just drunk.

He put his arm around Nick Carrollton's shoulder.

At 6:15 a.m., when the phone rang in the bedroom, Nick reached for the receiver and, with what seemed a practiced discretion, passed it silently to the older man. The cord lay across the boy's bare chest as Anders listened to the caller's familiar voice: "It's a good thing you don't have to get shots for Iceland on two days' notice. I suppose it's too damned cold for any germs to live there."

"Mr. President," he said.

Nick Carrollton's eyes doubled in size.

"I've got you on the plane," said Nixon. "It's the reward they gave me for not publicly crapping in advance on this foolish goddamned summit. Poindexter's allowing me my own set of eyes and ears in Reykjavik, and I told him I wanted those to be you. So talk to his assistant. You're wheels-up from Andrews at nine forty-five a.m., day after tomorrow. *Vaya con Dios*, Andy!"

Part Two

Iceland

OCTOBER 9–12, 1986

13

THURSDAY, OCTOBER 9, 1986

10:10 A.M. (EDT), WASHINGTON, D.C.

"Great *clip*," said Merv.

The California morning shows had just run footage of the first lady kissing the president goodbye as he boarded the helicopter on the South Lawn. Nancy was now back upstairs in the Residence.

"Aw, thanks, Merv. It's already lonesome here."

"How about going up to Camp David?"

"Oh, it'd be worse there! But they've scheduled a few things here to keep me busy." She had a Just Say No luncheon at the Capital Hilton a couple of hours from now, and on Saturday night she would be getting some award from Catholic University.

"Well," Merv suggested, "you can stay up late tonight, eat bon-bons, and watch Joan."

For a horrified moment Nancy thought that Joan Quigley would be giving a TV interview. Then she realized Merv meant the premiere of Joan Rivers's talk show, opposite Carson.

"Do you think she'll make it?" Nancy asked.

"She won't last a year," said Merv, who could be all business when the subject was business.

"You know," said Nancy, "I had to spell 'Reykjavik' for our other Joan—Quigley. I called her just after the summit invitation came and caught her at a bad moment. Her mother had just died. But I went ahead and asked her to do three charts on Ronnie for this weekend: one for Iceland, one for London—which they were also thinking about for a location—and one for Washington, just to see what would happen if he didn't go at all."

"I'm on the edge of my seat!" said Merv. "What was the spread?"

"I can't even remember London at this point. But the chart for Washington was 'mediocre to poor,' according to Joan. The one for Reykjavik was 'stupendous.' Her word."

"Oooh," said Merv.

"Every planet—this is with Reykjavik—went into the upper half of Ronnie's chart. She said it was one of the most 'visible' arrangements she'd ever seen."

"I'm getting chills," said Merv, though Nancy was sure he didn't understand the difference between the "upper half" and the lower one any more than she did.

"She picked the departure time from Andrews."

Imagine telling this to anyone but Merv! Still, she *didn't* tell him how Joan had said the "stupendous" results might be discernible only in the long term, or that Ronnie's first meeting with Gorbachev, scheduled for Saturday morning, *didn't* look all that promising. And she certainly couldn't tell him about Uranus and Saturn, further out.

Knowing that Nancy's silence indicated a wave of worry, Merv altered the conversational course. "Now you just need to ask Joan whether we should open with 'Fascinating Rhythm' or 'Strike Up the Band.'"

He was referring to the Gershwin evening at the White House, which he was helping her to organize. Nancy gave a tinkling laugh and said, "Okay, Mervyn. I'll see you on the twenty-sixth."

"Can't wait."

She soon heard a knock on the bedroom door, two soft taps and then a third slightly more committed one: Maureen's usual sequence. Had her stepdaughter been standing there, waiting for the call to end? The timidity of it touched Nancy. This poor fifth wheel!

"Come on in."

Maureen opened the door but didn't cross the threshold. "I always feel I'm back at Chadwick when I stay here!" she said with a laugh, referring to the boarding school that Jane had stuck her in after the divorce. "Except that all the other girls have somehow gone home!"

Nancy laughed too. "Sit down for a while."

"Oh, I can't," said Maureen. "I'm headed to the office." Her recently expanded role at the RNC was occasioning more White House stay-overs. Maybe Maureen would find her niche at last, thought Nancy. (But who would tell her that the burnt-orange jacket she was wearing made her look big as a house?)

"I really just wanted to give you this," said Maureen. "It was faxed up here a couple of minutes ago by one of Don Regan's mice."

Nancy took a look at the curled sheet of thermal paper. It was a revised schedule for the president, for Friday, October 24, which now had him going from Oklahoma to Tampa—an added stop on behalf of Paula Hawkins—instead of back to the White House. They were going to wear him out.

Without looking up from the paper, she said, "That'll be the second life preserver Ronnie's thrown your Paula."

Maureen looked uncomfortable, partly over Nancy's inability to say "your father" instead of "Ronnie," but mostly from the suggestion that Paula Hawkins, whom Maureen really had been pushing, was a kind of deadbeat. Alas, one couldn't deny that the president had already raised three hundred thousand dollars for the senator during a trip he'd made to Florida in July.

"Oh, I know," Maureen said. "I wish she could learn to do a little more swimming on her own. And I wish she hadn't just spent *three days* up in New York promoting that child-abuse book. She seems to think that doing a couple of two-minute network interviews is worth the time away from retail campaigning back home—when in fact those interviews only confuse things. Half the Florida voters who see them think she's an author instead of their senator."

Nancy said nothing.

"But it's *so* important that we pull this one out," continued Maureen. "And I still think we can. *Thank you*, again, for making that video. Oh! I forgot!" she exclaimed, interrupting herself to extract a VHS cassette from her faux-leather bag, as big and as awful as her jacket. "Here's a copy of the edited version. It's got a couple of bells and whistles on it now. Tomorrow night's the first donor dinner they'll be showing it at. Sarasota, I think."

"Great," said Nancy, putting it on an end table. "I'll take a look later."

She knew that Maureen, afraid to ask directly, was trying to get her to commit to this new Florida trip with Ronnie. But she couldn't now think about anything but the summit. She looked through the window and realized that her husband was already well out over the Atlantic.

Maureen gave up waiting for her stepmother to volunteer. Without Merv's aplomb, she changed the subject. "You know," she said, her expression suddenly troubled, "Dad came in to say goodbye to me an hour ago, just before everybody went down to the Lawn for the departure."

"Did he?" asked Nancy, who couldn't recall a moment when Ronnie had been out of her sight this morning.

"Just for a second," said Maureen.

How *proud* the poor girl was telling this! Nancy, sad just to look at her, felt almost ready to give in about the 24th. Really, it was such a crumb.

"He said something funny," Maureen continued.

Nancy guessed that, with Gorbachev on his mind, it had been a Russia joke. *Ten years from Thursday? The plumber's coming that afternoon!*

"Not funny ha-ha," Maureen added. "Funny . . . odd. He asked me to pray for him."

"Really?" said Nancy, whose mind began racing across a spectrum of catastrophes from more trouble with the Contras to a recurrence of colon cancer.

"I asked him, 'Is anything wrong?'"

"And what did he say?"

"Just 'Oh, no, Mermie.' He had the strangest, most faraway smile on his face. And then he turned around and was gone."

12:00 NOON (EDT)—ABOARD AIR FORCE ONE (SAM 27000)

This will be essentially a private meeting between the two of us.

That's what the president had said in his departure remarks, copies of which had now been distributed to everyone flying with him. *Air Force One* was full, and there was another plane, equally crammed with aides and luggage, flying right behind. It seemed likely that the Soviets would be arriving in Iceland with even more of a presence, making Reagan's suggestion of a cozy tête-à-tête seem comical.

Anders had heard that there wasn't even room for the man Don Regan called "the scribe," the president's official biographer, who was intermittently being permitted to "shadow" him during his second term. If Edmund Morris had made the cut, he would likely be doing what the rest of them were, every few minutes: looking, as nonchalantly as possible, toward Reagan's private cabin, hoping that the president might emerge for a break from his briefing books, cracking a joke about all the work Professor Shultz had assigned him. But Reagan had been hidden away for more than two hours now, ever since he'd boarded, waved to those already seated, and disappeared.

Once in a while, someone would come out of the Senior Staff cabin—Poindexter had done it ten minutes ago—to perform what old-timers called a "Nixon stroll," a prudent pacing of the aisle, designed to ward off coagulation and phlebitis. Anders, who had done a hard run between four and five a.m., sat behind Jack Matlock, the president's special Soviet affairs assistant, and next to a Secret Service agent whose name he had already forgotten.

That he was on this plane at all—instead of tailing after it, with the NSC staff of equal rank, on AF26000—seemed to indicate how much Poindexter wanted to keep Richard Nixon from objecting to the summit. Realizing this made Anders nervous. The purpose of his presence, unknown, he would guess, to anybody but the national security advisor, felt like a second secret he was being forced to conceal, when the other, more personal one was a volatile burden enough. He envied his office buddies and the clerical staff on the other aircraft, which had a history more exciting and macabre than any yet made by its replacement, the plane he was actually on. If they'd put him on 26000, he might, a week from now, be telling Anne Macmurray what it had felt like to fly inside the machine that had taken Nixon to China and brought Kennedy's body home from Dallas.

It would be easier to talk about those things than what he really wanted to confide. Yesterday he'd called Anne to say goodbye and had mentioned seeing Peter Cox. She'd been alarmed by what he'd said about her ex-husband's frail appearance and the company he was keeping. But close as Anders had come to asking if he might drop by, and for all that his instincts made him believe she was the one person who could calm or absolve him, he had kept the source of his panic bottled up.

A bon-voyage card had arrived at his in-box yesterday, a hand-delivery from the pouch that daily went between the RNC and the White House. The card showed a surfer who'd accidentally gotten on the wrong flight and was now standing beside an igloo. STAY WARM! read the printed greeting above the simple signature: NICK. Since receiving the card, Anders had resolutely tried to keep from thinking about it, even as he'd tucked it into the breast pocket of his jacket at six o'clock this morning.

Every hour of northeasterly travel left the interior of the plane notice-ably darker. Deciding that work was the best and most honorable medi-cine, Anders put on his glasses, sat up straight, and began reorganizing the last-minute looseleaf he'd been presented with. There was a strangely optimistic feeling throughout the plane, a festive sense that something might be brewing. Even short-tempered Don Regan, now doing a Nixon stroll with one of his mice, seemed to be in a good mood. As one of the fact sheets in his binder cheerily informed Anders, the chief of staff would be returning to a country where his Marine unit had been sta-tioned in 1941.

"Who decided to leave today and not Friday?" a reporter near the back of the plane called out. The protocol-defying journalist did have a point: this flight to Reykjavik (a word the president had mispronounced in his departure remarks) would take less than five hours, hardly time enough for jet lag to set in, and they would have a whole free day before only a day and a half of meetings.

"Oh, you'd have to ask a much higher authority than me about sched-uling," said Regan. The cryptic nature of his response didn't dampen his geniality. A White House photographer captured his smile and then, as if he'd been assigned to get a shot of every table at a wedding reception, snapped pictures row by row of all those aboard Anders's section of the plane. A click of the shutter just a foot from his face startled him, made Anders somehow feel found out; his hand actually went to his breast pocket.

He needed to calm down if he was going to make it through the weekend. Altering his strategy, he shut the looseleaf, closed his eyes, and attempted to doze. But within a minute the seat next to him, vacated by the Secret Service agent, was being filled by someone else. Before he could reopen his eyes, Anders recognized the voice of Pat Buchanan, the president's scrappy but convivial communications director.

"Not as roomy as you expected, is it?" Buchanan asked, with his staccato laugh.

Anders, who had met him only a couple of times, smiled politely and said, "Oh, it feels plenty big enough."

"They've finally ordered up a 747 to replace it. But I doubt it'll be ready in time to fly the boss off into the sunset." Buchanan laughed again.

"Really?" asked Anders. "With more than two years left?"

The communications chief, whose good spirits seemed a heightened manifestation of the plane's general atmosphere, pointed to the matchbox model of Air Force One on Anders's tray table. "Got your souvenir chum, I see. You know what the 'V' on that stands for?" He pointed to the delicately painted designation on the model's tail: VC-137C.

"No," said Anders.

"'VIP.' Reagan put it back. Carter had the letter erased for four years. Carried his own bags onto plain old C-137C!" Buchanan's snare-drum laugh burst forth again. "You know what the greatest form of egotism in the world is?"

"No," said Anders.

"False modesty."

Anders wished he had some reciprocal lore or insight that he could offer Buchanan, but he didn't, and he could feel his new seatmate losing interest in his monosyllabic responses. Buchanan seemed to recognize Anders as one of those people, a joyless silent minority within any administration, who respect politics but don't relish it. The communications director stood back up, excused himself, and got ready to go mix it up with some of the press at the rear of the aircraft. By way of farewell, he good-naturedly tapped Anders on the shoulder and said, "Don't let the Old Man down."

Like Nick Carrollton in bed the other morning, Anders incorrectly believed he was hearing a reference to Ronald Reagan. It took him a moment to realize that Buchanan, an old Nixon hand, meant the thirty-seventh president, not the fortieth—and that he knew the real reason Anders Little was on this plane.

1:00 P.M. (EDT), 2032 BELMONT ROAD NW, WASHINGTON, D.C.

Having skipped both breakfast and lunch, Spitz Channell drank from his third cup of coffee and looked out onto Connecticut Avenue, furtively, through the slats of his top-of-the-line MechoShade blinds.

"Are you *ever* going in to the office?" Eric called out from the bedroom.

"Maybe later," answered Spitz, who turned his attention away from the street and back to CNN.

"*The people I met in El Salvador, that I knew, were all Company people,*" said Eugene Hasenfus, the Contra-supplying "kicker" captured by the Sandinistas a few days earlier. The prisoner had at last been permitted—or forced—to make a public statement, which the cable-news channel had now run several times. Hasenfus's voice was halting and his manner fearful. He reminded Spitz of that tortured captain of the *Pueblo* from back in the sixties. Surely this confession of a link between the supply operation and the CIA (the "Company") had been coerced from him.

"*Phone rings, door chimes, in comes* compan-eeee," sang the Sondheim-loving Eric, holding the last syllable of the lyric as he passed through the living room.

"*Eric,*" scolded Spitz.

"Okay, okay."

The State Department's Elliott Abrams, whose face now filled half the screen, insisted there was "no relation at all" between the downed plane and the spy agency. Spitz groaned: it was—alas—the truth, more or less.

However sorry he felt for Hasenfus, that hapless figure wasn't terribly important. What Spitz wanted to know, and what the Sandinistas weren't revealing, was what information had been found on the bodies of the American crew—Hasenfus's superiors—who'd been killed in the crash.

The telephone rang. Spitz waited until he recognized the voice starting to leave a message before he picked up.

"I am *outraged*!" said Ellen Garwood, her Texas accent even thicker than it had been the other night at the Hay-Adams. "Look at how they're treatin' that poor fellow! He looks *starved*. What need has he got for any of that precious humanitarian *dental floss* when his teeth have very evidently not been allowed anywhere *near* food this week?"

"Yes, Mrs. Garwood," said Spitz. "I've been watching."

"I'll tell you what else I don't like: 'And together we can be true to the cause of freedom even while we're true to the cause of peace.' "

Having listened to CNN all morning, Spitz had heard this portion of the president's departure remarks at least three times.

Mrs. Garwood barreled on: "I taped it on my VCR, and then I *transcribed* it." She made it sound as if she alone now held evidence of this incriminating utterance. "I don't mind tellin' you, Spitz: the sound of that *worries* me. It's like somethin' Teddy Kennedy would say!"

"Mrs. Garwood," Spitz replied, as softly as he could, "we should probably all lie low for a bit. One of the best things about this summit may be the chance it provides us to do that. It'll take the spotlight away from what happened in Nicaragua on Monday."

"Hasn't so *far*!" Mrs. Garwood protested, before subsiding. "Well," she sighed, looking for substitute fronts to fight on, "Friday's the day I usually write checks. Which of those candidates we talked about the other night would you recommend for a contribution? Hawkins or Chavez?"

"Hawkins," Spitz answered, absently, thinking just hard enough about the choice to name the candidate who still had a fighting chance.

Mrs. Garwood's mind, like his, had already gone back to the problem in Central America. "Is someone going to come around asking me questions?" she wanted to know.

"I hope not," said Spitz, looking through the blinds again.

Mrs. Garwood's silence seemed to indicate a certain disappointment, one that would be deeper, Spitz thought, if she ever found out how modest her large contributions to the Contras had been compared to those made by a certain theocracy in the Middle East.

7:05 P.M. (RT [REYKJAVIK TIME]), U.S. NAVAL AIR STATION, KEFLAVÍK, ICELAND

"Christopher Hitchens," said the man himself, extending his hand to the president of Iceland, an attractive blonde in a wide-brimmed hat.

"Vigdís Finnbogadóttir," she responded, giving his hand a friendly shake.

He nearly replied, "And Bob's your uncle." Her name was so enchanting, so suggestive of fairy-tale incantation, that one could imagine Reagan and Gorbachev just saying it together—"Vigdís Finnbogadóttir"—and Bob's your uncle, there you go: world peace.

It was difficult, with all the umbrellas, to get close, and the patter of chilling rain made it hard to hear. But Hitchens raised his voice a notch and told the Icelandic president: "I understand you demonstrated against the presence of this air base back in the sixties."

"Well," said Vigdís Finnbogadóttir, whose looks and outfit created a younger, softer version of Mrs. Thatcher, "we are very happy to have it available for the arrival of a president who is seeking peace."

The Great Communicator was "wheels-down," but his plane still had a ways to taxi until it reached the velvet ropes and little welcoming stand. Hitchens had arrived two hours before at the nearby civilian airport, and spent most of the time in between drinking a ghastly sort of blueberry liquor—some local calamity—with two Swedish journalists who'd gotten hold of it in the Duty Free.

"Are you sure that 'seeking peace' is on his mind?" he now shouted, taking one last shot at getting something quotable from Vigdís Finnbogadóttir.

"It is on *everyone's* mind," she said, with a lovely smile, as she allowed an aide to coax her toward the red carpet.

It wasn't a *bad* retort, but it lacked the sort of sting one might expect from the Grocer's Daughter back in Westminster. Hitchens felt he'd just been swatted with a slipper instead of taking a spike heel to the groin.

For all the nip of the rain, it was hard not to feel suspended in a warm bath of purposelessness. The mass of reporters arriving in the little news-sequestered capital would these next few days be searching futilely for the Breakthrough, the crystal of peace that might be growing in some padlocked clean room. Hitchens had a few minutes ago spotted Nicholas Daniloff, in pursuit of the same nothingness and fending off what must be the fiftieth attempt by a fellow journalist, lacking any other available quarry, to interview *him*.

The doors of Ronnie's great Argo at last opened, spilling forth the Reaganauts. Spotting Buchanan and Don Regan, Hitchens realized that there were even more Irishmen in this administration than in the lace-curtained Camelot of yore. And now, here was Shultz, bulbous and sooth-ing, as if come to town to make the world safe for technocracy. Strange to think of him as a figure who could, on occasion, *roil* things, as he had this past January, when Norman Mailer, now PEN's president—as bad a choice for the job as the Gipper was for his—had invited the secretary of state to address the scribes' big international gathering in New York. La Sontag, always more cute than lucid when angry, had been distinctly displeased to have the organization's podium offered to the top diplomat of the Sandinista-butchering administration.

Hitchens scanned the other deplaning faces as quickly as he could, recognizing one of them as Mrs. Kirkpatrick's walker from the funeral of Ancient Ave. The same fellow who was Dolan's Nordic dreamboat. He looked, at the moment, as if he'd come back to his Hyperborean home. ANDERS LITTLE: the card he'd offered inside the cathedral was still in Hitchens's wallet, and some interesting facts about him, the result of a few Tuesday phone calls, had recently come into the Hitch's possession. The writer attempted a wave, which was noticed and refused. *Touchy*, Hitchens thought, and made a mental note to follow up.

At last, Reagan; smiling, but with lower wattage than usual. Fastening the top button of his white raincoat against the Arctic autumn. Sweet: one could almost hear Nancy singing to him: *Take good care of yourself, you belong to me*. And yet, it wasn't a terribly *courteous*, pleased-to-be-here gesture, was it? Was Ronnie indeed off his genial game? He'd just shaken hands with Vigdís Finnbogadóttir, and was already moving toward his limousine. No statement? Was he playing it safe or, right at the start, cutting his losses?

Hitchens stepped onto the press bus heading to the Hotel Loftleidir, where Spokesperson Speakes would be telling them that they had just seen Ronald Reagan get off a plane. He had no intention of going there, any more than he did of attending the Soviets' countershow at the Hotel Saga, a venue to which they might think of giving a less action-packed name for the duration of the weekend. No, he would take the bus to the center of town and then hop a cab, if there was one to be had, to the sort of watering hole where he might pick up a bit of useful intelligence, or at least some lively local opinion.

Coming here had been his idea, and he *had* after all taken Charles Moore's shilling. The *Spectator*'s editor had provided a flat that was waiting for him on the Bergstadastraeti, not far from the Americans' digs. Its owner had also taken Charles's shilling and vacated the premises: in a town now woefully short of hotel rooms, the natives were making a killing.

The bus traveled its thirty miles past rocks so square-edged they appeared to have been cut by a stonemason instead of volcanic nature. By the side of the roadway one or two sloganeering bedsheets, brandished with an approximation of intensity for passing reporters, went in and out of view too quickly for anyone to read. What did they say? IRISH OUT OF ICELAND? Most of the widely spaced humanity along the route had arranged itself in small grouplets of hopeful souls holding candles. Odd, somehow: with so much of the year here lived in the dark, one would expect the population to be unfretful over even winter of a nuclear kind.

Hitchens decided to attempt a quick nap. A late night with Ms. Proctor hadn't made today's crack-of-dawn departure any easier. The last thing he saw before closing his eyes was an advertising poster, at the front of the bus, depicting an Icelandair hostess who looked agreeably like dear

Kelly. Mrs. Harriman's assistant, and Florida, seemed impossibly distant prospects at this icy moment.

In about half an hour he awoke from a semisleep, surprised by the sight of trees. He hadn't noticed their absence at the journey's start and wouldn't particularly have missed them if he had. Still, it was peculiar to see trees multiply when one *entered* a city rather than left it. More betwixt-and-between-ness, he supposed.

"Any thoughts?" yet another reporter asked the put-upon Daniloff as they all extracted their bags from the underbelly of the bus. Grabbing his own, Hitchens bid farewell to his afternoon Swedish companions and succeeded in hailing a taxi.

"What would you say is the best hotel bar?"

"Hotel Borg," said the driver. "Very close by."

"I'm in your hands."

The cab was soon passing an enormous poster for *Top Gun* and, a bit up the street from that, a large American flag that had no equal-time Soviet banner flying beside it.

"Are you all taking sides?" asked Hitchens.

The driver shook his head. "It is Leif Eriksson Day."

"I see," said Hitchens. One of America's many discovery myths: the Vikings in competition with Columbus and the mostly on-foot Asiatics for having been the first to spot Ronnie's hill, even before the Puritans had put a city and a shine upon it.

At the Borg's brass rail Hitchens spotted one fellow he recognized, a writer for the *Telegraph* he'd encountered when reporting on Sharansky in Israel. Well, it was better than someone from the *Mail*.

"*Last* year in Jerusalem," Hitchens said, by way of a greeting.

"I think it was more like June."

"I gather that Mother Sharansky has now been permitted to join her son."

"Yes," said the reporter. "But I've got news of somebody's being sprung that will top that." As if to show Hitchens he'd been doing more than drinking today, the reporter pulled out a small pad with a recent jotting. Consulting it, he muttered in frustration: "Christ, I can never pronounce these damned names. Looks like Rat's-Ass. Hang on a second." He moved the little notebook closer to the light.

"Ratushinskaya?" asked Hitchens, incredulously. She was a poet he'd heard about from Brodsky back in the States; he'd even signed a PEN petition on her behalf. But there'd been no steady drumbeat for her release from the gulag, nothing to make one predict that the Soviets would toss her over the fence with Orlov as an additional "gesture of goodwill."

"Clever one you are," said the man from the *Telegraph*, peering again at the pad. "That's the name. Thirty-two years old. Inside for more than three years. A serious Christian."

"Yes," said Hitchens. "Still, one oughtn't be *punished* for it."

"I'll tell you an offense one *ought* to be punished for," said the man, who was further into his cups than Hitchens had supposed. "*Nancyism.*"

Hitchens sighed. If he was going to be treated to some tirade against the homosexuals, his companion might as *well* be from the *Mail*.

"What I'm picking up from some of the Yanks is that Nancy wants Reagan to give away the game. To come home with an agreement like it's some new piece of jewelry for her."

"Yes," said Hitchens, only slightly relieved to have "Nancyism" revealed as a new Blimpish geopolitical term. The news about Miss Ratushinskaya was what intrigued him. It looked as if the other side needed success from these talks even more than the first lady did.

4:00 P.M. (EDT), 3032 N STREET NW, WASHINGTON, D.C.

"The 'Peerage' is here," Janet informed Mrs. Harriman with a laugh. Along with a fresh set of poll numbers, she deposited, next to her boss's cup of afternoon tea, the newest, just-arrived edition of *The Social List of Washington, D.C.*—more often known as "The Green Book," for the color of its velvety cover.

"Anyone dropped?" asked Pamela.

"I shouldn't think so," said Janet. Neither inclusion nor exclusion from this snobbish anachronism mattered very much anymore. "Unless you count the ones so senile they forgot to mail back their forms."

Pamela had actually been asking who'd suffered a drop in the *polls;* only someone like her mother would care about this fusty annual. But she let the point, and Janet, go.

Alone again in her sun-filled office, she looked at the Senate figures, which were mostly encouraging but not without some trouble spots. In Florida, she could see that Graham had slipped a few points and been downgraded to a "slight favorite" by the *Post.* Bush was campaigning there today for a Republican gubernatorial candidate with a Spanish last name, and Pamela now felt cross to think this poll might hearten him enough to lend a hand to Mrs. Hawkins while he was close by.

She put down the charts, sipped her tea, and experienced, in spite of herself, a twinge of curiosity about the Green Book. Was Ave still listed, as if alive? Or had the editors had time enough to make a gentle deletion before going to press? Pamela rubbed her thumb along the plush cover before opening to the volume's alphabetical listing. She found herself on page 199, quite alone:

HARRIMAN, Mrs. W. Averell
(Hawyard—Churchill—Pamela
   Beryl Digby)
3038 N Street 20007
338-8330
and
"Willow Oaks"
Rt. 2, Box 28
Middleburg, Va. 22117

She did wish that all her past names could fit on one line instead of two, and hoped that anyone who consulted this sclerotic production wouldn't take "Beryl" and "Digby" for two more husbands. But she was glad to see that whoever had sent in the update—the normally delinquent Kelly Proctor?—had left the home phone number in: it was *so* arriviste and self-important to keep it unlisted.

But something *was* missing, besides Ave himself. Pamela couldn't put her finger on it, so she decided to retrieve last year's edition from a shelf across the room. And there it was: *HARRIMAN, The Honorable and Mrs. W. Averell.* Ave's "Hon." was gone with him, and she couldn't escape the sudden feeling that she, too, had been stripped of it, that she was somehow, in this one small respect, sliding back toward being Madame de Maintenon, whereas in all others she had been making such strides toward becoming Mrs. Roosevelt.

Once back at her desk, in a small fit of pique and curiosity, she began browsing the new edition of this book she hadn't seriously consulted in years. Just look what its "Reminders With Regard to Protocol" had to say about widows!

> *The wife of an official always assumes the rank held by her husband, whether he is present or not. . . . Widows of former officials have no rank at all but are usually given a courtesy position. This is not obligatory, however. The only exception to this ruling is that the widow of a former President of the United States has a definite ranking in official precedence.*

Transferring her ire from the author of the passage to its subjects, Pamela thought: *Jackie and Lady Bird can go fuck themselves.* This ridiculous continuation of *precedence* in a democracy!

I am an American by choice and a Democrat by conviction. She recalled her words from the convention two years ago and decided that she believed them. According to page 14, the Administrator of the General Services Administration outranked the Chairman of the Merit Systems Protection Board but fell below the head of the Federal Aviation Administration. Rubbish! She slammed the book with another strong certainty: there wasn't a single job on all of page 14 that she would settle for. To think she'd once considered that Chief of Protocol might be a nice reward for herself! Well, she was far beyond that now. And once she delivered a Senate majority, followed by a president, she'd be further beyond it still. She knew exactly the job she wanted: ambassador to France, in which position she would bloody well be at the head table when the queen, or anyone else, passed through Paris.

The thought picked her right up, as if it were an encouraging word from Kitty. But there was work to do between this day and that delightful future—hundreds of checks to write and dozens of dinners to give—so she would just get on with it, starting with the late supper she was hosting Saturday night, not here but at Nora. The restaurant was "organic" but still chic, and she had reserved a small private dining room for three senators, none of them on this year's ballot, along with their wives. She would be furious if anyone with a seat to defend wasn't home campaigning or out raising money.

"Kelly!" She strode, heels clicking, into the adjacent room. "Have we heard from Senator Moynihan's office?"

"We haven't."

"Well, call them *again*. Or is that too much effort? This is inexcusable." She left it unclear whether Kelly's dereliction, or the senator's, was being so deemed.

"All right," said Kelly, who at the moment was engaged in a bit of personal RSVP'ing. Her typewriter held a letter addressed to Hill & Knowlton, informing the public-relations firm that she would be delighted to accept the position they had offered her with a starting date of November 3.

As she waited, Pamela was drawn to the low hum of the TV near Janet's desk. It now ran all day, tuned to CNN, PamPAC having adopted the practice that currently prevailed in all legislative offices and federal agencies, as if cable news were air conditioning or heat.

The clip of Reagan's arrival in Reykjavik was running.

"That *hat*," muttered Pamela, looking at the Icelandic president. The rain was no excuse for its broad brim, which looked like Princess Margaret's idea of high fashion. Like all women her age, Pamela had hated the clothes of the sixties—except for the death warrant that had been issued for hats. Much better to be helmeted with one's own hair. "*Higher*," Kenneth always suggested when doing hers, as if he were Balanchine coaching an elderly ballerina.

Janet came over to watch with her. On top of the television sat the third "Fact Book" that PamPAC had prepared for this year's candidates; its talking points filled a volume far thicker than the Green Book, Mrs.

Harriman noted with satisfaction. Ronald Reagan, by contrast, looked anything but satisfied—less vacant, perhaps, than usual, but even more distant, mightily preoccupied, and rather frail with this buxom Icelander instead of tiny Nancy by his side. The picture made Pamela recollect what the dreadful Mr. Hitchens had asked her, downstairs, a month and a half ago: *Would you have married him?*

Preposterous, thought Pamela—and yet, she had for so long constructed so many spousal scenarios that she now began assembling this one. Where might she and Reagan have met? In London, in the late forties? She understood he'd made a picture there then—at a time when he was, in fact, quite miserable over the breakdown of his first marriage.

No, Pamela would never have given him a second look. As it was, at that point she'd still have been gone on Ed Murrow, who—she even now liked to remind people—had no money at all. So there. But waiting fifteen years for Ronald Reagan to make something of himself in politics? And then another fifteen until he got to the White House? It would have been a dull agony, same as just waiting for Ave would have been, if she'd actually *been* waiting for him all those years, rather than simply not knowing how one day, decades later, he would fall back into her lap.

Hitchens, Pamela now thought. "Kelly, have we set something up with that awful man from *Vanity Fair*?"

Ms. Proctor, on the phone with Moynihan's office, nodded. "On Monday, the twentieth," she informed Mrs. Harriman, once she hung up. "An interview after Graham's debate with Hawkins."

Pamela sighed. "Where will the interview be?"

"At the hotel. You're staying at the Langford in Winter Park."

Janet supplied some additional information from memory: "Before the debate you've also got a dinner with Jewish leaders for Bob Graham. Mr. Hitchens can also go with you to that—see you in action."

Pamela groaned. "Why that *particular* event? Why the—" She'd almost said "Why the Jews?" which wouldn't have sounded right, but all she meant was why were they spending time with a liberal constituency that was surely already in Graham's corner?

Janet, who could tell what she was thinking, shaded the picture a bit.

"Hawkins is wildly pro-Israel. If only because Israel is a prerequisite to the Second Coming."

"These dreadful fundamentalists," said Pamela, who was relishing the thought of a big turnout for the Reverend Robertson in the '88 Republican primaries.

"Actually," said Janet, "Hawkins is a Mormon. Born in Utah. I was kidding about Judgment Day, but not by much."

Losing interest in the theological complexities, as well as in Reagan's welcoming ceremony, Pamela looked at Kelly, over at the Xerox machine. "Well, what about Moynihan?" she snapped.

"He'll be there," Kelly responded, while collating three copies of the Florida schedule: one for the boss; one for herself; and one for the man she already liked calling "Hitch."

Walking over to Mrs. Harriman, she took two keys off her plastic ring and plopped them down, along with the itinerary. She looked around to make sure she had everything and, as she exited this room for the last time, said, "Cheerio, bitch. I quit."

11:45 P.M. (RT), HOTEL HOLT, REYKJAVIK

From his window in room 304, one floor below George Shultz and the senior arms controllers, Anders Little noticed all the security down in the street. The Icelandic police, recognizable by their black-and-white-checkered hatbands, had a deferential, even nervous, appearance, as if more frightened by their heavily armed American colleagues than the prospect of any Soviet or terrorist intrusion.

Anders himself was bothered by that little red house with the corrugated tin siding right across from the hotel: it was a private dwelling, no bigger than a prospector's cabin, built in 1897 according to the proud plaque he'd passed coming in. This city might be a charming architectural hodgepodge, full of hardy little holdouts amidst the larger modern structures, but the proximity of this little red house would make it, for the Soviets, an ideal spot from which to intercept U.S. communications.

Had its owners been cleared out in advance? He assumed so—and hoped that the Americans had done the clearing.

He would be working tomorrow inside a little school near Hofdi House, the site of the talks by the water. There would be, he'd been told, desks and supplies and a fax line that was secure. Maybe *too* secure for the one document he was likely to transmit from Reykjavik? He didn't want any American eyes on whatever he sent to Nixon in New York or New Jersey. Don Regan had been blunt during a last briefing on the plane: no phone calls to anyone back home. But did a fax count as a phone call? And didn't he have tacit approval—his very presence here was proof—to serve as Nixon's eyes and ears? Moreover: What good would his service to the former president be if it wasn't rendered before the summit was over with and being autopsied in the newspapers?

Anders checked to make sure he had his badge before putting on his overcoat. Late as it was, he'd decided on a midnight stroll that would allow him to map out a running route for the next three mornings—a more broadening way to exercise than the hotel treadmill would provide.

He pushed LYFTA for the old-fashioned elevator, whose door opened outward, and then made his way to the lobby. Three Icelanders were grouped around a small television behind the front desk, absorbed not so much by coverage of the summit as by the simple fact that *anything* was being broadcast on a Thursday night—the one evening of each week when, by government fiat, everybody took an evening away from the idiot box. Such a policy would displease the more libertarian Reaganites here inside the Holt, but Anders couldn't help thinking there was something to be said for it. Before leaving the desk, he bought a postcard with an aerial view of some volcanic rocks that almost resembled the black-and-white hallway tiles back in the EOB. To whom would he send it? His parents? Anne Macmurray? (Nick Carrollton?) Would Don Regan object to outgoing *mail*?

Paintings hung everywhere in the hotel, whose owner was a great collector and an artist himself. Anders entered the first of three interlocking lounges on the first floor, this one dominated by a huge canvas depicting a weather-beaten woman at the shore. It reminded him of the Hockney show that Sarah had taken him to a few years back. He now pretended to study the portrait's enormous lined face while eavesdropping on a conversation between two arms controllers, one from the NSC and the other from State. Recognizing him, they nodded and continued talking.

"Adelman says it's a bad idea to link a reduction in nuclear tests to a reduction in ballistic-missile warheads."

"How does he know it's a bad idea?"

"He came up with it. And Reagan liked it. It went into the General Assembly speech. Sort of. Remember? The point is, the more missiles you get rid of, the more you're going to need to test new ones. Think about it."

The second man in the conversation, the one from State, said nothing as he flipped through a document on his lap. "Is this a decision memo?"

"No, it's talking points."

"But there's nothing we're supposed to talk *about* to anyone but ourselves."

"Because nothing's going to happen here, remember?"

"Yes, we're meeting to decide about the next meeting. Reaching the summit so we can see the next summit over."

The NSC man began to sing: *"We'll be there, because we're here, because we're here . . ."* Then he summoned the waiter for another round.

Anders wondered if things were the same with the Soviets tonight: figuring out how to improvise the fate of the world, or only how to defer it a little longer. He experienced a sudden sense of futility, and felt more worn out than the Icelander in the painting. He could feel a blurring of the hard line he espoused, the softening agents being human nature and sheer absurdity. Jeane Kirkpatrick would be telling him to suppress such nonsense and keep his eye on the ball. But how did he suppress the strongest, most honest feeling, however childish, that he had at the moment— that right now the fate of the world seemed less important than his own personal confusion? He remembered the line from *Casablanca*, the one about the "hill of beans," and thought that Bogart might have had things exactly backwards.

He would clear his head with the ocean-chilled air.

After waving goodbye to his colleagues, he stepped out of the hotel and set off down Bergstadastraeti with its patchwork of apartment houses and cottages. He took out his illustrated street map and headed toward Skólavördustígur, where shops began to appear, some of their windows sporting sweaters with Reagan's and Gorbachev's knitted faces. There seemed to be a bookshop every hundred feet: it was hard to argue with these televisionless Thursday nights. Starting west on Laekjargata, a name that sounded more Indonesian than Icelandic, Anders knew that the street would bring him to the harbor.

And there he saw them: two Soviet ships, on one of which Gorbachev would be staying after he got here tomorrow by air. They glowered in the lamplight, creating the impression that these visitors had invaded rather than merely arrived. If Deaver were here, still part of things, he would be pronouncing the imagery a net loss for the Russians, a small win for the U.S.

Anders turned around and walked toward a big grassy square, gently inclined and embedded with a flight of steps that led to the statue of some helmeted Viking. He looked up at the figure even as he became aware of a presence behind him. Turning around, he saw a young man in a long blue coat. Expecting to see, attached to the boy's cap, the police's black-and-white checkerboard pattern, he noticed instead a small hammer-and-sickle pin.

"S'okay," said the sailor, reassuringly. "Is cold, no?"

"Yes," said Anders.

"Smoke?" the young man asked. It was unclear to Anders whether he was offering or requesting a cigarette.

"Go someplace warmer?" the sailor now asked, his hand now touching Anders's arm in a way that the American, for a hopeless second, tried to pretend was without meaning. Then he shook the boy off and gave him a small, unambiguous shove before double-timing it up the steps to the statue. When he reached the Viking's pedestal he turned around—the sailor was calmly walking away—and wondered exactly what had just happened. A "honey trap," as the spies would put it? The thought was ridiculous: How would anyone know to set him up that way, let alone that he would be here at this moment?

Another explanation seemed less ridiculous but even more fearsome. Had he just been made the sincere offer of someone's company? Had Monday night's events somehow rendered him not just different but *apparent* to everyone? A honey trap would at least have an aspect of Cold War dignity; this other possibility made him feel sickened and crippled.

He looked up at the helmeted stone man: INGÓLFR ARNARSON, the first Icelander, from Norway, who'd decided to drop anchor here in the "bay of smokes" eleven hundred years ago. It was hard to tell if the man's shield was resting against a horse or a dragon, or just the prow of his ship, and Anders was still trying to decide what the sculptor intended when he saw an emerald flash in the sky: the aurora borealis.

The heavens were clashing with themselves, trying to bring something forth.

10:30 P.M. (CDT), ADOLPHUS HOTEL, DALLAS, TEXAS

The Adolphus was more hotel than Anne could afford, but it was the only one in Dallas whose name she could remember when she'd arrived at DFW after her impulsive journey. She had decided that she would send all the bills to her son, without embarrassment. A Saturday-night stay-over would make the plane ticket cheaper, but who knew if there'd even be any purpose to her remaining that long? She had not told Peter she was coming and had no idea what sort of welcome she would get.

She had drawn the line at room service, going out instead to a cheap Mexican restaurant. After eating, she'd wandered down Commerce Street and found herself in the only part of town that didn't seem a lip-glossy, Plexiglas embodiment of the city's namesake TV series. In this more antique-looking precinct she had experienced the sensation of being in a familiar dream, and then realized that she was in Dealey Plaza—a place she'd been, like everyone else, a thousand times before, in those horrifying snapshots and jagged home movies. She'd looked up at the Book Depository and beaten a fast retreat, remembering the Friday when her children had come home early from school, both crying, and the three of them had waited for Peter. He was already, even then, so "out there" politically that her heart stayed in her mouth over the possibility that he'd come through the door saying something awful. But he'd entered and said nothing, just shook his head, tossed the paper onto the couch, and suggested—penitentially, she thought—that they skip cocktails and sit down to dinner, which they ate in near silence.

Now, half a mile from the scene of that long-ago crime, she took off her shoes, propped herself against the enormous pillows on the hotel bed, and went back to reading *The Man Who Mistook His Wife for a Hat*. She had mistaken *it* for a novel when she purchased it before boarding the plane. She'd assumed the title to be a metaphor and only later understood that the author wasn't kidding.

What would a case history of Peter reveal? she wondered. And what had *he* taken *her* for, during their years together? A Republican cloth coat?

Unable to concentrate on Dr. Sacks's book, she put on the television and found Joan Rivers talking about how unattractive she was to Edgar. No, thank you. Two clicks of the remote brought her to Carson, who had Bob Hope on his couch:

"*Reagan is expecting some tough arms negotiations over in Iceland. In fact, his aides want him to be downright Machiavellian—if need be, to cheat and lie and fake the numbers. Good thing he's brought along his old agent!*"

Anne lowered the volume and reached into her purse for the envelope that had brought last month's mortifying alimony. Since the turquoise gallery owner left him, Peter's return address had changed, from that of a house to what now looked like an apartment. (That the woman *did* leave him, something Anne herself could never manage, had become one last reason to feel inferior toward her successor.) Did a third wife reside at this new address? That was a definite possibility, one that would make her own mission here—and what exactly *was* that?—more misguided. Surely Ralph or Susan would have told her about a third Mrs. Peter Cox? Maybe; maybe not. Her children sometimes wound up being the most hurtful when trying to be the most protective.

She couldn't stop fidgeting. She got up to get one of the postcards on the mahogany table. They all depicted the Reunion Tower, which loomed over the western part of the city like an electrified lollipop. On impulse she jotted a greeting to Jane Hazard, her old convention pal, who was still a chum. She referred to Peter by the nickname they always used for him:

Do NOT *wish you were here. That One is ailing and I've taken it upon myself to fly down. Please* DON'T *advise. I know you'd have the sense to say turn around and go straight home.*

Back on the bed, she switched the TV to CNN, and there was Ronald Reagan in his white raincoat. She scanned the clusters of staff and reporters in the president's vicinity, hoping for a glimpse of Anders, whose troubles she'd been guessing at these last few days, when she wasn't focused on her own. Failing to see him, she shut off the television once and for all.

She would go mad if she stayed in this room. And so, a few minutes later, her shoes back on, she was sitting by a potted palm off the hotel's vast lobby, waiting for a waiter, as the all-hours cocktail pianist played "Buttons and Bows," a song that had never been off the radio in Owosso during the summer of '48. The *Times Herald*, Dallas's afternoon paper, rested on a nearby chair: Reagan in his white coat again, as if he'd arrived in Reykjavik to perform surgery on the world.

No, she would go mad here, too. She got up, quickly, walked out onto Commerce Street, and got the doorman to call her a cab.

"Okay, Turtle Creek," said the driver, nodding when she showed him the address on the envelope. His radio was broadcasting items about Iceland: something about "the highest ratio of bookstores to people in the world." More memories of Owosso came Anne's way: Peter and Jack fighting over her as if she were the '48 electorate. The town had lived and breathed the campaign until the local boy managed to lose—as she had, too, voting for Harry Truman but, on the same day, picking the golden-haired, sarcastic Mr. Wrong for herself.

The driver approached a building called The Claridge, a high-rise at odds with most of Turtle Creek's horizontal luxury. The tower was so swanky, so intent on its own perfection, that it looked more like an architect's model, something being offered in competition, than an actual residence. Anne peered into the lobby from a distance of fifty or so feet and saw, as she feared, a doorman: a slender, Spanish-looking man. Should she turn back? If she had him call up from the lobby, there was every chance Peter would refuse to see her.

But she kept her nerve. Using a trick she remembered from some TV drama—*Dallas?*—she fell in step with a handsome, middle-aged couple who were arriving home. She remarked upon the weather and, just like the man and wife, smiled at the doorman—letting him think she was the couple's guest, letting the couple think she was another resident of the building.

She took the elevator to the seventh floor, walking the hallway's thick carpet and passing its dimly lit sconces, until she came to 726, the apartment number on the envelope. She pressed the button on the door, which made an electronic sound not at all like a bell or a buzz. She pushed it three times without an answer. Had Peter gone to the hospital? Suddenly died? Just fallen asleep?

On the verge of fleeing, Anne at last thought she could hear, from somewhere well within the apartment, a heavy sliding door. She realized, from the sound of shuffling feet, that Peter was coming in from one of the balconies that ran up and down the building. All at once, without asking who was there, he was opening the apartment's front door, as if whatever harm might be on its other side could not compete with—or might put an end to—the disease that was killing him from within. She was still wondering what she would say—*Trick or Pete?*—when she saw his face.

Standing in a silk bathrobe—his skin yellow with sickness, an eerie still-golden strand of hair catching the light amidst the rest of the thinning gray—he was unable, for once, to fake nonchalance.

"Jesus Christ," Peter said. "Why *you?*"

He had a point. Why indeed her? Why not Ralph or Susan or the turquoise wife?

Because he was the father of her children; her husband for nearly twenty years; the poorly chosen love of her life.

"Because," she answered, "the buck stops here."

14

FRIDAY, OCTOBER 10, 1986

11:15 A.M. (RT), BRITISH AMBASSADOR'S RESIDENCE, 31 LAUFÁSVEGUR, REYKJAVIK

"I hope they don't serve us stewed tomatoes," said Pat Buchanan, with an Anglophobic laugh, as he sat down at the British ambassador's dining room table. Don Regan's staying here seemed to indicate that the president's chief of staff enjoyed a loftier status than his secretary of state, who was with the arms controllers at the Holt, a minute's walk away. Holding the regular staff meeting here seemed designed to rub it in.

Although his role as Richard Nixon's observer now seemed known to several people besides Admiral Poindexter and Buchanan, Anders Little would be the official NSC notetaker during this late breakfast. Buchanan had sat down on Anders's left, no doubt hoping the younger man would be livelier company than he'd been on the plane.

Regan walked into the dining room wearing not one of his Merrill Lynch pinstripe suits but a heavy white fisherman's sweater.

"He gets to go fish and *we* get to cut bait," Buchanan whispered to Anders.

Regan in fact intended to spend this day before the summit on the higher ground outside the city, revisiting the antiaircraft machine-gun emplacements his Marine outfit had once helped to build. One of Iceland's former prime ministers would be taking him around in a jeep—a far cry from the helicopters he'd developed a taste for back home.

Regan began the daily operations rundown in the same crisp manner he used in Washington: "The president will be talking by phone to

Speaker O'Neill today. He'll be urging the House to drop its nuclear-test-ban proposal and its insistence on SALT II compliance, so that he can have a free hand dealing with the general secretary tomorrow. The price for this is likely to be a small, temporary cut in SDI spending, but no more than that. So if that's the bone he has to throw Mr. O'Neill, he'll do it. But if the Democrats want to ask for more—and then look as if they're undermining the president while he's out of the country negotiating with our chief adversary—they're free to do that."

No one around the table commented. By temperament and conviction every man in the room was disinclined to take Congress seriously when it came to the making of foreign and defense policy.

"Moving on to domestic affairs for a moment," said Regan. "The majority leader is trying to get the Senate adjourned so that everybody can go home and campaign straight through Election Day. But he says he's not going to let them leave until they pass the first lady's drug bill. Well, it isn't *going* to pass if he doesn't remove its death-penalty provision. So good luck to him. We'll see if Mrs. Reagan gets what she wants."

Anders noted how the chief of staff made this legislation seem another of the first lady's extravagances, like the set of White House china she'd acquired, along with much disastrous publicity, back during the recession. Regan also seemed unsympathetic to Senator Dole's impatience over the drawn-out congressional session: "You know, our guys may want an adjournment, but once they get it, the other guys get to go home and campaign too. It's a zero-sum game, so I think the majority leader ought to relax."

Buchanan smiled. "It's not a zero-sum game if we've got more endangered incumbents than they've got. And we do. Those guys need to get out of Washington and go save their seats."

Regan ignored the objection. "Speakes is doing the morning shows right about now. The news blackout on the summit remains in effect, so he'll stick to local color and high hopes. But you should be aware of how we're being needled back home. Congressman Dicks"—he gave a schoolboy's emphasis to the Democrat's unfortunate surname—"just said, and

I quote, 'The president won't have anything to blame except divisions within his own administration if he doesn't achieve something out of the summit this weekend.' If you're provoked by the press, remember that there are *no* divisions within this administration. The president *is* the administration, and everybody else is an advisor, including the secretary of state."

"Ouch," said Buchanan, with his whinnying laugh. He leaned over to Anders and whispered, "The sound you just heard is a towel snapping against Shultz's tiger-tattooed behind."

Anders wondered what latest injury to Regan's *amour-propre* had made him offer the remark. Was he afraid that Shultz's relationship with the first lady—as excellent as Regan's was disastrous—would make the secretary of state overly susceptible to her supposed avidity for an agreement? Should any of this find its way into his report to Nixon?

"Is Shultz with the president right now?" Anders whispered to Buchanan.

"No, he's doing the *Today* show."

"On Central America," said Regan, raising his voice a bit, "Elliott Abrams reports that our people in Managua are not being permitted to talk to Hasenfus, the captured flyer. So we're trying to apply a little additional pressure. And the vice president's office is explaining to the press that this Max Gomez connection they're trying to exploit is way overblown. Bush isn't running these supply missions—*no one* here is. We've taken great care to see to that."

What exactly did that mean? That they'd been covering their tracks? Anders looked over at Poindexter, who puffed quietly on his pipe.

"Sam Nunn," continued Regan, "says that the Senate Select Committee on Intelligence will be investigating what you've all been seeing in the papers." Regan spoke as if this wouldn't be any particular problem; Nunn was more conservative on defense than some of his Republican colleagues.

Even so, having recovered some of his equanimity during an early-morning run to the Viking statue—ten times up and ten times down the steps—Anders felt his spirits sink. He wondered whether, thanks to

Spitz Channell, he himself had what a lawyer would call "vulnerability" in such an investigation.

Did he *need* a lawyer?

Lost in this thought, Anders missed hearing the last of Regan's updates and reminders. The meeting had begun to break up, its participants ready to head back to the Holt or over to the American embassy, or to the little schoolhouse near the site of tomorrow's talks. Regan's smile indicated to those departing that the rest of his own day would contain more fun than theirs.

"It must be nice to control the schedule," said one of the mice.

"You being funny?" snapped Regan, who'd overheard them.

"No, sir," said each of the aides.

"While we're on the subject of the schedule," Regan added, "we have to be out of here before night falls on Sunday. And, as you know, it falls pretty early."

"What's the urgency?" someone asked.

"Yom Kippur," explained Regan. "As it is, we're shaving things so close that a couple of Jewish reporters declined to make the trip. Dan Schorr for one."

"Good!" said Buchanan, whose memories of Watergate always combined fresh resentment with nostalgic delight. He earned a verbal swat from Regan. "We don't need some mini-Bitburg," said the chief of staff, referring to last year's debacle over the president's visit to a German cemetery where SS officers were enjoying an honored rest.

Regan and Buchanan, each worried he'd been abrupt toward the other, exited with a visible bonhomie. Anders followed behind them, remembering that Regan had been the man to bring Buchanan back into government, and that Buchanan hoped to get the NATO ambassadorship before the administration was through.

"That goddamned woman," Regan muttered, as an explanation for his crossness. "You want to know the real reason we've got to get out of here as early as we can on Sunday? Because *he* can't stand to be away from her for a fourth night in a row. He promised Mommy he'd make it home for dinner!"

Buchanan roared with laughter. The chief of staff was not amused.

7:35 A.M. (EDT), HOME OFFICE OF JIMMY CARTER, PLAINS, GEORGIA

With the television muted for a commercial break, Jimmy Carter regarded, with some impatience, a few souvenirs of his postpresidential travels: the little drum from Korea; the decorative roof tile from Costa Rica. Or did he have these backwards? He supposed that both objects would soon be joined by something from Bangladesh, which he'd be traveling to on November 1. The trip was blocked out on the pages of a calendar that now reserved early December for Haiti and Honduras. Before any of those journeys he would be hosting foes of the guinea worm and advocates for human rights here in Atlanta at the Carter Center; and he'd be hammering together a couple of Habitat for Humanity houses on the South Side of Chicago.

Absent from the calendar's October page were any campaign stops, not even one in support of Wyche Fowler, the Democrats' Senate candidate here in Georgia. No one anywhere had asked him to come in on their behalf, no matter that Reagan, whenever *he* was out on the stump this fall, sounded as if he were still running against Jimmy Carter, six years after the fact. The Republicans would be pretending he was the opposing candidate for another thirty years, the way the Democrats had with Hoover.

"I'm tired of making these phone calls," said Rosalynn, as soon as she entered the study. "You do it this morning." She left as quickly as she'd come in.

He knew what she wanted—that he call Amy up at Brown to make sure she would be attending classes today. His daughter was in danger of flunking out, a difficult feat at an institution where all the courses could be taken pass/fail. But he was proud of her nonetheless, living in that vegetarian co-op and getting herself arrested in protests against campus recruitment by the CIA.

Amy's activities, no matter how people mocked them, were further establishing *him*, in their minds, as a man of the left. He'd never been that, not while in office and no matter how much Reagan tried painting him as such. But more and more he was coming to realize that being remembered as an idealist, a visionary, was better than being recalled as just a failure, an incompetent who cowered inside a cardigan sweater. He'd won the presidency by pulling his party away from left-wing McGovernism; maybe he could salvage his *ex*-presidency by pitching his tent farther out on the quixotic fringes than McGovern had ever been.

He turned the sound back up once the TV began showing a long shot of the Reykjavik harbor with the Soviet ship on which the Gorbachevs would be staying. Looking at it, he affirmed to himself once again that he had been right to sell the *Sequoia*, the presidential yacht on whose piano Nixon liked to bang out "God Bless America" in mad, solitary moments, all at the taxpayers' expense. It had made sense to do this, just as it had for him to cancel all those water projects that O'Neill and so many others on the Hill had cherished. "Stop making people feel bad about themselves!" Tip had barked. "Bad?" he'd asked, sincerely perplexed. "*Dirty*," the speaker had explained. "As if they're supposed to be ashamed of spreading a little money around their districts."

The TV picture of the boat gave way to one of Reagan's press secretary, who was now talking to CBS from his Icelandic hotel: "The president is upbeat approaching the summit because he believes that possibilities exist for real progress to be made."

Never mind the progress *he* had made! And never mind that Reagan was set to dismantle what remained of it. The Senate might not have ratified SALT II, but Jimmy Carter had signed it and the country had abided by it. Now Reagan wanted it scrapped so that he could launch his Star Wars chimera.

The former president leaned back in his leatherette armchair and examined his conscience, as he made himself do three or four times a day. Did he, in his heart, that telltale organ wherein he sometimes lusted, truly fear the destabilizing effect of Star Wars, or was his real worry that, over in Iceland, Reagan might, against all expectations, wave some other magic light stick and produce peace with the Soviets? No, he decided, after closing his eyes for a contemplative moment, it *was* the former, the destabilizing effect, that truly bothered him, though in order to be sure of this he would reexamine his scruples, and pray for his own sincerity, sometime later this morning.

The CBS host was now asking Larry Speakes about the deal the administration hoped to work out with the House. "The president will be talking with Speaker O'Neill," said the press secretary, declining to give further detail.

Carter realized, rather suddenly, that failure to reach such an agreement could pose a significant last-minute problem for his successor. Should he himself make a few calls to the Hill—maybe even to Tip—to warn whomever he reached against backing off the test ban or allowing Reagan to ignore SALT II?

His spirit weakened at the thought of calling O'Neill. Tip had never wanted him as president; he'd been waiting for Teddy to run in '76. And when Teddy *did* run four years later, challenging a sitting president from his own party, the best that Tip could manage was to remain "neutral." And yet: surely Tip couldn't be happy with the idea of letting Reagan play fast and loose with the Russians. The whole myth of how the current president became the speaker's buddy whenever it was cocktail time or the chips were really down was just that, a pint of public-relations malarkey for both of them. When it came to foreign policy, O'Neill was way to the left of Jimmy Carter, let alone Reagan—thanks, it was said, to the enduring influence of an aunt, that Maryknoll nun. Carter had met her.

All at once he had an idea. He switched to the little swivel chair in front of his Kaypro computer. He reached into the file box and found the floppy disk for "Political Leaders—Relatives and Associates." After inserting it, he scrolled downward to Tip's name. A few keystrokes brought him to TOLAN, SISTER EUNICE ("ANNIE"). He pouted over an aide's electronic update—*Deceased 1981*—but then saw another annotation: *Met her with Sister Marian Pahl.* Yes, he remembered her, too, a second Maryknoll sister, the one who wrote letters all the time, to Tip and to him, about American overreachings in Central America.

He dialed the Carter Center in Atlanta and got the aide who kept these files up to date and faithfully observed—it was only 7:40 a.m.—

the same farmer's hours Carter always did. "Please locate Sister Marian Pahl—P-A-H-L—and call me back."

Within minutes he had the latest information on Sister Marian: she'd returned to the United States from Mexico in 1985 and was now at Maryknoll headquarters in Ossining, New York. The aide also supplied her phone number.

"Good morning, Sister Marian," said Carter, as soon as she answered her office phone. Apparently she, too, had a farmer's respect for the early morning. "I was just thinking of you and our meeting while I looked at my upcoming calendar," he said. "We have a number of Central American delegations that will soon be coming to the Carter Center to discuss the problems in Nicaragua and El Salvador."

"Oh, my goodness!" said Sister Marian.

"It's such an important part of the world. And yet, what happens there depends to some extent on what happens in Iceland this weekend. If President Reagan is allowed to operate without restraint in Reykjavik, it will only increase his recklessness in Managua and San Salvador."

"That's right," said Sister Marian, who impressed her unexpected caller by going on to acknowledge, quite specifically, what the papers and TV were saying the president would have to work out with Speaker O'Neill today.

"And that's why," said Carter, "I was wondering if this morning you might think of making a call to Sister Annie's famous nephew."

A sudden movement on the TV screen attracted his eye: a clip of Reagan, waving, from the garden of the American embassy in Reykjavik.

Was it more of a sin to make people feel dirty, or to make them feel unduly clean and shiny?

"I would be honored!" said Sister Marian.

2:35 P.M. (RT), DOCKING AREA NEAR THE *BALTIKA* AND THE *GEORGE OTS*

Hitchens got up from the bar at the Hotel Borg, where he'd read the London papers flown in this morning. Mrs. Thatcher would be speaking today at the Conservative Party conference in Bournemouth and was expected to attack Labour for promoting unilateral disarmament. But was her real worry the bilateral disarming that seemed to be in the nippy air of Reykjavik? Should she get wind of a wavering Ronnie, would she come bearing down upon Iceland as if it were the Falklands?

Exiting the hotel, Hitchens commenced a short walk to the harbor. Cold as it was, he would rather be at Reykjavik's shoreline than Bournemouth's, dotted as that one would be with Tory MPs in a rutting, holiday mood. He made it to the piers minutes before Gorbachev's motorcade completed its trip from the airport. Taking up position near a small group of demonstrators, Hitchens gave them a tiny encouraging nod instead of the big American thumbs-up they were used to. Then two Israelis proudly introduced themselves as the ones who'd just succeeded in disrupting a Soviet press briefing at the Hotel Saga. With greater interest, Hitchens observed several figures protesting U.S. policy in Nicaragua. Alas, presenting such a viewpoint to the Russians, knowing they could be counted upon as a sympathetic or collusive ear, seemed rather to substantiate La Kirkpatrick's point that the Sandinistas were a Soviet cat's-paw.

A string of cars approached, dominated by Gorbachev's personal ZiL, flown in like the London papers. No Vigdís Finnbogadóttir was on hand, however, for a greeting. Nor had she been at the airport: the Icelandic parliament, requiring her presence, was in session and sticking to its schedule—a plucky touch of independence and self-esteem.

Gorbachev emerged from his car to a smattering of applause, right as Hitchens felt a slithering movement against his lower left leg: a friendly black-and-white cat, one of the many felines he'd seen prowling the streets late last night, as if Reykjavik were a refrigerated Rome. Gazing down at the creature, he said, reassuringly: "A cat may look at a general secretary."

Having already spoken at the airport, Gorbachev used this moment to give only a brief, on-message reminder of Soviet generosity—their one-sided decision to suspend nuclear testing and general willingness to think big: "We are prepared to look for solutions to the burning problems which concern people all over the world and to reach the goal which we in the Soviet Union have set for ourselves—that is, the final elimination of nuclear weapons by the year 2000."

It sounded like reverse-Armageddon, the mushroom cloud shrinking to a toadstool as Gorby reached his eighth decade and Reagan got ready to crack ninety. And yet, for all this millenarianism, the general secretary's manner seemed that of an American businessman. Indeed, he resembled the breed rather more than raincoated Ron had yesterday on the tarmac, though Hitchens would admit he wasn't now close enough to observe whether Gorbachev's suit showed any improvement over the boxy cut always sported by yesteryear's apparatchiks.

The general secretary began introducing the current crop of those to the Reykjavik city fathers on hand. Almost all the Soviets still wore fedoras, and Hitchens noticed only one or two pieces of military headgear. Had the brass been left at home in order to assure more peaceful imagery here—or had they stayed behind because they were busy plotting a coup? How much leeway did Gorbachev really have? What did he need to deliver to his army if he wanted to keep *perestroika* perking along and not take up residence in one of the cells just vacated by Orlov and Ratushinskaya? According to the boys at the Borg, the *Baltika* now floating behind the leader had carried Khrushchev around the world and ferried Soviet soldiers home from Cuba after the '62 contretemps. Had the military selected it for this trip as a little *memento mori*?

It was Raisa's turn to step front and center, in a hat that looked like a pillbox struggling to become a turban: half Jackie, half Edith Sitwell. She offered a box of chocolates to a wary Icelandic lad nudged forward to greet her. If the fairy-tale pronunciation of "Vigdís Finnbogadóttir" might conjure instant world peace, rolling out the syllables of "Raisa Maximovna Gorbacheva" seemed likely to summon an armada of the Furies. This doctor of sociology informed the assembled press that over the next thirty-six hours she would be visiting parliament, a museum, and a junior high school, while taking a keen interest in the general secretary's negotiations. Inevitably, one scribe asked her about Nancy's absence. "There must be a cause for her not coming," replied RMG.

"Maybe she isn't well. Or maybe she had something else to do."

"Meow," said Hitchens to the cat still at his feet.

10:40 A.M. (EDT), JOHN HOWARD PAVILION, ST. ELIZABETHS HOSPITAL, WASHINGTON, D.C.

Donahue was not the typical morning TV choice here in the patients' lounge of the Forensic Unit. But a new, very serious young doctor had made today's selection after pretending to consult with the residents. No one—in fact, not even he—was looking up at the television.

John W. Hinckley, Jr., had been elected president of his elementary school class in two separate years, and he had some seniority here at St. Elizabeths, but he refused to participate in any of these occasional sham exercises designed to build "leadership skills" and democratic values among the patients. The place remained a totalitarian state; the concrete wall surrounding it, more than three times Hinckley's own height, was even more visible than usual through the barred windows now that the magnolia trees were losing a few of their leaves. This morning Hinckley's irritability had been further heightened by the unmistakable smell of a McDonald's Happy Meal, brought to the young doctor by some brown-nosing resident from one of the noncriminal wards, somebody allowed to walk around the neighborhood on a two-hour pass.

Such a pass had become the assassin's own near-term goal and the object of his latest letter to the court. While Donahue kept telling a single mother how great she was doing, Hinckley continued revising his personal progress report to Judge Parker, who had the same name as a comic strip that ran in the *Washington Post*. From time to time Hinckley had to remind himself that the two Parkers were not the same man. And yet, he would not be entering a new phase of his life, one he'd been promised would start today, were he not the sort of person who could, with a little effort, maintain such distinctions.

Donahue had reached a commercial break, and the station was previewing its noontime news show. Reagan and Gorbachev still wouldn't meet until tomorrow, but the channel was split-screening their separate arrival photos: Gorbachev wearing black, Reagan white. Hinckley looked up with mild interest, thinking that—if the picture stayed onscreen for a few seconds more—he might begin to see the white coat turn red, from blood spilling out of a small hole near Reagan's lung.

The Iceland negotiations had nothing on the ones that had been going on here for months. Washington, D.C., was about to take control of the hospital from the federal government, which would put the black patients, who already had the numbers, even more firmly on top, since Marion Barry, and not Reagan, would become the head man.

But the real number to focus on, the one to which Hinckley paid attention whenever he heard the administrators and nurses talking amongst themselves, was 800. That was the number of patients—half of everybody here—who'd have to be let go within the next several years. *Deinstitutionalization:* it was a word he could spell correctly if he broke it down into syllables, the way he had long ago managed to spell "*anti-disestablishmentarianism*," a feat that had played a part in his election to those two class presidencies. The administrators here said that deinstitutionalization wasn't *their* idea; they were up against the lawyers and psychiatrists who argued that the 800 could survive on the outside if they got the right drugs. The nurses would shake their heads and talk about how on the way to work they were *already* tripping over all the disturbed people living on the street amongst crack addicts. No matter: Hinckley was determined to be among the 800.

Leslie, now that she was a secretary here instead of a patient, had her own opinions about deinstitutionalization. She was moderately against it, which Hinckley found personally insulting and definitely illogical, since she'd been released after spending time here for killing her daughter and then blowing off her own arm with a shotgun.

She remained, on paper, his girlfriend. Judge Parker liked stability, and their relationship probably looked healthy to him. But the more cautiously Leslie talks and behaves, the more his desire for her fades. He has recently been nostalgic for Penny, who once wrote him with an offer to kill Jodie. He'd like to be back in touch with *her*, but contact with Penny will not make him day-pass material, or one of the 800.

Distracted now by the sound of approaching footsteps, he looked up from the letter to Judge Parker and saw Dr. Miller standing in front of him. The doctor was holding a clipboard and two plastic prescription bottles, and he was smiling. His expression, in fact, resembled the one Donahue used with the single mother.

"These are two mild sedatives, John," said Dr. Miller. "No more Haldol and no more chlorpromazine."

It was official. What had been promised was happening. He was being taken off antipsychotics.

"If all goes well," said Dr. Miller, "at some point down the line we'll start talking about day release."

Hinckley nodded.

"If we feel that it will test the skills you've learned in here, and provide a boost to your confidence, we'll support it," said Dr. Miller. "What we want is to increase your self-esteem," he added, as if that quality, like the drugs, could be measured in milligrams.

Dr. Miller shook hands with him. Hinckley nodded and thought: *I do not even require the medications that the 800 will need.*

He looked at two patients playing Ping-Pong in a corner of the big room. Back and forth, back and forth went their volley, which ultimately went nowhere. His own situation was not like that at all. It involved, as he resumed writing to Judge Parker, nothing but progress.

4:30 P.M. (RT), BESSASTADIR, THE RESIDENCE OF ICELAND'S PRESIDENT, OUTSIDE REYKJAVIK

"I appreciate the tour, Madame President!" said Ronald Reagan.

The "tour" was really a three-minute circling of the lawn, a fast photo op before Vigdís Finnbogadóttir's champagne reception for her American counterpart.

"Please call me Vigdís. We are very informal here in Iceland."

Reagan cocked his head and blushed, as if not sure that he could allow himself such a liberty.

President Finnbogadóttir was wearing a short, bright-red coat; light and unbuttoned, it was really just a cape. Reagan, having expected much colder weather, was attired in a heavy trench coat belted at the waist. An enormous brown fur collar ran all the way down its long lapels. He looked, thought Vigdís, as if he'd been draped with a funeral wreath.

"What an extraordinary coat," she said.

Reagan lit up, taking the remark for a compliment. He waved to the photographers, and Vigdís followed suit, directing her gaze at Nicholas Daniloff, to whom Don Regan had earlier introduced her. The cameras kept clicking while she and the president resumed their private conversation a little farther down the lawn. She realized that he had no memory of meeting her in Washington in 1982, though he'd even made a toast to her presence then. True, she'd been among a whole host of Scandinavian officials. Would it be rude to remind him of the occasion?

"You've had a busy day," he observed. The flap over parliament's being in session during Gorbachev's arrival had gotten a lot of play.

She laughed. "We were doing only routine business, but there is no rescheduling the Althing."

"I was just riding herd on *my* parliament, over the phone." Reagan winked at her.

"I wish you had time to see more while you are here, Mr. President. Your Mr. Regan was just telling me about *his* sightseeing!" She pointed to the higher ground outside the capital.

"Oh, yes," said Reagan, rather gravely. "Those old machine-gun emplacements. Antiaircraft guns; very long ones."

Vigdís nodded.

"That's why SDI is so important," said the U.S. president, startling her. "Imagine how much more effective *it* would be as a defensive weapon than those 90-millimeter guns. You know, Madame President, we don't have a War Department in the United States. We have a Department of Defense, and the way I see it, defense is the moral part of war. It's the harder part, too. Just about anyone can throw a javelin. But who can *catch* one without getting hurt?"

Vigdís, nodding, was nonplussed.

"I shouldn't be getting into all that with you," said Reagan. It was unclear if he thought it inappropriate to be advocating such a position with the host of the talks or if he'd decided not to bother her pretty head with such matters. Vigdís's expression couldn't conceal disappointment— not with his courtliness but with his apparent hard line. Would every- thing at Hofdi House revolve around his Star Wars?

Politely proceeding with a change of subject, Reagan declared, "They've told me about all the theater you've done."

Vigdís laughed. "Only as a producer and manager. I am scared to be on the stage myself. But yes, I have helped to put on many plays, espe- cially French ones. I also introduced them, on camera, in a television series. Quite a while back."

"No fooling!" said Reagan, with delight. "*General Geothermal Theater*," he remarked, looking toward the distant landscape.

Vigdís didn't get the joke, but she smiled.

"I never liked being onstage myself," said Reagan. "Never even liked going live on TV. After-the-fact always suited me best." He started to tell her about how, fifty years ago, while working as an announcer for WHO, he would reenact baseball games, from wire copy, as *if* they were live.

"Why the preference for delay?" asked Vigdís, gently interrupting him. "Less danger of mistakes?"

"Maybe," said Reagan, with a smile. "Or maybe things just seem a little more real once they're in the past. Some of the pictures I did felt pretty silly while I was making them, but six months later I'd see them onscreen and they'd look almost important! I guess you never know the real meaning or real effect of something at the moment it's going on." He pointed to the already fading sun. "That light we're seeing is really eight and a half minutes old. That's how long it took to get to us."

Vigdís was already thinking that she'd never be able to tell her friends what he was like. He seemed all at once very close and far away; rather silly and a little mystical. Like the canvas-and-fur coat, he was composed of two elements that seemed to alternate but never add up. She could hear herself telling those friends that he might be the most deeply shallow man she'd ever met. It would not be a witticism, and she would mean it, she thought, more as a compliment than criticism.

She realized she'd gotten lost in thought and that, having made their circuit, they were no more than fifty feet from the edges of the reception. She had to say something. "I hope that everything inside Hofdi House will be satisfactory to you and to General Secretary Gorbachev. We have tried to think of everything in the last two weeks."

"They tell me the place is haunted!"

She laughed. She knew the stories that had been told by a British ambassador from just after the war: the nighttime crashes; the wine bottles sailing through the air. She smiled reassuringly. "I don't believe that it is haunted, Mr. President."

Reagan responded with an expression of gentle sadness. "Maybe not *yet*, Vigdís."

3:00 P.M. (EDT), EAST WING, THE WHITE HOUSE, WASHINGTON, D.C.

"Lose the coat!" ordered Nancy Reagan, on the phone to Reykjavik.

"Yes, ma'am," replied Jim Kuhn, one of her husband's executive assistants.

"It's *awful*," said the first lady. "He must have packed it himself! It predates *me*."

"Yes, ma'am," said Kuhn, wary of further response. Agreeing that that was a very long time ago might suggest Mrs. Reagan's own antiquity; but a gentlemanly protest—saying that that didn't make the coat all *that* old—would acknowledge that Mrs. Reagan hadn't entered the president's adult life at its dawn.

"Lose it *literally*, if you need to."

She hung the phone up rather hard. She'd been rattled by that Russian dame, whose comments had just come over the television: *Maybe she had something else to do.* And then the pictures of Ronnie in that coat! It looked like something he'd been given by Francis X. Bushman.

She again picked up the phone and this time asked for Elaine Crispen, her press secretary. "What are the arrangements for tomorrow?" the first lady wanted to know. She'd be getting that medal for Just Say No from Catholic University.

"No availability," said Elaine. "The press will just report the podium and they'll have the text of the speech in advance."

"Give me a couple of minutes with a few reporters beforehand. I've got to respond to her with *something*. I don't even know if I can wait that long."

"Let's wait at least until then," said Mrs. Crispen. "We don't want it to look as if you're overreacting."

"Elaine, how long have you been in this job? Overreacting is what I *do*."

As soon as she put down the phone, Nancy picked it back up and asked the operator to get Bob Dole.

"Sorry, Mrs. Reagan," said the majority leader, knowing she was calling about the drug bill. "It's still bottled up."

"Is the death penalty the problem?" asked Nancy.

"Yes. And I've got a dozen people here who are going to impose it on *me* if I don't let them go home and campaign soon."

She was never much in the mood for his quips. She responded with silence.

Dole at last elaborated: "Biden and a few of the others aren't going to budge."

The first lady tightened her grip on the phone and thought about pulling out the Delaware senator's hair plugs, one by one, as excruciatingly as she could. "I don't like the Senate bill at all," she said. "The Democratic House gives me six billion dollars and the death penalty. The *Republican* Senate gives me only 1.8 billion and a lot of hand-wringing."

Dole offered her an explanation she scarcely needed: "If I had as many conservative Democrats over here as they've got in the House, we'd get somewhere. But I don't. Fact remains: the House will *accept* a version of the bill without the death penalty; the Senate *won't* accept one with it."

"A death penalty for drug-related *murders*," she reminded the majority leader.

"I'm trying to arrange a fielder's choice, Mrs. Reagan. Even if I can get a bill out of here, the House-Senate conference is going to be a lulu."

Again she replied with silence, this time because she was thinking.

Ronnie had once, as governor, nobly stayed the execution of a brain-damaged man. On the other hand, thanks to the California Supreme Court, Charles Manson also remained disgracefully alive.

"Who loses the most if the Senate bill doesn't pass? Them or us?" she asked.

"With no bill the Senate looks like a do-nothing outfit," said Dole. "And that hurts us more, because we still control the place."

Nancy took one more pause, a brief one, during which she thought about Paula Hawkins. "Okay," she said. "Kill it."

"Kill the bill?" asked Dole.

"No, kill the death-penalty provision. Drop it." Her mind was already jumping from Florida to Iceland. *If killing SDI is what it takes for a deal in Reykjavik, Ronnie needs to do it.*

"Okay," said Dole. "Stay tuned."

"I will," said Nancy, with what she judged to be a healthy hint of menace. "Say hi to Sug—" she added, catching herself before completing the word "Sugarlips," the name everyone here used for Dole's Southern wife. "Say hello to Elizabeth."

She wondered, as she hung up but kept her hand on the receiver, what was going on in the House—not with the drug bill but in the standoff over nuclear testing and SALT. She could have someone call down to Don Regan's mice for an update, but half of them were in Reykjavik. If Mike were still here, he would already have gotten her word of any afternoon developments.

Where *was* Mike? No one had heard a word from him in weeks.

She felt unusually edgy. Maybe she shouldn't have let Joan pick such an early departure time. This extra day over in Iceland, before anything got started, was driving her crazy. She kept thinking about these "prayers" that Ronnie had requested of Maureen: Would they interfere, like some sort of radio jamming, with Joan's own celestial manipulations?

She walked upstairs from her office to the Residence, and by the time she arrived a phone message was already waiting. "Mrs. Hart" was "calling at the suggestion of Mr. Griffin."

Gary Hart's long-suffering (from what she'd heard) wife? Trying to muscle in on the drug bill in advance of his next presidential campaign?

Better to be safe than sorry: Nancy dialed the operator downstairs and allowed her to return the call.

"*Nothing* could make me bother you except a one-two punch from Merv and Marvin Hamlisch!" said the delightful, solicitous voice that came on the line. Nancy recognized it at once as belonging to Kitty Carlisle—Mrs. Moss Hart—though she'd met her only once or twice.

"Kitty!" she said, with the same giggle she'd have given Merv himself.

"I'll come right to the point," said Mrs. Hart. "Merv and Marvin asked me to sing 'Love Is Here to Stay' at the Gershwin event. I said 'Oh, no!' and suggested they give that one to Sarah Vaughan, and then they had an even better idea."

"Oh?" asked Nancy.

"Yes. That *you* sing it—to the president, in the front row."

"Oh," said Nancy, immediately sensing a dozen things that could go wrong with that.

"Merv told me: 'If she hesitates, just say "Second-Hand Clothes." ' "

Nancy laughed. Merv wanted to remind her of the hit she'd made at the Gridiron dinner several years back, sending up her spendthrift image with a parody of the old Fanny Brice song.

"Let me sleep on it, Kitty." As if she ever slept! "I'll let you or Merv know."

"I'll be crossing my fingers," said Mrs. Hart. "I'm so looking forward to the twenty-sixth."

"We're looking forward to it, too."

Merv would of course be staying at the Willard, but Nancy now realized she hadn't thought to ask if anyone else connected to the Gershwin program would like to stay at the White House—assuming they could get Maureen out of the Lincoln Bedroom for a night.

As if intuiting the first lady's thoughts, Mrs. Hart said, "I'll be staying with Pam Harriman in Georgetown. When she's in New York, she always 'crashes' with me, as my son would say."

"We've never met," said Nancy, who didn't feel one could count a single receiving-line moment—at the British embassy, when Maggie Thatcher had been here between the first inaugural and the shooting.

"Oh, you two should get to know each other!" exclaimed Mrs. Hart.

"Let me think about that, too," said Nancy, with another giggle, as "Second-Hand Rose" played in her head.

7:10 P.M. (RT), HOTEL LOFTLEIDIR AND HOFDI HOUSE, REYKJAVIK

Larry Speakes was finishing his statement to a roomful of underemployed reporters: "The congressional leadership has responded to the president in a bipartisan spirit. He is grateful for the show of unity. Broad, deep, equitable, and verifiable reductions in offensive arms remain our highest priority."

A woman from the *Washington Post* said to a man from the *Los Angeles Times:* "I hear one of Tip's nuns made a run at him this morning, but that it didn't work. He doesn't want the Democrats to look obstinate. Even *he's* less focused on the House than on taking back the Senate."

The man from the *Telegraph,* who'd noted Speakes's deliberate reference to "reductions in *offensive* arms," snorted. "The Democrats just figure they'll have a better time crucifying Reagan on Monday if they look 'big' about things now."

Don Regan, standing nearby and thinking more or less the same thing, had changed back into his fisherman's sweater after the Icelandic president's champagne reception. His tour guide and new pal, Geir Hall-grímsson, the ex–prime minister, remained with him.

"I'm on my way to Hofdi House with a fellow from the mayor's office," said Regan. "I'm going to check on the setup. Want to come along?"

The three men were soon driving along Faxa Bay, a mile or so from the moored Soviet ships. Two chimneys, rising from a genial-looking white frame house, came into view. Waved through the cordon, the men mounted the house's front steps and entered. The mayor's man directed their attention to the official poster celebrating the summit; he smiled sheepishly at Regan, pointing to the dates "October 10–12," which in the manner of a concert advertisement were not followed by the year. "Haste makes waste," he said in his good idiomatic English. "The proofreader noticed it too late."

Leading them upstairs, he explained that Hofdi House, a handsome dwelling with several spacious rooms on each of its three floors, had actually been purchased and assembled, early in the century, from a Norwegian catalogue.

"Christ," said Regan. "Like the one Nixon's old man got from Montgomery Ward, or wherever the hell it was."

Regan said hello to a group of Secret Service who ushered the three men into the largest second-floor room, one dominated by three big windows and a crystal chandelier. It was here that tomorrow's meetings would take place. Regan noticed that the ocean came so close one almost thought the house was floating. You couldn't see the ribbon of road running along the coastline unless you walked up to the window and looked straight down.

The sound of staple guns came from a couple of spots within the house, whose top floor, up another flight of stairs, appeared more woody and Nordic than what was below. The mayor's man showed Regan and the ex–prime minister two rooms that were bare except for some plain tables and chairs. They'd been set up for use by American and Soviet support staff.

"There won't be much need for that," said Regan, as politely as he could. "This thing is going to be mostly one-on-one—or two-on-two when Shultz and Shevardnadze are around. If you count the translators, there'll be six people downstairs at most. The policy guys will be back at the hotel and the embassy, or over at that schoolhouse." It was a good thing, too, Regan thought: so far he'd seen only one toilet in this place.

Back in the hallway, the mayor's man showed off the staircase landing that connected the two halves of the upper house. The thick dowels of the banister had hearts carved into them. The house had been a present from a French consul to his wife; the man's name was carved into one of the cornices downstairs. "But the whole dwelling was deserted by the 1950s," the mayor's man explained. "Abandoned except for some—how do you now say?—homeless?"

"Squatters," said Regan, bristling a little, suspecting the man had learned this new word from reports on what he himself regarded as an overblown problem back in the States.

"I have heard that we may be on the top of an old Viking burial site," said the ex–prime minister.

"I keep hearing about that ghost, too," said Regan, resisting an impulse to spill the beans about Nancy Reagan's paid fortune-teller.

A distant crash and then a shriek interrupted the men. "What the hell was that?" asked Regan.

"I'm sure it was nothing," said the mayor's man, who nonetheless led them back downstairs to find out. They reached the bottom floor before they had their answer.

Two armed Russian security officers had claimed the biggest room down here for their own. They didn't even turn around when the American and two Icelanders entered, so intently were they watching a Tom and Jerry cartoon on the VCR. Jerry, the mouse, had just brought a window down on Tom's tail, one of the Soviets finally explained to the mayor's man, who had been chosen for this detail because he spoke Russian as well as English. What they'd heard was the crash of the cartoon window and Tom's subsequent yelp.

Regan shook his head and said, "Sufferin' succotash. Let's get the hell out of here."

The chief of staff and his two companions left Hofdi House and emerged into what looked, at least to the American, like deep middle-of-the-night darkness. On the way to the car they heard a loud shout from one of the Russians they'd left behind.

"What did he just say?" Regan asked.

"'Rewind,'" the mayor's man explained.

11:30 P.M. (EDT), THE LINCOLN BEDROOM

Having just checked in with her husband in California, Maureen Reagan felt an impulse to call her mother, Jane Wyman, the way she always had when spending a night with "the folks" during her adolescence. It didn't matter that Dad wasn't here tonight; she was at Dad's *house*. And years ago that had always prompted her to make a small triumphal gesture— *See? HE loves me*—toward her difficult mother.

Tonight she tried jauntiness: "It isn't every Friday night that *Falcon Crest* gets tuned in from *this* house," Maureen said, once she'd explained where she was calling from. Alas, she could hear the overheartiness in her voice, a mark of the failed politician, trying to win someone over by dialing things up a notch too high. Her humorless mother wouldn't acknowledge the joke, in any case. She'd be thinking: I don't understand. Why should Ronnie and Nancy ignore my TV series?

"What did you think of the episode?" asked Jane Wyman, as if talking to a fan of the still-popular wine-country drama.

Maureen hadn't actually watched it, and she could feel sudden panic competing with equally sudden resentment: already this conversation was all about Mother. She knew there wouldn't be any questions about how it felt to be in the White House during such a momentous weekend.

"You were wonderful," she said.

Her mother ignored the compliment. "Six seasons ought to be enough," she declared, "but they're determined to keep it going with guest stars. Kim Novak is a handful. How's your brother?"

Mother probably wanted to save herself a phone call. "Mike is fine, so far as I know," Maureen answered. "I was in Africa a week ago. My second trip. They've got me cultivating the leader of Mozambique. He's far left but likes Dad a lot."

"Was it in the papers?"

Hopeless. Only *that* could make it important, or even real, to Mother. The newspaper would also do the service of rendering it impersonal, of providing the remove at which everything in this family had to be experienced. As a child of divorce, Maureen knew she reminded each of her parents of a previous spouse. But there were all the other filters and "step" relationships, too: Michael had been adopted; so had Nancy; and so, probably, had Jane Wyman, though she'd been no more honest with her children than she'd been with movie magazines about the details of her early life. Remoteness upon remoteness.

And then there was that creepy remark of Dad's that always got quoted: "The wonderful thing about having a daughter is that you get to see your wife as a little girl, growing up." He sounded like Roman Polanski! Had he actually been seeing Jane all the time that she, Maureen, had been his child? And had he repeated the process with Nancy and Patti? The country might now be full of step-families making the best of a complicated square dance, but the Reagans glided by one another like distant planets, a solar system ruled by two long-separated stars.

"Is there anything you want, Maureen?" her mother asked.

For a moment what Maureen really wanted was to be out of it all, to hide herself away, just as Dad's first campaign team had insisted, with very little resistance from the candidate, during the '66 governor's race. Everyone had acted as if there'd never been a first set of children from a first wife.

"I've been wondering about something Dad said to me when he left yesterday morning."

"Left for where?"

"*Iceland*, Mother! *That* was in the papers."

"You know I hate politics," said Jane Wyman.

"He asked me to pray for him," said Maureen. "It surprised me." The person she really ought to be asking about this was her stepbrother, Ron, who had the most insight of all the children into their father—not that that was saying much. But Ron was an atheist and didn't seem a reliable source on this topic. Maureen herself was nothing in particular, though she'd long ago been meaninglessly baptized into the Catholic Church, when Jane, after one of her divorces, went through a brief religious phase.

"Mermie, if your father said 'Pray for me,' he just meant 'Love me while I'm gone.' He *prefers* being loved from far away."

"That's not true, Mother. Nancy is always close by. He mopes when she's away."

"Nancy may think she's close to him. But he's *always* in Iceland. Nancy is kidding herself, dear."

"Oh, Mother, really."

"I'm telling you the truth."

Maureen thought of Nancy, already in bed a few rooms away. She had lately felt more connected to her than to her own mother. Common enemies, like Don Regan, helped to solidify the bond, though they had both always known better than to make an enemy out of Jane Wyman. They owed Jane too much for remaining as mute as her character in *Johnny Belinda* on the subject of Ronald Reagan these past twenty years, no matter how hard the press tried to draw her out.

"Do you know why I could never truly love your father?" asked Jane.

"No. Why?"

"He wouldn't fight back."

"I remember some fights," said Maureen.

"I won all of them."

"Maybe that's just because he's a gentleman around women," said Maureen.

"It doesn't mean there isn't anger inside him," said Jane. "Somewhere."

"But *where*, Mother?"

"If I'd ever found it, I might still be married to him. Do you remember what 'our' song supposedly was? It was really his song. He used to sing it around the house. 'Deep Purple.'"

"I remember," said Maureen. "Sort of."

"Think about that song."

"All right."

"Well," Jane said, "it's getting late."

It was all of a quarter to nine in Beverly Hills. "Good night, Mother."

"I'm glad you called, Mermie."

After hanging up, Maureen went over to the window and looked out onto the South Lawn, from which her father's helicopter had taken off yesterday morning. She shut her eyes and set about trying to remember the lyrics to "Deep Purple." Yes, she *could* remember him singing it—in the car, with her and Michael, but not their mother. The singer's lost love returns to him through a fog of remembrance, *breathing my name with a sigh.*

It was *his* name he heard being spoken—through a mist. By someone he was happy wasn't there?

15

SATURDAY, OCTOBER 11, 1986

**5:05 A.M. (RT), ALONG BERGSTADASTRAETI, AND AT HALLGRÍMSKIRKJA,
REYKJAVIK**

Anders jogged down the street in the predawn dark, thinking he'd put
on speed closer to the harbor. But a couple of blocks beyond the Holt
he became aware of a dark-haired figure coming toward him. The man,
wearing a raincoat and smoking a cigarette, seemed impervious to the
cold, and to everything else, and as the two of them prepared to pass each
other, he very calmly said, "Hello, Mr. Little," as if they ran into each
other every day.

Anders recognized the face and remembered avoiding its glance at the
airport; he knew the man was press but still couldn't recall where he'd
first seen him. Even in the faint glow of the streetlamp, he appeared to
be flushed with wine.

"You're having a late night," said Anders.

"So much better than an early morning. But I don't suppose you'd
agree."

"I'm due at my post at eight."

"Except Ron keepeth the city, the watchman waketh but in vain."

Anders looked perplexed. "I'm trying to remember where we—"

Hitchens produced the business card. "You gave this to me in the
cathedral, at the service for Honest Ave. I'm Christopher Hitchens."

"Oh, yes."

"You were with Mrs. Kirkpatrick. Your choice for '88? Or is she just
a friendly ex-boss?"

Anders managed a smile. "A lot can happen between now and then."

"Yes," said Hitchens. "Her beloved *commandantes* may march the resistance straight into Managua. A triumphal validation of her *Dictatorships and Double Standards.*"

"Yes, it's a sacred text," said Anders, playing along. "We just call it *DDS.*"

"Hmmm," said Hitchens. "A tribute to the dentist in *Marathon Man*?"

Anders began running in place, to ward off the cold and indicate his need to get going. "Want to run with me?" he asked, knowing the invitation was sure to be rejected.

"Let's pretend that this is the arms race," said Hitchens. "And that you've agreed to slow it down to a crawl. Shall we?" He turned and set off with Anders toward the harbor. The American had no polite choice but to stay at his side and slacken his pace. "Do you ever exercise?" Anders asked.

"Perhaps I'll start when I get to be your age, which I know to be thirty-eight."

Startled, Anders tried to keep his cool. "How old are *you*?" he asked.

"Thirty-seven," answered Hitchens.

"Then you don't have much time."

"Not enough to waste running in circles."

"How do you know my age?" Anders asked, unable to stave off the kind of alarm he'd felt with the Soviet sailor on Thursday night. Even so, something about the Englishman's personality, for all its apparent aggression, felt as soothing as his voice.

"I did a bit of research," said Hitchens.

"Obviously." Anders couldn't imagine that the writer's effort had been prompted only by a desire to know more about someone he'd seen walking with Mrs. Kirkpatrick. "Who are you writing for while you're here?" he asked.

"The *Spectator.*"

"The one out of Indiana?" asked Anders, referring with a hopeful surprise to the Reaganite monthly.

"Dear boy, don't be mad. The one out of London."

"What kind of article?"

"The kind that won't be filed until a week from Wednesday. So you can ignore this news 'blackout' and tell me everything."

"What would you like to know?"

"I'd like to know who's winning."

"The talks haven't even started."

"Who's winning on your side?"

"Shouldn't that be *our* side?"

"No," said Hitchens. "You're strolling with Switzerland."

"I'll bet you're the sort of commentator who now refers to the hardline Communists in the U.S.S.R. as 'the right wing'—the new conservatives. It's a neat rhetorical trick, when you know of course that they're really to Gorbachev's left."

"Not at all true," said Hitchens. "The 'spectrum' is actually a circumference. It bends in such a way that the extremes meet each other."

The two men paused for a passing car before crossing a street called Laugavegur. Anders looked up at the sky and said, "It really *is* darkest before dawn."

Hitchens disputed even this: "Only celestially. In all other respects, it's always darkest before doom."

Anders laughed. "I can't keep up with you."

"I'm relieved," said Hitchens. "I'd be disappointed if anyone on the National Security Council showed signs of quickness."

"Chris—"

"Please. Christopher."

"Christopher, what exactly are you trying to find out?"

"For starters, you can suggest to me whether the 'moderates'—Shultz and Nitze *et alii*—or the Vulcans—Weinberger and Perle and your bluestocking mentor—have won the battle for what passes for the president's mind. Who besides Nancy is going to be in his head when he sits down at the table this morning?"

"There are no divisions within this administration. The president *is* the administration."

"Mr. Little, it's not so dark that I can't detect an unstraight face."

Anders laughed. "You're right, that was a talking point."

They were now close to the harbor, which showed a surprising amount of activity. Small patrol boats were cutting vigilant arcs around the *Baltika* and *George Ots*, lest another Greenpeace ship try to grab the world's attention by sidling up to them, as had happened a day ago.

"I make you out as a member of the Shultz camp," said Hitchens.

"Why would you do that?" asked Anders.

"As a litmus-testing lie. The tone of your response confirms what I actually thought all along: you're a hard-liner."

"Score one more for you," said Anders, a bit sharply.

"Does that hard line extend through Central America?"

"You don't need subterfuge to figure *that* out. You saw me standing side by side with Dr. Kirkpatrick."

"True," said Hitchens. "But that was in broad daylight. The shadows often provide a clearer view."

Anders pointed toward the steps leading to the Viking statue. "If you don't mind, I'm going to sprint those. Ten times up and ten times down."

"I think I'll wait here," said Hitchens. He watched as Anders's lean form began its absurd ascent, and decided to see if he could smoke a cigarette in less time than it took Little to perform his Sisyphean repetitions. He also wondered: Would the release of endorphins reduce or increase the man's resistance to questions? Hitchens had made phone calls to Terry Dolan and a couple of others just before he'd left the States, and he was beginning to connect a few dots. Of course, like dots, connections themselves could be random, but there seemed to be a good case for learning more. If only he had Ms. Kelly Proctor's administrative skills here on hand to keep the findings straight. Perhaps she'd get him organized down in Florida.

"Beat you," said Hitchens, a few minutes later, pointing to a cigarette stubbed out on the ground.

Anders was glistening with the thinnest patina of sweat but still not even breathing through his mouth. How fetching this sight would be, thought Hitchens, to Dolan and Grover and the one each of them had called "Spitz."

"Let's go to church," Hitchens suggested.

"Really?"

"The Lutheran cathedral up the hill." He explained that yesterday he had caught a glimpse of the steeple, which was made of concrete flanges rising hundreds of feet into the air. It looked like some Soviet power plant for which Stephen Spender might have composed an ode in the 1930s.

Anders consulted his sports watch. "Okay."

The two men walked up the gently inclined Skólavördustígur, and a few minutes later the church came into view—to Anders's astonishment.

Noticing his companion's look of sudden reverence, Hitchens declared, or quoted: "So many spires can hardly point in vain." Anders appeared puzzled, so Hitchens explained: "Verse. A chap from the Great War. No reason to know him." Looking toward the church, Hitchens also thought of Hardy, the greatest poet of that war, who'd recognized the railway station as the modern world's replacement for the cathedral. Here in Iceland the sacred and the scientific seemed to be lying down like the lion and the lamb: the steeple played host to a radio antenna.

Actually, for all its monstrous size, this wasn't a cathedral at all—just a Lutheran parish church, according to a sign near its mosaic-tiled front doors. Moreover, though it had been under construction for decades, the great pile was only now being deemed complete. It was due to be consecrated two weeks from Sunday.

Anders pointed to the date range of the building work: 1945–1986.

"Hmmm," murmured Hitchens.

"The length of the Cold War," said Anders. "More or less."

"Yes, I have chills. But I ascribe them to the fact that it's below zero Celsius, and quite possibly Fahrenheit."

Hitchens opened one of the doors, and as soon as he did an elderly verger, who for days had been letting reporters in at all hours, beckoned both men to enter. Inviting their appreciation, he gestured toward the organ, the pulpit, and a sort of wagon wheel with votive candles for the faithful to light. Finally, he pointed to an elevator, which traveled to an observation deck near the top of the steeple.

"Are there stairs, too?" asked Anders.

"Oh, Christ," said Hitchens, who made for the lift.

Up on the deck he found it was even colder. Freezing inside the stony space, which was open to the air, he looked down upon the city from all four sides of the tower. It was still too dark to distinguish the colors of the painted rooftops.

Anders soon arrived at the summit of the winding steps.

"Beat you again," said Hitchens.

Anders smiled and walked over to a side of the deck directly above a statue of Leif Eriksson. In the first glimmers of dawn he also searched for the Hotel Holt.

"It all looks so rational from up here," he told Hitchens.

"It?"

"The world."

"You find that pleasing?"

"I think it's an illusion," said Anders, as a gust of wind hit his face. He wasn't used to talking expansively, but he now said just what he was thinking: "Inside all those neat, square houses you have everybody dreaming their messy dreams."

Hitchens considered the use of "messy," the degree to which it bespoke sex hatred or just the technocrat's disgust with imprecision. He then pushed the conversation back to the sign they'd seen below, with its span of construction dates: "So, *does* the Cold War end in 1986?"

"Doubtful," said Anders. He rubbed his hands together while Hitchens lit a cigarette.

"But if it *were* to end—how would you see that happening?"

"Oh, that's easy," said Anders, turning away from the view and trying to smile. "Just like Reagan said: 'We win; they lose.'"

Hitchens said nothing. He could for a moment hear his own younger self singing "The Internationale." "Do you pray?" he asked.

"Not as much as I should," said Anders, adopting a look of conventional humility.

"Would you pray for Terry Dolan?"

Anders's expression gave way to something stricken. "Of course," he said, turning back to look at the city below. After a few seconds Hitchens noticed that the man's shoulders were gently heaving beneath the wind-breaker. Mr. Little was struggling to get back "on message" but couldn't do it. The personal and political strands of his being had become two downed power lines, sparking and spasming, overwhelming the electrical grid of an overorganized personality.

When Anders turned back around, tears were running down his face.

Hitchens moved a step toward him. "When they shot down that plane over Nicaragua, Hasenfus was the only one who had a parachute."

Anders said nothing, but allowed Hitchens to come another step closer and put a comradely arm over his shoulder. "Have *you* got one, dear boy?" the Englishman asked, gently.

7:05 A.M. (EDT), DUPONT CIRCLE APARTMENT OF TERRY DOLAN, WASHINGTON, D.C.

It was crazy coming over this early, but Terry had said, "Hey, I can never sleep anyway with all these meds," and with the election coming up Nick had to work a full day, no matter that it was Saturday—so here he was, at seven in the morning!

He could hear Olivia Newton-John as he climbed the stairs to Terry's apartment. *Let's get* phys-*ical*, phys-*ical* . . . The stereo wasn't quite loud enough to wake the neighbors, some of whom had probably crawled into bed only a couple of hours ago.

"That's the spirit!" he said, entering the apartment.

"Trust me, Nick Carrollton," said Terry. "You don't want to hear my body talk."

"No negative thinking!" countered Nick, with a big smile, though he had to wonder, just looking at him, how soon it would be until Terry's next hospitalization. He handed him the wheatgrass drink he'd bought last night in Arlington and kept in his fridge. "Have you seen the store windows out on Connecticut? They're crammed with Halloween costumes already!" He felt like somebody bringing news from another world.

He put a bag of groceries on the kitchen counter along with some "buddies" paperwork from Whitman-Walker. The whole apartment still had the look of someone's office. On previous visits Nick had had some of the stuff on the walls explained to him, like the HONOR AMER-ICA poster from a prowar rally that Terry had organized way back in 1970, as a college student. Of course the HAWKINS '80! bumper sticker hadn't needed any explanation: one of NCPAC's biggest—and most endangered!—achievements. On an end table near the couch lay a two-week-old newspaper clipping about the organization's supposed decline and four-million-dollar debt; in the margins Terry had written, in red ink, words like "WRONG" and "PROVE."

"Think you might be up for a walk?"

"Thanks, Nicky. But I can barely get between here and the bedroom today. And, God, my mouth is so *dry*. I feel like I need water to wash down what I'm *drinking*."

Nick's sympathetic grimace conceded that the wheatgrass did look pretty awful. He now worried that it might make the nausea worse, too.

"Hope you won't burn out on me," said Terry, while Nick got a glass of water. "Not that I'd blame you if you did."

"Never!" said Nick, who pointed to Terry's mustache and asked, "How about a trim?" The neuropathy in Terry's fingers made it hard for him to handle a pair of manicure scissors.

"I'm starting to look like Fu Manchu," said Terry. Unsure of who that was, Nick laughed anyway, while he snipped.

The *Washington Times*, Reverend Moon's conservative alternative to the *Post*, lay on the couch. Done with his trim, Terry picked it up, pointed to a story about the summit, and sighed. "A year ago NCPAC was saying Shultz should resign. Now he'll be spending the whole day in the same room with Reagan and that birthmarked Cossack!" He laughed. "I wish your boyfriend would lock him out of that little house in Iceland."

"He's not my boyfriend!" said Nick, who couldn't hide his thrill at the suggestion. "I can't tell you anything," he added with a laugh.

"Of course you can," said Terry. "We're 'buddies,' right?" He was thinking he probably shouldn't have told Hitchens quite so much on

Tuesday—all that secondhand stuff he'd heard about Spitz's party—but maybe it would make Chris grateful enough to really stick it to Pamela Harriman, who was being talked about these days as if she were some combination of Dolley Madison and Mark Hanna. It made him want to puke even more.

"Here," said Terry, handing Nick a videocassette. "Could you pop that into the VCR?"

"Sure." Once he hit play, the picture switched from MTV to the tape. A Jimmy Buffett song from a couple of years back, "Who's the Blonde Stranger?" came on. Nick watched for half a minute. God, this felt slow if you were used to videos by A-ha and Wham! But it was kind of funny, too: about some good ol' boy partying and cheating on his wife.

"Freeze it right . . . *there*!" said Terry.

Nick complied and made the screen hold a shaky image of some middle-aged dude in a fisherman's hat. He was clutching a younger woman and hoisting some goofy drink inside a carved-out pineapple.

"So?" said Nick. The guy under the hat looked sort of familiar, but that was it.

Terry said nothing, just noted the tape time on the VCR and wrote out a Post-it: *Check out 1:01. Great photo for 30-second ad in Florida Panhandle, no? Maybe one that features Mrs. Reagan?* He asked Nick to put the tape and the note into an envelope he'd already addressed to "Democrats for the 80s" at 3032 N Street. "Can you messenger this for me?"

"Whatever," said Nick, with a laugh. He would dispatch it this morning from the RNC.

Terry seemed to be experiencing a moment of peace. "So tell me about *your* Halloween costume. You going to run the high-heeled race out of J.R.'s?"

"Me?" said Nick, plucking at his preppy J.Crew sweater. "I'll tell you something, though. Anders Little could *win* that race, even if he had to wear platforms. Oh my God, I almost stole a pair of his running shorts Tuesday morning! They had WAKE FOREST on them. Sounds like the name of a fairy tale," he said, sighing.

Terry laughed.

"I guess it is!" said Nick, before adding, more seriously, "Do you think I'm in love?"

Terry gave him a wistful smile. "You're going to forget to messenger the video."

"Not a chance," said Nick. "See you Monday!"

11:20 A.M. (RT), HOFDI HOUSE, REYKJAVIK

"Let me, Mr. President."

The general secretary got up from his chair to retrieve two note cards that had dropped from Ronald Reagan's hands onto the Oriental carpet. Both the startled translator and notetaker had remained locked in their seats.

"Thank you," said the president, who bent down to get the cards himself. "I'm afraid I'd get a scolding from our intelligence people if I allowed you to do that." Reagan smiled at the Soviet leader as he put the two cards back on top of the stack in front of him.

Gorbachev thought of something Nixon had said to him this past summer: that Reagan took his responsibilities to defend the United States as if he were still the lifeguard he'd been in his youth. Should *he* be reimagining himself at the same age, riding the combine beside his father during the summer harvest?

He looked at Reagan from the opposite end of the not-very-long table. The glass bowl atop it was empty. "No jellybeans," he said, pointing. The remark had been prompted by a flash of fondness, a feeling somehow permitted by his overall contempt for the president. Even a modest respect for his opposite number would have blocked it.

The translator struggled with "jellybeans" while Reagan looked out at the ocean. After a morning of rain, the waters seemed to have risen even higher.

The president smiled again. "It's a lovely house. Peaceful." He could feel the footsteps of the staffers overhead, and actually hear the tick of the grandfather clock a floor below, near the front entrance. His deafness to louder, higher frequencies made him, the doctor had once explained, somehow more alert to lower and softer ones.

"You know," he said, "they tell me that I'm technically the host for this first session, so I feel I should thank you, Mr. General Secretary—not just for coming, but for proposing this meeting in your letter last month. I'm ready to talk about anything, and I'm glad that much of our time together will be one on one—not that you fellows are invisible," he added, with a wink to the notetaker and translators.

"Yes," said Gorbachev, "we can go to two-two"—meaning they could add Shultz and Shevardnadze—"when I've finished outlining our basic proposals." He had been at it for a while already, unsure how much of what he'd said was registering with Reagan in even the most basic way.

"I know you pledged a fifty-percent cut at Geneva," said the president. "In strategic arms."

Irritated by the jumping around, Gorbachev sought to organize the agenda. "All right: We'll go into the armaments details now? Then this afternoon do the regional and bilateral and humanitarian issues?"

"Oh, yes," said Reagan, rushing straight to the last one. "You'll find that I have quite a soliloquy to give you on human rights. We really can't have progress on arms without progress on that."

Gorbachev pressed on with his attempt to systematize matters. "We have had too many arms-control proposals, both during Geneva and afterwards. The result has been confusion. I think that a radical simplification is in order."

"I thought we got to fifty percent there," Reagan reiterated. "But then I found out how our side takes that to mean forty-five hundred missiles apiece while your fellows interpret it as sixty-five hundred."

"I would like to wait on specific numbers," said Gorbachev, as politely as he could. "And I would like to emphasize that our goal is getting to *zero*—so long as there is parity at every step on the way down to that."

Dmitri Zarechnak, the American translator, supplemented his oral work by tracing a staircase, with his index finger, on the air.

"*Doveryai no proveryai*," said Reagan. "Have I got that right, Dmitri?"

"Yes," interrupted Gorbachev. "'Trust but verify.' You have said it before."

"I understand that it's a proverb," said Reagan.

"It is a witticism. I am telling you, as I told you some minutes ago, that we are now willing to permit on-site inspection where ballistic missiles are concerned."

"When do you think you'd like to make your trip to the United States?" asked Reagan.

"I was going to get to that later. It depends of course on whatever progress we make here."

"Oh, yes. And they tell me we've got to consider throw weight along with the number of missiles. They're not all equal, you know."

"Perhaps," said Gorbachev, genuinely at a loss, "it is time to call for our foreign ministers."

Reagan seemed delighted with the idea. He joined his counterpart in waving them in. As Shultz and Shevardnadze took seats across from each other, the American secretary of state thought to make a little joke about a game of bridge, but abandoned the idea when he realized that even in translation it might mean nothing to the Soviet leader.

"I was about to tell the president," said Gorbachev, directly to Shultz, "that in addition to cutting fifty percent of ballistic missiles—with the eventual goal of reaching zero—we are prepared to see the elimination of all *medium*-range missiles in Europe, both American and Soviet, *even* as we allow the British and French to retain their own. And we are willing to continue negotiating a reduction of Soviet intermediate-range missiles in Asia."

Shultz said nothing for a moment.

"That is the essence of our proposal," said Gorbachev. "It represents an enormous move toward compromise on our part." He looked at the secretary of state, whose blandly intelligent face now appeared to belong to a man who couldn't believe his ears. Then Gorbachev turned toward Reagan, to see whether he would take an actor's cue from Shultz's barely suppressed pleasure. But the general secretary could detect no change in the president's own expression.

"Additionally," Gorbachev declared, "as soon as we make significant progress on strategic-arms reduction, we are prepared to negotiate a new nuclear test-ban treaty. Such a treaty is, of course, essential; the Soviet

Union cannot forever continue its unilateral moratorium on testing. And so, if you are willing to observe the ABM treaty for another ten years, and for that same period to confine testing of your Strategic Defense Initiative to the laboratory, we could reach a comprehensive agreement that will set us on our way toward 'zero'—a world free of nuclear weapons. We could acknowledge the basic arrangements here; the staffs of Mr. Shultz and Mr. Shevardnadze could work out the details in the months ahead; and then we could sign the treaty when I come to Washington."

Shultz, observing protocol, waited for Reagan to speak, which the president did only after a pause. "You know, some of those Asian missiles, if they were just swiveled into a different position, could hit Europe."

Had he heard nothing? thought Gorbachev. Could he not take yes for an answer? The Soviet leader looked imploringly toward Shultz.

"SDI is what will *get* us to zero," continued Reagan. "We'll let you watch us test. We'll share the results with you. We'll share them with *everyone*. After all, what happens if, once *our* missiles are gone, some madman like Qadaffi acquires nuclear weapons of his own? How does the world protect itself from that?"

"Please focus on what we've proposed," said Gorbachev. "Even the Asian missiles are negotiable. But not if you transport the arms race into space—which would be a clear violation of the ABM treaty negotiated by your President Nixon. There was no greater antagonist of the Soviet Union in his day. And yet *we* are proposing to strengthen and extend *his* treaty. You propose to renounce it, just as you continually fail to observe the SALT agreements."

"Well," said Reagan, gently, "we'll take a serious look."

"I know that this is a lot to digest," said Gorbachev. "But you will study the matter between our sessions?"

"Oh, yes," said Reagan, smiling now. He turned to his secretary of state. "You look excited, George."

Gorbachev saw the quiet elation on Shultz's face, as if the full import of everything just proposed was truly sinking in.

A faint but sharp sound, like the snap of a mousetrap, could be heard from the floor below. Shevardnadze appeared startled. The sound was followed by a gale of Russian-sounding laughter.

"I hope it's not too early to call," said Richard Nixon, who for the last dozen years, since his near-fatal illness, had been a "morning person."

"Heavens, no," said Jeane Kirkpatrick, from Bethesda, Maryland.

"Oh, good." Nine-thirty on a Saturday still *felt* early to Nixon, no matter that his medications had had him up since five. Even now he missed the brooding late nights with a legal pad on his lap, the hours when he would let the bold and dark thoughts chase one another inside his head.

"I just heard from our friend," he informed Mrs. Kirkpatrick.

"I have fewer friends than I'd like to," she replied, "but I don't know which one you mean."

"Little. Over in Reykjavik."

"Oh, Anders. I hope he took some mittens for when he goes out *jogging*." She pronounced the word as if it were a distasteful compulsion.

"Ever been to Iceland?" asked Nixon.

"No."

"Godforsaken place. I was there in '56, and again in '71, to see Pompidou. The location was his idea."

"As it was apparently Gorbachev's this time."

"Reagan probably thought he said *Ireland*! And then Shultz went off and made the arrangements."

Mrs. Kirkpatrick laughed her guttural laugh. "So what does Anders say?"

"Sounds like a hell of a morning," said Nixon. "The American staff just finished meeting over lunch." He reached for his glasses and for Little's lightly coded but still indiscreet fax. It was only a paragraph long, hastily handwritten minutes ago. Nixon boiled it down to a couple of sentences: "Gorbachev is willing to go for a fifty-percent cut in heavy offensive missiles and to come way down on the strategic kind—even the ones they've got in Asia. Of course they can't even agree on what fifty percent means. But *why* the big concessions? That question may be more important than the concessions themselves."

"Why indeed?" asked Mrs. Kirkpatrick. "You know, I signed Courter's letter." A Republican congressman had sent Reagan a pre-summit petition asking that the president speed up work on SDI and be sure not to trade it away for anything in Reykjavik.

"Kissinger wouldn't sign, but I know he agrees with it," said Nixon.

"It wouldn't have killed him to say so," said Mrs. Kirkpatrick. "How about you?"

"*My* signature?" Nixon asked, with a laugh. "I wouldn't want to give Courter's letter the kiss of death."

"Come now. That wouldn't happen on a matter like this."

"Maybe, maybe not." He didn't want to tell her about the way he always had to suppress himself in order to preserve influence inside the White House. "You know, SDI's all right, but I can't get excited about it. I've never believed in a defense deterrence. It's *offensive* weaponry that keeps the peace. Guns, not shields, deter an enemy from attacking. I've always been at odds with Shultz on this."

"I'm at odds with him on a great many things," said Mrs. Kirkpatrick. "Perhaps especially Israel, about which I've never found him to be all that robust."

Nixon knew that her real grievance against Shultz concerned his refusal to back her for the NSA job, which had gone first to McFarlane and then to Poindexter. But that was life. "I'm less worried about Reagan giving away SDI than I am about his giving away too many warheads," he told her. "If we get down to some sort of low-level parity with the Soviets, they'll overrun us on the ground. He did the right thing putting in the Pershings a couple of years ago, and I hope he doesn't *un*do it now because Nancy and some others are telling him this is his big chance to be a goddamned 'peacemaker.' When we last talked, I told him not to accept a bad deal and not to accept the appearance of a good one."

"Well," mused Mrs. Kirkpatrick, "I'd say Reagan has less to worry about than Gorbachev does this weekend. If *he* gives away too much, the Russian army may tell him not to bother coming home."

Nixon, who retained the sense that he himself had been overthrown, instinctively veered toward another subject: "Know anything about this

Max Gomez character?" The press had begun exploring a connection between George Bush and a figure they'd just linked to the rogue resupply operation in Central America. Given her championship of the Contras, Nixon suspected that Mrs. Kirkpatrick knew plenty.

But it was her turn to avoid a subject. "He's apparently been involved with this sort of thing all the way back to the Bay of Pigs" was all she would say.

"Christ," said Nixon. "Howard Hunt and his Cuban burglars will be turning up there next!" It was hard even for him to tell whether he meant this as a joke. Whatever the case, Mrs. Kirkpatrick remained silent, and Nixon moved on: "You've got this big shindig coming up in New York." Friends and political boosters would be throwing the former UN ambassador a sixtieth-birthday party just before Thanksgiving.

She groaned. "Sixty is a dreadful birthday. Especially for a woman."

"No, no," Nixon protested. "My own sixtieth was my last good one!" It had come two months after his landslide reelection, and two months before Watergate exploded.

"I'm not sure whether that makes me look forward to it or dread it all the more." Mrs. Kirkpatrick sighed.

"There's a lot more than Georgetown ahead for you, Jeane." Strange that this tough woman seemed almost to need the Nixon pep talk. "I'm hearing a lot of vice-presidential chatter about you," he said. "You know, you'd be especially helpful to Bush. Is he qualified for the job? Yes. But does he come across as strong? No. But you do."

"Well," said Mrs. Kirkpatrick, as dismissively as she could. "There's no way to make such a thing happen. It either does or it doesn't."

"Not true," said Nixon. "Tom Dewey more or less made it happen with me and Ike. Back in the old days when you were still mad for Hubert and Adlai."

She laughed, but let this subject drop, too.

"Well," said Nixon, "Reagan's got two sessions to go over there, though only the last one will count. How do you think he'll do? You've seen him face-to-face more than I have in recent years."

After a pause, Mrs. Kirkpatrick spoke deliberately. "I told this to my husband when I first met Reagan, all of six years ago: he doesn't talk like anybody I'm familiar with. He doesn't sound like a politician, or an academic, or a journalist. But I can also tell you that he's the most impersonally warm man I've ever encountered. They won't know how to figure him out over there."

"Well, they've already met him at Geneva."

"I'm not talking about the Soviets. I'm talking about his own staff— Shultz and Adelman and all the others who'll be trying to get him to do things." She paused again. "Mr. President, I don't know *you* very well, but I do know that you can be clasped. You're complex, yes, but *palpable*. Reagan is smoke."

"But where there's smoke there's fire?"

"Oh, yes," Mrs. Kirkpatrick answered. "But nobody knows where the fire *is*. And nobody knows who started it or how to keep it going."

3:30 P.M. (RT), HOFDI HOUSE, REYKJAVIK

Shultz's pulse had been elevated during the lunchtime strategy session inside the embassy's glassy anti-eavesdropping bubble, built during the past week—a piece of Cold War construction almost certain never to be used again once they left Reykjavik. Gorbachev's proposals were potentially so momentous that they encouraged the secretary of state to imagine a world from which all such contrivances, including ballistic missiles, would disappear. Three days ago, back in Washington, they had all been thinking of this as a "pre-summit"; now it looked as if it might become a coda to the world they'd been living in for forty years.

Throughout lunch, Reagan had continued to act as if back at Hofdi House he'd participated in nothing more consequential than a summertime cabinet meeting. He joked about keeping goldfish in the glass security bubble and nodded happily during all the strategizing, as if they were in some tree-house fort, hatching a plan to capture the rival gang's domain before their mothers called them home to supper.

The goldfish remark had reminded Shultz of Geneva, where last year the president had awakened in a bedroom of the Aga Khan's borrowed mansion and noticed that one of the pet fish he'd promised to feed had gone to its eternal reward. Don Regan and the Secret Service were enlisted to find a lookalike substitute that might satisfy the owner of the original, the prince's young son, for whom the president left an apologetic note. The story had gotten around, and if asked whether it illustrated some wild sentimentality in Reagan or, alternatively, the bedrock human qualities that made him exactly the right person to be negotiating the fate of the world, Shultz would of course have said it was the latter. But he didn't believe he would ever know for sure.

Now, at 3:30 p.m., once more climbing the steps into Hofdi House, Shultz regarded the president's blue-suited form just in front of him. No, despite the reverential swoons of the party's base, there wasn't a Lincolnesque particle to him. And yet, having read the Gore Vidal novel over a dozen of last year's plane trips, Shultz knew that he'd spent as much time trying to figure out Reagan as Lincoln's own secretary of state, Seward, had expended contemplating the enigma *he* served. Of one thing he was certain: Gorbachev didn't know what to make of the sweetness that suffused Reagan's stubbornness. One could see the Russian choosing to dismiss and disdain it—because he feared it? At the very least it kept him off balance, and as Shultz now shook hands with Shevardnadze, and then the notetaker and translator, he wondered if this might work to their advantage, as so many things seemed to be working, unexpectedly.

"My turn to read," said Reagan, who had genially resumed his seat at one end of the table. Shultz knew that the stapled sheaf of papers wouldn't hold the president's attention: he would skip and paraphrase and extemporize as soon as something eluded or bored him.

"I'm happy that you're focused on ballistic missiles," he began. "And I'm glad to hear your willingness to go below sixty-five hundred. Let's limit bombers, too, to three-fifty apiece. I also hope you'll go beyond just a willingness to *talk* about those INFs in Asia. We need to reduce those, not just freeze them. We can quickly go down to a hundred each in Europe if you'll go down to a hundred in Asia. In fact, let's settle on one hundred/one hundred now. We're *getting* somewhere."

Shultz kept hearing *let's* and *now*. These were the two dominant notes in the melody, which played all afternoon.

"About SDI," said Reagan, looking fully present. "We know that it can be developed within the confines of the ABM treaty—maybe with a small modification or two. And we must develop it. It's the key to eliminating *all* offensive ballistic missiles."

With dismay, Shultz noted how the reintroduction of this subject made Gorbachev's hostility rise in proportion to Reagan's enthusiasm.

"We're not looking to acquire a first-strike capability," the president assured the Soviet leader. "Basing our security on a *defensive* system will add to the stability of things between us. And SDI will prevent—"

"We can discuss this later," said Gorbachev.

Reagan nodded, with a sort of disappointed surprise, as if unable to grasp why anyone would turn down the chance to celebrate a miracle. "We *could* start work on a new test-ban treaty," he declared, with less energy. "But before that—while we're here—we should fix the verification procedures in the existing test-ban treaties. That's easily done. You know," he added, with a sorrowful shake of the head, "I've made the decisions I have regarding SALT because of Soviet noncompliance."

Gorbachev gave him a stony look, and for a moment Shultz wondered whether there was, finally, all that much difference between the current general secretary and the bullies of yesteryear, the Molotovs and Malenkovs, that parade forever being purged but still somehow always marching at full strength.

"Let's put our experts to work, right here, tonight," said Reagan. "They tell me there are some big rooms upstairs. Let's let them go all night if they need to—adding details to the basics on which we seem to be moving toward agreement."

Let's, let's. It was, thought Shultz, as if he were courting the girl in one of his old films.

"Believe it or not," said the president, pushing the stapled papers aside, "I'm done." For a moment Shultz thought he might even wink.

Gorbachev took a cautious pause, before saying, "Yes to forty-five hundred. A fifty-percent reduction." Shultz, a bit crestfallen, decided that once the Soviets gave a little on SDI this might be as far as things would go. He had to remind himself that it could hardly be called a bad weekend's work: the Democrats in Congress would have to express delight, and the president's poll numbers would go even higher.

But as Gorbachev continued to speak, the translation astonished the secretary of state: "Let's reduce *everything* by fifty percent, at once: ballistic missiles; submarine-launched missiles; bombers. We should untie the knot, Mr. President. Otherwise Karpov and Kampelman and the rest of our arms controllers will continue beating around the bush. We need to take political decisions."

Reagan nodded. Shultz looked quickly from one leader's face to the other and saw both beginning to think of themselves as what in fact they were: a club of two.

"It's an interesting idea," said Reagan. But his expression was shifting. It now indicated some alarm that the girl he'd been wooing had gotten overeager. "There's one problem. If we cut everything by fifty percent, that still leaves you with more."

Gorbachev pushed a sheet of figures across the table. "Here is the data. Let us cut this in half. Let us have bold ideas instead of all the porridge we've been eating since Geneva."

"May I keep this?" asked Reagan.

"Yes," said Gorbachev. "Now you have all our secrets." He smiled, but as Reagan regarded the numbers, the general secretary became grave and then almost belligerent. "We need to get out of the forest, Mr. President. I agree to this all-night session that you propose. But I must warn you: if you try to outsmart us, to be duplicitous, negotiations will stop forever." The translator winced, even as he spoke words Shultz guessed were more polite than Gorbachev's original locution.

"Here's why you can trust us," said Reagan. "At the end of the Second World War, we offered to put nuclear weapons under international control, no matter that we were the only country that had them. We could have dictated our will to everyone."

Gorbachev, unimpressed, ignored the debating point and said, wearily, "We are seeking the zero option."

"Yes," said Reagan. "We are, too. But on a global basis."

"Let us solve Europe and then do Asia. We are making far more concessions than you are."

Reagan, looking a bit hurt, reminded him: "We *have* no missiles in Asia."

Gorbachev scoffed. "You have *bases* there, Mr. President. In the Philippines, Korea." He looked at his watch. "The experts can discuss Asia."

As if Asia were a detail! thought Shultz. Nothing got this freewheeling in even the hypothetical war-gaming sessions back home.

"Okay," said Reagan.

"You mistakenly believe that our Asian missiles can hit Europe," Gorbachev pointed out.

"You know," said Reagan, getting drawn into a tit-for-tat quarrel, "we've deployed our missiles in Europe only because you put the SS-20s there."

He made an indisputable point, thought Shultz. And if they got past this rough moment, succeeded in bringing Europe to 100/100, the administration's much-mocked policy—*build up to build down*—would prove itself vindicated.

"*Why* do we mistrust each other?" asked Reagan. "If we could figure *that* out—"

For all the big thinking they'd engaged in, Gorbachev was not in the mood for philosophy. He wished to remain practical: "Mr. President, the ABM treaty will be more important than ever if we make dramatic reductions. It is what will keep things stable. Commit to abiding by it for ten years, and confine your SDI research to the laboratory."

"You're currently *breaking* the ABM rules," Reagan responded, with some heat. "And why should there be *any* limitations on SDI? It's the greatest force for peace in the twentieth century! It's not *civilized* for us to depend on mutually assured destruction instead of an actual defense. Besides, SDI is now coming along so fast it won't take ten years. We want everybody to have it, and if you don't believe we'll share it, then let's build it together."

Gorbachev said nothing. Shultz looked at Shevardnadze, who kept his eyes on the empty glass bowl.

Reagan spoke as if a camera had come in for a close-up. "Think of us standing there together, Mr. General Secretary, a few years from now. Telling the world that we have succeeded in developing this capacity. And then telling other nations to get rid of their own terrible weapons—because they're now useless."

"Let's turn our experts loose," said Gorbachev, as if weary of repeating himself.

Reagan looked at his own watch. "You know, we haven't had any talk of human rights. Do you think we could have a working group for that, too, tonight? George?"

Sarcasm was not one of the president's modes, but Shultz didn't see what else this could be. Still, deciding to play things literally, he answered, "We could put Roz Ridgway at the head of our team—"

"Yes," said Gorbachev. "We can form such a group."

Shevardnadze nodded.

"Okay," said Reagan, rising to his feet. "We'll let all of them go at it—and I'll see you back here tomorrow at ten?"

Gorbachev agreed and then stood. Reagan, in the manner of Detective Columbo—*just one more thing*—detained him for a moment: "If you don't want to work together on it, why don't you develop your own SDI? If you come up with something better, you can give it to *us*."

"Mr. President," replied Gorbachev, "I cannot take this talk of *sharing* seriously. You won't even *sell* us oil-drilling bits!"

Shevardnadze, embarrassed, muttered something, but Shultz kept his eyes on Gorbachev. *They don't have the money to build their own*, he realized. Everyone knew the Soviets were working on a version of SDI, but only now did Gorbachev's agitation make sense. *They don't have the money to continue.*

"You know," said Reagan, "I'd give up the whole idea of SDI if I didn't believe the United States would share it."

"Are you sure your CIA would let you? Are you even sure what's *in* this system?" The implication was clear: the CIA, America's *real* government, hadn't informed the president of SDI's true, sinister *raison d'être*.

Shultz tried to urge the men forward, physically, toward the stairs that would lead them out of the house and into their cars, before they could change their minds about the all-night session.

Reagan smiled and shook Gorbachev's hand. "Back there you gave me a sheet of paper," he said. "Let me return the favor." He handed his counterpart almost fifty pages secured with a binder clip. It was a list of twelve hundred dissidents who wanted out of the Soviet Union.

5:00 P.M. (CDT), THE CLARIDGE, 3510 TURTLE CREEK BOULEVARD, DALLAS, TEXAS

Peter's apartment was so impersonally decorated that, in the early hours of the past two mornings, Anne Macmurray had half expected to see a hotel bill slide under the door of the bedroom she occupied. On Friday she'd gone back to the Adolphus, her actual hotel, to check out, after Peter told her it would be foolish not to stay here. He was right: it felt no more awkward than being in the same Hilton during the weekend of their daughter's wedding.

Except of course for the matter of his now being desperately ill. The prognosis was not good. Peter faced weeks of chemotherapy, starting Monday, and although he maintained his casually scornful persona, Anne could tell he was relieved to have her here.

At the moment he sat in the huge glassy living room, wearing his bathrobe, while here in the kitchen she tried to concoct for him a fruit drink more nutritious than the straight-up martinis he continued to favor. She now understood that the children *had* known more or less everything since their father's first signs of sickness early in the summer. But neither Ralph nor Susan had yet made the sort of extended visit during which things actually get *done*. For the past two days Anne had shopped up a storm, organized the bachelor jumble of Peter's medications, and arranged for the visiting nurse who would be here during the worst of chemo's aftereffects. Even so, and for all she'd said about the buck stopping here, she sometimes tried to make herself believe that she was doing all this not for Peter but to spare Susan and Ralph the trouble.

She had also begun setting up regular supermarket deliveries through the building's concierge—being Texas *nouveau riche* had its advantages—and Peter had said "be my guest" when she asked if it would be all right to use his shambolic home office to do the paperwork required by the service. Strewn across his desk were campaign brochures and contribution receipts from Republican officeholders she'd never heard of, as well as evidence of donations to a few better-known figures (Paula Hawkins) and several sinister-sounding organizations (Sentinel? the Western Goals Foundation?). Above the desk she'd found grip-and-grin pictures of Peter with Nixon and John Connally and a certificate identifying him as an "Eagle" donor to the '84 Reagan campaign.

Nowhere, to her disappointment and vague shame, could she find anything signifying the payment of alimony to his second wife.

In the kitchen she stirred the fruit drink and poured herself a glass of white wine. She carried both into the living room on a tray, as if it were the old cocktail hour in Owosso. Lights were coming on throughout Dallas; she noticed how many of the downtown skyscrapers sported little bulbs or fluorescent tubing up and down their exteriors, as if decked out for Christmas the year round. Getting up with some effort, Peter walked over to the floor-to-ceiling windows and pointed toward properties on which John Connally had lost portions of his shirt.

He also pointed out the city's West End, which included the plaza where Connally had almost been killed along with Kennedy. The seedy area was slowly coming back to life, he explained; plans existed to transform the assassination site into an enormous tourist draw with a museum. "They'll get the whole area landmarked. Connally's wife is ready to cut the ribbon once it's done. She told me herself."

"Really?" asked Anne. "The place where she was covered in her own husband's blood?" She shook her head over the Texas-sized grotesquerie of this, but made no other argument. Peter was already giving her his "what's your point?" look.

"Do you remember the Dewey Walk?" she asked.

This unexpected question was the closest either had come since Thursday night to a mention of their romantic past. Peter actually smiled, recalling a local businessman's scheme, during Owosso's delusional summer of '48, to turn the center of town into a theme-park commemoration of Thomas E. Dewey's early career. But the recollection did not lead them any deeper into nostalgia or even toward politics. When they hadn't been concerned with medical practicalities over the past two days, their conversation had been a part of the condo's decor, a neutral gray rug, no matter that it covered a lava bed of still-molten resentments and attraction. They talked as if the hollow apartment were full of other people and they'd both arrived here for a college reunion.

When the phone rang, Anne strode across the room, relieved at having something to do. "It's Mr. Channell," she said, waiting for Peter to get across the carpet and take the receiver.

"Hello, Spitz," he said. After a pause, Anne heard a grave and slightly self-important tone enter his voice: "Yes. I saw what Bush said about Gomez." And then, after a longer gap, with exasperation rising almost to a shout, he lambasted the caller: "One minute you're telling me they're going to name a base or a plane after me—and now you're saying you want my money for a legal-defense fund!"

Trick or Pete.

Anne realized he must be talking to one of the people Anders had seen him with on Monday night. What was the extent of his involvement with them? The only encouraging inference she could make was that it had been brief, that Peter had been acquainted with "Spitz" and his crowd only long enough to be set up for some bait-and-switch scheme. Or had the news from Central America, to which she'd barely paid attention this week, suddenly changed what was required of her ex-husband and his friends?

Short of breath, Peter walked back to his chair and made no attempt to explain the phone conversation.

"We have a mutual friend," Anne said, as deliberately as she could, picking up her glass of wine. "The young man your pal Nixon got me a White House tour with."

"Who's that?" Peter only half-remembered asking for that favor back in August.

"Anders Little. I think you actually met him the other night."

Peter seemed unsure of the name, but once he recollected the encounter, he smirked. "I wouldn't say he's marriage material. If he's like the rest of the group I saw him with."

Despite the crispness of this dismissal, she could see that he was even more confused than she was.

She'd heard, mostly in the form of jokes, about such odd political-sexual alignments: the old "Bonnie, Bonnie, and Clyde" joke about Joe McCarthy and his two young acolytes; and there was that true-believer congressman who'd lost his seat a few years back after picking somebody up in the wrong kind of bar. She wasn't *completely* naïve. But she couldn't fit Anders, her lean, tightly wound friend in Arlington, into this strange political cellar that Peter was hinting at.

"He's in Reykjavik right now."

"Who?" asked Peter.

"Anders Little."

Peter shrugged, as if the summit were of no more interest to him than how Anne, a nuclear freezenik, had become chums with this young man on the National Security Council. "Why don't you go fetch the *Times Herald*? It ought to be on the mat outside the door by now."

"Don't say 'fetch,' buster. I didn't put up with that even thirty years ago."

The two of them laughed, but she did go out to the hall and bring in the afternoon paper. They divided up sections of it as if the ancient cocktail hour had turned into a long-ago Sunday breakfast.

She ignored the Nicaragua story but summarized for Peter what the front page had to say about the superpower talks: a feeling of surprise, a sense of momentum, seemed to be in the Icelandic air, a sense that this might be a real summit after all and not just an overture.

"I hope Reagan doesn't disappoint you by making peace," said Peter.

"He'd disappoint *you* by making peace."

"I could bring up the inconvenient point that *you* voted for the only man in the history of the world to drop an atomic bomb. Two of them, in fact."

"Yes, and my punishment was to spend the next thirty years in the Republican Party, even though I vowed to remain a Democrat when I accepted your marriage proposal. God, the things I did for you!"

Peter managed to smile, but he was beginning to fade. He accepted Anne's suggestion that he lie down while she made dinner, though he refused her help getting to his bedroom.

In the kitchen she decided she should add the latest medication, picked up this afternoon, to the little day-by-day plastic holder whose compartments resembled a set of false teeth. This particular pill needed to be halved—was that hopeful?—and she opened a kitchen drawer to see if Peter might have a tiny chopper suited to the purpose. Another farrago of male disorganization greeted her, but she plunged her hands into the mess of can openers and matches and swizzle sticks until her fingers felt a metal campaign button, which she lifted from the drawer, thinking it must be one for Reagan or Connally—or maybe even one of Peter's own, from an old state senate race. But then she saw the simple old-fashioned lettering: I'M JUST WILD ABOUT HARRY. It was the button *she'd* been wearing thirty-eight years ago this month, one that Peter had snatched off her best polka-dot blouse on a Saturday night when they were parked in his brand-new '49 Ford. "I can't kiss you if you're wearing *that*," he'd informed her.

She had always believed he'd dropped it on the floor by the front seat, and gotten rid of it the next time he cleaned the car.

1:45 A.M. (RT), HOFDI HOUSE AND HOTEL HOLT, REYKJAVIK

"S-L-C-*M*," Anders Little heard Ken Adelman explaining, when he passed an open door on the second floor of Hofdi House. Adelman and one of the Russians were confusing each other about "sea-launched cruise missiles."

There was noise everywhere in the house, all of it cacophonically doubled by the translations. No one had enough room. Anders's own work station was in the large bathroom upstairs; boards had been laid across the tub to turn it into a desk. He and two others had to vacate the room whenever someone needed to use the toilet. It was as if an exchange students' frat house had fallen from the sky onto a remote island and they were all scrambling to improvise a new society. The feeling was heightened by a few eerily terrible paintings, works of art inspired by some training once conducted here by the American space program. They showed astronauts gamboling over the volcanic landscape.

It wasn't clear to Anders what his job consisted of tonight, besides of course listening in for Nixon. Nobody had anticipated this nighttime session, but everyone preferred its excitement to the aimless day they'd put in at the schoolhouse or embassy. Anders had been elated to find himself included in the all-hands-on-deck order that Don Regan issued before dinner.

On his knees by the bathtub, he sorted through some papers containing interpretations of several ABM-treaty provisions. Two or three times he heard cries of "Yes!" from some American voice in another room—not exasperated reiterations of whatever position the man was arguing, but yelps of pleasure over a Soviet counterpart's unexpected capitulation. He had also heard "*Da!*"—though only once, he now thought—when the dynamic ran in the opposite direction.

An NSC colleague burst into the bathroom. "Is there a Xerox machine anywhere? The basement maybe?"

"One of the Russians has carbon paper," Anders answered. "Let me go find the guy."

But before he could move he was surprised by the entry of State's Rozanne Ridgway, who with her sensible hairdo and oversized glasses looked like his high school French teacher. He could see, for all the calm she was trying to project, an astonished look behind her spectacles, an undeniable admission that nothing from her years negotiating fishing treaties in South America, or even serving as ambassador to the deep freeze that was East Germany, had prepared her for the night she was having with Aleksandr Bessmertnykh, the Soviets' deputy foreign minister.

She held a handwritten note. Anders rose from his knees, almost like a Senate page, to ask if he could be of any help.

Ms. Ridgway told him she understood that Paul Nitze and a few others would be heading over to the Holt—no matter that it was almost two a.m.—to consult with George Shultz. "I can't leave here myself. We've just passed a crucial point and are trying to solidify something. Could you bring this to the secretary?"

"Of course," said Anders. He took the note she'd been holding. It lacked even an envelope—there were none of those around, either— and Ms. Ridgway hadn't bothered to fold it. Anders did not hesitate to read the contents as she stood in front of him: *"Human rights will now be openly, officially and regularly on the agenda."* He knew instantly what this meant: those issues would no longer be confined to meaningless Soviet PR announcements in places like Helsinki. The Russians would now be negotiating them with the Americans, abuse by abuse, dissident by dissident, whenever armaments were discussed. It was the ultimate "linkage." Progress would from this point on involve not only, say, the Soviets scaling back their support of "liberation movements" in Africa; it would also require changes within jail cells an hour outside Moscow.

"I'd be honored to carry this," Anders told Ms. Ridgway.

"Thank you," she said, before rushing back to Bessmertnykh, as if afraid the Russian might change his mind while waiting for her at a table on the other side of the stair landing.

Minutes later, Anders was packing himself into a car with Paul Nitze, Max Kampelman, and Charles Hill, one of Shultz's men. All of them, followed by a second car, set out along the shoreline and headed back to town. The lights of the *George Ots*, aboard which the Gorbachevs were presumably asleep, shimmered in the harbor, and Anders caught a glimpse of this morning's cathedral as the driver made an eastward turn not far from the Holt.

The occupants of both cars quietly entered the lobby of the hotel, whose bar and lounges all remained open. Anders took the stairs, not to seek yet more exercise, but because the small elevator car wouldn't hold everyone. A security man hit him with several questions before letting him go higher than the third floor. By the time he reached Shultz's room, number 413, the secretary was already in conversation with Nitze and Richard Perle, who'd just arrived from his own hotel. "Agree to the fifty-percent cuts," Shultz was saying. "Agree to them for everything if you can get the Russians to soften on SDI." There was a pause. "Yes?" Shultz asked Anders, having just noticed him.

"I have this from Ms. Ridgway."

Shultz read the note, and some invisible part of his emotional makeup, maybe the same component that had long ago made him tattoo that Princeton tiger on his behind, sent tears into his eyes. Anders heard him whisper "Jericho" before one of the other visitors reminded everyone to be at the front door of the hotel no more than twenty minutes from now for the ride back to Hofdi House. The working groups would resume activity at three, said Nitze.

Downstairs, in the front lounge, Anders avoided several how-about-it looks from reporters who had guessed that all kinds of unexpected, even festive, turbulence was occurring inside the news blackout. He made his way to the bar to see if he could buy a bottle of mineral water—supplies at Hofdi House had run out—and felt a sudden distress, as well as peculiar comfort, from the unexpected sight of Hitchens, who waved him over from a seat near the painting of the weatherbeaten woman.

Anders flinched, recalling the abrupt, tearful departure he'd made at dawn, when he'd slipped from the writer's embrace as if it were something he both couldn't tolerate and didn't deserve. But he gathered his courage and went over to the couch, telling himself that he was not the rattled, unguarded person he'd allowed himself to be this morning. He was Mercury, swift and fit, conveying messages about the new and better world being birthed.

Hitchens introduced him to one man from the London *Telegraph* and another from the British embassy, before asking, "Long day?"

Bent on erasing his earlier display of weakness, Anders smiled and said, "We have it in our power to begin the world over again." It was the Tom Paine quotation from Reagan's declaration of candidacy.

Hitchens took a sip of port. "Yes. I'm afraid Ron wouldn't much like the rest of the book his speechwriter got that from."

The man from the British embassy asked Anders, "Any tidbit I should bring home to your Mr. Regan? He's bunking with us, you know. Something worth waking him up for?"

Anders smiled and went off to get his water. But once he had it in hand, he came back to the couch to further remake himself in Hitchens's eyes. What he *could* tell them wasn't, after all, a military secret, and if he put it *hypothetically* . . .

"Would you consider it a breakthrough," he asked the man from the embassy, "if I told you that from this point on, human-rights issues will be a regular, open, and legitimate part of every Soviet-American meeting?"

As he spoke, he wished that Anne Macmurray were here listening, too. He would prove to her it was the hard-liners who were softening the world. He would experience with her and Hitchens a Nixonian comeback, a regaining of self-possession.

Hitchens wrote down the phrasing that Anders had gotten from Rozanne Ridgway; he knew exactly the person to whom he would immediately pass it on.

10:00 P.M. (EDT), RESTAURANT NORA, 2132 FLORIDA AVENUE NW, WASHINGTON, D.C.

Pamela Harriman glanced, severely, at John Carter Brown: *This is not going well.* She wondered if asking for one of the restaurant's private dining rooms had made things worse. Perhaps her guests would be on better behavior if they were in public view.

It should have been *so* simple: inviting three of the party's most popular senators to a late supper. Aside from not being on this fall's ballot, all of them had some conservative inclination in foreign or domestic affairs that made them reassuring to independents and "swing" voters. In short, these were three men positioned to offer a little extra help, in the form of personal appearances or the dispersal of funds from their own political coffers, during these last crucial weeks of Pamela's crusade to recapture the Senate. That was to be her pitch, that they do all the law would allow in transferring money, and that they get out on the campaign trail once Dole turned everyone loose.

And, of course, none of it was proving simple at all.

Al Gore and Tipper, who even *looked* like Republicans, had been the first to arrive. If not so adroit as young Governor Clinton, Al was just as hungry. In fact, what somebody—perhaps Tipper?—needed to do was stop him from going too far too fast. Still not forty and in the Senate for exactly twenty-one months, he might foolishly begin trying to make himself president a year from now.

The Gores had been followed by the Hollingses. Fritz now sat on Pamela's right, across from his wife, Peatsy. They even *sounded* like Republicans, the new Southern type, their voices full of South Carolina molasses. And with his handsome face and silver hair, Fritz looked like someone Leland might have cast in a road-company production of *Mr. President*. It had been ridiculous of Senator Hollings to try for the *actual* job in '84, but the temptation must have been irresistible when he looked around and saw that his competitors for the nomination would be on the order of Glenn and Mondale. Fortunately, his campaign had flamed out so quickly that almost no one remembered it had ever occurred.

Last to arrive—and the reason Pamela never should have allowed herself to think this evening would be easy—was Pat Moynihan. She had been hoping that her invitation would be interpreted as a modest request for rapprochement, but the second he came into the room— and gave her a barely civil hello—she had realized her mistake. He was without his wife, who had no doubt decided against any friendly return signal. He'd chosen to come instead with dear Lindy Boggs, the Louisiana congresswoman and a great favorite of everybody even before she took over her dead husband's seat in the House. Mrs. Boggs and Moynihan had become pals, Pamela remembered, while helping to preserve some stretch of Pennsylvania Avenue in all its unattractive glory, and the senior senator from New York was clearly enjoying a chance to escort this popular old belle. (Tipper, Peatsy, and Lindy! Dear God, it was like some Faulknerian version of *Winnie-the-Pooh*.)

The strange thing about Moynihan: one minute he was plummier than Lord Digby's friends; the next, he seemed to be back on a street corner in Hell's Kitchen. Well, it would be a bumpy night. But at least he'd decided to show up and, presumably, help out the team.

The drinks tray arrived at last.

"I hope *this* isn't oh-ganic, too," said Hollings, taking a glass of white wine. He found the restaurant a peculiar choice.

"Oh, but it is!" Pamela exclaimed. "These are Virginia grapes. They come from a vineyard not far from my little place in Middleburg."

"I hope you won't mind my having *one*," said Moynihan, glaring at her as he lifted a glass from the tray.

"Cheers," said Pamela, suppressing a groan. It was going to be worse than she'd thought.

Their history was terrible, she had to admit. Thirty years ago, during Ave's single, less-than-successful term in Albany, Moynihan had been one of his most important aides. A decade later, she'd become Mrs. Harriman and begun dabbling in Democratic politics. She had plunged herself and Ave into Bella Abzug's '76 campaign for the Senate nomination in New York, and yes, she *had* made rather a point of telling people that Bella's main foe, Mr. Moynihan, had a decided problem with drink. It was the truth, but she had been maybe a bit aggressive in spreading it the way she had. When Moynihan found out, he naturally was enraged. Today, of course, she would do things differently; and maybe it wasn't too late to begin placating him.

"I must say, the news from Iceland, or what we heard of it on the car radio, sounds quite encouraging," observed John Carter Brown. Rumors of bold proposals and unexpected breakthroughs were continuing to find their way through the press blackout.

"That depends on how one looks at it," said Pamela, with the smile of a scolding spouse. Indeed, for all that she might like him to share her interests, her expression seemed to be telling Brown that if he wanted the van Gogh he would leave the punditry to her.

"They should have sent some Senate observers over there with Reagan, like last year," said Hollings. "We ate pretty well in Geneva, I must say."

"It would be interesting to know what those 'working groups' are up to tonight," said Senator Gore. Stories of the "all-nighter," which by now must be in progress, were everywhere.

"That's what *we* are tonight," said Pamela. "A *working* group." She smiled with the purposeful cheer of a girl chairing the decorations committee for the prom.

"Already?" asked Hollings, frowning. He wanted at least a second drink and a good look at the suspicious menu before Mrs. Harriman got them down to business.

Carter Brown tried to slow things down by remarking that Nora, a risky proposition at first, had now enjoyed seven years of success. He seemed to be starting a brief lecture, as if the restaurant were a piece of colonial furniture.

"I can remember when this buildin' was a grocery store," said Peatsy Hollings.

"You eat here often?" her husband asked Brown. "You look like you're starvin'. Skinny as a rail."

"Everything looks grand," Mrs. Boggs said, convivially, though a stolen glance at the bill of fare had revealed the cuisine to be a bit *minceur* for her New Orleans taste. "You know, my friend Paul Prudhomme just opened up in New York a while ago. They gave him all *kinds* of trouble with permits!" She pronounced it, pleasingly, as *POI-mits*. "But I gave Eddie Koch a call and got him to speed things up. We always had such a nice time workin' together on Banking and Currency when he was in the House."

"We need to get back to regulatin' trade instead of restaurants," said Hollings.

Peatsy, who had run her husband's office while he was still married to his first wife, was taking her own look at the menu. "I'm regulatin' *you*," she told Hollings, "but I'm goin' to let you have the *tres leches* cake for dessert. I don't see any point in anybody even *tryin'* to resist that."

"I want that, too," said Tipper.

"I'm going to pass, when we get there," said Al Gore, who clearly paid attention to his trim physique and whose remark left the unfortunate impression that he wished his wife would pay more attention to hers.

"Where did we once have that cake, Al? Mexico?" asked Tipper.

Moynihan, flamboyantly bored, all but begged for them to go on to a more interesting topic. "That dessert is all over Central America," he said. "Just like us."

Everyone became alert. They sometimes had to remind themselves that this charter neoconservative, whose foreign-policy apostasy predated Jeane Kirkpatrick's, had a while back split from Reagan on the matter of the Contras. Seeing that they could use a refresher course, the former Harvard professor explained, "I was *personally* offended by not being told by the administration that we were mining the Nicaraguan harbors. I was offended on behalf of my Republican committee chairman as well."

Pamela nodded her agreement, hoping to inch back into Moynihan's good graces, though she wondered if it mightn't be true, as she'd heard, that the chairman and vice chairman of the Intelligence Committee *had* been briefed. Senators Goldwater and Moynihan had just been a little too sozzled to remember it later.

"I have never objected to Mrs. Kirkpatrick's tough-mindedness," Moynihan continued—his bowtie seemed to smile while the head above it bobbed and preened—"but I would like that intellectual condition to be accompanied by a certain respect for international law. The ability to effect such a combination is one of the qualities so many of us find admirable in the junior senator from Tennessee." He raised his glass to Al Gore, who if he did jump into the '88 race would be the most conservative Democrat in the field, at least when it came to defense. Tipper rewarded him with a little neck squeeze, and Gore, accustomed all his life to praise from older men, nodded bashfully.

Nineteen eighty-eight was the last subject Pamela wanted to get into, and she decided that the moment had come to cajole and flatter. "I'd like to talk about who's *not* here tonight," she began. "I'm speaking of the wonderful challengers and incumbents that we have in the field, such as John Breaux in Louisiana"—Mrs. Boggs nodded—"and Harriett Woods in Missouri. There's Harry Reid out in Nevada, and even further west, Alan Cranston is facing a tough race in California, whose voters have never made him quite the *institution* that all of *your* voters have been wise enough to make *you*."

"Even young Al?" asked Hollings, who reached around Tipper to give Gore a good-natured poke. "Pammy, that's layin' it on pretty thick for a fella who's been with us less'n two years."

Mrs. Harriman flashed her boxy smile and pressed on: "I'm hoping that you'll all be willing to consider ways of extending yourselves even further in the little more than three weeks we have left. Especially in Florida, where Bob Graham needs all our help. Mrs. Hawkins"—she pronounced it like the name of some awful governess—"is preparing an enormous barrage of ads later this month. And while Governor Graham has been offering the voters a sensible array of moderate proposals on Social Security, the economy, and international affairs, the incumbent's only issue seems to be *children*."

Peatsy Hollings turned to Lindy Boggs and said, "Speakin' of which, how's your wonderful Cokie?"

"Oh, she's just great," said Mrs. Boggs about her daughter, who was familiar to them all from National Public Radio, and to Al Gore from his own Washington childhood. "You know," the congresswoman said as gently as she could to Mrs. Harriman, "children's issues can be mighty powerful in a campaign . . ."

"Well, of *course*," said Pamela. "But—"

"She went to bat for us," said Tipper, remembering something. "Paula Hawkins. She showed the Twisted Sister video. She was good!"

"That was a wonderful thing you did organizin' those hearings, Tipper," said Lindy Boggs. She referred to Mrs. Gore's young-motherly crusade to get rock'n'roll songs, with their often filthy lyrics, rated according to the same kind of system the movies had.

"What was the worst one?" asked Hollings, with a grin. "I remember you talkin' about it."

Peatsy tried to squelch her husband's question. "Darlin', I don't think we need—"

"Oh, I don't mind," said Tipper. "You're thinking of 'Darling Nikki.' It was number one on our Filthy Fifteen." The wife of Tennessee's junior senator proceeded to sing several lines of the song, in which a young man remarks upon a girl "masturbating with a magazine" in a public space. "This is the sort of thing my daughter was listening to!" Mrs. Gore added.

"Oh, my," said Mrs. Boggs, after hearing Prince's lyrics. "Well, it's wonderful what congressional wives get up to nowadays. When Hale was in the House, I just did a lot of hospital committees."

"The participle appears to dangle," said Moynihan, with more than visible contempt.

"What?" asked Pamela.

"Just what I said. The song clearly means to indicate that the young lady is pleasuring herself. But the grammar suggests it might be the gentleman doing that to *him*self. I don't suppose the sheet music provided clear punctuation?"

In the ensuing silence, Carter Brown began remarking on the Amish quilts with which Nora was decorated.

"Let's get back to Florida," Mrs. Harriman declared. "Governor Graham needs to put this race away. As you know, Mrs. Hawkins has many vulnerabilities, especially ones involving her health. She has lied about her hospitalizations for back pain and lied about the amount of time she spends in traction."

Moynihan fairly exploded. "Have you changed at *all*, madam? The lady's health is her own affair! She doesn't have her finger on the nuclear trigger. She's entitled to be indisposed now and again. Yes, she spends some of that time in traction in a hospital bed near Senator Thurmond's office; and she gets *out* of it in order to come to the floor and *vote*. I should think the people of Florida might be pleased to hear of such zeal."

Hollings knew what this was really about. Mrs. Boggs wasn't sure, but she politely changed the subject, expressing a hope that New Orleans might host both party conventions the year after next. She'd be happy to open her Bourbon Street home even to the Republicans.

Pamela, determined not to inflame Moynihan any further, turned to the congresswoman and smiled. "I'm afraid I'll be making the case for Washington, D.C., when the site-selection committee comes to town next month. There'll be a party for them at the Riverview and I shall be arguing how nice it would be to fight Ronald Reagan in his own backyard! Not to mention the thirty million dollars' worth of business the convention would bring to this poor city that's been so neglected by Mr. Reagan."

"More nonsense!" cried Moynihan. "Ronald Reagan got reelected—with fifty-nine percent of the vote—by continuing to run as an 'outsider.' And *you* want to make despised Washington look like the Democrats' natural habitat! Why don't you just write the city a check for the thirty million?"

Carter Brown, who knew the van Gogh to be worth even more than that, wondered whether he should put a stop to this. But Pamela looked straight at Moynihan and said, with a certain steel, "Well, perhaps this summit, before it's over, will drive the president's numbers *down*. We can only hope."

"You don't support your country? You—an 'American by choice'—want your president to fail?"

For a moment no one uttered a word. Then Mrs. Harriman, through neatly clenched teeth, said, "Of *course* I support the country. Unfortunately, the president who is negotiating for it won't even agree to a test-ban treaty, which Mr. Gorbachev most sincerely wants."

Moynihan, after finishing off his wine, scoffed at her. "That sounds like a transcript of the last tutorial Ave must have given you. What you fail to understand is that Mr. Gorbachev wants to reduce the number of missiles because he can scarcely pay for the maintenance of the ones he already *has*—let alone develop any new ones through testing. We need simply to wait out the U.S.S.R.; I've been pointing this out for some time. My only fear is that the president will overplay a strong hand, panic the Soviets, and make them grab a piece of the Middle East, or do something even worse, to distract the peoples—yes, that's an ethnic plural—of their fractious and crumbling empire. There's no need to throw 'evil' onto the pile of adjectives. 'Easy does it' and 'wait them out.' As I've been saying."

Mrs. Harriman glared, as if any talk about the disappearance of the Soviet Union was a further insult to Ave—and thus a cheapening of the prestige he had bequeathed her, along with the van Gogh. She signaled to the waiter that they were ready to order, though no one had yet made a full study of the menu. While people took a fast look, she made a final, restrained effort at reconciliation.

"I'm glad you accepted my invitation nonetheless," she said to Moynihan, with something like a smile.

"I accepted it only because it asked me to come to this restaurant," said Moynihan.

"You like oh-ganic food that much?" asked Hollings, hoping to rescue things with a little raillery.

"No," said Moynihan. "Because by coming here I could assist my party without breaking my pledge."

"Pledge?" asked Mrs. Boggs.

"Yes," said Moynihan, staring at Pamela. "My pledge never to set foot in that woman's house."

6:30 A.M. (MOSCOW TIME), ZHKH-385/3-4, "SMALL ZONE," BARASHEVO PRISON, MORDOVIA, U.S.S.R.

Sofya Kornilov lay awake thinking, pleasurably, of the two occasions that she and the rest of the women in this enclosure—something between a house and a hut—had celebrated in just the past week. First had come news of Yuri Orlov's release, for which the eight prisoners had split four pieces of contraband chocolate into halves. And then, on Thursday, had come the news that Irina, one of *them*, was being freed! Only thirty-two years old, but she'd already done three years, and had at least that many to go, if you counted the portion of her sentence that would eventually banish her into "internal exile," like Sakharov. To be freed instead! There was no chocolate left, but the women had rejoiced. A feeling that something *big* was afoot in the vast wretched country outside the gates of the gulag had begun to act like a kind of champagne on them.

"Agitation" may have been the offense leading to Sofya's own imprisonment, but her "criminal activity" actually derived from a serene nature. She took pleasure in at least *knowing* what she was in here for—violating Articles 70 and 72 of the Soviet Penal Code—which is more than her father could do when he was picked up for no stated reason at all in the 1930s. Sofya was not a refusenik. She desired just to leave jail, not the country—same as Irina Ratushinskaya, who even now was bent on keeping her citizenship. Sofya *was* guilty, proudly, of editing a *samizdat* that monitored international opposition to the *psikhushki*, the psychiatric hospitals for political dissidents. Unlike Irina, she was not the least bit literary. She had published her underground journal in the plainest possible style.

Right now the far-off sound of squabbling amongst the *zeks*—the actual, nonpolitical criminals—seemed almost peaceful. Sofya was glad to be back here where she could see the watchtower, and to be once more on the ordinary regimen; she had returned to it two weeks ago, after her latest hunger strike earned her a stretch in an isolation cell. Bad as that had been, she was happy not to have been put in a *psikhushka*, which might have been somebody's ironic idea of "justice."

She was glad, too, that she had no husband and no children, no one to miss or make suffer. Irina had been permitted but one visit with her Igor (so handsome!) during all the time she'd been here. She was a brave, headstrong girl, saving her paper ration for letters to him, writing her poems on soap bars. Once she had them memorized, the evidence of their existence would go down the drain. *Lather—rinse—repeat!* they used to joke, to encourage her—not that she ever needed much cheering on. She had always been full of schemes and pluck, like having them all write that letter to Reagan, congratulating him on winning reelection, and then actually getting it to him! There was help both inside and outside the gates now—journalists and diplomats passed all kinds of information to sympathetic guards—but that particular success had been a miracle of mischief. "Well," she'd reasoned, "why shouldn't I write to Ronald Reagan? I was sentenced in the same month he talked of the 'evil empire.'" News of the president's speech had spread joyously through the camps, faster than the usual flu.

It would be nice to have some *real* champagne, although a part of Sofya was able to concede the reasonableness of Gorbachev's inveighings against alcohol. The country would probably come out of its political stupor only after it shook off the even longer one induced by vodka.

A knock on the window. Through the cloudy old glass she could see a guard motioning her to the front door. She opened it, and he gave her two cigarettes, knowing that she didn't smoke. She took them, closed the door and peeled off what she knew would be the extra rolling paper on each one of them.

SHE SIGNED NO CONFESSION, TOOK NO CLEMENCY, read the first of the messages.

Brave Irina!

Nina, a religious ecstatic whose arms were always raising themselves toward heaven, had begun to stir. Sofya put her finger to her lips but urged her to come have a look. The second rolling paper contained a message about Shevardnadze, the foreign minister, and themselves:

EDUARD AMBROSIS CONCEDES SOVIET POLITICALS HENCEFORTH LEGITIMATE MATTER FOR DISCUSSION AND AGENDA.
   YOU EXIST.

Nina crossed herself and Sofya rolled her eyes, as though to say: Well, if you *must*. And then, in the dawn's early light, the two women embraced.

16

SUNDAY, OCTOBER 12, 1986

9:25 A.M. (EDT), WHITE HOUSE RESIDENCE, WASHINGTON, D.C.

"I'm sorry, it must be early out there," said Nancy Reagan. As if she didn't know the time difference between Washington and California! At even falsely apologetic moments like this she was used to getting replies on the order of "Oh, no, not at all!" but Joan Quigley could be as assertive as she was expensive. "It's still dark!" the astrologer replied from San Francisco. Even so, Nancy could hear her rousing herself from bed.

Nancy had been up since six, reading the new Sinatra biography by that awful little blonde who lived across town and was now said to be gunning for *her*. After reaching the end of the Ava Gardner marriage, the first lady had forced herself to stop and open up the *Post*, which she saw contained her response to Raisa, made last night before the Catholic University event. *"I heard over the air that I didn't feel fine."* It read as a nice combination of innocence and cattiness, Nancy decided, though a part of her wished she'd been bitchier: *I see she's been wearing some wonderful outfits* was the remark she'd squelched at the last minute.

The paper reported that Ninotchka would be touring a sheep farm today—no doubt putting in a good word for collectivization as she trudged from lamb to lamb.

No, thought Nancy, she had to keep holding her tongue. Too much was at stake, and the payoff might turn out to exceed anybody's imagining.

"I'm hearing all kinds of things from over there," she told Joan.

"Were they really at it all night?" the astrologer asked.

"That's what Ronnie told me when he called a few hours ago—just before he headed into this morning's session. I'm surprised everyone isn't punchy." If Don Regan, or even George Shultz, had tried to drag Ronnie himself into those post-midnight meetings, she'd have pitched a fit.

Joan Quigley wondered if the first lady wanted anything in particular. "Are you concerned about the departure time?" she asked.

"There's still nothing fixed, but Ronnie did promise he'd be back for supper. So I expect they'll be taking off soon." She looked over at her plaid suit with the big buttons, already laid out for the trip to Andrews. A sudden worry: had she been photographed in it only a few weeks ago? Maybe even at some event with Dole and Sugarlips, who might be in today's welcome-home delegation?

"The meeting really should go on for as long as possible," said Joan.

"But CNN just said it's close to finishing! And it's the last one."

Joan sighed, something almost no one else around the first lady had done audibly for years. "Nancy, I've said it from the beginning: no matter how spectacular the charts look for this summit, it all requires *time*, both for the meetings themselves and for the results to *play out*." As she went on about the alignments of Aquarius (Ronnie) and Pisces (Gorbachev), Nancy did her best, as usual, to hide how the technical points of astrology bored her. But she knew there might be something to this business of letting things play out over time—even Sydney Omarr, in today's *Post*, was telling Aquarians to "*look beyond the immediate; perceive potential. You are on the right track.*"

"It's a shame they can't have a fourth session," said Joan. "That was always the optimum number."

"You never told me that!"

"Nancy, my mandate has never extended much beyond arrival and departure times. We got the president there a day early, as we should have, but the number of meetings and the wrap-up on Sunday has always depended on the Russians. Six o'clock today—Iceland time—still looks crucial. But crucial can mean a lot of things."

Nancy closed her eyes for a moment, wishing she'd gone with him, even if reversing course would have looked like dancing to that Russian dame's tune.

"Okay, Joan. Thanks. And I'm sorry about the early call. I won't bother you again until this is over and we've all had a breather. But you and I have some big talks coming up after that."

She was more than ever determined to get herself and Ronnie out of here.

Joan made a professional-sounding goodbye, and Nancy turned back toward CNN, unmuting it with the remote. Frank Sesno, who looked no older than the interns downstairs, was saying:

There you have it. On this American football Sunday we've got a summit that's gone into overtime. This is a quite unexpected development, perhaps unprecedented in the annals of Cold War diplomacy, and you can bet that we will all be spending this late lunch hour in Reykjavik wondering if it means that a major agreement is at hand.

She suddenly saw Ronnie and Gorbachev pulling away in their limousines—to return, as Sesno now explained, at three o'clock.

Going into overtime. God, Joan really did know her stuff.

A knock on the door brought Maureen, who was wearing an apron, bent on making chili for some friends who'd be coming over this afternoon to watch one of the football games. She was raising both her hands to show crossed fingers on each. "Do you think my prayers have been answered? I did as Dad asked!"

1:55 P.M. (RT), ROOM 324, HOTEL HOLT, REYKJAVIK

Anders made a quick stop back at the Holt in order to calm himself—*everyone* needed calming—and to brush his teeth. He would grab a sandwich at the embassy, three blocks away, and then try to make it back to Hofdi House before the president did.

But the phone was ringing.

"What the hell's going on there? This clown Velikhov is all over the tube."

"Mr. President," said Anders. "Velikhov?"

"Soviet Academy of Sciences," said Nixon. "He's having a press conference at the Russians' hotel near you. Saying Gorbachev and Reagan are on the verge of a big agreement—and don't blame the Soviets if it falls through."

"He's violating the news blackout," said Anders, at a loss for anything else.

"Big goddamn surprise!" exclaimed the former president, who nevertheless seemed to appreciate the Soviets' chess move. "The Russians have put him in front of the cameras to whip the media into a frenzy—to make them start begging Reagan not to leave without a deal. Christ, Barbara Walters will be on any minute asking him to 'be good to us.'" He paused. "Between all this and what Nancy's telling him, it's going to be very tough for him to do the right thing."

"Despite what this guy may be saying, the morning had plenty of rough moments," Anders assured the former president, remembering that he was supposed to be the one conveying news. "I was upstairs but I got the gist of what happened during the ride back to town."

"Tell me what you heard," said Nixon.

Anders looked at the notes he'd just made in the car. "The two of them began with jokes about the Book of Genesis. Gorbachev told Reagan it was only the second day, so they had five more to go before they got a day of rest."

Nixon harrumphed. "Godless son of a bitch."

"Then Reagan reminded him it was Sunday—so it *is* a day of rest."

Anders could detect Nixon's impatience on the other end of the line. Was it over the inconsequence of the story or the thought of Reagan's casual work habits?

"They reviewed the reports from last night's working groups," Anders continued. "Gorbachev said his conscience was clear about the 'bold' proposals he came here with and what they added up to: the elimination of all U.S. and Soviet strategic nuclear weapons within a decade—two five-year phases."

"All!" cried Nixon, with a horror that couldn't catch up to his disbelief.

"Yes, and he said he had one more big concession to make in the short run. The Soviets will allow the Americans to put one hundred more missiles on U.S. territory if the Russians can keep one hundred in Asia. For now. After ten years those will be gone, too."

"Christ," said Nixon.

"It does sound like a crazy meeting, sir. Sort of like the weather here all morning. Fifteen minutes of sunshine, then fifteen minutes of cold rain. The rough spots of the discussion all involved SDI. The president says that developing it doesn't violate the ABM treaty—' "

"The hell it doesn't!" said Nixon.

"—and that we'll share it with the Soviets. Gorbachev doesn't believe him and insists that the research be confined to the laboratory. The president got mad enough to swear at one point, something like, 'Why the hell should anyone have to live another ten years with the threat of nuclear weapons if we've already decided to get rid of them?' "

"He said *we've*?" asked Nixon.

"I believe so. And he also said 'hell.' "

Nixon snorted. "When he uses that word in a letter he writes it with a dash: 'h,' blank-blank, 'l.' Goddamned affectation."

Anders looked at his watch. He knew he had to speed up. "Gorbachev told the president it 'takes two to tango,' and he wondered where the American concessions were."

"Reagan's conceding *everything*! Who's going to tango with *him* in the Congress, when the only way he'll get a treaty like this approved would be with a massive buildup of troops and tanks to match what the Russians have ready to roll into Berlin once the missiles are gone."

"Reagan got sort of philosophical at one point," said Anders, trying to make sense of a sentence he'd written while the car was crossing a cobblestoned intersection. "Or historical, I suppose. He said that we distrust the Soviets because they've always talked about wanting a 'worldwide Communist state.' And then Gorbachev reminded Reagan that *he* had suggested putting *them* on the 'ash heap of history,' which isn't exactly peaceful coexistence."

Nixon groaned. "He knows nothing about history."

"Gorbachev?"

"No. Reagan."

Anders struggled to finish. "Shultz kept watching the clock and ended up proposing that he and Shevardnadze use lunchtime to work on a statement about the reductions—"

"*Reductions?* He and Reagan have become a bunch of goddamned *abolitionists!*"

"—and leave ABM and SDI to be solved later. Gorbachev said that maybe they'll have to go home from here with nothing, and Reagan indicated he thought that would be a shame. The notetaker in the meeting said he looked kind of sad."

"This scares the hell out of me," said Nixon. "It sounds like Yalta—and they don't even have Hiss whispering into their ears!"

"Shultz and Shevardnadze are still at Hofdi House," explained Anders, "trying to see if they can agree on language. The president and Gorbachev are supposed to get back there by three." If he himself didn't get out of here soon, he would miss lunch *and* his ride.

"What's everybody else doing now?" asked Nixon. "The staff, I mean."

"Calling our allies—to give them a heads-up in case the deal goes through."

"They ought to be telling them to build another goddamned Maginot Line!"

Anders was silent, and Nixon said nothing more for a moment or two. Finally, he issued an instruction: "Don't leave the hotel for ten minutes. And stop at the front desk before you do."

11:00 A.M. (CDT), AMERICAN AIRLINES DEPARTURES TERMINAL,
DALLAS/FORT WORTH

Standing near her gate, Anne looked out the window at DFW's monorail, which made the airport look like the ugliest ski resort ever built. She was coming to understand how Peter could have seen this scorned and brutally bumptious city as just the place for his attempted reinvention. It was harder to convince herself that *she* had done the right thing—just been useful, and not put herself into deep emotional water—by coming here three days ago.

The trip had at least turned out to be economical. She was probably the last person in the United States still using traveler's checks and, having spent only one night at the Adolphus, the packet of them in her purse remained nearly as thick as when she'd arrived. She *had* modernized herself to the point of having a telephone credit card—it had come automatically when she established service in Arlington—and she knew that if she punched the right codes into a pay phone she could "access" the messages on her new answering machine.

The sight of a phone by the next gate filled her with a pointless urgency to do that; surely this could wait another few hours, until she was back inside her apartment? But the weekend's atmosphere of emergency would not abate, and with a few minutes left before boarding she picked up her suitcase and went to the phone. It took her two tries to make the codes work.

The first message was from her daughter, an exasperated little speech that was only technically an apology: *Mother, it's Susan. Daddy called me yesterday when you were napping. I'm sorry Ralph and I didn't tell you. We were going to wait and see what the situation is after the chemo. You know, you didn't need to do this, rush down there and . . .*

She wished she were in the room with the machine and could fastforward through this childish scolding that treated *her* like a child. There was probably a way to do that by punching yet another code, but she didn't know it, so she let Susan's voice play on until the tape came to a second message—this one from the girl in the WAND office whom she'd thought about fixing up with Anders. It must have been recorded only minutes before: *Hi, Anne. It's Lisa. Let's see, it's Sunday, a little before lunchtime. Some news, huh? It sounds like peace is breaking out over there! Give me a call if you get this and have a chance.*

Anne looked over at the TV near her own gate, wishing she were close enough to hear what the onscreen reporter was saying. But there was a third message, even more recent than the second, for her to hear—something from Helen Caldicott's least pleasant lieutenant, a woman from the Boston office who always managed to be grim and manic at the same time, someone Anne and Lisa called Alma Geddon: *Ms. Macmurray, I was hoping to get you at home. It's important that you be at your desk tomorrow by eight a.m. We're likely to be issuing a statement on what's happening—whenever it becomes clear what that man is* doing *over there! Eight o'clock, please—and keep an eye on the fax machine.*

Anne realized that "Alma" was too young to remember when FDR had been "that man" in the White House. The epithet's use in this message made it appear that whatever was going on in Iceland, progress or conflict, would soon become something bad in the world of WAND, simply because it was Ronald Reagan helping to bring it about. The deduction made Anne uncomfortable, while three beeps signaled that there were no further messages for her.

As she picked up her bag and returned to her gate, she made a mental note to buy one of these new suitcases with wheels and a leash. Looking up at the television, she could see the CNN man standing not far from the little white wooden house in Reykjavik. Patched into one of the Sunday talk shows, he was explaining: *Moments ago one mid-level American official said, "It's a bold and breathtaking business." Extraordinary reductions in nuclear weaponry may be imminent. Once Mr. Velikhov's statement broke the news blackout, this American source was willing to speak on the record—but still not willing to be named. As we've been reporting all weekend, Hofdi House is thought to be haunted. Well, everyone here is beginning to wonder if it's not a very benevolent ghost that's worked whatever magic will be making Mr. Reagan and Mr. Gorbachev return to the table on the second floor for this afternoon's surprise session . . .*

4:05 P.M. (RT), HOFDI HOUSE, REYKJAVIK

Anders tried to scrutinize the face of Don Regan. Across one of the big upstairs rooms, the chief of staff was taking another look at what Anders recognized to be Nixon's lunchtime fax—a document Anders had more or less committed to memory:

The proposed agreement will strengthen the Soviet position immeasurably. I myself do not believe that SDI will ever be deployed—except, in effect, at this meeting. If you insist on it to the point where the Soviets walk away from the proposed sweeping reductions, then SDI will have done more for American security than its actual development could ever achieve.

Regan's expression definitely showed annoyance. He was seeing none of Nixon's usual cagey deference in this document; the tone reflected a sense of emergency, even dread, about what was going on here. Anders guessed that Regan didn't disagree with the fax's substance, but it was in the nature of his position, as the president's steward, to crave short-term, immediate success for his administration. Even though Anders had gotten him the fax before Reagan and Gorbachev went back into session downstairs, Regan had declined to show it to his boss.

Anders made a bleak psychological calculation. If Nixon's advice provoked a sense of guilt in the chief of staff, Regan's subconscious would soon sour on the former president. References to the Sage of Saddle River, often heard around the White House, would lose their affection and express only mockery—and at that point no one would be more vulnerable to the chief of staff's displeasure than Anders Little, Nixon's eyes and ears.

The room was quiet, tense with a feeling that the die had been cast, that there would now be an astonishing agreement or nothing at all. Some of the staff read paperback books; others made notes they could show to future employers or will to grandchildren. From time to time the saturnine Perle and the silvery Nitze looked far out the windows, as if the negotiations downstairs were incidental to their own competing visions.

Anders decided to get some air—and to make himself scarce for a few minutes. He descended the stairs, passed the closed doors on the second floor, and exited into the cold air. The lights were now on in all the rooms of Hofdi House, and from the gathering darkness outside, the old dwelling place looked more cozy than haunted. The press had assembled in the middle distance, a tenterhooked mob, quiet for the moment, reminding Anders of the birds in Alfred Hitchcock. Especially eager to avoid the sight of Hitchens, he turned away from all the microphones and lights and cables and looked instead in the direction of Keflavík, imagining Air Force One, which had been on the runway ready to take off for the past several hours.

Back inside, he was startled to see Tom Simons, the notetaker for the current session, double-timing it up from the second floor to the third. "Secretary Shultz," Simons breathlessly explained to Regan, "asked me to type up this translation of the latest Soviet draft." By this point confidentiality and the chain of command had pretty much collapsed. The silence in the room allowed the whole American team to hear what Simons was telling the chief of staff: "Everyone's still fine with the reductions, but Gorbachev keeps insisting that SDI be confined to the lab. Even so, the president seems to think that they're getting close."

"What's *wrong* with Shultz?" barked Regan. "You're not a typist! We need somebody in there!" His glance fell on Anders. "Didn't you take notes at the staff meeting the other morning? Get down there! We're not going to rely on some goddamned translation of the Russian guy's notes!"

Anders raced to the second floor with a legal pad and pen, which he held up to the American security man at the door. "I'm in for Simons," he said, as if this were a track meet back at Wake Forest.

Ronald Reagan, used to the unexplained scurryings of staff, smiled as Anders took a seat at the table. Gorbachev said nothing. Looking out the window, at the encroaching sea, Anders himself felt almost sick with excitement.

"You can confine SDI to the laboratory and trust us," said the general secretary. "We would not have made the proposals we did if you couldn't."

"SDI will guarantee that the agreement *sticks*," said Reagan. "As I've said before, we'll share it and we'll use it to see that a madman—Qadaffi, or that fellow my age over in North Korea—doesn't start something with his own nuclear weapons." He took a long pause and looked out at the ocean. When his eyes returned to Gorbachev's, his voice was low and confidential, and his eyes, much younger than the rest of him, were glistening: "Ten years from now I'll be a very old man. We can come back here together and bury the last atomic weapon and have a party for the whole world. You'll say, 'Ron, is that you?' and I'll say, 'Mikhail, it's wonderful to see you again.' "

He's seeing it as a movie, thought Anders: *Mike and Ron Save the World*. It was absurd and frightening and, in some eerie way, brilliant. Anders felt a surge of protectiveness toward Reagan, as if he were Grandfather Little back in North Carolina. Whatever happened here, he wasn't going to tell Nixon the lines that had just been spoken; they would only provoke an explosion of scorn. But he recorded the little speech as best he could, using any abbreviations that came to mind. In the midst of everything else, he wondered: Would he be able to keep this original piece of paper?

Shultz was leaning forward in his chair. Gorbachev bitterly joked: "You will outlive me, Mr. President! You'll make it to one hundred. But you are killing me with this desire to *win*, with your refusal to make concessions."

"I won't make it to a hundred if I have to keep worrying about Soviet missiles," said Reagan. Anders thought this was an excellent line, the kind that earns a comedian a rimshot from the drummer, but when he looked up from his pad he saw that Reagan's face lacked any hint of a smile. He said nothing more.

"We are on the verge of eliminating those missiles," said Gorbachev, wearily, through his translator. "And we are *not* eliminating your SDI by restricting it to the laboratory."

"And *we're* not going to be putting weapons into space as you keep contending. SDI is purely defensive. Why don't we leave it as an issue to be settled when you come to Washington?"

"No," said Gorbachev, immediately. "This must be a package."

"We're not getting anywhere," said Reagan, flinging down a pencil he'd never used. "Let's take a recess."

At that moment Simons came back to the room carrying a single freshly typed page. Anders was crushed, as if one of his parents had come to drag him home from a party. The restored notetaker sat down next to him just as Gorbachev was refusing to take a break. No one seemed to care, Anders realized, whether he stayed or left. So he would stay! He doubted he would ever again, for longer than a handshake, be this close to Reagan. People in the White House were always taking the president's measure, figuring him out, and reporting back on their five minutes in his company. They would describe Reagan's mental terrain as being vastly more complicated than anything yet reckoned—or else they would worry that the cupboard really *was* bare. The questions about him remained so basic, the hypotheses so far apart, that there was still no agreement even as to what instrument was required to read him, a microscope or a telescope. Anders now felt himself wishing his own ten minutes here would stretch toward twenty, so that he, too, could at last make a personal, perhaps seminal, reading of the president.

Gorbachev went back to SDI and how it was a violation of the ABM treaty; if Reagan would only concede this simple point, he said, they could begin the ten-year-long abolition of nuclear weapons within the next ten minutes. But he got no response. Reagan looked briefly at the draft language Simons had brought in, and Gorbachev at last agreed to the recess that the president had proposed. Within seconds everyone was standing up, heading toward their respective precincts upstairs, where, unlike last night, the staircase now operated as a kind of Berlin Wall between the American and Soviet sides. Anders had no choice but to follow Reagan and Shultz and Simons, and to accept the unlikelihood of his ever getting back down to the second floor. He felt, for a split second, the understudy's impulse to trip Simons and break his leg.

The last round, they all knew, would start in minutes. For now, while listening to Shultz, Don Regan made every effort to exert his authority: he was the champ's manager and Shultz merely the corner man. The president himself looked as if he were waiting to have his cheeks slapped with liniment. He remained silent except for the utterance of a firm *nyet* when his chief of staff raised the possibility of their all staying another night. The one-word response provoked a small burst of laughter from Buchanan.

"This is taking too long," Reagan added—not, Anders realized, with irritation at the prospect of being late for dinner, but with a despairing pit-of-the-stomach sense that the patient downstairs had been on the operating table for too many hours and was unlikely to pull through.

Trying to figure out what, if anything, could be done, Don Regan, as if in spite of himself, reached into his breast pocket. He handed Nixon's fax to the president, who read it with a cryptic cock of his head. Some staffers always swore that a rightward tilt meant one thing, a leftward pitch another. Was the president just mystified that someone could seem lukewarm toward SDI? Grateful that one of his predecessors had thought of something he hadn't? Saying nothing, he handed the paper back to his chief of staff with an expression that said only: Interesting.

It was five thirty when the president and Gorbachev returned to the second floor—without Anders, who remained behind to look out at the ocean. Like everyone else, he waited. The devil was not in the details but in the most basic of basics, and one way or another they would all soon be going home. What would he do when he got there? Call Anne Macmurray? Call someone else? His hand felt in his pocket for Nick Carrollton's card. As the minutes wore on, the guy next to him put down *The Hunt for Red October* and asked if Anders wanted to share the long-cord earbuds on his Walkman.

Before he could answer, one of Regan's mice, who'd been idly gazing out the window, shouted, "Christ! It's Gorbachev!"

A rush to confirm the sighting ensued, and sure enough, there below on the steps of Hofdi House were the general secretary's fedora and Reagan's white raincoat. Don Regan raced to the stairs and everyone followed in a scramble to the bottom floor. Within what felt like seconds, aides with clipboards began hustling people into cars, telling them they didn't know if the farewell reception at the embassy had been canceled, or how long everyone would have to check out of their hotels. At one point Anders stood close enough to Gorbachev to hear him urging Don Regan: "You should speak to the president." It was clear from the principals' body language how everything had just gone upstairs, and the chief of staff's response was sharp: "The president makes up his own mind."

Anders heard one Soviet agent shout a reminder to another—a fast flurry of Russian words that somehow contained the phrase "Tom and Jerry." The man being addressed held up a videocassette as if to say

"Don't worry, I've got it!" And at the point of maximum chaos, Anders spotted Hitchens in the row of press closest to the rope line. He didn't think he could prudently, or humanly, refuse a quick hello.

"Bad vibes," said Hitchens, imitating an American accent.

"I don't know any details," Anders replied.

"I'd say that Reagan had *his* parachute, and that somebody pulled the cord for him."

Anders thought of borrowing Don Regan's retort—*The president makes up his own mind*—but a sudden exhaustion, immediately apparent to Hitchens, overtook him.

"We'll talk back in the States," said the writer. He spoke the sentence not as a question or request or command. It came out as a statement of fact, the rhetorical mode Anders had already come to recognize as Hitchens's method for expressing whatever desires he thought reasonable.

"Yes," said Anders. "We'll talk."

"Anyone else's perspective I should seek? For *this* part of the story?" He was reminding Anders that he'd not forgotten about Central America.

Anders couldn't think straight. "You should talk to Anne Macmurray in Washington," he said. "She works for WAND—Women's Action for Nuclear Disarmament." He was surprised by whatever impulse had made him speak her name. Was he offering it to knock Hitchens off guard, to make him believe that people like Anders Little actually cast a much wider net for divergent opinions than was generally supposed? Or was this just an utterance from his dead-tired, unmoored self, a protective invocation of his moral and motherly guardian angel? He looked at Hitchens with similar uncertainty: Did the man behind the rope line represent danger or asylum? *You're strolling with Switzerland.*

"Get going!" cried one of the mice, tugging Anders toward a van, not even a car, as if his temporary statuses—former president's eyes and ears, current president's notetaker—had already vanished. He waved goodbye to Hitchens.

Inside the vehicle, speeding back to town, he heard fragments of scuttlebutt mixed with eyewitness observations from the American translator who'd been on the second floor at the end:

Shultz actually said, "Let's do it!" like they were about to pop a cork or cut a ribbon—

Gorbachev told Reagan that this was his last chance to be a great president.

Shevardnadze said history would never forgive any of them if Reagan said no.

Riding past the *Baltika*, Anders looked out the van window and thought of the buddy movie Reagan had proposed and then canceled. *Ten years from now . . .*

It should be easy to picture an already-old man being ten years older, but when he tried to envision Reagan a decade hence, he saw him wrapped in fog.

3:45 P.M. (EDT), 3038 N STREET NW, WASHINGTON, D.C.

Pamela had begun the day in poor spirits, waking with the thought that she should have gone to Middleburg for the weekend instead of hosting last night's fiasco at Nora. But what's done is done, and she had made herself get some fresh fall air with a lunchtime walk along the towpath of the canal that still ran through Georgetown.

She had brightened up considerably—and then come home to news of the summit's collapse! Moynihan's patriotic piety be damned: she simply could not get enough of it. Except for the housekeeper, she was home alone this afternoon. In her office, in front of CNN, she drank from a gin and diet tonic and allowed herself two handfuls of unsalted peanuts. Senator Hart had just condemned the president's terribly destructive choice, and Senator Pell was calling it "a sad day for mankind."

The pollsters were already at work, and Pamela anticipated the sheet of results that would be brought to her tomorrow morning—the brightest, most buttery item on her breakfast tray. Right now she was experiencing a slight sensation of Destiny, a feeling that it had fallen to her—in this year of our Lord, nineteen hundred and eighty-six, as the vicar at Minterne might say—to bring the Reagan Revolution to its end.

She could surely be forgiven a desire to plant, without delay, the first seed of an idea for her truly long-term future, an idea that involved posterity. It required a telephone call, which she would make herself, while no one was around.

She dialed Arthur Schlesinger's number and could soon hear him hastening to the line—an avidity she found hopeful, though she knew he considered her a bit tiresome, even something of a poacher, on the subject of present-day American politics. He'd prefer having her talk about old Winston and old Joe Kennedy, because that would lead him into his own monologue on Camelot. Then he'd bore *her*, talking as if she somehow lacked bona fides because of all the time she'd spent along the Great White Way when she should have been on the New Frontier. As if the latter had been history's most crucial epoch. Really: How many of the Camelot crowd, all of them beginning to age very fast these days, could say that they'd met *Hitler*? Well, she had, thanks to the craziest of the Mitford girls, who'd taken her to call on him during her one term at that awful German boarding school.

Nonetheless, Arthur was really the only person for the job she had in mind. Well, two jobs; there was a smaller one first. She would tell him that Moynihan had been a boor last night, and would count on his own dislike of the senator—old Harvard rivalry; disgust that Moynihan had consented to work for Nixon—to ensure that Arthur spread *her* version of last night around the Century Club and the rest of Manhattan.

Indeed, it was only after she'd set this in motion that she began easing toward her second, larger purpose.

"Arthur," she asked, "have you been approached by this man Hitchens?" She explained the nuisance of the *Vanity Fair* article.

"No," answered Schlesinger, "but if I am, should I speak to him?"

"Oh, I hope so! You'll know just what to say. You always do." What one loved about Arthur was the way fealty to his subjects was never compromised by too much devotion to historical truth. And if *she* were telling the truth at this moment, she would be admitting that she didn't especially care whether Arthur talked to Hitchens or not; it was a larger biographical project toward which she was moving the conversation.

"I'm rather missing Ave this afternoon," she said.

"I imagine you are," Arthur responded. "It was such a special pleasure"—she wished all those s's didn't sound so much like her Water-pik toothbrush—"to be 'present at the creation' of you two—or I should say the *re*-creation."

He referred to the party Kay Graham had thrown in '71, the event at which she and Ave had reconnected for the first time since London and the war.

"Oh, Arthur," said Pamela. "You're always everywhere important, and that's because you *make* each place and occasion important. I also remember that wonderful weekend you were with us in Middleburg."

"Yes," said Schlesinger, "doing that interview with Ave for *American Heritage*—mixing business with pleasure, though it was really mixing pleasure with pleasure."

That's what she meant. He was so different from other writers, who were often so hostile, such pests.

"Oh, that was a *splendid* piece," she replied. "You know, I do think it's time for someone to capture the entire life. To expand the vision of your eulogy for Ave into a whole book."

"Well," said Schlesinger, "there are a lot of the young ones who could do it. Isaacson. Or Evan Thomas's boy."

"Hmmm," said Pamela, who meant for him to hear a gentle scolding, a suggestion that he was passing the buck. She didn't want some tyro; she wanted Arthur's name and his loyalist's touch. And beyond that she wanted from him a very particular approach.

"I almost *went* to Middleburg this weekend," she said, plunging in from a side angle.

"It's such a delightful hamlet. When Jack and Jackie were there—"

"Yes," she said, cutting him off. "I'm now not sorry that I stayed in town, but I do realize that I left my book out there last time."

"What is it that you're reading?" Schlesinger asked.

"*Eleanor and Franklin*," she answered. "Joe—what's the author's name?"

"Lash," Arthur informed her. "You know, I found myself thinking of Mrs. Roosevelt the other night, when—"

"Fortunately, I have another book going here. *Nicholas and Alexandra*. I think these joint biographies are really wonderful. The excitement of two stories becoming one; the way the doubleness gives a broader perspective on the whole era in which they're set." How long, she thought, tapping her fingers against the dish of peanuts, would it take for the penny to drop? She could already picture, on the shelf, a book called *Averell and Pamela*, its title rolling off the tongue as musically as "lilacs and lavender."

But she could hear Arthur trying to change the subject. Perhaps the penny had dropped and fallen on its side. "I can't help thinking that this administration," he was saying, "has today chosen a Flash Gordon fantasy over arms control. Mrs. Roosevelt would be weeping—Ave, too, I suspect."

"Yes," Pamela responded, "but the right sort of biography could show how, despite setbacks, his work is being carried on. Think of what you wrote for—I mean, *about*—Bobby, after writing about Jack. Imagine someone doing all that in a single volume."

Silence told her that she'd overplayed her hand, not something easy to do with Arthur.

"Think about it," said Pamela, though no proposition had been explicitly stated. "And in the meantime, tell me how your spring diary looks."

"Busy as ever. I'm—"

"Janet will be asking you to find a few dates for our issues evenings. I'll have the next president for you at one of them! And I'll sit you beside the Senate's new *majority* leader."

"What an exciting, satisfying prospect."

All those s's. They had her grinding her teeth.

"Love to your wife!" Pamela declared, signing off and hanging up. She hoped that he and Moynihan would get strangled in each other's bow ties at the Century.

Well, there was work to be done. She looked at a pile of things that Janet, who'd come in even yesterday, had left for her attention. What was this curious videocassette, apparently hand-delivered?

The trees disappeared from the landscape as soon as the motorcade passed beyond the city limits. Inside the second car, Pat Buchanan was still writing, in his clear, Catholic-school hand, some departure remarks for the president. During the private reception for embassy employees, which Reagan had gamely endured, the press had raced either to the Soviet leader's news conference or out to Keflavík for the president's goodbye.

Hitchens stood inside a building near the tarmac, waiting for Reagan and watching on television a tired-looking Mikhail Gorbachev at a movie theater back in the capital. Volunteer guards in orange coats gave the televised venue a festive, cultish air. "Only madmen," the general secretary was saying, "would accept such a deal, and madmen are in hospitals."

What, thought Hitchens, had put psychiatric hospitals on the leader's mind? Was he worried that one of them—or just a pensioner's small flat—lay in his near future? Reagan might be coming home empty-handed, but then so, too, was Gorbachev, without SDI's carcass strapped to the roof of his ZiL.

And now here was Ron, being cheered by the troops. Hitchens stepped reluctantly into the cold and listened to the president, over the loud-speakers, doing his adorable-henpecked-hubby routine: "I called Nancy and told her I'd be late for dinner. She said she understood; in about six and a half hours, I'll find out." The boys in green loved it.

"Idiot or idiot savant?" Hitchens asked the man from the *Telegraph*, who offered him a gulp from his flask.

"Geopolitical genius," the man replied.

"I'm so relieved to know that," said Hitchens. "To think it had some-how eluded me."

"I'm not having you on," the man from the *Telegraph* responded.

Waving goodbye and moving toward the plane, Reagan became an inaudible white speck. At the bottom of the airstairs Vigdís Finnboga-dóttir waited to say goodbye to him.

"Madame President, I wish we could have done better," said Reagan.

"You can return," she assured him.

"No," said the president, bashfully shaking his head. "I'm afraid we're passing out of each other's lives." He said it with a wistful sort of wonder, as if he were boarding a starship that would take eight and a half minutes to reach the Sun.

"I would like to see you again," said the Icelandic president, almost pleadingly.

Reagan winked. "Just go back to Hofdi House any time you like. You'll find my ghost there."

———

Inside the plane the hardliners and the accommodationists took seats on different sides of the aisle. Perle's group and Nitze's weren't saying much, amongst themselves or to one another. All of them waited for Reagan to board the aircraft, which he did without a wave or even a grin. He headed straight to his quarters.

In the minute or two before wheels-up, the television playing at the front of the cabin cut to a hollow-eyed George Shultz. Back in Reykjavik, he was conducting his own press conference before flying, as scheduled, to Brussels, where he would now have nothing to persuade the Allies about. He defended SDI to the reporters—said it was what had gotten the two sides as close as they came—but he looked so drained and downbeat that Admiral Poindexter decided he'd better get up and go counter that impression with the press at the back of the plane.

A moment later Don Regan followed him down the aisle, stopping at Anders Little. He reached into his breast pocket and took out what Anders recognized as Nixon's fax. "Get rid of this thing," said the chief of staff.

9:35 P.M. (EDT), CLIFF ISLAND, MAINE

"*God*, it's cold here!" cried Bette Davis, who pulled the mink coat she was using as a blanket up toward her chin. The film crew for *The Whales of August* had made two bonfires on the beach—one of them close to the picture's three aging stars—but there was no taking the chill off this October night on the shore of Casco Bay. After several weeks of shooting, with a couple more to go, the actresses had spent a lot of time with the crew but very little with one another. The assistant director had grouped them together for a kind of playdate at this Sunday-night cook-out; every so often he would look over at the elderly women to see if the experiment in camaraderie was yielding any results.

"*Cold!*" cried Davis once more. She was unaccustomed to going without a response. Lillian Gish, eighty-eight or ninety-three, depending on whom you asked, was bundled up and asleep in her lawn chair, thus sparing them yet another reverential mention of D. W. Griffith. Ann Sothern was tucking into a second hamburger.

"Gary Merrill and I lived up here for seven years and I never got used to it—*never!*" said Davis by way of elaboration. At this mention of Bette's ex-husband and costar, Ann Sothern cheerfully patted her mouth with a napkin and offered, at last, a reply. "You know, it's a terrible confession to make, but I never saw *All About Eve* until maybe ten years ago, when they ran it one night on the late show. Boy, you were good."

Davis brought the jelly glass containing her martini up to her lips. She supposed it could be worse. Ann could have said she'd never seen the picture at all, or seen only the stage version—with Bacall! God! Anyway, she would excuse the lapse. She liked Ann, though the poor thing was enormous these days. People were going to think she was playing one of the whales. Still, she was a good, hearty soul, and at least two comfortable echelons down the movie-history pantheon from herself. She envied Ann her good humor and the peaceful relationship she had with her daughter, who was even playing a part in the movie. What had *she* gotten from *her* daughter? A memoir that made her sound worse than Crawford! How long had JC been dead? she now found herself wondering, while she looked at some pine trees further down the little island's coast. Ten years? Not long enough.

"Did they cut it to ribbons?" she asked Ann.

"Cut what?" replied Miss Sothern, crunching a pickle.

"*Eve.*"

"I suppose so. Don't they always for TV?"

"I suppose so," said Davis, who couldn't keep her response free of mimicry. A stiff breeze prompted her to pull the mink even closer. She had always hated location shooting, but her part was good and she needed the money. She needed the *work*, if she weren't to die altogether. Still, if only they could be on a soundstage instead of this awful island! The ferry came once a day, resupplying them like some prison colony, bringing in groceries and the papers from Portland. This morning's front page was flapping at Ann's feet, its headline still visible in the light of the bonfire: ICE BREAKER: RON, GORBY SEEM TO CLICK.

"Did you know," she asked Ann, "that both Ronnie *and* Nancy were nearly in *Eve*?"

"No, I didn't," said Ann, finishing the last of her pickle.

"I'm not kidding. He was on the list for Merrill's part and Miss Nancy was up for what went to Celeste Holm."

"Really?" said Ann, with a laugh.

"They'd have had to call it *All About Heave!*"

She shouldn't have said it. For all she knew Ann was some tiresome Republican like Irene Dunne. She now lived in *Idaho*, for God's sake. Cliff Island must feel like Venice to her! Still, she shouldn't have made the remark. A couple of months from now she was supposed to get—at last—a Kennedy Center Honor from Reagan. And until that happened she should hold her New Dealer's tongue.

"Was Reagan any good as an actor?" asked Ann. "I can't recall."

"Terrible! A passable moment here and there, maybe. But look at the films he did—or *don't* look at them. Most of them were junk. How can *anyone* get good if they're not given good *material*?"

"Did you ever work with him?"

This could get *very* annoying. Had the Idaho late show never run *Dark Victory*? It was her own favorite among her films, beyond even *Eve*.

"Ronald Reagan—" she began, but was interrupted by Miss Gish, who'd been recalled to life by this talk about the president.

"Mr. Griffith used to quote Charles Dickens: 'The more real the man, the more genuine the actor.'"

Davis rolled her eyes and fought off a flash of rage toward this sweetheart of the silents. Here *she* was, after cancer and hip surgery, and a stroke. And what exactly had Miss Gish suffered? Second childhood? Had she ever emerged from her *first*? God, that cutesy-pie manner! To be stuck on this island having to play her blind sister. Blindness was the single disability Bette Davis *didn't* have!

"Reagan was *awful* in *Dark Victory*," she informed Miss Gish.

"Oh, I wouldn't say that."

"I was *there*, Lillian. He was terrible. But at least he was terrible because he was stubborn. That counts for something. Edmund Goulding wanted him to play the part like a pansy. And he refused to do it. Actually, Reagan was a *very* stubborn boy. All those years heading the screen-actors' union and he *still* always pointed out how much he'd hated being *required* to join it."

Miss Gish, thankfully, had once more nodded off.

"That reminds me," said Davis. "What are you going to give our *non*-union crew for a present?"

"I haven't thought that far ahead," said Ann. "They've taken enough off me in poker—they should get *me* a present! Have you already chosen something?"

"I brought mine with me: 'Bette Davis Eyes' T-shirts. *Too* wonderful!" She loved the song.

One of the crew, a set designer gayer than Reagan's old nemesis, Goulding, had been eavesdropping. He now looked away, afraid of being reprimanded.

"Don't worry," said Davis. "We're through talking about Mr. President."

"We were just talking about him too," said the assistant director who'd organized the cookout. "He's flying home empty-handed. The radio says he could have abolished nuclear weapons—but he refused to let go of fucking Star Wars!" Three members of the crew sharing a bottle of tequila began "singing" the theme from the film series: Di-DA! Di-da-di-DA-DA!

"He totally blew it!" the assistant director shouted.

"Perhaps *he* doesn't do well on location either!" answered Miss Davis. Then she looked away. It was always best not to get too chummy.

As someone who knew something about stubbornness, she found herself having a thought. *Interesting.* She had fought against a cheap happy ending for *Dark Victory*, and she'd gotten her way. She wondered if, maybe in this case, her callow old colleague knew what he was doing over there in Iceland. After noticing that Ann had joined Miss Gish in the arms of Morpheus, she looked up at a pinprick of light in the night sky: A star? Somebody's plane? For a moment she pretended it was the president's. Taken by the improbability, the majestic absurdity of it all, she raised her glass and cried, "Little Ronnie Reagan! Ha!"

Part Three

OCTOBER 17, 1986–JANUARY 1, 1987

17

OCTOBER 17, 1986

"*Oooh*," said Merv. "Great *movie*."

Nancy Reagan had just told him that here at Camp David she and the president were watching *Kings Row*, generally regarded as the best of Ronald Reagan's films and one that he, honestly, claimed not to have seen since 1942. Nancy had slipped away, with a third of the picture to go, to make a few calls from the bedroom in Aspen Lodge.

"Yes," she said. "It *is* great."

In fact movies made her impatient; she almost never remembered having seen them, because all through her viewing—same as when listening to a speech—she would be thinking and worrying about something else. *Kings Row*, which she dimly recalled watching forty-five years ago at Smith, was no exception. And back then she'd certainly taken no special notice of Ronald Reagan.

"The president should have gotten a Best Supporting Actor nomination," said Merv.

Nancy laughed at the ancient slight. "There's no justice." But then a related thought made her serious. "Look at Elie Wiesel." The author had recently won the Nobel Peace Prize.

"Exactly," said Merv.

"You know what that was really about, don't you?"

"Oh, of course," said Merv, who agreed with Nancy's implication that Wiesel had been honored by the liberal Scandinavians not for decades of witness to the Holocaust but for his criticism of Reagan's cemetery visit to Bitburg last year. "There's so often another reason," Merv added. "Look at Elizabeth's first Oscar. She didn't get it for *Butterfield 8*. She got it for surviving that tracheotomy."

"You bet," said Nancy, comforted by their shared frame of reference. She sighed. "It's been a hard couple of weeks. I'm really down on Joan Quigley."

"How so?" asked Merv.

"Her advice about Iceland was so confusing. A big piece of it came too late to be of any use—and then everything fell apart."

"But people think he did fine!" Merv assured the first lady. "George Will said it was his 'finest hour.' That gave me chills. And the polls after the speech on Monday? *Oooh.* Off the charts."

"For now," said Nancy. "People always rally 'round right after one of those speeches. They even did for Nixon. It doesn't last."

Merv responded with a soothing purr, but Nancy, who knew anger to be one of her few, intermittently effective weapons against gloom, turned some more of it on Joan. "And then today! A fighter jet came within four miles of Ronnie's plane, over Pennsylvania. That's dangerous, Merv."

"Did Joan pick the departure time?"

"She did."

"That's a heckuva thing to be off on," Merv conceded. But he didn't want to get between the first lady and the astrologer he'd brought into her life. "I should let you get back to the movie. Don't let Ann Sheridan steal your man!"

Nancy forced a silvery giggle. "Okay, Mervyn. I'll see you on the twenty-sixth."

There would be so much campaigning between now and then. Ronnie had been heading to North Dakota this morning to stump for another "moderate" Republican senator, Mark Andrews. Why couldn't everyone just be honest and call them liberals? Andrews was one of those who always acted as if they were doing Ronnie a favor, and dirtying themselves in the process, when they managed to support a president from their own party.

The political people were running her husband ragged, just as poor George Shultz was running himself into the ground. In the five days since Reykjavik, the secretary of state had been to Brussels and then El Salvador—not because of the Contras, but to help out after an earthquake. In between, during the glimpse she'd had of him, Nancy could tell—no matter what he loyally said—how much George wished (same as herself!) that Ronnie had taken the deal in Iceland. If he had, then next March *he*, instead of some left-winger like Paul Newman, might be getting the Jean Hersholt Humanitarian Award from the Academy, which had never given an honorary Oscar to the only one of its members to become president of the United States. It would *kill* them to give Ronnie something, but if anything could force their hand it would be what had almost happened in Iceland, inside that white frame house; it looked from the pictures she'd seen like the false fronts behind which the burghers of *Kings Row* lived.

Maureen had been here all afternoon, flipping through polling data as fast as she went through a plate of chocolate-chip cookies. She'd shown Nancy some of the awful numbers: Breaux up by seven in Louisiana; that horrible little fireplug Mikulski ahead by *twenty-four* in Maryland; and Graham back in double digits in Florida. How were she and Ronnie supposed to make a dent in that when they flew to Tampa next week?

She went back into the living room and over to her stepdaughter, who was on the couch between Ronnie and the Huttons, the White House physician and his wife.

"How about a little walk?" she whispered. "I know *you've* seen this picture."

"Never at Mother's," whispered Maureen, with a laugh. "But yes."

The two women donned parkas and, outside the lodge, with a pair of agents falling in behind, set off on one of the paths Nixon had paved over. Ronnie had restored most of the others to dirt and horse riding.

"Really," the first lady asked her stepdaughter, "what's the strategy for the next three weeks? Other than driving your father into the ground."

"To nationalize the election," said Maureen, with a firmness acquired from much recent practice with this phrase. "To make it about Dad, about the voters sticking with *him*, since he's a lot more popular than most of our guys—and a few of our policies, too."

"It won't work," said Nancy. "Two years ago your father won forty-nine states—and we still lost two Senate seats."

Maureen had no answer.

"Any bright spots for 'Paula'?" The first lady still couldn't pronounce the name without mockery.

"Not many," Maureen admitted. "Some sympathy votes for her health problems. One poll shows that some attacks on that have backfired."

Nancy groaned.

"I agree," said Maureen. "It isn't much."

Lucky, the sheepdog puppy now almost fully grown, bounded up and rammed his nose into Maureen's right thigh. She reached into a pocket of her parka and gave him a potato chip from a small bag.

"Don't," said Nancy. "He'll get fat."

Embarrassed, Maureen tried to ignore the dog. "Can you get Paula in on the drug-bill signing?" she asked. "Maybe even do it in Florida?"

Nancy hesitated. On Wednesday, once the death penalty was out of it, the Senate had at last passed the legislation, and on Friday the House had followed through. She wasn't at all sure she wanted to share her own show with "General" Hawkins.

"Don Regan doesn't want her there," said Maureen.

"Okay, then tell Mitch Daniels I insist. I'll tell your father."

Maureen savored her small victory for a few silent steps along the path. "You haven't told me about the Princess Grace thing. How did that go?"

A couple of nights ago, along with Prince Rainier and his two daughters, the first lady had helped unveil a bust of Grace Kelly at the National Portrait Gallery. Looking at the small bronze sculpture, she'd had the same feelings of longing she'd experienced back in August when gazing at the model of Ronnie's library. Grace seemed to be enjoying such peace and completeness. No, Nancy didn't want to plunge off a mountain to attain those things—but, still.

"Stephanie's dating Rob Lowe," she now informed Maureen.

"Well, that'll at least keep Patti away from him."

Nancy laughed.

"I imagine Stephanie's mother would kill her, if she were still here," Maureen speculated.

"Mermie, if Grace were in Hollywood today, she'd be sleeping with Rob Lowe *and* his brother." Tapping Maureen's broad back, Nancy indicated that the two of them should probably start returning to the lodge. "You know, there's a dinner up in the Residence, another one for the library foundation, on Monday night. I don't think I can face it—not without Bets there to host it. Do you think you could fill in for me?"

Surprised and flattered, Maureen agreed. While Lucky gamboled around them, she asked Nancy: "What has Dad said to you about last weekend?"

Nancy, who'd been on the verge of taking her stepdaughter's arm, winced. She hated talking about the summit and the confusion it had produced—thanks to Don Regan, who had let everything get out of control even though he still liked to describe himself as the guy in a parade who sweeps up after the elephant. Unable to manage even the past few days since their return, he'd allowed Ronnie to tell some senators an off-kilter version of what the U.S. proposal in Reykjavik had been, and then had to make Larry Speakes issue a clarification.

Nancy finally answered Maureen with words she could have addressed to any newsman: "Right at Andrews he told me that he couldn't break his promise to the country not to trade away SDI. That was it." And that *had* been it! He'd said those very words, and she'd lacked the heart to press him further. "What's he said to *you*?" she asked Maureen.

"Well, I said to *him*, 'I'm sorry my prayers weren't answered.' And he replied, 'Are you sure they weren't?'"

They entered the lodge and hung up their parkas. On a table near the door sat the bag of nuts that Ronnie would bring back on Monday for the squirrels outside the Oval Office.

For Pete's sake, let's give a party! I feel swell!

Reagan's voice, recorded almost half a century before, was shouting from the screen. Resigned to the loss of his legs, he was reaffirming a desire to live. The music for the closing credits had begun to crescendo. The Huttons and Eddie Serrano, the valet who'd done the cooking tonight, looked ready to applaud, but the old picture's second lead, still jet-lagged after five days, was asleep on the couch.

"Dad's in a deep purple dream," said Maureen to Nancy, who had no idea what she meant.

Eddie began putting away the snacks, and Maureen gathered up her papers. It would be, as usual, an early night.

Dr. Hutton, who had kept the first lady informed of everything during last year's cancer surgery—no detail could be too small, she insisted— quietly approached her now. "This is as good a time as any," he said, nodding toward his dozing patient.

"For what?" asked Nancy, eyes instantly wide.

"I want you to know I'm going to test the president for the AIDS virus at his next full physical, in January."

"What!"

"Just a precaution, against the very small chance some of the transfused blood he got after the shooting might have been tainted. The test for the virus has finally become simple and reliable, and—"

"Oh, my God," said Nancy. It was the one contingency she had never thought of.

"Really, Mrs. Reagan, there's no reason to be afraid."

She looked at him as if he were terribly naïve. There was, always, every reason to be afraid.

———

"Hit TRACKING," said Anders, on his knees in front of Anne's new VCR.

"Okay," she replied, searching the remote for the right button. "Wait a minute. There!" All at once the young Englishmen running on the beach came into a graceful, unified focus.

Anders had agreed to set up the machine in exchange for another home-cooked meal. Anne told him that she'd been tempted by *Silkwood* but had chosen *Chariots of Fire* for a test-drive video from the rental store on Wilson Boulevard. Now that it was successfully teed up, Anders shut off the VCR so they could first eat dinner.

As the meal finished cooking, Anne told him: "I *have* mastered, all on my own, the other modern marvel here, my answering machine, and I thought you should hear this." She reached over to the end table and pressed a button. After the mouse-squeaks of rewinding, a by-now familiarly dulcet voice reached Anders's ears: "Ms. Macmurray," it began, playfully emphasizing the new female appellation that actually abbreviated nothing, "Christopher Hitchens here. I'm writing a piece on the recent summit meeting and on things nuclear in general. Anders Little, our mutual friend—as Dickens would redundantly put it—suggested that you might give me an interesting dissident's perspective on what Mr. Reagan failed to accomplish in Iceland. My number—"

Anne clicked off the machine. "You're full of surprises, Anders. Why would you want him talking to *me*?"

"To show the administration's broadmindedness?"

Anders would be hard-pressed to explain the logic to himself, or to articulate what lay beneath it. Hitchens still claimed to be a neutral, and Anne was the friendliest of enemies. Did the two of them together somehow offer him a circle of protection, a safe-conduct pass from one side to another, in the event of catastrophe?

"I haven't called him back yet," she explained.

"You'd better do it soon—if you want to, of course. I think his article is due on Wednesday."

"I'm still too depressed."

"By the lack of an agreement?"

"Yes, and by . . ." She didn't want to tell him how WAND was depressing her, too, by making Reagan as much the enemy as the missiles.

"Why do you think the summit 'failed'?" asked Anders, a bit too tutorially for her taste.

"Reagan's pigheadedness." She *did* believe this. "Wanting his Star Wars fantasy more than he wants arms reduction."

"You don't think he was sincere."

"Not entirely." Alas, she could concede that he might be *partly* sincere, and for that reason alone she didn't like the shrillness of the press releases she and Lisa had been required to turn out all week.

"I can't show this to Hitchens," said Anders, extracting a folded piece of paper from his khakis. "But I'll show it to you if you won't tell him about it."

She took the paper. He'd mentioned his several minutes of service as a notetaker, and here she was now, holding the proof of it.

"'Mikhail'? 'Ron'?" she asked, disbelievingly.

"It was weirdly . . . intimate," Anders explained.

He had left Nixon's fax at home, though he might have brought that to show Anne as well. He'd spoken to the former president only once this week, asking if he thought his Sunday-lunchtime warning had been decisive. Nixon had replied with a modest grunt. But rumors of this fax were spreading through the administration. Had Don Regan talked about it with someone else? Anders wondered. Was he *imagining* that over the past few days he'd gotten a couple of cold shoulders at the office—for overstepping, and thereby perhaps helping scuttle Reagan's chance to astonish the world?

"Well," said Anne, "it's hopeless now. They didn't even arrange for the *real* summit—which was supposed to have been the purpose of the one they had!"

"I wouldn't call things hopeless," said Anders. "Something is up. Something's in the air. Look at David Goldfarb." The Soviets had released another dissident, who was at a hospital in New York, being treated for heart disease and diabetes. He'd had a phone call today from Ronald Reagan.

"I heard," said Anne. "The poor man sounds in worse shape than Peter."

She had shared with Anders news of her ex-husband's physical condition, but until this moment had waited to broach the other, equally troubling part of Peter's story. "Down in Texas, there was a phone call from Mr. Channell. They argued a little about money and whether, I think, it should be going to fund someone's legal defense instead of some air base. And Peter mentioned the connection between George Bush and Max Gomez."

Gomez had been further connected, in today's paper, to the U.S. ambassador in San Salvador. Anne now offered a prediction: "Something tells me that all these earthquake-relief funds aren't going to reach their announced destination."

Anders said nothing.

"It's my turn to show you something," Anne continued. "I spent a lot of time at Peter's desk last weekend, and I found this." She handed Anders a yellow Post-it note on which her ex-husband had written:

APPLES - 35K

PEARS - 50K

Anders shrugged. But he knew what the jottings meant. The Sandinistas continued to dribble out "revelations" acquired from the Hasenfus plane. What they claimed to be radio codes—"apples" were guns, "oranges" ammunition, "pears" explosives—had yesterday reached the NSC and would no doubt find their way into the *Post* tomorrow or Sunday.

"What does that note mean?" Anne asked. "I'm sure that Peter has no sudden new interest in agriculture. How deep in is he?"

"I don't know," said Anders. Anne didn't realize she was putting *him* in deeper: the Senate Foreign Relations Committee had said it would soon begin taking voluntary depositions in connection with the supply missions. If the Democrats captured the majority a few weeks from now, there would be subpoenas.

"I don't know what Peter's trying to prove," said Anne. "Or what sort of legacy he's hoping to leave. But cancer is enough for him to be dealing with. These people should stop exploiting his weaknesses. Can't you get them to back off?"

She knew how uneasy she must look: about being drawn into both this Cold War skirmish and back into her own past. But she realized, too, and for the first time, that irrespective of cancer she was stronger than Peter—and probably always had been.

Anders thought of Hitchens's parachute question: *Have you got one, dear boy?* It seemed that he was flying deeper into a jungle, without any say in the matter, and that it was too soon to bail out.

"I'll see what I can do," he told Anne.

18

OCTOBER 20–24, 1986

"It's easy to fight for something that has no opposition," said Bob Graham.

From the middle of the audience Hitchens experienced a first twinkle of interest in this televised debate between the Florida governor and Senator Hawkins. He felt almost inclined to make a note on his pad but couldn't quite get over the threshold required for genuine engagement.

"*Really?*" replied the senator, looking like a cocktail waitress who'd been stiffed on a tip. "You think it's *easy* to fight for missing children? Do you know how hard it was for my bill mandating . . . ?"

Hitchens could so easily be watching this on the telly in his hotel room. Kelly Proctor remained there, though not from any fear of running into Mrs. Harriman, who was showing the national party flag here in Orlando tonight. Rather, Ms. Proctor had simply pronounced herself tired out from her day at Disney World with the Hitch. She had insisted that he see the Magic Kingdom and take the teacup ride—"you being English and all." He had pronounced its gyrations to be the least good reason he'd ever had for throwing up, but he acquiesced.

"This from a man who seconded Jimmy Carter's nomination and called Ronald Reagan 'simpleminded'!" cried Senator Hawkins, a Molly Pitcher of the strip mall.

"I said some of the president's *ideas* were simpleminded," Governor Graham responded. He failed to achieve any decibel reduction in the jeers from the Ron-revering side of the house.

Hitchens was tonight paying most of his visual heed to the nimbus of expensively cut blond hair in the front row. During Governor Graham's utterances, most of them pitched to the state's electorally ferocious "seniors," it bobbed with the enthusiasm befitting *an American by choice, a Democrat by conviction.* When Senator Hawkins spoke, with a volume that attempted to compensate for an absence of grammar and fact, Mrs. Harriman's hair-sprayed halo remained severely, respectfully still. The candidates made their closing statements looking straight into the camera, in the time-honored way of talking over the heads of the immediate audience to all those wonderful people out there in the magic U.S. kingdom of subdivisions and time shares.

In the period following the moderator's farewell, Mrs. Harriman joined others in mounting the stage to congratulate the challenger, who had decided to wait around for a couple of hours, until he could congratulate himself, live and for free, on the eleven-o'clock news. Hitchens lingered on the edges of Senator Hawkins's retinue, close enough to hear a bit of self-description: "I'm Joan of Arc, running against a robot!"

The polls, taken more frequently than a surgical patient's blood pressure, had today been showing the senator to be back within single digits of the governor. If she could get the Cubans and the right-to-lifers to turn out with a zeal matching that of the "seniors" Graham had done the better job of scaring . . . and if she could keep the newspapers from getting hold of more health records . . . and if the Gipper was strong enough to carry her another ten yards or so . . . she might yet make it into the end zone. (When, Hitchens wondered, had he started making football metaphors from *their* sort of football?)

He caught a ride, in the front passenger seat of his subject's limousine, back to the old Langford Hotel in Winter Park. Throughout the trip silence prevailed, as Mrs. Harriman made a great bespectacled show of studying data and memoranda in the limo's soft light. In the hotel elevator she pointedly issued the same instruction she had in August: "We're off the record until I say we're on."

"Off we, not on we," Hitchens responded, to her incomprehension. "And how was the political rabbinate?" he asked, referring to the earlier event she'd attended with leaders of Jewish groups. "Did you convince them that Governor Graham shares the eagerness of the Reverend Robertson and Mrs. Hawkins's Tabernacle Choir for an Israeli-driven Armageddon?"

"Oh, I don't want to talk about that. Let's begin with the senator's misstatements—"

"Sorry that didn't hit your G-spot," Hitchens murmured. He could see she didn't know the term, but if anyone knew where it *was* . . .

Janet hovered watchfully in the hotel suite's sitting room. She presented Hitchens with the scotch he'd "preordered" during the elaborate back-and-forth faxing and phoning required to arrange this last audience, which Mrs. Harriman seemed determined to get through with the speed of Roger Bannister. She had a page of notes—typed by Kelly, before her departure?

"This senator talks of criminalizing food-stamp fraud," she began, on the record now. "Such fraud is *minimal*. But Mrs. Hawkins made her proposal for hunting down its perpetrators at a luncheon where she served strawberries and steak to the receptive listeners. That seems to me emblematic of 'where she's at,' as they say, and of the Reagan administration in general."

With what he recognized as his own morbid compulsion for combat—even with those on his own side of an issue—he felt the urge to point out that her suite's square footage significantly exceeded that contained by most of the houses that had gone unpurchased during the prevalence of fourteen-percent-interest rates under the previous Democratic president. But he decided to move Mrs. Harriman toward matters immediate and strategic: "Mrs. Hawkins is reported to have more money left on hand than the governor does."

The interviewee dismissed this as a trifling matter. "A hundred thousand dollars or so."

"Speaking of hundreds. The governor has signed more than a hundred death warrants during his time in office. Does that bother you?"

"The state of Florida executes people, not Governor Graham."

"He signed the warrants."

"Do your research and you'll find that the Democratic Party is surprisingly tough on crime. Any other notion is a Republican myth," said Mrs. Harriman, visibly pleased with herself.

"But let's talk about Governor Graham's personal values, shall we?" asked Hitchens.

"A thoughtful man. An exemplary friend."

"Is it appropriate for him to appear in a music video that seems to promote alcohol abuse and philandering? I refer to the song stylings of Mr. Jimmy Buffett."

"Can we really be talking about this?" asked Mrs. Harriman, feigning disbelief. "Can *you* really be talking about this? Yes, I've seen the two seconds of videotape in question. The governor participated as a light-hearted favor to a singer who had supported one of his own charities. *Really*, Mr. Hitchens."

He smiled. "Have I at long last no decency?"

Dolan had confessed the video ploy to him over the phone. He could now see that Mrs. Harriman hadn't made up her mind about what to do. But she was nervous. And was it really up to him, a mere objective journalist, to protect her from folly and embarrassment?

———

"If you liked Jimmy Carter as president, you'll love Bob Graham as your senator!"

Four days after the debate, Hitchens listened to the president address a rally in Tampa. His own Florida sunburn had rendered his face even more rosy than Ron's made-up visage. Kelly had again declined to tag along, choosing to make her own trip to the Salvador Dalí museum across the bay in St. Petersburg.

Reagan, with Nancy by his side, had drawn a good crowd; the only empty portion of the bleachers was the one reserved for the White House press corps, most of whom had been left behind in Norman, Oklahoma—Ron's morning stop—when their chartered plane developed mechanical problems. Hitchens for a moment wondered if the people sending those iffy aircraft to Central America weren't running the White House travel office, too.

He didn't need to be here—he had more than enough material—but Ms. Proctor wanted to extend their Florida idyll, and Tina Brown appeared happy to pay mountains of expense money for a few extra molehills of local color no matter how far afield they might lie from his actual subject, Mrs. Harriman, who had long since returned to Washington.

I have to tell you that Nancy and Paula have impressed me so much with their work on Just Say No that I found myself saying those words the other day in Iceland.

Cheers for Mommy. Cheers for toughness. Reykjavik would apparently now stand for brinkmanship instead of the spontaneous little acid trip toward comity that it had actually been. Ms. Macmurray, Little's friend, had been gentler in her characterization of Reagan's behavior—*I think he imagined he wanted it*—than had almost all the others, both accommodationists and hard-liners, to whom Hitchens had spoken.

Mr. Gorbachev demanded that we, in effect, kill our Strategic Defense Initiative.

Why, Hitchens suddenly thought, was it the *Strategic* Defense Initiative? Did not the name somehow imply that the system *would* be used aggressively, thrown into operation in the course of an American first strike upon the Soviets? He wished he'd included this point in his piece, and he now made a mental note to bring it up with Little.

Four more years! the crowd began to chant, with a strange Nixonian atavism.

"The Constitution says that can't be," Reagan replied, by way of a rare ad-lib, "but I'll tell you what. I'll settle for two more years of a Republican Senate!"

Passionate agreement rose from the crowd, so many of whom, here in this University of Something stadium, were dismayingly young.

Paula's opponent and the Washington liberal crowd would like you to believe that the last five and a half years happened by accident.

Oh no, conceded the Hitch to the Gipper. They'd been no accident. The deliberateness of the counterrevolution was enough to make him wonder whether the outcome of Reykjavik had been no accident either. Had the blustery last-minute walkout all been theater, planned from the start?

Hitchens began his descent from the bleachers, prematurely enough to excite a security officer's notice, as if the writer might be carrying his own Hinckleyesque torch for Jodie Foster. But within twenty minutes, unthwarted, he was back inside his Tampa hotel room while Kelly splashed in the shower, sloughing off the curated dust of surrealism. He decided to call the subject of his profile and see if she could provide something additional and quotable about Ron.

"The *General*!" sputtered Mrs. Harriman, who cooperatively enough had just finished watching the president's performance on C-SPAN and been revolted by his military compliment to the drug-averse Senator Hawkins.

"I'd say that speech is worth about ten ad buys to them, wouldn't you?" asked Hitchens.

"How did they react to *Nancy*?" She spoke the first lady's name as if it were between little scare quotes.

"*Wildly*," Hitchens assured her.

"Well, we shall be purchasing a new block of ads ourselves. To counter this advertisement featuring *her* that's about to air, and to mop up whatever slurs against the governor they decide to attach her image to."

"Must be awfully expensive this late in the game."

"I've just decided it, so there's some news for you."

He could tell that she was trying to impress him, show herself off as some hands-on Wonder Woman. But the specter of Mommy had rattled her, and the lingering rhetorical powers of Ron—why was *he*, come to think of it, never called "Daddy"?—had charmed her only into fury.

"Do you think you finally have everything you need?" asked Mrs. Harriman.

"Oh, yes. I'm certain I've at last got enough. Ever so many thanks."

Emerging from the bathroom in a large white towel, Kelly said, "Oh, I've still got *plenty* more on her to give you."

"Ah, the persistence of memory," said Hitchens, falling back onto the bed like a foldable clock.

19

OCTOBER 26–27, 1986

'S awful nice! 'S paradise! 'S what I love to see!

From her seat in the East Room, a few feet from Marvin Hamlisch's piano, Nancy listened to Sarah Vaughan sing Gershwin and watched her sway inside a loose purple gown. The first lady was touched to notice that the singer—the standard of perfection in all things Gershwin, Merv had assured her—was *nervous,* a little awed by her surroundings, something not always the case with those who came to the White House to entertain. When the number finished, Nancy applauded and shot Merv a glance that said *You're a genius.*

Ronnie was glowing; Nancy knew it without even turning to her left. The two of them, she would admit, looked a little tired lately, but she was pleased with the black-and-silver cocktail dress she'd chosen. Kitty Carlisle had called again the other day, terribly worried after realizing she'd chosen for herself something red—by now so much the first lady's color that no one else dared to wear it here.

Kitty stood at the microphone, telling some anecdotes with that unfailing gift for putting people at their ease. Nancy decided she would let it go to work on her, too, that for the next hour she would just *enjoy* herself. But when she turned to her right, to smile at Frances Gershwin, who'd outlived her brother George by fifty years, she recalled that the other day she'd promised a man at the National Symphony she would try to get Rostropovich's sister a visa out of Russia. If she didn't follow through, there'd be one more East-West setback, and somebody would probably repeat Raisa's crack about her having "something else to do."

About 130 people sat in the East Room's frail, gilded wooden chairs, and Anne Macmurray was rather astonished to be one of them. Aside from the performers and Merv Griffin, few of the guests, she noticed, were celebrities of any kind. Anders, her escort, had explained to her that passes to an event like this weren't much different from White House parking spaces and tickets to the president's box at the Kennedy Center: items in a buffet of small perks that kept an administration's mid- and even low-level staffers feeling grateful and fervent. On Friday afternoon he'd been offered two tickets, and when he'd asked Anne to accompany him, she'd reflexively responded, "No girl to take?" even though she'd begun to get the sense, not just from Peter's insinuations, that there might never be a girl.

So here she was in the White House on a Sunday afternoon, listening to Kitty Carlisle recall the opening night of *Porgy and Bess* ("George was sort of a beau of mine"). Marvin Hamlisch played "Rhapsody in Blue," and the Manhattan Transfer—the girls all big hair and shoulder pads—sang a couple of numbers that threw Anne back to her 1930s childhood, with its radio soundtrack. As emotions, most of them good, rose to the surface of her lately overworked nerves, she felt glad that George Gershwin's brief life hadn't extended into the forties. If his compositions included songs that had once played on Peter's up-to-the-minute car radio, she wouldn't trust herself not to cry. As it was, when Sarah Vaughan started on "Someone to Watch Over Me," she reached over and tapped Anders on the arm, unsure if she was making herself the song's watcher or protectee, or if the tap was just some electrical excess of feeling. Anders predictably flinched. Embarrassed, she turned her eyes toward the front row, and made them settle on Nancy Reagan's head, which in three-quarter profile looked even more than usually big for her body.

She was trying almost studiously to dislike the first lady—that lethal little doll she'd first seen in the convention skybox back in '76—but at this moment found herself unable to summon any scorn. The woman's enormous, attentive eyes made her look as if she were wishing for someone to watch over *her*, someone different from the man sitting next to her. Even with her eyes on Sarah Vaughan, Nancy was clearly watching over *him*.

Hamlisch had begun singing directly to the first lady. The song was "Love Is Here to Stay," and the two of them now commenced a bit of stage business they must have worked out in advance. Nancy got up to sing to *him*, and then of course took the hand mic and turned to Ronnie: *But, oh my dear* . . . This seemed to be the finale. The president smiled and stood up next to his wife without, Anne realized, any sense that this was a woman who every day of her life expected the Rockies to crumble and Gibraltar to tumble.

To conclude the program, Reagan went over to a little lectern by the piano and told of how he'd been a young actor on a Hollywood sound-stage the day all the studios observed a minute of silence over the celebrated composer's sudden death. "I didn't know George Gershwin, but the intensity of that moment somehow made me feel that our paths had crossed . . ." Anne peered at the president, struck by this astral sentiment but otherwise unable to feel anything toward him. Nancy might provoke an alternation of sympathy and annoyance, all of it human and basic, but her husband? This man who might still *blow up* the Rockies and Gibraltar? Anne had the sense that *no* path had ever really crossed his, that the only way he encountered anyone was by drifting past them on a moving walkway.

"There's a reception now," Anders whispered.

"You're kidding," said Anne.

"Something else they give us instead of the higher salaries available at a think tank."

The two of them headed down the hall. On one side of its red carpet Anne noticed a portrait of Harry Truman, which sent her mind back to Peter. Her daughter's latest report said that he was already quite bald from chemotherapy and determined to quit the treatments before they ran their course.

A clutch of guests and press surrounded Nancy Reagan near the entrance to the State Dining Room, which had been filled a few nights ago with a dinner for the West German chancellor.

"What was your favorite moment of the program?" one reporter asked.

"When Sarah Vaughan told me I had a nice voice," the first lady replied.

"*Oooh*," said Merv. "Great *compliment*."

———

Half an hour later, out on East Executive Drive, Anders apologized to Anne and said he needed to go to his office next door rather than accompany her back to Arlington on the Metro.

He knew he ought to be heading there for real, getting a jump on tomorrow's meeting of the National Security Planning Group, which was bound to be a contentious affair: divisions between the Shultz and Weinberger factions had worsened steadily since the summit, with the former side arguing it had been a visionary near-success, the latter calling it a catastrophe averted. But Anders did not go to the EOB. As soon as Anne was out of sight he hailed a taxi.

He had lately become accustomed to lying, to others and to himself. And yet, as he rode up Connecticut Avenue, he decided that today's fib was partially redeemed by its being made on someone else's behalf and not just his own. He got out of the cab at 2032 Belmont Road and buzzed the second-floor apartment, whose owner knew he was coming.

Spitz Channell looked thinner and paler than he had a few weeks ago; his mustache had a certain droop to it.

"Make yourself at home," he said. "Eric is out with friends."

"I won't stay long." Anders looked around and remembered the paintings, less interesting than the ones on the walls of the Hotel Holt.

Channell lit a cigarette and put the match into a "Fort Knox" ashtray. He saw Anders looking at it. "I was stationed there before going to Germany," he explained. "Back in the sixties. The only gold bricks I saw there were lazy GIs. Get you anything?"

"No, thanks."

"You're all dressed up. Been to church?"

"No, I've got a dinner to go to." Another lie. "Look, I want to ask you about somebody I met here."

"Dugan? He's still hoping you'll call him."

"No, Peter Cox, the guy from Dallas."

"Dallas," sighed Channell, looking momentarily more cheerful and robust. "The mother lode for contributions, though I never succeeded in getting anything out of Bunker Hunt, the biggest prize there. Not even when Ollie and I flew down to make a run at him, maybe a year ago."

"Peter Cox. Do you know much about him?"

"I know that he smokes even more than I do."

"He's dying," said Anders, who thought to add, reassuringly, "Not lung cancer. Liver."

"Did he tell you that?" Channell seemed to find the news suspicious.

"Someone close to him is alarmed by the amount of his money that's going to 'apples,' 'pears,' and 'oranges.' "

Channell smiled and shook his head. The supply codes had indeed gotten into the papers last week. "Cox has been a good contributor."

"How much longer until the press find out where all this NEPL money really goes?" asked Anders. "The Foreign Relations Committee is already investigating the airdrops."

"Money from the National Endowment for the Preservation of Liberty goes to a good cause," said Channell.

Anders almost laughed at the pomposity.

"What matters," Channell continued, "is that my *warriors* know where it's going. Cox knew what he was buying because I always made that clear to the donors. And they wanted nothing in return. Wait—let me correct myself on that. Ellen Garwood asked me to show her the cherry blossoms one time she was up here."

"What do you think Cox might want?"

"A non-Communist Central America?"

"I'm sure he does," said Anders. "So do I. But there's something else at work with him. I'm not sure what you'd call it—the vanity of a dying man who never made much of a splash politically. Do you think it's right to put him in a position where he might wind up having to spend his last months in courtrooms as well as hospitals?"

"Don't you think you're being a bit of a drama queen?"

Annoyed that he was apparently *expected* to know a term like that, Anders replied with another question. "Then why did you call him a couple of weeks ago about making contributions to a legal defense fund?"

Channell looked up at him distrustfully and didn't answer.

"You know that this thing is about to blow up and—"

"You have no idea," Channell finally replied, with a scornful laugh.

"If it's that big," said Anders, "then Peter Cox can't matter very much. Give him back his money and put him in the clear."

"I don't see how Cox is a victim here. He's *made* money off this business—at least temporarily."

"I don't follow you, Spitz."

"Let's just say that money from other places has had to be parked with various people. With different individuals, for camouflage purposes. Peter Cox has a very flush bank account right now, even if its contents will eventually go to an offshoot of this cause."

"How many other 'individuals' are involved like that?"

"You sound as if you're from the Foreign Relations Committee."

"No," said Anders, "but I'm not happy at the prospect of being called before it. Who else that you connected me to—at the Hay-Adams or here—is getting temporarily rich? Besides Peter Cox."

Channell said nothing.

"Dugan?"

Channell laughed. "Think much younger. Cuter. Sillier. Less likely to be suspected."

He saw Anders's startled expression and added, "Relax. It's only for a short while. He'll be *fine*."

———

At 2:40 p.m. the following day Nancy Reagan was back in the East Room, standing in front of Bob Dole, part of a little group clustered around a desk that had been set up for Ronnie.

"I'd like to single out Senator Paula Hawkins in particular," said the president, as the camera shutters clicked like a hundred crickets. "She took this battle to the public and has been a driving force behind the effort to rid our country of drug abuse."

Nancy smiled at the senator, who was about as much involved in this particular bill as her Aunt Fanny—but with the election eight days away, you had to do what you had to do. If the little wirephoto bonanza that would result from this bill-signing helped to bring General Paula a come-from-behind victory, the president's wish would be Senator Hawkins's command.

"And now, Paula, if you and your colleagues will join Nancy and me, we'll get on with the signing of this bill, making HR 5484 the law of the land."

Once he'd affixed his signature, the president passed his wife the pen with a dash of showbiz pizzazz. The cameras went to work and Nancy realized that *this* would be tomorrow morning's photo and that Paula would be lucky to make the caption. Well, so be it. She flashed Ronnie a smile even bigger than his own and took his hand along with the pen. The poor man had rallies in North Carolina, Alabama, and Georgia ahead of him tomorrow, and a slew of western states at the end of the week. She noticed a purplish spot below one of his knuckles and forcefully reminded herself that there was no good reason to think it indicated anything but aging.

———

Across town, watching CNN, Pamela heard Kelly Proctor's replacement, whose name she couldn't remember, say "Mrs. Hart's on the line."

"Kitty, darling," said Pamela. "Have you made it home safely?" Her houseguest had left on the 8:00 a.m. shuttle after two nights here on N Street.

"Oh, yes. You made me marvelously comfortable. Can't thank you enough!"

"It's no more than you do for me in New York. And I forgive you for serenading the enemy. I'm looking at that dreadful woman right now."

"What dreadful woman?"

"*Nancy.*"

"Oh, Pam. She was perfectly lovely to everyone."

"She's on the television with that Florida grotesque, Senator Hawkins."

"*That's* what I forgot to tell you last night!" exclaimed Mrs. Hart. "I knew there was something."

"What is that?"

"I got to talking with Mrs. Reagan at the reception, after the little performance. I complimented her, told her what a formidable force you know her to be. I mentioned, *lightly*, how you'd just ordered up all that advertising to deal with *her* ad. I was very nice about it."

"I'm sure you were," said Pamela.

"But so was she," explained Mrs. Hart. "She told me there *is* no ad. Just some little piece of film to show contributors—something not very special that was put together weeks ago. Nothing to be broadcast."

"Kitty, darling, don't be naïve. Of course there's an ad. And it's going to have her smearing Bob Graham in the most cheap and ludicrous way."

Mrs. Hart, who knew better than to get started with Pamela, signed off with a touch of Gershwin. "All right, dear girl. Let's call the whole thing off!"

20

NOVEMBER 4, 1986—ELECTION DAY

At 8:30 p.m., a little after CBS called the North Carolina Senate race for Terry Sanford, the Democrat, a chef's assistant brought a platter of California fruits and chocolate puffs to the White House Solarium.

"I thought you'd be giving us lame duck," said the president, winking.

"Ronnie!" said the first lady, with a smile that collapsed as soon as the man exited with his serving cart.

Maureen, here with her husband, was experiencing a one-two punch of chagrin and exhaustion. Sitting near one of the Solarium's half-moon windows, she knew she should be on Capitol Hill right now, bucking up the troops at the RNC, but she didn't have the heart or the energy for it. She'd only just gotten back from Africa, where she had represented the United States at the funeral of Samora Machel. The Mozambican leader who'd "hit it off with Dad" had been killed in a more than slightly suspicious plane crash near the South African border.

"You know," said Maureen, as CBS went to a commercial, "I liked him a lot. It seemed to me a shame that a Soviet tank should be pulling the caisson with his coffin. True, he was very left, but I still think with a little effort we could tilt them our way. I mean, there I was, having to exchange nods with Arafat and Castro's brother, with only Jesse Jackson for American company! We could have sent a bigger delegation. And we should be helping Mozambique to get more from the IMF."

The president ate a chocolate puff, evincing no displeasure that his daughter might be criticizing him, while Nancy, taking a small slice of melon, just nodded. This was so Maureen, she thought: keen and earnest and fleeting; unable to stick with anything, from acting to newscasting to husbands, for very long. The clipboard on her lap, with its RNC scorecard of the Senate races, already looked like the souvenir from one more former career.

But Nancy could scarcely blame Maureen for looking downcast. By nine o'clock another two seats thought to have been "in play" fell to the Democrats. The whole thing was turning out even worse than she'd feared, and when the phone rang—it could only be Don Regan—she said, "Don't take it."

Ronnie complied, with an abashed look. "At some point I'm going to have to call Frank Fahrenkopf," he said, referring to the head of the National Committee. "With at least an encouraging word."

"Do it now and get it over with," said Nancy.

Once the RNC leader was on the line, Reagan focused on the governorships the party seemed to be winning, and told Fahrenkopf to tell anyone who was worried about this administration being out of gas that "they ain't seen nothin' yet." Nancy twirled her index finger in a wrap-it-up gesture. She didn't mind the Hollywood allusion, but she wished he hadn't picked one that went back to the dawn of talkies.

Paula Hawkins, who went down by a full ten points, conceded at a quarter past nine, claiming to have fulfilled her six-year-old pledge: "I told you that if I went to Washington you would know I was there." She looked as if *she* barely knew where she was, thought Nancy—painkillers?—and appeared to be taking her own defeat less hard than Maureen, who was guiltily avoiding her stepmother's gaze.

They'd allowed Ronnie only a single day at the ranch, Sunday, amidst all his stops in the West, but all the travels had been for nothing. "Switch to *Moonlighting*," she told Dennis, who had the remote. ABC wasn't bothering with continuous coverage of just a midterm.

Dennis obeyed, although as soon as he changed the channel Maureen said to Nancy, "If I don't stay with it, I'll feel even worse than I do." She and Dennis rose and left the room for a television down on the second floor.

"I'll stay here," said the president.

As she watched *Moonlighting*'s comically noir L.A., and heard its soft jazzy soundtrack, Nancy felt a strong longing to be home, as if Los Angeles, compared to Washington, were a haven of wholesomeness. And then the phone rang again. Ronnie gave her a look that asked for guidance.

"I'll take it," she said, deciding she would handle Don Regan herself.

"Yes?" she said, icing the syllable.

"Mrs. Reagan, it's Mike."

"Mike!" The only person who could ever make things like this better. The president raised an eyebrow.

"Where have you been?" the first lady asked. "I've left message after message, and—"

"I'm in the hospital."

————

PamPAC's celebration, in full swing by eleven p.m., was the evening's hot ticket. Pamela herself, positioned in front of the van Gogh, continued to receive handshakes and kisses as the woman who had led all those here out of six years' bondage.

Mayor Barry, high on the evening's results, kissed her on both cheeks.

"Next we'll get the convention!" Pamela assured him. The site-selection committee would meet ten days from now. "And maybe we'll be nominating *you!*" she exclaimed to Gary Hart, who was next in the receiving line.

A cheer went up when one of the room's two televisions showed Barbara Mikulski in Baltimore celebrating her Senate landslide. Elsewhere in Maryland, Ethel Kennedy's daughter had failed to win a House seat, which Pamela thought just as well, since the family name now seemed a drag toward the past. Young Joe's ascension was quite enough.

A small crowd arrived from the Four Seasons, where the decorators' big benefit for the city's hospices had been unaccountably scheduled for election night. As they made their way into the room, the increasing noise prompted inevitable comparisons to Andrew Jackson's riotous inaugural. Nancy Dickerson told Pamela that she'd seen the first lady's hairdresser, Robin Weir, at the benefit. "And why not?" cried Peatsy Hollings. "He's got some time *off* coming. She won't be showing herself in public for at least a *week*!"

Bob Strauss gave Pamela a Texas-sized buss before standing up on a sofa—Carter Brown would have died, had he been here—in order to shout: "I'd like all you ladies and gentlemen to know that out of nine candidates Ronald Reagan campaigned for last week, six of 'em—and it may end up being seven—have lost!" When the cheers for this subsided, Helen Strauss, helping her husband down from the couch, could be heard to declare: "Somebody should tell that to the underappreciated Jimmy Carter!"

An awkward silence followed.

Stoop-shouldered Ed Muskie, Carter's last secretary of state, filled it by informing the group: "It would be an expensive call. President Carter is in Bangladesh tonight—working for the poor."

Polite, unfestive applause rippled through the room.

Bob Strauss tried to keep things aloft. "There'll be no tears tonight, Ed!"

At 11:37 CBS called Alan Cranston the winner in California and predicted that the Democrats had not only taken the Senate but would control it with a 55–45 majority. A general jubilation fueled the rush of a dozen guests out onto N Street, where the portly, retiring speaker of the House, recognizable through the window by the frozen custard of his hair, was getting out of a town car. Tip O'Neill bellowed to a reporter, "This is the first even-numbered year since '52 that I haven't had to be at my own headquarters up in Cambridge!"

Mrs. Harriman, informed of his arrival, decided that she would stand still and wait for the speaker to come to her. She whispered to Janet that *that* was the moment the video cameraman must capture; she'd be damned if O'Neill's sidewalk stemwinding would be the piece of film to air on the morning shows. As space was cleared around her and the speaker continued his solo performance outside, Pamela caught the eye of Mr. Hitchens, whom she'd taken the chance of inviting on the theory that her moment of triumph would make exactly the right scene with which to conclude his piece.

Still waiting for O'Neill, she decided to go over to the writer and ask, "Are you being taken care of?"

"Very nicely," he answered, raising the glass in his hand. "Care to say something, even off the record?"

"*Yes*," said Pamela. "*On* the record!" Her angular smile created a large portal through which a *bon mot*, ghostwritten for her moments ago by Bob Shrum, could issue: "This is a political earthquake. A *fifty-five* on the Richter scale!"

"Shame about that last advertising buy," said Hitchens.

The smile disappeared. Pamela pretended not to know what he was talking about.

"The ads that talked so defensively about Governor Graham's character," Hitchens explained. "After no one, let alone Mrs. Reagan, ever raised the matter."

Pamela forced herself to redeploy the smile and said, evenly, "We took no chances. And it hardly matters now. Just look at *Senator-elect* Graham's margin. Another 55–45!"

"But imagine what another hundred or two thousand dollars might have done for poor Harriett Woods in Missouri." Hitchens referred to one of the Democrats' few senatorial failures tonight.

"Mr. Hitchens," said Pamela, "look at *this*." A sweep of her hand indicated the whole reveling room. "*This* is your story." The hand came gently to rest on her emerald-draped décolletage.

"I'm afraid my article has already 'closed,' as we say in the biz. It went to the printer this afternoon."

Annoyed by her wasted effort, Pamela curtly nodded and moved away. Her hand remained on her bosom, to which she should never have brought this viper.

————

Richard Nixon returned the flashlight to its kitchen drawer and noticed the time: 12:30 a.m. He had just come back from an extra walk with the current dog, this one a hell of a lot better behaved than Checkers, whose yapping all those years ago would drive Pat up the wall. Nixon could scarcely remember the dogs who'd come in between, least of all King Timahoe, the Irish setter blurred by the convulsions of his presidency.

He would pay a price for staying up so late tonight, but a little nocturnal indulgence felt good. He picked up his yellow pad from the hassock and made a check mark. Now that the networks had declared Washington State for Brock Adams over Slade Gorton, a strange Ichabod Crane character, he could compare the complete results against his Sunday-night predictions and see that he had correctly called thirty-three of the thirty-four Senate races. He'd missed only North Dakota, having guessed that Andrews—that Lowell Weicker of the Plains—would squeak through. He couldn't say he was displeased to be wrong.

After spinning his Rolodex, he picked up the phone and called Dole's office in the Capitol, opening their exchange with an observation about the senator's own reelection: "I see from the tube that you're going to go over seventy percent in Kansas."

Dole replied with a couple of unsyntactical grunts: "Nothing like a landslide against token opposition. Can't say it's much consolation." His job as majority leader was gone.

"I was out with the dog," said Nixon. "Have you done all the networks?" The rest of them had joined CBS in its election coverage once prime time was over.

"Couple of them. I'd rather talk to you than to Brinkley."

"You know, Bob, tough as it may look, you're better off."

Dole snorted. "You think?"

"I do. If you want to go for the big prize in '88, it's better to spend two years in opposition. There isn't going to be any administration program to push through after tonight. You can get on the attack instead of having to make nice and beg for votes across the aisle. You can carry your own water instead of Reagan's."

"Carried a lot of your water back then," said Dole. This throwaway grumble, a reference to his chairmanship of the RNC during some of the first Watergate days, was made almost tenderly.

"Of course," the ex-president said, "there's an even better alternative."

"Yeah?"

"Quit. Don't waste your time as minority leader. Get out of the Senate altogether. Run from the outside. Christ, just look at it from a practical standpoint! I don't know how I'd have won in '68 if I'd had to hold down a goddamned *job* while I was running."

"Well," said Dole. "I'd miss the charms of Al D'Amato."

"I've got a feeling Reagan's water is about to get a lot heavier. Let Bush carry it into '88." Nixon was thinking of a conversation earlier tonight with Anders Little, who'd suggested that this Nicaragua crap might soon blow sky high in ways no one had anticipated.

"I wonder whether we might have squeaked through tonight," said Dole, "if Reagan had come home with some big deal from Reykjavik. As it is, I don't think the summit hurt us much, but we needed a boost."

"And lose the goddamned Cold War? Hell, no! Worst bargain he could have made. Christ, when I think of the cracks he used to make about détente—just go back to '76. This would have been de-*bacle*."

The majority leader, a pure pol, was engrossed only by the kind of tallies on the yellow pad. For all the electoral acumen he'd shown tonight, that had never been true of Nixon himself. "I lived with two Democratic houses of Congress for my whole goddamned presidency," he needlessly reminded Dole. "Reagan will only have to do it for two years. But it will change him."

Dole harrumphed. "I don't understand him to begin with. So I'm not so sure as I'd notice any change."

Nixon laughed. "Well, what the hell. He'll soon be the fourth monkey."

He knew Dole knew what he meant. The majority leader had gotten off a line a while back about the three ex-presidents, Ford, Carter, and Nixon. "See no evil; hear no evil; and Evil," he'd called them.

Reminded of it now, Dole gave a small, sheepish laugh, but Nixon fairly roared. "Some goddamned Rushmore the four of us will make, don't you think! Night, Bobby!"

———

Anders Little had turned in early, not long after getting a call from Nixon. "'Eighty-eight starts tonight, my boy," the former president had explained. "If Jeane Kirkpatrick is going to make a move, now's the time—either to get out on her own or attach herself to Bush or Dole and hope for the VP slot. Christ, Robertson was all over the tube tonight. The others need to keep him from gumming up the primaries and making the whole party look like a bunch of snake handlers."

Anders, who both craved and feared Nixon's advice on his own burgeoning predicament, now tossed and turned. Nicaragua might be the main cause of that, but there were others, too. Being offered those tickets to the Gershwin concert gave no real indication that he was on solid ground at the office, and since attending the event with Anne he'd sensed more and more of a cold shoulder there. He could connect it to both his presentation of Nixon's fax in Reykjavik and to a whole new atmosphere of suspicion within the NSC, one that was bound to get worse now that Senate approval of any arms-control treaty would be in the hostile hands of the other party, who could defund SDI whenever they liked.

Anders had lost five pounds since Iceland. He could feel his stomach clench whenever the phone rang with anyone at all, let alone Hitchens, on the other end. No, he'd told Christopher the other day, he didn't know *why* it was called the *Strategic* Defense Initiative.

He'd made plane reservations to go home for both Thanksgiving and Christmas, no matter that he would be the divorced sibling while his brother and sister and their mates kept busily increasing the population of the kids' table. Tickets for the two trips sat on the night table by the digital alarm clock, which now showed 12:50 a.m.

What had happened four weeks ago—and not since—was an *incident*, he told himself, something that would never happen again. And its drunken brevity argued against his having any responsibility for the flaky kid who'd provoked it.

It was 12:55 a.m. when the phone rang.

"Hello?"

"Oh, I woke you up! Sorry!" said the voice with a young person's disbelief that anyone could go to bed this early. "It's Nick." He was laughing; half nervous, half drunk.

"I guessed. What are you doing? Where are you?"

The boy groaned. "On First Street," he said, meaning the RNC's offices. "Everybody's drinking. Some old Irish guy said it's like a wake."

You couldn't tell it from the music, thought Anders. He could hear "Walking on Sunshine" pounding in the background. "You're up a lot of governorships, no? Aren't they as important as Senate seats?"

"I know!" shouted Nick, as if it were totally amazing that Anders could be thinking the same thing. "I keep *saying* that! But tell it to David Brinkley! Nobody *here* seems to believe it, either. I wish *you* were on TV instead of all those commentators. Much more fun to listen to—and look at."

Anders could feel his flat stomach clenching. He kept his voice perfectly neutral. "What did they have you doing today?"

Nick groaned again. "It was the worst. I fielded about thirty angry phone calls from Texas."

"Texas? That should have been a bright spot, no?"

"Not if you have to deal with people who've got a parent in this one Houston nursing home. Something went wrong with the automatic calling operation down there and all these bedridden old people got like a jillion recorded calls in a row from Reagan!"

Anders laughed. His stomach began to relax. Feelings of his own vulnerability gave way to ones of lust and then protectiveness. "Nick," he said, "I think I need to see you."

"Hallelujah! I've been waiting to hear that for a month!"

"No," said Anders, gravely. "I'm afraid you may be in trouble."

Nick laughed. "Me?"

"I don't even want to talk about it over the phone."

"Good! I'll be right over—I remember the address."

"No," said Anders. "It's late."

"I'll be there in fifteen minutes! I'll take a cab! I'm loaded these days."

"You are?"

"Well, it's not actually *mine*—but my cash flow is really good. It's a long story, and hard to explain—and, hey! I'm drunk!"

"I can tell."

"See you in fifteen!"

21

NOVEMBER 13, 1986

Shielded by the limousine's darkened windows, and with only a single security car ahead and behind, Nancy Reagan read the draft of a Just Say No speech she would be giving at Boys Town two days before Thanksgiving at the ranch.

For most of this morning's ride, to a spot forty miles beyond Baltimore, she had ignored the stack of folders on the backseat in favor of looking out the tinted window. She was worried, mostly about Ronnie—the last several days had brought a whole new political calamity—but also about Mike, and whether this clandestine trip to the Ashley Center for Alcohol and Drug Rehabilitation was a good idea.

Boys Town of course made her think of Spencer Tracy and Father Flanagan, and now here was another priest approaching to greet her, coming right to the limousine door.

"It's a privilege to have you here," said plump Father Joseph Martin, the center's director.

"I hope you're taking good care of Mike," said Nancy, softly, hoping it didn't sound like a command.

"We're doing our best," said Father Martin, ushering her inside. "Let him know that he's loved."

Only Catholics ever struck her as being truly holy. Not just the movie ones like Tracy and Pat O'Brien, but the several converts she'd met, and sometimes even Bets. She felt a twinge of shame remembering the social relief she'd felt, decades ago, upon finding out that Ronald Reagan, despite the Irish name, was actually Protestant.

"Is he getting better?" she asked Father Martin, as they started down a hall.

"I was drunk for sixteen years, Mrs. Reagan. And I got better. He can, too."

On her way to a lounge set up for the visit, Nancy avoided the eyes of the curious staff—there would be no meet-and-greet here—and braced herself for how far gone Mike might appear; he'd had to spend ten days here before even his wife was allowed to visit.

"Mike," said Father Martin, opening the door to the lounge, "I'll leave you with the friend I've brought you."

He looked awful. His hair had grayed and he'd gotten so much thinner his glasses looked as if they'd slide off his face. She decided to start off with a joke: "I only *called* Frank. But I'm *visiting* you." She gave him a kiss.

He looked confused for a moment, but then she could see that he got it: news of Sinatra's operation out in Rancho Mirage, for diverticulitis, had penetrated the rehab center's walls.

"It means a lot that you tried to hunt me down," he said.

It now seemed ridiculous to have listened to the White House counsel all those months ago, when she was told not to speak with Mike directly anymore.

"No more secrets, Mike. You've got a problem, but you're going to get well. You *look* well."

"Well, I don't know about that."

"You know what I feared? Cancer. *This?* You can beat it. This is a treatable disease." She believed that. She was Dr. Davis's daughter, unsentimental when it came to illness and medical procedure of any kind—including, though she'd never say it, abortion. Once she'd gotten over the initial jolt from Dr. Hutton, she'd become resigned even to the AIDS test.

"You know," said Mike, "you told me that the *Time* cover was a big mistake. But I was too far gone to hear you." He'd let himself be photographed using a limo's phone—and wound up with "Who's This Man Calling? Influence Peddling in Washington" as the article's title. "It's funny how I could be that indiscreet with a photographer and still be able to keep a secret, the drinking, from even you."

She sat across from him and let him talk, gave him the legendary attentiveness of The Gaze. Sometimes he met it and sometimes he didn't, but the disclosures he needed to make kept coming: how he'd dried out for a few days in Georgetown Hospital, early in '85; been drunk through most of Bitburg a few months later; had kept bottles in his desk for years. She tried to look as if none of it shocked her. Little of it did.

"I still need you, Mike. I wish you could be there tonight!"

Ronnie would be giving a televised address at eight p.m., trying to explain the whole nightmarish week they'd had since the election. Some magazine in Lebanon had lit a match to Washington, raised a great blaze of indignation over how the administration was having secret contacts with Iran, selling them weapons and spare military parts in exchange for a handful of hostages. On the first day of the story she'd been *happy* about it, glad for the way it finally took Reykjavik off the front page; but by last weekend she knew there was no controlling it, that this story was going to be worse than anything else in their six years here.

Mike poured her a glass of ice water from the pitcher on the table. He displayed, for a moment, a serene expression that she didn't recognize. Maybe he'd learned it from Father Martin.

"Ronnie had the congressional leadership over to the White House yesterday," she told him.

"Not as much fun, I'll bet, as bringing the Mets to the Rose Garden." He twinkled, however wanly, letting her know that he still watched the news.

"Mike, I think people are going to believe the Ayatollah's version of what happened before they believe Ronnie's. And that's worse than all the jokes being made."

The peace overtures to Iranian "moderates" had been clownish— Poindexter's predecessor, Bud McFarlane, bringing over a cake in the shape of a key, to symbolize new beginnings. God!

When Mike said nothing, Nancy sighed, before adding: "McFarlane is supposed to be on *Nightline* tonight. And before that we have to get through this speech."

"I'm afraid a speech isn't going to do it," said Deaver.

"Oh, you and *I* know that—but tell it to Don Regan!"

"Poindexter needs to be fired."

"At the *least!*" said Nancy.

"And then get rid of North."

He said it as if she had the power to make it happen—which sometimes she did and sometimes she didn't. She still wasn't sure who North even *was*—somebody on the NSC whose name kept coming up in stories about two different "scandals," first Nicaragua and now Iran.

"I'm guessing he's an egomaniac," said Mike.

"You know, George Shultz was completely against this Iran business."

"I'm sure he was."

This was no good, thought Nancy. She was having to tell *him* things. Before his fall, he'd always been her first source of news.

"Ronnie told me he thinks George will keep being a team player," she explained.

"Shultz or Bush?"

"Oh, both. But he was referring to Shultz."

"Jimmy Carter claims to be 'distressed,'" said Deaver, who had always been able to get a rise out of the first lady with any mention of the former president. But Nancy just shook her head, sadly, thinking of how Kay had allowed the words "Reagan went Carter" to appear in a *Post* editorial the other day. The lack of proportion was crazy! She knew Kay had her job to do, and she'd never asked for favors or kid gloves, but you'd think that after *all* the shared lunches and all the phone calls Kay might have spared her at least something as egregious as that. It was all going haywire—Joan's astrological chickens coming home to roost months ahead of schedule.

"Mondale says Carter would have been shot for this," said Nancy, as much to herself as to Mike.

He just laughed.

"It's our own side I really worry about," she continued. "There's nobody to count on. Even George—George Will—is writing about the 'bender' of appeasement Ronnie's been on since Daniloff."

"Ouch," said Deaver, with a wince.

"Oh, I'm sorry!" She realized he'd been stung not by the politics of Will's observation but by the word "bender."

"I miss the 'troika,'" she said, trying to soothe him with a compliment. She referred to the first-term team of Mike and Jim Baker and Ed Meese—never mind that Meese was too right-wing and that Baker, however efficient, was always out for himself, always waiting for the bigger prize that might come from George Bush. She'd now take a little dig at him, she decided, to pump Mike up and make him feel he'd always been the first among equals.

"You know, when Jim Baker would tell me it was raining, I'd look out the window. I never have to do that with you or George Shultz."

"Ah, the rain," said Deaver, returning to his own plight. "I was going to be the ultimate 'rainmaker' out there on K Street. And now? TWA, Boeing, CBS: all of them gone as clients, as fast as I acquired them. The business is in ruins."

"You're still Mike the Magician."

She regretted saying it the moment she did. If this really was a disease that he could master, he needed realism. "Mike, you have to get well and get strong for *me*," she now declared. "It might be too late to help Ronnie, but—"

She stopped herself; that hadn't come out right, either. She didn't mean that Ronnie was finished! Just, of course, that it was too late for Mike to come back to the White House.

"What I meant—" she said, trying again.

"You know, I never put the touch on the president. Never asked for any favor."

He seemed to be having another conversation entirely.

"Oh, Mike, *I* know that."

"Did he ever say anything?"

"About that? No, why would he? You never *did* put the touch on him."

"No. About the drinking. I sometimes wondered if he noticed."

"No, I'm sure he didn't. And neither did I."

"I guess I was never as obvious as his dad."

Everyone knew the story of young Ronnie having to drag his inebriated father in off the snow-covered porch.

Nancy felt *herself* being dragged, as if by a current, toward a question she'd never been able to ask. "Mike, how did you do it? For twenty years."

"Do what? Hide the drinking?"

"No, how did you understand Ronnie? How did you always know what he needed?"

"Nancy, I've told you a dozen times: all I ever did for Ronald Reagan was see that they lighted him well. He's the one who did everything for me, and this is how I go and repay him."

"Mike, stop." She hated anyone's self-pity but her own, which she excused as a coping mechanism instead of a character flaw. But she hadn't said "stop" to put an end to Mike's indulgence; she'd said it to make him focus on what she'd actually brought herself to ask.

Now, all at once, he seemed to get it, to appreciate the enormity of the question.

Deaver paused, then shook his head, very slightly, before stopping.

No, he knew better than to admit the truth, which was that he did *not* understand Ronald Reagan. He might understand his interests, might have learned to read his commands the way a nurse learns to interpret the blinkings of a patient in isolation, but he did not understand the shallows and the depths behind Reagan's genial countenance. He had flown over them but never been permitted to land and explore on foot, up close. He had obtained what knowledge he had by staring, intensely and at length, from a high altitude.

So he said nothing.

Nancy, grateful without quite knowing why, looked straight at him and said, truthfully, not because Father Martin had recommended it: "I love you, Mike."

———

John Hinckley was on his way to the second of three weekly psychotherapy sessions. The endless green wall tiles of the John Howard Pavilion made him think of Evergreen, Colorado, where he had lived just after high school and which he had much disliked: the tall, never-denuded trees always felt like obstacles, dense hindrances to a clear path. He came to prefer the vast flat brown stretches of Lubbock, Texas, during his failed college years.

The tiles here in the Howard Pavilion were not really *ever*green; they were interrupted every ten or fifteen feet for doorways to private offices like the one he was now passing, the one that belonged to Dr. Patterson, the pavilion's medical director, a man not much older than himself, and a black—even though the District of Columbia had yet to take over the hospital. Hinckley wondered for a moment if there might be a connection between Howard *Pavilion* and Howard *University*.

His parents had done "family therapy" with Patterson and they liked him, but the doctor did not even look up as Hinckley passed his open door. He continued feeding Tender Vittles to the snapping turtle in his office fish tank. He had never fully supported John Hinckley's petitions to Judge Parker, and as Hinckley moved past—and the green tiles resumed—the patient experienced a surge of his greatest fear, that he would become one of those residents who eventually became senior to every staff member. No one who worked here was allowed to remain more than twenty years: too much tension and burnout.

He heard footsteps behind him. The hardness of the sound indicated a leather-shod doctor and not some nurse or patient in running shoes. The loud heels got closer, but he didn't turn around until he felt a hand on his shoulder and heard a soft voice saying "John."

It was Dr. Miller, giving him his usual soothing smile.

"I want to try something new, and I want to talk to you about it," said the physician.

Hinckley shrugged, more wary than indifferent, before starting back down the corridor.

"Come see me when you're done with therapy," Dr. Miller called after him. He thought he saw Hinckley nod in agreement, and almost decided just to wait and see if he actually showed up. But Dr. Miller couldn't resist spilling the beans of his bright idea. "John," he called out to the receding patient, "I'm thinking of putting your case for expanded privileges before the Forensic Review Board."

Hinckley stopped. He turned around, curious.

"It's the hospital's own panel and can make a limited number of decisions without court approval," Dr. Miller explained. "Such as a supervised day release—what's called a 'pass with staff.' There'd be somebody with you, but you'd be out. At least for several hours."

Now deeply interested, Hinckley retraced his steps until he stood only a foot from Dr. Miller, who smiled. "There's no guarantee this will go through, but I think it's an avenue worth pursuing."

"Okay."

"The Secret Service won't like it," said Dr. Miller.

Hinckley rolled his eyes, and the doctor gently cocked his head, looking almost like Ronald Reagan for a moment, as if agreeing with his patient that the Secret Service were a bunch of fussbudgets whom together they would outwit.

Hinckley continued on to therapy after promising Dr. Miller he would come to his office as soon as the session was over. He did not mention the draft of a letter inside his pocket, a second attempt to communicate with Ted Bundy in Florida, whose "awkward position," living on Death Row, the letter politely acknowledged.

———

Ronald Reagan was scheduled to begin his brief address on the Iranian situation at eight p.m. The Democratic Party's convention site-selection committee was prolonging its cocktail hour in the Riverview restaurant of the Watergate complex so that its members could hear the president before sitting down to dinner. Nearly all those assembled before two television screens, no matter which city they were pushing for, wore GREAT IN '88! buttons.

"It's a shame we ever moved the party headquarters away from here," said Pamela Harriman, gazing out over the Potomac. The Democratic National Committee had vacated its fabled, burgled offices in the Watergate even before Nixon resigned, but the whole series of swirling buildings here on the river still shimmered with the glow of liberty redeemed. Nathan Landow, the Maryland developer in charge of the site-selection committee, nodded his agreement, even as he silently bet the Watergate's management was glad to be rid of a tenant with such chronically up-and-down finances as the DNC.

The presidential seal appeared on the television screens.

"Instead of moving downtown," said Mayor Barry, "the party should have relocated itself to Ward 8." He didn't have to explain that such a move would have been a gesture to its poorest and most loyal voters, who also happened to be his base. Mrs. Harriman gave him a momentary look of fascination before urging John Carter Brown to help Landow in shushing the crowd to a decibel level that would make Reagan's incoherence at least audible. Brown was doing double duty tonight: he was here not only as escort but also to talk up all the museums and monuments that delegates could visit in the unlikely event Washington's bid for the convention prevailed.

Good evening, said the president. *I know you've been reading, seeing, and hearing a lot of stories the past several days attributed to Danish sailors, unnamed observers at Italian ports and Spanish harbors, and especially unnamed government officials of my administration. Well, now you're going to hear the facts from a White House source, and you know my name.*

"Lose one for the Gipper!" cried a high roller from Atlanta, the front-running city in the selection contest.

"*Sssh!*" ordered Mrs. Harriman.

Reagan began explaining how the weapons sent to Iran were a sort of gesture, a token of his sincerity in seeking reconciliation: *These modest deliveries, taken together, could easily fit into a single cargo plane.*

"They sound *o*-most as small as these *o*-d'oeuvres," said Senator Hollings, one of the few office-holders permitted here tonight, his own presidential ambitions having been so thoroughly finished off in '84. The site-selection committee actually prided itself on the absence of big-name pols; it made them feel more in charge of their appointed task.

"You know what this administration's problem is?" Bob Strauss told Hollings. "It's all cattle and no hat. They only understand guns but don't know anything about how to make a *deal*."

Hollings nodded at the reversed Texas aphorism. Signs of diplomatic collapse were indeed everywhere. Last week Shultz and Shevardnadze had had an eight-hour fiasco of follow-up meetings in Vienna; the Cold War was reheating, and now there was *this*, too. The senator and the superlawyer returned their eyes to one of the televisions.

There is ample precedent for this kind of secret diplomacy, Reagan explained. *In 1971 then-president Nixon sent his national security advisor on a secret mission to China . . .*

"Oh," purred Clark Clifford, "there are going to be rather more parallels to Nixon than that one."

Pamela almost shushed *him*. At this stage there was something depressing about Clark, even if he *had* done so much to make her a hundred million dollars richer. He was too old-guard; it was almost as if Arthur were here—Arthur, with whom she'd so far gotten nowhere about the book, though surely her election-night triumph had nudged him at least a half inch toward seeing the wisdom of the thing?

Our government has a firm policy not to capitulate to terrorist demands. That no-concessions policy remains in force, in spite of the wildly speculative and false stories about arms for hostages and alleged ransom payments. We did not—repeat—did not trade weapons or anything else for hostages, nor will we.

"*Alleged* payments?" shouted the wealthy, drunken Georgian. "Tell it to Jacobsen!" He referred to the most recently released of the hostages, while standing in front of a giant cartoon that rested on an easel and showed Republican candidates slipping off Reagan's coattails, now said to be the only Teflon part of him.

. . . the relevant committees of Congress are being, and will be, fully informed.

"They will be *now*," said Hollings, with more than a chuckle. "Wait till he tries dealin' with Bobby Byrd." The wiliness of the incoming majority leader was such that he had survived even an early association with the Ku Klux Klan.

"I see Ed Muskie over there," said Clifford to Strauss, who wasn't listening. "A shame he's not still in the Senate. He'd be perfect for one of the investigating committees. I'd advise him to go after the foreign banks. They have to have been involved in this thing."

Carter Brown pointed to Reagan's image and whispered to Mrs. Harriman, "You know what's really scary? He thinks he's telling the truth."

Pamela didn't consider this much of an insight. In fact she thought it the only sympathetic thing one could say about Ronald Reagan. She, for ages, had practiced exactly what Carter Brown was now accusing the president of. "What *other* way is there to go through life?" she replied sternly, before resuming a contemptuous regard of the screen.

Thank you, and God bless you, said the president.

22

NOVEMBER 15, 1986

As her helicopter entered the airspace of northwest Washington, Prime Minister Margaret Thatcher flicked a thistle from her camel-hair coat. She had acquired the offending piece of vegetation several hours before, while riding in a golf cart from the Camp David helipad to Aspen Lodge. During the afternoon, she had listened to Ronald Reagan deliver his weekly radio address and given him a severe talking-to over lunch.

Ambassador Acland, sharing this return journey with her, would be taking the prime minister, once they landed, to a press conference at the British embassy. Right now, however, he concentrated on picking up the thistle, which had landed near his shoe. As if it had been insufficiently punished, he deposited it in one of the helicopter's less-and-less-used ashtrays.

Mrs. Thatcher reached into her handbag for a copy of the communiqué that had been issued upon her departure from the president's weekend retreat. It stipulated that she and Reagan had

> *... confirmed that NATO's strategy of forward defense and flexible response would continue to require effective nuclear deterrence ... The United States and the United Kingdom agree that these matters should continue to be the subject of close consultation within the alliance ...*

"We are pleased," said the prime minister, without looking up at the ambassador.

Two days after the collapse of last month's summit she had called the president to request—or more nearly demand—today's meeting. She now believed that, after his near-fatal slip on the utopian ice of Reyk-javik, she had gotten Reagan back onto the solid ground of mutually assured destruction.

"Yes," said Acland, who'd sifted through his briefcase for a copy of the communiqué. "It's very sound."

"It ought to be," said Mrs. Thatcher. She had rehearsed her arguments to Reagan by trying them out, yesterday, on Shultz and Weinberger, and had perfected them this morning over breakfast with George Bush.

The helicopter began its descent. Within another few minutes, Acland and the prime minister, her suit the same shade of blue as his own, were striding into the embassy's auditorium, taking up positions near a blown-up photo of Mrs. Thatcher and Reagan. It had been taken only hours ago, during their golf-cart gambol in the Catoctin Mountains, and released to the press along with the communiqué. She had requested display of the enlargement because she knew the president's leather bomber jacket would infuriate the peacenik women still camped out back home on Greenham Common.

After several questions about the language of the communiqué, the back-and-forth between the prime minister and the press grew more expansive:

"Have you at times been exasperated by the president's casual style and what's been described as his inattentiveness to detail?"

Mrs. Thatcher narrowed her nostrils: "The president's broader brush reflects the differences between executive and parliamentary government. His grasp of essentials is quite acute."

"Over in Iceland, didn't the president nearly bargain away European security for unclear reasons of his own? And do you now have a sense of what those reasons were?"

The prime minister pointed her finger and shook it twice, slowly, like the blade of a scissors. "Your second question is premised on your first, and since the answer to the first question is no, the second question is moot and I needn't answer it. But I shall, in my own fashion. Before President Reagan came along, the West was *losing* the Cold War. With his election—as I said in a speech here in Washington in 1981—the tide

began to turn. Bargain *away* European security? I think you'll find that
the president drove a very hard bargain indeed—just ask Mr. Gorbachev."

"Prime Minister Trudeau of Canada has long urged that we speak
more softly to the Soviets. Is that advice not more urgent after the failure
of the talks in Reykjavik?"

Mrs. Thatcher noticed, unbelievably enough, a second thistle that had
managed to get underneath the camel-hair coat and onto her navy-blue
skirt. She removed it without taking her eyes off the questioner. "It was
never urgent. We must speak firmly, and must remember that nuclear
weapons have given us, over four decades, *more* security, not less."

The man from the *Telegraph*, seated in the front row, smiled as he
wrote on his pad. He would bet that she had cuffed Reagan around something awful this afternoon, no matter that she was making it sound as
if there'd never been a shade of disagreement between them. The writer
sitting next to him, the chap he'd met over in Reykjavik last month,
seemed to be thinking the same: "Is it true," Christopher Hitchens now
asked, "that there was no notetaker at Camp David because the president
knew you would get into a discussion of Iran?"

The prime minister prepared to mock the pseudo-knowingness of this
question, which must be coming from the *Guardian*, or perhaps, even
worse, the *New Statesman*. The man asking it looked handsomely familiar, but she could not place him, a failure that she knew would drive her
response to a higher level of irritability. Worse still, she realized that the
question's presupposition was correct: she herself often relied on notes
she dictated only after a meeting had finished, but Reagan—except for
today—always had someone writing things down. She decided to execute
a simple evasive maneuver: "The president and I discussed, as always,
anything we cared to. As for Iran, I believe implicitly in the president's
total integrity on that subject."

She looked at her watch. Nothing had really gone amiss, but she had
ceased to enjoy herself and was ready to conclude things. "I'm sorry my
stay in the United States will be so short, and almost sorry that my welcome has been so warm. I find nothing more soothing than falling asleep
to the chants of protesters in the middle distance, but there have been
none to be found here. Good evening, ladies and gentlemen."

"Will you be leaving before breakfast tomorrow?"

"After. I have requested my usual from the ambassador: vitamins and black coffee."

Acland gave two staffers the signal to wrap things up. The pair set about ushering the reporters out, and as they went, Mrs. Thatcher had another look at the dark-haired man in the front row, recognizing him this time. She had once, as leader of the opposition, swatted him on the rear end with a sheaf of papers.

He waved hello, and then made a series of hand gestures to Acland: *Me? Her? Together? Two minutes?*

Acland signaled back: *Sorry. Out of the question.*

"No," said Mrs. Thatcher, noticing the dumb show and overruling the ambassador. "It's all right."

Rather astonished, Acland arranged for Mr. Hitchens to stand with the prime minister on a carpet in a hall outside the library. "Off the record, of course," he stipulated.

"Story of my life," said Hitchens.

"Yes, I do remember you," said Mrs. Thatcher. "I even *read* you from time to time. I saw for instance, what you wrote a week or so ago for the *Spectator.* Quite *colossally wrong*—as if someone had taken the muddled thinking of the Foreign Office, turned it inside out, and managed to make it even *more* wrong."

Hitchens was disappointed to notice that the teeth through which she was more or less smiling had been straightened since their last encounter; he found their improved arrangement to be a dash less arousing than what he'd seen up close a decade ago, when she'd briefly disciplined him.

"Are you pleased, Prime Minister, that everything in arms negotiations with the president is allowed to depend on hypothetical laser beams?"

"I'm quite in *favor* of SDI, Mr. Hitchens. I simply don't believe that it will or should make nuclear weapons obsolete. I'm delighted that the Soviets are so preoccupied by it, so desperate to stop it."

"If you did indeed read my piece, Prime Minister, you know what it says about a 'wasteful, dangerous militarization of space.'"

"Wasteful, perhaps, but an obliquely effective scheme for tilting the military balance back toward us. And, yes, I shall continue my 'sub-Churchillian rhetoric' about deterrence, as I believe you called it."

Hitchens thought: Who needs the jagged teeth? Was there any arousal equal to what came from being quoted to oneself?

Mrs. Thatcher continued: "In 1983, President Reagan told me that the Soviets would soon not be able to keep up the pace of the arms race, that their economic system wouldn't be up to it. He said the same thing again to me in 1984. We may actually be seeing that now."

"Build up to build down," said Hitchens.

"No," said the prime minister. "Build up to *wear* down. I am *not* in favor of discarding nuclear weapons within ten years—or twenty. And that is not what the president proposed."

"Do you think he *knows* what he proposed?"

She stared at him more severely, as if he were an adolescent who'd just tried out a dirty joke. She would tolerate no talk of senescence or bewilderment. Met with silence, Hitchens continued speaking: "Now that you've got this president back on the right path, are you prepared to deal with the *next* one? I discuss Mr. Reagan's political eclipse in my latest column."

"Perhaps I'll catch up with that one on the plane home."

"I'm sure it will prove useful."

She slid her pocketbook up toward her elbow and waggled her empty hands. "I'm afraid I'm unarmed today."

She meant that she was carrying no roll of papers. It was thrilling that she remembered.

Acland led her toward the library, but before they entered it she turned back around. "Mr. Hitchens?"

"Yes?"

"Do you know any astronomy?"

"I know that there's an observatory next door. Where Mr. Bush gets a free house."

"Go have a look through their telescope. You will be reminded that eclipses are, by definition, temporary."

"I don't know the source of the money," said Anders Little to Anne Macmurray, wondering how much more he could tell her. Almost three weeks had passed since Spitz Channell told him about money being parked with donors, and ten days since Nick Carrollton had confirmed—*"It's not a big deal!"*—that funds had been hidden with him too. That he was only now broaching the subject with Anne, here in his Arlington apartment, told him how scared he was of it.

"It makes no sense," she said, picking up a Triscuit with a slab of Swiss cheese, Anders's bachelor idea of an hors d'oeuvre. "Why would they give money to Peter, even temporarily, at the same time he's giving money to *them*?"

"I know," said Anders, wishing they hadn't made a plan to have dinner at Whitlow's, which was always crowded; he was finding it hard enough to talk to her here. "There's at least one other person," he finally managed to say, "who's in the same boat as Peter."

She waited to hear more, but he couldn't bring himself to go further. "Peter and I are in touch every week or so now," Anne explained. "Do you want *me* to warn him?"

"No," said Anders, hastily.

"Anders, what is it? Are they parking money with you, too?" She had arrived only ten minutes ago, following an afternoon of local errands, and was feeling less and less relaxed.

"Oh, no, no. I have this young friend who . . ." He left the sentence unfinished.

"Someone from work?" Anne asked, taking a sip of wine and trying to appear matter-of-fact.

"No, not exactly—although, yeah, part of, you know, the whole general mix, the administration—"

"A *personal* friend?" Anne asked.

"Well, uh, yeah, sort of. I mean, not really—" He looked to her for help.

"I don't want to pry, but for a while now I've been wondering—"

"Wondering?"

"Whether you wanted to talk about . . ."

"Something."

"Yes, something."

Anders nodded. "I don't know if I can."

"If not now, whenever you feel ready."

"No," said Anders, quickly, almost exclaiming the word, as if afraid the opportunity to talk might never come again. "I *do* want to talk. I mean, it's just—" The buzzer sounded, and he fairly leapt to the kitchen intercom.

"Yes?"

"It's a Mr. Hitchens," said the doorman. "He thought he might 'pop up.'"

"Okay," answered Anders, who didn't know what else to say.

"We can get back to this later," said Anne, when he returned to the living room. Now fully on guard, Anders shrugged and said, "Sure," as if whatever subject they'd been about to discuss was so unimportant he couldn't remember it.

"I didn't know you had company," said Hitchens, once he entered the apartment. He extended his hand to Anne once Anders introduced them. "We've spoken over the phone," he reminded her. "I appreciated your help with that article."

"Can I get you a drink, Christopher?" asked Anders.

"What an extraordinary question," Hitchens replied, eyeing the half-drunk bottle of white wine with a distinct lack of enthusiasm. His host went off to the kitchen to gather the components for a cocktail.

Sitting down, Hitchens noticed a copy of the Oliver Sacks book through the wire mesh of Anne's tote bag. He pointed to it. "Have you gotten to the part about Reagan and the aphasics?"

"No," Anne said with some embarrassment. "I've more or less been carrying it around for a month."

"It's quite remarkable, really. Aphasics can no longer understand the meanings of words, but they're uncannily sensitive to affect—the way the blind can supposedly smell more acutely than the rest of us. They're particularly good at distinguishing sincerity from mendacity when listening to someone, even though they don't know what's being said."

Anders returned with a tray of liquors and mixers. Hitchens appeared delighted by the chance to construct his own drink, but first he would finish his tutorial with Ms. Macmurray. "Apparently when a group of aphasics were played a videotape of Mr. Reagan giving a speech—Dr. Sacks documents this—they broke into fits of laughter."

"Ha. Ha," said Anders, without cracking a smile.

Anne did laugh, then looked at Anders, wondering if she was right that he'd been on the verge of a sexual revelation just before. It would make perfect sense for the poor man to be chronically buttoned up, to have been rendered aphasic when it came to a whole part of life, forced by the world to keep a secret that must be harder to conceal than any acquired in the National Security Council.

As they both watched Hitchens mix a small amount of Perrier with a large amount of Johnnie Walker, she felt a sudden fear that Anders's revelation might have two stages: He wasn't gay and *sick*, was he? Oh, God, no. That was impossible to believe. But then why should it be? AIDS itself was impossible to believe—and he did look even leaner than just a month ago.

"I wasn't interrupting anything important, was I?" asked Hitchens, as he put the cap back on a bottle.

Anne now felt glad to have him here. "Oh, no," she answered. "Just conversation. What have you been up to since we spoke?"

"I was talking with Mrs. Thatcher about an hour ago." He said it off-handedly. "She takes a rather different view of the arms race from the one you hold, Ms. Macmurray."

"Don't tell me you were up at Camp David," said Anders, as if Hitchens's presence there would have been on the level of a terrorist attack.

"Relax, dear boy," said Hitchens. "Attila the Hen had a press conference at the embassy, and the ambassador let me have an unpublishable word or two with her afterwards. I must say, Iceland is beginning to seem a bit . . . yesterday. The press were getting rather more interested in Iran before their time expired."

"I suppose you want to interrogate me on that subject, too," said Anders, who seemed more relieved than testy. At least Hitchens wasn't asking about Central America or boys.

"Yes, of course," said the writer. "This exceptional president of yours first denies trading arms for hostages, and then asks for credit when *quo* follows *quid*. I don't know whether they've yet shown Thursday night's tape to the aphasics."

"Well, what can I do for you?" asked Anders, who had no intention of saying anything.

"Tell me about that whole bats' nest you're working in. I'm halfway through a draft of my next piece, and so far that's my image from the animal kingdom for the NSC. I also today used an *exclamation point*—a mark I try to avoid as rigorously as I do most adverbs. But outlandish times call for outlandish punctuation. Was this mad initiative news to you? The key-shaped cake and all the rest of it?"

"You know I'm not going to tell you one way or the other," said Anders. In fact, the whole McFarlane-North mission had come as a surprise to him. "But I can tell you that the NSC sometimes, not often but sometimes, has to do things like that."

"Why?" asked Anne, who looked at Hitchens while she put the question to Anders. For once she would have an ally in a conversation like this!

"Because," Anders explained, reverting to the voice she remembered from the White House Mess, "Congress has had things set up for the past ten years in such a way that the CIA has to give them notice of just about everything it does. Our own intelligence agency can't do anything in secret!"

"But if that's the case—" said Anne, before the doorbell interrupted her.

"What the hell?" muttered Anders. He sprang to his feet, brushing the Triscuit crumbs from his khakis.

"Hi!"

Hitchens and Anne looked closely at the well-groomed young man at the door.

"The guy downstairs recognized me and let me up!" the arrival explained with an enthusiasm even younger than his years. "He said, 'Oh, you must be going to the party!' " The boy waved hello to Hitchens, who was intrigued, and then to Anne, who tried to reassure herself with the obvious health of this fresh-faced preppie.

Both she and Hitchens could detect, from the slight crumpling of the young man's expression, that Anders, who had his back to them, was mouthing a reprimand, something on the order of *You shouldn't be here.*

"Oh, wow," said Nick Carrollton, after Anders introduced him. "Real drinks!" He pointed to the bottle of Johnnie Walker.

"And how was *your* day?" asked Hitchens.

"Lazy! I really haven't done anything except fix lunch for my friend Terry."

"Terry?" asked Hitchens.

"My AIDS buddy."

Anne looked alarmed and Hitchens looked delighted, with recognition: luck and deduction had just high-fived each other in his brain.

"Terry has told me quite a lot," said Hitchens, "but he's never told me about you." He paused before saying, "Little, where are your manners?"

Anders began fixing Nick a cocktail.

"I see you know what he likes," said the writer.

23

NOVEMBER 19, 1986

"Sit down, Mr. Keen," said Ronald Reagan, with a somewhat weary smile. "Anyone new you've dug up for me today?"

Old-time radio's Tracer of Lost Persons had provided Reagan with a nickname for Edmund Morris, his authorized biographer, who frequently brought news of the president's distant past into the Oval Office. Lately Morris had even discovered the daughter of a minister, back in Illinois, to whom Reagan had once been engaged.

"No, Mr. President," said Morris, in his soft South African accent. "Today, while it's fresh in your mind, I'd like to take you through Reykjavik."

"I see."

The biographer scratched his neat beard. He was hoping to keep Reagan away from Hollywood anecdote, where so many of his conversations, even ones with foreign leaders, tended to stray.

The president looked at a card listing his afternoon appointments. Morris stole a glance at it too: Pat Buchanan, Senator Laxalt, and George Bush would all, one by one, be following his own forty-five-minute allotment of time. When through with them, the president would rehearse for tonight's press conference, an ordeal necessitated by the failure of last Thursday's speech to quiet the Iran controversy.

"It's been a lonely twenty-four hours here," said Reagan, despite the string of appointed visitors. The first lady was up in New York, seeing friends and having lunch with the designer Valentino. "But Nancy will be home for dinner," the president explained, "before I go in front of that lynch mob."

The phrase was spoken without the usual glint of humor. Morris was interested by this, but didn't want his subject digressing into even a topic as serious as Iran. He said nothing.

"How long have we been at this, Edmund?"

"Less than two years, Mr. President. I know it must seem more." Almost four years had passed since Senator Hatfield, at his home in Georgetown, put a small array of biographers in front of the Reagans, tempting the president and first lady with the idea of allowing a history-as-it-happens chronicler to be underfoot in the White House. Deaver liked the idea, but it took two years for the rest of the troika to get over their skepticism, and about as long for Morris, known even to the president for his book on Theodore Roosevelt, to make up his own mind.

"We met once before that night at Hatfield's, didn't we?"

"We did," said Morris, quite surprised. "At a state dinner during your first year here."

Reagan nodded, and said, "Well, Reykjavik," like a boy ready to take his punishment.

"Yes," said Morris. "Tell me the first thing you now recall when you hear that word: Reykjavik." He feared getting a pol's auto-answer—*I remember the warmth of the Icelandic people*—but he knew that Dutch, whom he'd begun thinking of by this childhood tag, was likely to respond with something more peculiar.

"The porch," said Reagan.

"The porch?"

"At Hofdi House, where we had the talks. I was struck by the fact that there wasn't a porch; just some concrete steps, a kind of stoop. I remember thinking a house as fine as that one should have a big front porch."

Morris made a note.

"Did you detect any changes in Mr. Gorbachev? Since you'd last seen him in Geneva?"

"Changes?" asked Reagan, who politely pretended to give Morris's new question some thought before returning to the previous one. "You know," he said, "I do remember the ticking of the grandfather clock."

Morris's ears pricked up. "What did it make you think?" He anticipated, hopefully, a reference to nuclear Doomsday.

"I was surprised that I could hear it," said Reagan. He often had to ask Morris to repeat things. "It's a very old-fashioned sound, just right for that kind of house. Maybe that added to the oddness of there being no porch."

Morris nodded, hiding aggravation as he made a note. "Let me go right to the last session. I hear from"—he almost said "the mice"—"from people who were there, about your anger with Mr. Gorbachev."

"Anger?" asked Reagan. "No," he added, shaking his head, as if not wanting to admit to something so unseemly.

" 'Distress' perhaps?"

"No, not quite that."

"I've seen the photos of you emerging from Hofdi House, Mr. President. 'Disappointed,' surely."

"Well, a bit frustrated, I suppose."

"You were coming out empty-handed."

"Yes, that was it." He flashed Morris a large, sincere smile, glad that they had finally cleared up the matter.

Morris made a note and the president looked once more at the schedule card. Fearing he might lose his subject's attention altogether, the biographer pleaded for a bit of elaboration: "What had Mr. Gorbachev failed to give you? Failed to put in your hands."

"Oh, no," said Reagan, the smile suddenly gone. "That wasn't it. I felt as if I'd left something behind, forgotten something inside the house."

"What was it?" asked Morris, leaning forward.

"Oh, if I'd known, I'd have gone back in."

———

"I'm honored to have played a small part in our great victory!" declared Mrs. Harriman from a lectern in the Senate Caucus Room.

"Ha!" cried Fritz Hollings, with a kind of courtly rudeness, from the front row. "Small part? You were the heart and soul of it, Pammy!"

Mrs. Harriman gave him a pleased, forgiving look before casting her gaze more generally upon those gathered here for a luncheon in her honor. "And I would like to acknowledge someone else who would have been heartened by the success that finally came to us—my late husband, Averell Harriman."

This small tribute was greeted with brief, funereal applause. Al Gore's unlined, well-brought-up face instinctively assumed the most respectful expression in the room.

"We won because so many gave their commitment and their hearts."

Pamela scanned the premises for Moynihan. No sign of him, of course; so she settled for the sight of a tepidly applauding George Mitchell, who had headed the Senate Democrats' own campaign committee and been put well into the shade by PamPAC.

"We overcame the Republicans' financial margin; we caught up with them technologically; we surpassed them creatively. We even out-communicated the Great Communicator!"

"We'll see how well he manages to communicate *tonight!*" cried Senator Hollings.

"Now, we have *more* work to do—in the Senate and the nation. So it's on to 1988—to another victory and a new Democratic White House!"

She took the applause and sat down to the poached salmon being brought in while Mitchell introduced the party's senators-elect. Pamela had begun to learn that the star's job was decidedly less tiring than the supporting player's. Last night young Winston had given a talk at the English Speaking Union up in New York, and she'd been there, silently encouraging him as if he were Leland or Ave. But muteness had taken more out of her than being center stage was doing now. She had never, of course, had to perform audience-adoration on the daily basis or public scale required of Nancy Reagan, who now crossed her mind almost sympathetically. The extinction that woman must feel threatened with! Unless, of course, Nancy had somehow learned to reverse the polarity and be energized rather than drained by all the gazing. No, thought Pamela: if that were the case, the dreadful lady in red wouldn't show the peculiar emaciation that comes from being eaten alive.

Mrs. Harriman left the luncheon early, there being no surer sign of centrality than making oneself scarce. Only when her car pulled away from the Delaware Avenue curb did Janet hand her a Federal Express envelope she'd been carrying all morning. "I kept this from you so that you could enjoy yourself back there." The envelope, overnighted to N Street by a *Vanity Fair* staffer, contained the proofs of a still-untitled article along with an unsigned cover note: *Forewarned is forearmed—from an ardent, grateful Democrat.*

"Oh, dear," said Pamela, who put on her glasses and flipped backwards through the proofs with a pink-polished thumbnail. A paragraph on the penultimate page caught her eye:

> *Mrs. Harriman's touch is hardly infallible. In Florida, imagining herself up against a phantom Nancy Reagan, she spent hundreds of thousands of PamPAC dollars, in a last-minute panic buy, for an ad designed to rebut another ad that didn't exist. Outsmarted by the other side and looking foolish to those who have been playing this game longer than herself, she failed to realize how it was the Zeitgeist, rather than any bright strategy or command from her coral lips, that blew Senator Hawkins back into the fever swamps of the Everglades. Indeed, Mrs. Harriman's life history demonstrates more proficiency at acquiring money than at spending it wisely. If she truly craves an ambassadorship . . .*

Pamela resumed flipping through the proofs and was stopped by another of Mr. Hitchens's paragraphs, this one on galley number four:

> *She keeps in the desk of her N Street office an item deriving from the brief play she made for Sinatra in the months of 1971 between Hayward's expiration and Ave's taking of the bait: a gold charm, suitable for a bracelet or necklace, saying THIRD TIME'S THE. Engraved on the back is the name of the giver, "Francis Albert," who no doubt found it a small price to pay for being rid of her attentions.*

Pamela handed the proofs to Janet. "Am I to assume he burgled my desk?"

"No," said Janet. "That information comes from Kelly Proctor's for-agings, I'm certain. There are other things in here, too, that he could only have gotten from her."

"Yes, of course," said Pamela.

"Shall I start preparing a response? Something really forceful about his tactics?"

"No," answered Mrs. Harriman, looking straight ahead. "We're going to make friends with Mr. Hitchens."

———

The president looked at the schedule card—only two hurdles until Nancy's arrival—as the phone rang with the appointed call from Saddle River, New Jersey.

"Good afternoon, Mr. President."

"Hello, Dick."

"I imagine they're getting you ready for tonight," said Richard Nixon.

"Yes, they're giving me a good working over!"

"Is Buchanan in on the prep?"

"Yes, he's been there."

"Good, he's the best one at it. He was the *only* one of our guys to turn the tables on Ervin and Dash when he testified. Made them look like a bunch of jackasses. He was so good on live TV that Mrs. Nixon rushed downstairs to hug him when he got back to the White House from Capitol Hill. Threw her arms around him and did a little dance."

"How is Pat?" asked Reagan.

"All things considered, she's pretty well."

"Good," said the current president. "Please give her our love. And thanks for your memo about the election results. Don thought it very shrewd."

"Hmmm," said Nixon, wondering if the memo had stopped with the chief of staff or if Reagan had read it himself. "Well, I meant what I said. You've done a hell of a lot more for Social Security than we ever did—bargaining with goddamned O'Neill—and yet the Democrats are still managing to knock the crap out of us on the issue. Because we didn't line up with FDR fifty years ago. Christ, *we* might as well still be blaming *them* for the Civil War! But it boils down to this: we had too many lousy candidates with too much money and not enough brains to get on top of that issue—or most of the others."

"Well," said Reagan, "our political director here thinks we may get a little more cooperation from the Hill next year than people believe."

"I addressed that kind of talk in my memo," said Nixon. "This guy of yours is smoking crack."

"Oh," said Reagan, surprised.

Nixon forced himself to laugh. "I promise I won't use that analogy in Nancy's presence." What was the point of the White House's setting up this call, whose purpose was to thank the former president for his memo, when Reagan hadn't even read the goddamned thing? Should he, Nixon wondered, even bother trying to tell him how to handle Shultz? This past Sunday, on *Face the Nation*, the secretary of state, once Nixon's man at Labor and Treasury, had more or less threatened to quit over Iran. No surprise about that: Shultz was solid enough, but the former president still remembered how this born professor had gotten on his high horse back when Nixon and Haldeman had flirted with the idea of auditing a few people's taxes. There was a way to deal with Shultz at an awkward moment like this, but Reagan probably regarded the potential resignation of his own secretary of state as a mere detail. Nixon decided to sign off by drawing him the biggest picture he could think of.

"It's going to be rough out there for you tonight, in front of the press."

"Oh, I know that," said Reagan. "A regular lynch mob."

"That's right. And there's only one thing you can really do."

"I'm all ears," said the current president.

"Tell 'em you made a mistake on this goddamned Iran thing. And then apologize."

———

Upstairs in the Residence, Nancy Reagan sat on a couch in front of the television. She fingered the tissue paper inside a box that held a beautiful red cashmere jacket Valentino had insisted she bring home to Washington. The soft crinkle of the paper soothed her as she began witnessing Ronnie's second televised ordeal in the space of a week. He was starting his press conference with a statement that would satisfy no one:

... to eliminate the widespread but mistaken perception that we have been exchanging arms for hostages, I have directed that no further sales of arms of any kind be sent to Iran. I have further directed that all information relating to our initiative be provided to the appropriate members of Congress.

If you give them what they want, thought Nancy, they'll only cry for more. It would be the same with the press. Here came Helen Thomas, always allowed to ask the first question. The first lady braced herself: Helen was typically rough on the administration but sometimes displayed a soft spot toward Ronnie himself. No good, alas: she was bringing up his "credibility," mentioning the "trading" of Zakharov for Daniloff as if that were an established fact.

Nancy crinkled the tissue; she dreaded Ronnie's answers even more than the questions. Should she call Bets in order to get through this? For years they'd simultaneously watched movies and TV programs over the phone. The past couple of days she'd done very little calling from the hotel in New York—she didn't trust the lines or the operators—and by now she was jonesing (a word she always heard during Just Say No Q-and-A's) for the instrument.

But she couldn't sit still. She got up to redo some of the unpacking the maid had performed with the luggage that came back from New York. After rearranging things more to her liking, she came back to the television. Chris Wallace was standing to ask a question. Would *he* show a touch of mercy? She had met his father *fifty years ago*, at WBBM in Chicago, when Mother was doing radio soaps. Oh God, she mustn't think of Mother now. Should she send the red jacket out to her in Phoenix? Would she be able to appreciate the surprise?

"Mr. President, aren't you saying to terrorists that either you or your state sponsor—which in this case was Iran—can gain from the holding of hostages?"

"No," said Ronnie, *"because I don't see where the kidnappers or the hostage-holders gained anything. They didn't get anything. They let the hostages go. Now, whatever is the pressure that brought that about, I'm just grateful for the*

fact that we got them. As a matter of fact, if there had not been so much publicity, we would have had two more . . ."

This was a disaster. What was the message: We didn't do it, but if you'd only shut up we'd have done it better? She could feel the hostility in the East Room without even being down there. Her mind went back to two miserable weeks she'd spent in Las Vegas, more than thirty years ago, watching Ronnie every night perform the nightclub act that marked the low point of his career. He had, strangely enough, been a hit; the crowds were kind. But the night she best remembered was the second-to-last one, when she felt herself getting sick from the smell of cigarettes and cheap scotch and the realization that this show was *different*, that the audience was strangely hostile and unforgiving. It may have been just a fluke, a night when the chemistry was off, but the change was so total that it spooked her. She and Ronnie left two days later and never went back.

"How can you justify this duplicity?" Sam Donaldson now asked, sounding more like a heckler than a reporter.

She skipped Ronnie's answer, walking into the bathroom to splash water on her face. She returned in time to hear Bill Plante from CBS: *"Isn't it possible that the Iraqis, sir, might think that a thousand antitank missiles was enough to alter the balance of the war they're fighting with Iran?"*

Ronnie pursed his lips. *"No, this is a purely defensive weapon. It is a shoulder-carried weapon."*

She knew, instinctively, that he would turn out to be wrong about this, because Poindexter, who reminded her of some pompous, pipe-puffing dean out of an old campus comedy, hadn't briefed him properly.

She pressed the HALF MUTE button on the remote and called Don Regan's office, knowing he'd be there instead of in the East Room, so as not to expose himself to shouting reporters *after* the session.

"This is a catastrophe," she told the chief of staff.

"Your 'friend' approved the scheduling."

"I'm not talking about the scheduling," the first lady replied, though it was true that she had called Joan—in a moment of weakness, after seeing the polls on last week's speech. "He hasn't been briefed!"

"He was *over*briefed," Regan shot back. "I was at every session, including the rehearsal in the theater."

"Who did the preparation? *Before* the rehearsal."

"The admiral, principally."

"Why didn't you tell him to stop?"

"Actually, I did, once I realized how he was convincing the president he'd been told certain things, months ago, that he *hadn't* been told."

A moment of dead air passed between her and Regan, but it wasn't strategic; she'd been stunned into silence.

"Admiral Poindexter is a nervous man these days," continued the chief of staff. "It showed during the rehearsal, and that made the president nervous."

"Then get rid of him," Nancy said, evenly.

"I think the president might want some say in that."

"Don, I think you should make this happen while *you* still have some say—in anything." She hung up on him—a new low—and unmuted the TV.

Mr. President, what would be wrong in saying that a mistake was made on a very high-risk gamble so that you can get on with the next two years?

Nancy leaned forward and recognized the reporter as being from the *Washington Times.* My God, they were losing the Moonies!

I don't see that it has been a fiasco or a great failure of any kind . . .

She shut off the television and went to get the cookies and juice that had been delivered from the kitchen and left on a cart in the hall. Returning to the bedroom, she made a call to Ron and Doria, whom she'd never gotten around to seeing in New York. Neither of them had watched any of the press conference, a fact that replaced a small piece of her panic with exasperation.

Before saying goodbye to them, she heard Ronnie come into the other room. He'd switched the television back on. Sam Nunn, one of the Democrats they could sometimes count on, was wondering if the president had been "capable of assimilating all the information his staff gave him." The implication was that this might now be a problem with *any* issue.

"Don Regan says you were overbriefed," said Nancy, as if the chief of staff were some trusted source she frequently quoted.

"I was," said the president.

Dole had come onscreen, saying it was time to move on from Iran.

Nancy now doubted her own recommendation to Regan: What if they ousted Poindexter before he told Ronnie or George Shultz everything he knew? And what if, once gone, he decided to tell the truth to some investigating committee or, God forbid, a prosecutor?

She took the remote from her husband's hand, loosened his tie, and gave him a peck on the cheek. She flipped past all the channels offering instant analysis of the news conference and then suddenly saw herself looking up at Sarah Vaughan singing "Swanee." The public TV station was at last airing the Gershwin show, nearly a month after the taping.

Ronnie smiled, took a cookie, and sat down to watch; then Nancy tried to relax by watching her husband. The press conference, returning as one or two clips on the morning shows, would look better tomorrow, but only to him.

24

NOVEMBER 23, 1986

Ed Koch, much taller than people usually imagined, stood at the back of Sign of the Dove and welcomed everyone here to New York City, no matter that most of them were lifelong residents. He thanked Happy Rockefeller, Nelson's widow, for bringing people to this Upper East Side restaurant on a Sunday night to celebrate the sixtieth birthday of Jeane Kirkpatrick, who Koch now reminded them "took an institution I used to call a 'cesspool' and *drained* it. When Jeane got through telling the truth at the UN, especially to the enemies of Israel, the place was practically a *garden*. So we're all here to wish her sixty more years of health and chutzpah! I gotta run—being mayor's a big job!—but I had to come and say what I just said. And, by the way, I'm still a Democrat!"

He glad-handed his way out the door, receiving answers to his signature question, "How'm I doin'?" without even asking it. Although the unbidden answer was invariably *You're doin' great!* everyone knew that the buoyancy of Hizzoner's first two terms was rapidly dissipating into the scandals of his third.

"Well, I guess it's just us now!" Richard Nixon told the crowd while the mayor receded, as if Koch's departure would leave behind a uniform coven of Republicans.

"Nixon seems almost charming," Barbara Walters mused to her companions.

"You also once called him *sexy*," Happy Rockefeller reminded the newswoman, while rolling her eyes.

"That was a moment of off-air madness," Walters conceded. "But I still find him weirdly more magnetic than Reagan. Maybe 'magnetic' amounts to the same thing as 'sexy.'"

"Barbara, *for God's sake*," chortled Liz Smith, the gossip columnist.
"*Think* about it," said Walters.

The women debated the question of magnetism for a minute or two, agreeing only that Reagan's *lack* of intensity might be the nature of *his* sexual attractiveness, at least to Nancy: the current president was a sort of nimbus in which she could be safely enveloped. Happy Rockefeller's participation in this discussion—given Nelson's famously reckless, maybe even fatal, philandering—made the conversation more difficult than it might have been.

Anders Little, a late arrival from Washington, was the last person in the restaurant to be backslapped by Koch. The young man made his way to a spot near Nixon and Henry Kissinger, whose just-begun conversation he was permitted to hear but not invited to enter. Anders noticed that no handshake had accompanied the pair's greetings: only a simple nod between "Henry" and "Mr. President."

Nixon acted as if his former advisor had just come down the hall and into his office. "*You* usually get rumors before I do," he said. "Let me ask you about one that's going around." He was interested in a report that Shultz's departure was not only imminent, but that it would also be involuntary.

Kissinger shook his head. "Not as long as Nancy is around."

Nixon indicated agreement, and added, with a tilt of his own head toward the guest of honor, "I don't see her as secretary of state, whatever happens." He meant, Anders knew from his tone and from other conversations, that Mrs. Kirkpatrick was too good for a job whose honorific masked a lack of authority—no matter that Kissinger had once panted after it, insisting it be added to his national security advisor's portfolio while Nixon made him wait and wait.

"I don't see it either," said Kissinger. "When Jeane was at the UN, she wouldn't even clear her speeches with State."

"Hell, Henry, *you* wouldn't do that before you went over there."

"Exactly," said Kissinger. "That is why I needed to have both jobs." The point was made jocularly, but Anders could see there was no real warmth between the two men. Kissinger had survived the wreckage of Watergate to become a lord of the Upper East Side, while Nixon remained a ghostlike curiosity here, revisiting the neighborhood he'd lived in so briefly at the decade's beginning.

"Well," he said, "it's the president who makes the policy."

"Not always," replied Kissinger. "It is unclear to me *who* is making policy in this current administration. It was very different in yours."

Nixon had already made plain to Anders that he did not like Reagan's comparison of the Iran initiative and his own approach to China, but even so, he appeared dissatisfied with Kissinger's answer, which didn't actually concede *who* had made the Nixon administration's foreign policy a decade and a half ago—the president or his NSA. "In our case, Henry, the tapes show who was in charge."

Along with a great deal else, Kissinger seemed to be thinking. He settled for saying, "Yes, of course."

Mike Wallace approached the two of them, but after a quick hello Nixon went off to talk with Happy Rockefeller. Anders knew the back stories here, too. The former president had never been comfortable with Wallace, even if he had once toyed with the idea of making him his press secretary. Nixon and Nelson Rockefeller also had never been pals, but they'd warmed to each other near "the end," those two words that never signified anything but the sudden conclusion of his presidency. Rockefeller's mortal close had arrived several years later, when he died with his pants down, in the arms of his mistress, about ten blocks south of here.

"Where's Nancy?" Wallace asked Kissinger.

"You mean my Nancy. Somewhere in Mexico, taking a vacation from me. And from this kind of thing. Where is *your* Nancy?" Everyone knew of Wallace's old connections to the first lady and her mother.

"She's chewing off the last of her nails, I suspect. She's probably just gotten off the helicopter from Camp David." The CBS reporter, nearing seventy with hair as dark as Reagan's, directed Kissinger's attention to two nearby figures: "Shouldn't the birthday girl be getting advice from *you* instead of *him*?"

Mrs. Kirkpatrick was talking to William F. Buckley, Jr.

"Aware of your love for things French, I've been struggling to rhyme *charmante* with *soixante* for my toast," said the editor of *National Review*, whose long, quick tongue took a sip of martini the way a cat goes to work on a saucer of milk.

Mrs. Kirkpatrick gave his versifying efforts an appreciative smile, before Buckley presented her with a tidbit he'd picked up from his old friend the CIA director: "Bill Casey wants you to replace Shultz. 'It's over,' he told me when we talked yesterday. There was no antecedent to the pronoun, but I have a pretty good idea that 'it' means the whole administration."

Mrs. Kirkpatrick switched the subject by switching scandals. "I now find myself appointed to a panel that's charged with overseeing the *legally* appropriated aid to the Contras." She'd been named to it by Bob Dole, though both she and Buckley knew that Byrd, the incoming majority leader, would probably disband the group in short order. "My fellow panelists," Mrs. Kirkpatrick elaborated, "are a member of Tip O'Neill's staff and a Methodist minister."

Buckley laughed. "I saw your column, by the way."

On the subject of the Iran adventure, she had come out against only its optimism and naïveté, defending it in principle with the argument that governments engage in both arms selling and back-channel initiatives all the time. "If I'd had *that* job—I mean the one so gloriously held by McFarlane and Poindexter—I think I can say with a fair degree of confidence that this would not have happened." But Deaver and Shultz had long ago kept her from getting the national security advisor's post; she'd been too hard-line for the first lady as well.

Borrowing a line from Bill Safire, Buckley told Mrs. Kirkpatrick, "You have the courage of Ronald Reagan's convictions."

Kissinger, whose curiosity had been piqued by Wallace, came over and kissed the evening's honoree. "I saw two people wearing I DREAM OF JEANNIE—IN '88 buttons," he informed Mrs. Kirkpatrick.

"An absurdity," she said, before Buckley's tall, fashionable wife swept her away from the two men.

"You've got to stop *fussing* like that, dear." Pat Buckley swatted Mrs. Kirkpatrick's hands, which were always nervously picking at her collar or earrings. "And I'm going to take that away from you if you keep rummaging inside it." The former ambassador was also forever looking for things in her purse. Unlike Mrs. Thatcher, she rarely seemed able to locate them.

Jeane Kirkpatrick looked hurt. The exotic, boldly made-up Mrs. Buckley, whose black-and-red dress cost more than the contents of her own entire closet, had struck a nerve. She didn't like being excluded from the ranks of femininity any more than she enjoyed being barred, by her politics, from the pantheon of feminism. "Gloria Steinem says I'm a female impersonator."

"Gloria Steinem is a cunt," said Mrs. Buckley, who dragged on her cigarette as calmly as if she'd just made an approving remark upon the weather.

"You might at least have said it in French," replied Mrs. Kirkpatrick.

"Did you hear what Sam Donaldson called Nancy Reagan this morning—on TV? A 'smiling mamba.' A poisonous snake, apparently." Mrs. Buckley gave no indication of whether she found the comparison ungentlemanly or accurate. "I want you to meet Mary McFadden."

Mrs. Kirkpatrick knew, vaguely, that McFadden was a dress designer, but had no idea why she, or many of the other guests, were here. Ron Galella, the photographer, was now passing by and snapping pictures of Mrs. Buckley. When he had secured enough of them, he began looking around, disappointed. "When he came in, he noticed a few liberals," Mrs. Buckley explained to Mrs. Kirkpatrick. "And he got his hopes up for Betty Bacall, maybe even Jackie."

"Pat," said Mrs. Kirkpatrick, who had begun to grasp why she was being pressed to make the acquaintance of Mary McFadden, "no one's going to vote for me because of my clothes. And I already have a date for the prom." She looked toward Evron Kirkpatrick, once her mentor and for thirty years her husband. At the moment she was wishing the two of them were back home in Bethesda, or maybe somewhere on the high seas. Even the caramelized sea bass, which she'd noticed on the little menu cards at each place setting, had her longing for something else—specifically, fried chicken. Most of her new, high-rolling admirers tended to forget that *au fond*, underneath the advanced degrees and Francophilia, she remained the daughter of Fat Jordan, an oil driller from Duncan, Oklahoma.

"All right, Jeane," said Pat Buckley, putting her empty glass on a waiter's tray. "But I'm not giving up." She went over to Liz Smith, leaving Mrs. Kirkpatrick with Anders Little, who had waited for this moment to address her: "Congratulations on being appointed to the Contra panel."

Mrs. Kirkpatrick gave him a hangdog smile. "Thank you, Anders. But I suspect there will soon be some other, more consequential, panels looking into Central America."

"Yes," said Anders, hoping his nervousness didn't show.

"It's hardly the *official* appropriations that Congress wants to keep track of. If I may state the obvious."

"Do you think the Contras' other sources are illegal?" Anders was surprised by his sudden boldness. All these weeks past he hadn't been able to ask Mrs. Kirkpatrick if she knew about Spitz Channell's operation, let alone whether she might be aware of what sources had parked their money with designated intermediaries.

The former ambassador arched an eyebrow and allowed her lower lip to protrude. "The United States has a lot of friends whose primary interests may be elsewhere, but who like to show us their goodwill. The Saudis, for instance." She did sound as if she'd like to oversee not just Congress's grudging appropriations but the more secretive funding as well—if only to satisfy her own curiosity. And she now had Anders considering whether the Saudis might be the ones who'd put money into Peter Cox's and Nick Carrollton's bank accounts. He also began thinking of Nick's tousled curls, a couple of which, in the early-morning hours, tended to dangle onto his forehead like the scimitar-shaped letters of the Arabic alphabet. He suppressed the mental image.

Mrs. Kirkpatrick noted that he appeared to be drinking only Coke. "Good for you," she offered by way of a compliment. "I can't say much for all that running you do, but you're wise to stick with that." Anders knew it wasn't any political consideration, but rather the sorrow she had at home—the severe alcoholism of her son—that would likely keep her from running for anything, in '88 or beyond.

Nixon now approached her and Anders. "Oh, to be sixty again," he told Mrs. Kirkpatrick, with only a nod. Anders had never seen the former president give anyone so much as an air kiss.

Mrs. Kirkpatrick smiled. "We've had this conversation, about being sixty."

She had tried warming up to Nixon for years now but was still, at some deep level, aghast at having had to vote for him in '72. The problem was bigger than him, of course. Despite the almost adolescent ardor she these days received from conservative Republicans, she missed the Democratic Party the way a principled apostate misses the church. But remaining in the fold had been out of the question. She couldn't understand how Koch managed it; she wasn't a politician, no matter how much so many people in this room wished to turn her into one.

"How's your book going?" she asked Nixon, and as soon as she did she felt guilty about the lack of progress with her own. Her next *column*, all of 850 words, was already overdue.

Nixon, whose book was right on schedule, ignored the question. He'd always regarded writing as a relief instead of the agony people made it. "I haven't spoken to you since Reykjavik," he reminded Mrs. Kirkpatrick. "And I haven't seen you approach that subject in print." He smiled, underlining the implication that she was still hoping to go back into the administration.

"I do enjoy seeing some of our more feckless European allies in a snit," replied Mrs. Kirkpatrick. "I don't of course mean Mrs. Thatcher, but my cherished French are another story." She'd given Anders an earful just after the summit, but he knew—as Hitchens had pointed out some nights ago—that among people's preoccupations Iceland was quickly melting into Iran.

He now chimed in: "The attorney general's been told to prepare a chronology of the Iran business and have it to Don Regan by Monday." It wasn't much, but Anders was glad he had at least this in the way of news to offer his two patrons.

"Watch somebody leak it," Nixon prophesied. "It'll become the basis for one of those tick-tock, how-it-happened articles in the *Post*. The truth is, internal investigations aren't worth a goddamn. Sorry," he said to Mrs. Kirkpatrick; he always reserved his Olympian-level profanity for men. "In my time I ordered up a few of those in-house inquiries. Did the Dean Report convince either of you?"

The Podhoretzes, Norman and Midge, eager for a neoconservative word with Mrs. Kirkpatrick, approached. Nixon relinquished her to them and tapped Anders on the arm, suggesting that he do the same. The two men stepped away.

"Isn't that Cox over there?" asked Nixon, pointing toward the back of the restaurant.

Anders saw a man who, with some difficulty, was sitting himself down at an empty table near a cart of hors d'oeuvres. He appeared to be catching his breath.

"Christ, he looks awful," said Nixon. "I ought to go over there and pep him up with the never-say-die talk." But the former president didn't relish the idea of giving it. This party, like the handful of others he chose to attend only after careful consideration, took a particular effort that threatened to exhaust him. He was always the most famous person in the room, the one people were most interested to see, yet he could never be sure that he was fully welcome, that someone whose presence he hadn't figured on wasn't waiting for him with a cutting remark, or even a glass of booze to throw in his face.

"I could go over and say hello to him," Anders volunteered. "I saw his ex-wife recently. I could bring him her greetings."

"Good, good," said Nixon, sending him off, as if he were one of the ex-president's erstwhile young go-getters, the Jeb Magruders who could be counted on for bright ideas that were likely to skirt a couple of laws in the course of being executed.

"Mr. Cox," Anders said, when he reached the distant table. "We met in Washington a month or two back."

Peter looked up with an invalid's face nearly as yellow as his drink. His hair was just a patchy fuzz. "Yes, you're a friend of Wife Number One, I've since learned. Sit down if you like." It seemed clear that he lacked the strength to get back up.

Anders took a chair across from him. Loyalty to Anne made him bristle at the Wife Number One crack, but how could he not indulge the wreck he saw before him?

"You want to know why I'm here," said Peter.

"Well," said Anders. "Same reason we all are, I guess. To celebrate Mrs. Kirk—"

"*They* invited me up," said Peter, pointing to two men Anders didn't recognize. "They're putting together an exploratory committee for her for '88, and I've got plenty of money I can give them, along with a couple of ideas for ways that other people can, let's say, maximize their contributions—despite the ridiculous laws now governing this kind of thing."

Anders said nothing. He was a government official, for God's sake, and he didn't want to be hearing this kind of stuff on top of all the Spitz Channell business.

"Don't you think she'd make a good president?" asked Peter. "Or vice president?"

"Oh, that goes without saying."

"I wouldn't mind still being around to see her sworn in. Not that I have a chance in hell of that."

"How are you doing?" asked Anders. "Anne told me—"

Peter looked as if he didn't especially care to hear this probable fag first-naming the mother of his children, but after a second or two his animosity seemed to collapse into simple gladness that his former wife had found a friend in her new city. As his face brightened, Anders thought he might be getting a glimpse of what Anne had first seen in Peter, forty years before.

"She worries too much about me," said the older man. "Tell her not to."

"All right," Anders responded, imagining this was the last time he'd see this man alive. "Mr. Cox?" he asked, after a pause.

"Peter."

"Could I ask you something? In connection with the group I spoke to back in October?"

"Ask away."

"I know of course that you and others were donating generously to the NEPL."

"That's right."

"But do you know about money from other sources that's being parked, temporarily, with *donors*? For purposes that—"

Peter brightened further. Some of the years and the sickness appeared to fall away, making *him* look like one of Nixon's bright young malefactors. "The purpose of that," he said, leaning confidentially forward, "is—"

But he was interrupted, and then drowned out, by a familiar baritone voice filling the restaurant. "Ladies and gentlemen," said the thirty-seventh president of the United States, who'd seated himself at the piano and beside a microphone. "I hope you'll join me in singing 'Happy Birthday' to Jeane Kirkpatrick. And I hope you'll do me the great favor of singing it in the key of G!"

————

Anders never got to finish the conversation. Once Nixon's serenade was through, he and Peter were separated and sent to their assigned tables; after dinner there was no trace of the older man. It seemed scarcely believable that he'd made it to New York from Dallas in the first place.

Catching the last Sunday-night shuttle from LaGuardia to National, Anders reflected on how it had been an expensive day trip, but with Mrs. Kirkpatrick for a public mentor, and Nixon a semiprivate one, he really couldn't have missed making it. Aside from all else, it had taken his mind off a call he'd had late last night from Neal Grover, who'd told him that all hell was breaking loose in the office—at ten p.m. on a Saturday—but wouldn't say more over the phone. That was alarming enough, given Neal's standard indiscretion; but the call's real ominousness lay in its seeming to be a conspiratorial heads-up, one that Anders was expected to understand despite the absence of detail.

He planned to be at work extra early tomorrow morning, but as he stepped into a taxi outside National's small white terminal, an impulse made him tell the driver to head downtown instead of to his apartment in Arlington. He wouldn't sleep anyway; he might as well see what was on his desk, and who was around.

Lights always burned late in the massive Victorian pile of the EOB, illuminating the offices of those doing genuinely urgent work, and here and there the desks of young men just thrilling themselves with an illusion of their own necessity at the pinpoint center of the world. At eleven p.m. on this Sunday, it seemed to Anders that a good many more lights were on than usual. He speed-walked down the third-floor corridor with no thought of aerobic benefit, just an acute need to see whether Neal's light was one of those on. Tawny/Dawn/Whoever raced past him, without a Walkman or a hello, riffling through a stack of telexes as she went, intent on finding—what? Anders wondered.

He found Neal in room 368, which he entered with a *What gives?* gesture.

"Guys from Justice were here all day yesterday," Grover explained. "Going through documents in North's office. And Ollie was there the whole time. It was all very friendly; you'd have thought they were working side by side."

"The 'chronology,'" said Anders. "I heard about that on Friday."

"Yeah. Well, they can end that chronology with 'Sunday, November twenty-third.' Today. Which is when Ollie got called over to DOJ and shown one of his own memos—a 'problematic' one—that Meese's guys found yesterday."

Reminded of last night's vague phone call, Anders grew impatient. "You know, *I* don't have any Iran problems; I have a Central American one—thanks to you and your pal Channell."

Lowering his voice, Neal said, "I'm afraid it's all *one* problem, Andy."

"How's that?" was Anders's angry response.

"Well, you know the sale of the arms and the spare parts? It seems Ollie made a very good deal with the Iranians—cleared a nice little profit."

"Oh, Christ, now there's personal corruption, too?"

"Our boy Ollie? Don't be ridiculous," said Neal, who gave a campy salute. "Straight in every sense of the term."

"So where did the profits go?"

"*Nic-a-rag-u-a*," said Neal, pronouncing it with the exaggerated Spanish of a politically correct newscaster.

Anders could only stand there. *Let's just say that money from other places has had to be parked with various people.*

"If you hear the *tapokata-pokata* sound of a keyboard tonight," said Neal, "that'll be Ollie typing his letter of resignation. I saw him ten minutes ago."

At last unfrozen, Anders double-timed it down the stairs and out of the building. On Seventeenth Street he jumped into another taxi, but once inside didn't know whether to give the driver Anne's address or Nick's.

25

NOVEMBER 27, 1986—THANKSGIVING DAY

The frozen turkey that had flown west with them on Air Force One was browning in the oven, while Ronnie worked up an appetite outside, clearing brush with Barney. Nancy felt as solitary as it was possible to feel in the adobe house, what with agents by the front door and walking past the windows. For all the radical reduction in size and bustle that this place presented, she had several times today imagined herself to be still upstairs in the White House, looking at the Chinese wallpaper with which Ted Graber had decorated her and Ronnie's bedroom.

She had been staring at its hand-painted Oriental birds on Monday afternoon when Ronnie told her. The calamity that Joan had foreseen was now here for certain, ahead of schedule, and it was too late to run. Or maybe they already *had* run; maybe the ranch was about to become Elba, their presence here lonely and permanent.

"He has little to look forward to. The glittering popularity, the acclaim, will be dissipated in a welter of hearings, snickers, questions, rumors." Mary McGrory was a Boston-Irish witch, a kind of scullery maid for the Kennedys, and she had put it this way in today's *Post*. The worst of it? She was probably right.

It had turned out to be all one scandal. The two separate plotlines, each dark enough, had collided and taken a sudden twist that had the audience jumping out of its seats. North and Poindexter had figured out a way to take more than $10 million from the Iranian arms sales and send it to the Contras. A "diversion," it was being called, the word seeming to stand for both the reallocation and the giddy amusement of a grateful press. The pipe-smoking admiral and the gap-toothed soldier boy had both just been fired, but no one believed they could have cooked this up on their own. Even Kissinger, never more than half on Ronnie's side, was saying that higher-ups had to be involved.

She had nearly canceled Tuesday's trip to Boys Town, but Elaine and everyone else told her she mustn't, that that would only amplify the buzz of panic emanating from the White House. So she had gone to Nebraska, and while there at lunchtime, on a TV in the holding area, had seen Ronnie venture into the press room to introduce Ed Meese, who imparted news of the discovery once his boss ran away. Ed had stood there answering whatever question he could make out from a whole shouted hurricane of them, looking like a flatfoot who'd arrived late to the scene.

Yesterday had been even worse. She'd been at the Century Plaza, watching Ronnie on the suite's TV as he stood in the Rose Garden and pardoned a turkey raised on the same farm as the one now cooking. He'd looked afraid for the bird as the reporters *screamed* their questions. "HOW MUCH TROUBLE ARE YOU IN?" one of them—Andrea? Helen?—had asked, as if aware that he was more bewildered than guilty. Would *that* finally save him? Or would it be what did him in?

She'd gone out to the naval air station at Point Megu to meet *Air Force One*, and when the helicopter lifted off for the ranch, it felt as if she and Ronnie were escaping from that rooftop in Saigon.

No one was using the word "caper" for this, the way they had during the early days of Watergate. Ronnie had already been forced to appoint an investigative board that would be headed by John Tower—that little patent-leather martinet, a drunk, whom none of his former colleagues in the Senate missed any more than Nancy did. A special prosecutor was sure to follow: the *Post* had just run a sidebar listing five different laws that had probably been violated by now—and who knew what sort of cover-up might still be violating others?

Only the smallest rats would be able to swim away from the ship. Larry Speakes had already made it known that he'd be departing in February—for a job at Merrill Lynch! Maybe Don Regan could go back to his old firm with him. The only hopeful development? The press were beginning to blame Don for a lot of it. David Broder, hardly a firebrand, had called him "a manipulator surrounded by midgets." But Nancy knew that Don wouldn't go anytime soon, not without a push, not when it would mean looking incompetent or guilty.

The same logic would make it impossible for Ronnie to go, too. The idea she'd had of his resigning in glory on his seventy-sixth birthday, in advance of Joan's predicted doom? Too late for that now! Ronnie would stay in the presidency until '89 or until the two of them were pried from the White House and set down here in the Santa Ynez Mountains. There had last week been protests about the plans for the library up in Palo Alto—environmental objections, supposedly; but the real fault lines were shifting right here, below their own feet.

When she'd tried, only once, to suggest that he get rid of Regan, Ronnie had actually said, "Don't start," before tacking on an apologetic "please." This morning they hadn't said much at all, and when the chief of staff phoned from his hotel in Santa Barbara, Ronnie had given her a sheepish look before going off to take the call in the bedroom. He came out smiling ten minutes later, but only because Margaret had just called as well, to offer some encouraging words from London.

Now he was back from clearing brush, and the family were starting to arrive: Ron and Doria, Maureen and Dennis. Nancy had gotten over disliking the children's spouses, but they were still strangers to her, and she would never be comfortable with the bad casting. It always seemed to her that Doria, too old for Ron, and Dennis, too young for Maureen, should be married to each other. And when Moon, Ronnie's older brother, showed up with his wife, Bess, things got even worse. Sure enough, Moon—who still knew how to push his kid brother's buttons, who deep down didn't even *like* Ronnie—couldn't resist a few jabs. "It's okay, Dutch. *I* still trust you," he said, with a wink for the whole table, knowing how the plummeting polls on that particular issue hurt Ronnie more than anything else.

"Not funny, sonny," she replied.

Ron could usually lighten her mood for a moment or two; she'd always allowed him a certain irreverence and mischief that she never permitted Patti. But now, while Ronnie had some trouble carving the bird, his son was saying, "Maybe you could *shred* it, Dad." The destruction of documents, by North, was the latest rumor to have made it up the mountain from Santa Barbara.

"Skipper, enough," she reprimanded, as if Ron were six years old and ready to be sent to his room.

"Colonel North says he's going back to the Marines," Maureen pointed out. "I say let him go, and then court-martial him along with Poindexter." She was dead serious.

"Now, Mermie," said her father. "Good intentions count for something. I called North the other night to say how bad I felt about all this. It's a heckuva thing for a young man to get caught up in."

"Caught *up* in?" cried Maureen. "Dad, he *created* this 'heckuva thing'!"

The first lady rose from the table, trying to speed the evening along by taking her coffee to a living room chair.

"I've got a treat for everybody," said the president, once they'd all made the move with her. He handed a VHS cassette to Ron, who put it into the player. It was a tape of the Boys Town ceremony, with Nancy's speech:

When I was young, my mother was an actress, and so she had to travel. I missed her and she missed me. My father left us, so I stayed with my aunt and uncle. They were very good people but they weren't my parents. And what I wished for more than anything else was a normal family. I finally got my wish when my mother married a wonderful man, who became my wonderful father. And at last I knew where I belonged . . .

She couldn't stand listening to herself. It wasn't that her remarks had been dishonest; they were just obsolete. She didn't need family, not anymore; right now she needed friends—Bets or Harriet—who always felt closer at the other end of a phone line than her own flesh and blood did sitting across the room.

The tape neared its end after an interminable few minutes.

"Wasn't she swell?" asked Ronnie. She got up to kiss him. What he'd called a "treat" had been more in the way of a peace offering, a form of currency they almost never had to exchange. She went into the bedroom, and Maureen immediately followed.

"I was going to phone Mike," the first lady explained. Deaver was out of the rehab facility and had been spotted having lunch at the Jockey Club on Monday.

Maureen couldn't hide her disappointment. For twenty years she'd judged Mike Deaver to be a snake. Even worse, he was a crutch, one her stepmother had finally begun to do without last year.

The first lady put down the receiver.

"Dad needs you to go on the warpath," said Maureen. "Back at the White House it's what people actually *want*. Even people who are usually scared of you."

Nancy could tell from the look on her face that Mermie still belonged to that group.

"But what can I do from here?" She felt paralyzed by the remoteness of this sagebrush outpost that had to be supplied from civilization.

"You know why this happened? How it started?" asked Maureen.

"No," said Nancy, eager to hear the name of a mastermind, a person who could be made to pay.

"They showed Dad a videotape, ages ago, of one of the hostages, the one named Buckley. A tape of him being tortured that the CIA got hold of. It was awful, and he watched it, the whole thing, in the office."

Neither said anything. They both knew how this tape would have prompted the president's strangely remote tenderness; he would have been more affected by the video than by seeing the torture in person. His feelings were real, but they were best stimulated by a messenger, not through the nerve endings of direct experience.

"Oh, *Mo*-ther!" Ron playfully called from the next room. "Your favorite costar's on!"

Nancy went to the door, forcing herself to smile as she looked back out toward the family. She wasn't going to let Dennis and Doria, let alone Moon, see how upset she was.

"June Allyson?" she asked, pointing to the TV. "I never—"

"Wait for it," said Ron. "There!" The chubby face of Gary Coleman, starring as a mischievous angel in a holiday movie, appeared onscreen. June, grouchily playing against type, seemed to be his foil.

Nancy gave a comic shudder. They all knew that this kid had given her the creeps when she made a Just Say No cameo on his TV series.

She shut the door and turned back to Maureen. "I'm stuck here until Sunday, and I think I'm going to die of panic. Things are so bad I'm afraid that *Patti* will call. If she does, I'll know it's really the end."

Maureen enveloped her in a hug. "It'll be okay," she said. And then, for the first time in their up-and-down thirty-five-year acquaintance, she added the word "Mom."

———

Pamela Harriman flicked her coral-colored nails against a small card she had several days ago instructed Janet to retrieve from Kelly Proctor's Rolodex. HITCH, it said simply, above a phone number.

This same number could have been recovered from the folder containing the interview arrangements for the unfortunate *Vanity Fair* piece that would reach newsstands next week—Pamela could imagine Paula Hawkins reading it under a hair dryer—but securing the phone number from Miss Proctor's old desk was a foray into enemy territory, a warm-up for the little telephone mission Pamela was readying herself to perform.

She had been here at Willow Oaks since Sunday night. The Vances, Cy and his wife, had arrived the following afternoon and would be around until tomorrow. The big, rather senseless holiday dinner was over and her guests were downstairs watching the hour-long interview Pamela had recorded with C-SPAN last Friday, and which the network—*was* it a network?—had chosen to broadcast this evening. She had pretended to the Vances that self-consciousness wouldn't permit her to view it with them.

Actually, Pamela had already watched the interview, on a videocassette the producers had provided to Janet. Appearing on television was still a fairly new experience, but she'd not done badly. (The interviewer, mercifully, had yet to see the *Vanity Fair* piece.) Anyone watching would find her responses crisp and disciplined; she had stayed out of the Iranian thicket and remembered to credit all the right people for the election results. Still, there was room for improvement, especially when it came to her neck. Dr. Aston's phone number remained in her desk drawer on N Street.

The C-SPAN chap had had her doing lots of reminiscence: what it had been like with Old Winston in the bunker beneath Number 10; with Ave at his old haunts inside the Kremlin. It made for odd Thanksgiving fare, she thought. But this was a holiday she had never really warmed to. Getting into the spirit of it seemed to require a certain treachery. Hadn't the settlers, after all, been thanking God, at least in part, for deliverance from English tyranny?

She looked at the little card with the phone number, and after a moment's wonder as to whether Mr. Hitchens shared her British feelings about Thanksgiving, she took the plunge and rang him.

"I hope I haven't interrupted a family celebration," she said, knowing that her voice would be identification enough.

"I'm with my two-year-old son and some twelve-year-old port. What could be more agreeable?"

"And what is your little boy's name?"

"Alexander. I'm explaining to him the religious neuroses of the pilgrims."

"I see."

"I assume you've managed to see the piece, and that you're not calling to offer thanks for it, despite the day."

"No," said Mrs. Harriman. "The past is past. I'm calling about something else, something I'd *like* you to write. Perhaps the *second* time, not the third, will be the charm."

"Oh, good, I can tell you read it thoroughly."

"Yes, but there's a much different subject that I'd prefer to read you on. A subject you might pursue for one of your less glossy outlets."

"Ah, you're eager to see me banished from Mammon to mendicancy—to send me back from Newhouse to Navasky."

Uncertain of his analogies, Pamela decided she had better come to the point. "Have you heard rumors about some of the Iranian funds going to a cause other than the Contras?"

"One or two whispers," replied Hitchens.

"Have you heard anything about such money having gone into this fall's Republican Senate campaigns?"

"Into the coffers of Mrs. Hawkins?" He wondered if this was going to be Mrs. Harriman's backdoor way of excoriating him for the profile.

"No, not hers, but some others'."

"And the source of this intelligence?" Hitchens asked.

It had been Clark Clifford, but she didn't think it wise to mention that now.

"A *credible* source," she replied. "But the story needs someone fearless, like yourself, to dig in and substantiate it."

"I see your compelling interest in the matter." It appeared that Churchill's daughter–in-law had adopted Stalin's scorched-earth policy: having removed Dole from the majority leader's chair, she was now after Reagan himself, and wasn't going to wait until '88 to be rid of him. "Alas," Hitchens continued, "this tip feels more tantalizing than *propulsive*, shall we say."

"Well, do think about it. And have a happy Thanksgiving."

"And you *have a nice day,*" Hitchens said, with his best American accent.

He had in fact thought about it. Simple logic showed that, once North's cronies were presented with that windfall of rials, ecumenically laundered into shekels and Swiss francs, they must have been beguiled by the possibility of "diverting" them to a whole smorgasbord of fascistic persons and causes, not just the Contras or even this fall's Senate hopefuls. The matter demanded rangy pursuit, not Mrs. Harriman's one-track mind.

He tousled Alexander's hair. The clever boy was pointing to the just re-cradled receiver, as if to ask, who was that?

"Once upon a time," Hitchens began, "there was a lady with too many husbands and much too much money . . ."

DECEMBER 4, 1986

"So, Mr. Little," asked Senator Hollings, "could you tell us what you were asked to speak to these folks about?"

Behind the witness table in the Hart Building, determined not to look nervous, Anders resisted the urge to pour himself a glass of water.

"Senator, I was to brief them on arms-control issues prior to the president's departure for the Reykjavik summit."

Anders had been summoned by the Senate Select Committee on Intelligence two days ago for this inquiry that everyone knew was more or less moot. A Democratic majority—along with the independent counsel, whose appointment the president had now agreed to—would do the real investigating come January, but the electorally chastened Republicans still wanted to appear conscientious by going through the motions. They had gotten Poindexter to come and take the Fifth yesterday, just as Colonel North had taken it on Monday. Now it was time, behind closed doors, for a low-level assortment of NSC personnel to put some facts into the record being created.

"They didn't ask you anythin' about El Salvador or Nicaragua?" Senator Hollings further inquired.

"No, sir, that was outside my area of expertise."

"Would you also say that Mr. Channell's activities were outside the domain of the National Security Council?"

Anders mentally composed his answer before speaking it.

"The NSC has many varied responsibilities, and personnel with a wide range of specialties. I don't think I'm on a level there that qualifies me to answer."

"At this dinner," asked Senator Hollings, "was there any talk of dealings with Iran?" A long-"i" pronunciation of the country's name usually indicated a hard-liner, but Anders had to remind himself that they'd all gone through the looking-glass: Middle East hawks might now pose more of a political threat to the president than Middle East doves.

"No, sir."

Anders hadn't had any idea of the Iran connection until a week ago Sunday night, when Neal Grover dropped that anvil on him. In the event, after bolting from the EOB, he had gone not to Anne's or Nick's but to Spitz Channell's place on Belmont Road, where he woke up the occupant and demanded to know about the "parked" money. "Relax, relax," had been the bleary-eyed response: the sums, by Channell's standard, were so small—no more than fifty thousand dollars with either Peter Cox or Nick Carrollton, he said—that there was little to fear. What's more, the money was in cash. Spitz explained to an almost physically threatening Anders that the money with Peter had been intended for organizing some events that would gin up political enthusiasm for Jeane Kirkpatrick, demonstrations that might persuade the reluctant ex-ambassador to become a candidate in '88. The cash with Nick was ultimately bound for yet another of Channell's advocacy groups, one still being set up, to be called the National Endowment for the Protection of American Values. Its concerns would be domestic rather than foreign.

"Mr. Little . . . ," began Senator Durenberger, evidently still figuring out his question. As the committee's Republican chair, his clout had already waned to something less than what the ranking minority member now possessed. His query turned out to be a softball, pitched with a gentle underhand across the witness table. "Yesterday, in his speech at the American Enterprise Institute, Vice President Bush said that 'mistakes were made' in the initiative now being investigated. Did you, Mr. Little, make a mistake by not asking more questions about the group you were asked to meet with at the Hay-Adams?"

Anders had called Nixon early this morning and been advised by the former president to go before the committee without a lawyer. "You're fine. You're Hugh Sloan," Nixon had assured him, explaining that Sloan had been a minor player, a good guy, enmeshed in the early phases of

Watergate; he'd wound up being praised for his honesty by the Democratic investigators. Anders didn't tell Nixon about his private conversations with Channell, and was hoping the committee wouldn't be aware of them. This wasn't, he knew, much of a legal strategy, and he couldn't allow himself to meditate on the slightly sordid fact that he was now hiding something from *Richard Nixon* as well as the committee.

"Sir," he now replied to Durenberger, "it would probably have been wise for me to ask additional questions."

"Were you compensated for your remarks to that group?" asked Senator Specter. The pointedness of the question—*follow the money*—startled Anders.

"No, sir. Mr. Channell paid for my dinner. And a cocktail," Anders added, a meticulous touch whose application caused in him a swelling of self-disgust. He made no mention of the party afterwards at Channell's apartment, where *he* had been offered, like airline miles, to James Dugan, and where he had himself picked up the little gift bag—however voluntarily presented—that was Nick Carrollton.

"Do you know anyone else who may have been compensated for speaking to Mr. Channell's group?" Specter persisted.

For *speaking* to it? "No, sir."

Anders could no longer resist pouring himself some water from the pitcher, whose chips of ice reminded him of the ground that might now be breaking beneath his feet.

But a moment later Senator Durenberger was thanking him and calling the next witness.

Anders exited the committee room, expecting to see Anne but surprised to find Hitchens beside her on a bench halfway down the corridor. The writer had broken away from the other reporters.

"Any questions from Specter?" Hitchens asked.

Anders felt as if he'd picked up the phone and been pulled into one of Nixon's *in medias res* conversations.

"He asked me about money."

"Ah," said Hitchens, assuming that the senator's question had been more complicated than it was. "It would make sense for the evangelist of the single-bullet theory to follow such a line of inquiry." He referred to Specter's long-ago service as a staff attorney on the Warren Commission. "Money from Iran to Israel to Switzerland to Managua—rather like the shot that managed to travel through Kennedy's throat and then Connally's chest and wrist and thigh."

Anders said nothing.

"I'm trying to cheer you up," explained Hitchens.

"Thanks," Anders replied, without much of a smile. "Will you wait for me here?" he asked Anne. "I need to make a call." He took off for one of the pay phones down the hall.

It would be impersonal and awful to do it this way, but he felt an urgent need to get it over with. He dialed Nick at the RNC and braced himself for the big happy-boy hello that remained as arousing as it was irritating.

"How did it go?" came the exclamatory interrogative.

"All right. Nick, look, I've got to . . . I can't see you anymore. This is all very dangerous. You need to go see Channell one last time and have him get you out of this."

"I want to see *you*, not him!"

And I, thought Anders, want my life back. He wanted to give up his nighttime forays into a more personal freedom that he clearly couldn't handle.

"Grow up and stop being stupid," he told Nick.

"What am I? Ferris-fucking-Bueller?" Nick was crying now. "Are you telling me to lie low? Telling me to call you six months from now?"

"I'm telling you not to call me at all." Anders put the pay phone's receiver down hard; its taut coiled wire flipped into a figure-8 that seemed somehow sarcastic.

Anne and Hitchens had been watching him from a distance.

"I suspect he's talking to his own . . . *diversion*," said Hitchens.

Anne did, too, but loyalty kept her from saying so.

Hitchens pointed back to the committee room. "Has your ex-husband been summoned?"

Anne looked at him in surprise.

He reassured her. "It wasn't Mr. Little who told me of his involvement. Mr. Little is so discreet it's killing him."

"I know that," said Anne. Anders had yet to talk frankly about Nick Carrollton. "But how *do* you know? About Peter."

He had gone to work after Mrs. Harriman's Thanksgiving call, and told Anne about the investigative paths he'd followed: a bit of conversation with Anders about what the committee might ask; then a call to Neal Grover, easily seducible, who produced an unshredded guest list for the Hay-Adams dinner on October 6. PETER COX: he'd recognized the name from his post-Reykjavik phone chat with Anne, as well as the cocktail conversation they'd had at Little's apartment.

"There's something I wish I could tell you," said Anne, thinking of the money that had been parked with Peter.

"Really?" asked Hitchens.

"But I can't." She shook her head, disgusted by her impulse toward frankness.

"I so wish you would. After all, whom would you rather have finding it out first? Me or the FBI?"

Anne, pondering Hitchens's question, looked straight at the writer's blue eyes and decided that somewhere inside him, along with the silver tongue, was a warm flannel lining.

"You," she said.

But Anders was coming back down the corridor.

———

"If you let me," said Ted Graber to Ronald and Nancy Reagan, "I'll show you something that will make you feel a little more at home." Having just dined with the president and his wife, the couple's longtime decorator led them upstairs to the Solarium, which his crew had only this afternoon festooned with red-and-white spray-painted wreaths, all of them fashioned from madrone branches, the kind one saw everywhere at Rancho del Cielo.

"How did you do that?" asked the president, delighted by the intricacy of the example he was fingering.

"There's another bunch I'm doing for the Annenbergs," said Graber. "So you'll be seeing them again at New Year's."

"I'm going to scoot and let Ted reveal his trade secrets to you," said the first lady. She'd be working with Graber tomorrow morning, getting a jump on arrangements for the Nakasone state dinner. It was still months away and required the assumption that things wouldn't collapse entirely between now and then.

At the moment she needed to get to a phone. She gave both men a kiss and headed back to the second floor, where she sat down in her bedroom, facing the Chinese wallpaper.

Had Ted sensed tension between herself and Ronnie in the dining room? She knew, of course, that he didn't gossip: he'd never have lasted as long as he had with Bets and the rest of their crowd if he did. But things *had* been a little off between the Reagans because of a move she'd made this afternoon, a bold one whose usefulness remained uncertain.

"Would you get me Mr. Strauss, please?" the first lady asked one of the White House operators.

"With pleasure," said the girl, giggling. "He sent us all some Christmas candy the other day."

Nancy laughed, pleased with this additional evidence of how Bob, the city's best fixer, thought of everything.

Although she'd pretended it was Mike's idea, the meeting between Strauss and Ronnie, just before dinner, had been hers. She'd cultivated Bob the way she had Kay Graham, from the moment they got here. A couple of days ago she'd appealed to his vanity, said she knew she could count on him to put patriotism above party and help save a presidency in terrible trouble. Lest it appear that she was consorting with only the enemy, she'd added Bill Rogers, a tired old Nixon stalwart, to the meeting, like some throw pillow Ted had decided couldn't do any harm. And so, just a couple of hours ago—while the chief of staff attended Poindexter's farewell party in the Indian Treaty Room—she and Rogers had mostly sat silent while Bob talked to Ronnie like a Dutch uncle and made the case that Don Regan had to go.

Now she was back on the phone with him.

"That was quite the military-style operation!" Strauss joked.

Nancy took her eyes off the Chinese birds and laughed. She had arranged for Strauss and Rogers and Mike to gather at Jim Baker's offices inside the Treasury Building next door and to come over to the East Wing through a tunnel.

"Must be the first time anybody didn't *want* to be photographed comin' into the White House!" the lifelong Democrat added.

Nancy hoped the secret would hold for at least a while. "Bob, I just wanted to call and thank you." She paused. "But I'm not sure he's listening."

"Give it a little time," said Strauss, reassuringly. "And let me know if there's anything else I can do."

"I don't suppose you could actually join us? When it gets done? If it *does* get done?" Was it too preposterous to think that Strauss himself might be persuaded to take the chief of staff's job, like the deputy prime minister in a coalition government, once they were rid of Regan? Hadn't John Connally, one of Bob's closest old associates, gone so far as to switch parties?

"Well, darlin', we don't want to get ahead of ourselves. But when the first deed's done, we'll celebrate."

Nancy looked back at the Chinese birds and wondered if it would all prove too little too late.

———

Rogers didn't often call the former president. He checked in every six months or so, and the conversation was usually stiff. But Nixon had an idea about how the mind of his first secretary of state had worked tonight: *get the Christmas call over with early in the season; take advantage of having something interesting to report*—this thing with Strauss.

And interesting it was, thought Nixon. Bringing Strauss around might prove a hell of a lot more useful than clinging to Rabbi Korff had been in '74! And if Rogers wanted to believe that Strauss was Deaver's idea, fine; but this had Nancy written all over it.

Pat was downstairs with one of the grandchildren, while Nixon remained upstairs in his study, turning a giant Rolodex that his latest secretary tried to sustain as an up-to-date replica of the one in the New York office. Christ, sitting behind this thing, he must look like Gandhi at his spinning wheel.

He found what seemed to be a home telephone number with a 202 area code.

"President Strauss?" he said into an answering machine, which cut off after its startled owner raced to pick up. The Washington lawyer said hello to Nixon with the boardroom version of a good ol' boy's chortle. "President Strauss" had been a joke between them for the past couple of years, ever since Nixon had given a speech to the Economic Club of New York and told everyone that Bob Strauss, whom he knew to be in the audience, would make a better presidential candidate than Mondale.

"I hear you've been busy," said Nixon.

Strauss chuckled—"Word travels fast!"—and figured that Rogers had been the one to call the former president; but he couldn't quite rule out Deaver, who was these days so desperate for friends that he might be looking for them in peculiar places. "Mr. President," said Strauss, "I'm going to put you on speakerphone. It always gives me the pleasant illusion that I'm having an actual visit with someone here in my study."

"Be my guest," said Nixon, who began hearing his own amplified voice. "I've talked to Reagan a couple of times myself since this situation broke." He waited before saying anything else, hoping the silence would prompt Strauss toward a more revealing account of this afternoon's meeting than Rogers had given.

"I'm sure you gave him some wise counsel, too. Have you talked to *Re*-gan as well?"

"Not since the midterms."

"That poor fella," said Strauss. "Come January he'll have even fewer friends on the Hill than he does now. He doesn't know how to *make* 'em! Never goes out, for one thing."

Nixon inwardly disputed the analysis. As if things would have turned out differently a dozen years ago had Haldeman gotten sozzled at the Sans Souci every day instead of eating a tuna sandwich at his desk. But he could glean from Strauss what he hadn't from Rogers: Don Regan had been the focus of the meeting, with Nancy and Strauss pushing to get rid of him—and with Reagan foolishly resisting.

"A new broom wouldn't hurt," Nixon said, as blandly as he could.

"No, it wouldn't," replied Strauss. "The president also shouldn't be puttin' Meese out in front of the cameras anymore."

"I agree," said Nixon. "I hope you also told the president to lay off the press conferences. He's no damned good at them." *He* hadn't been, either, but only because he came across as contemptuous, not unprepared.

"I did tell him," said Strauss, who'd noticed this afternoon how that was the only part of his advice Reagan had liked, as if an exam were being canceled. Otherwise the president had kept saying that he wouldn't throw Don Regan to the wolves. Strauss now in fact wondered if the meeting hadn't *allayed* the president's fears: If a big Democrat wants to help me, he may have thought, how bad can things be?

"How far up do you think this thing goes?" Strauss now asked Nixon, the subtext being *You're the expert, after all.* "Henry says it can't be just North and Poindexter."

Nixon paused before going out on a bit of a limb. "You can be certain Casey knew—if not at the beginning, then at some point. You can be certain Shultz did not. And I hope to hell that Weinberger, the best man of the three, didn't either."

"How about the Big Enchilada?"

"That was Mitchell," answered Nixon, with a trace of exasperation. Strauss needed to brush up on his Watergate. "That was never a nickname for the president." He felt a smidgen of shame as soon as he heard his own pedantry.

"I forgot," said Strauss. "Any thoughts on involvement by the current incumbent?"

"I'll let the *Post* figure that out."

Nixon's own guess was no, that Reagan had not taken part in the hatching of the scheme or any cover-up. And if the former president were to tell the truth—which he did, to himself, with greater frequency than many people did—he would have to admit that he thought the less of

Reagan for it. He himself had not known in advance about the burglary, but once he'd gotten involved in the cover-up, his actions had seemed to him as much a matter of honor (albeit among thieves) as of survival. "Speaking of the *Post*," he now added, "how long will it be before you leak this afternoon's meeting to them?"

Strauss gave him a big laugh. "Oh, I'll wait a decent interval."

Nixon laughed, too, but his heart had gone out of the conversation. His Watergate reflections of a moment ago had depressed him, and at bottom he still couldn't stomach leakers. "Well, Bob," he said, searching for the name of Strauss's wife on the Rolodex card, "I wish you and Helen very happy holidays."

Strauss looked at the 1,200 Christmas cards ready to go out from his study and thought of the other 2,800 being prepared in the offices of Akin Gump downtown. "Same to you, Mr. President. And to Mrs. Nixon. I've enjoyed our chat—felt like I had you right here with me. Sorry my apartment has to be in the Watergate."

Nixon, surprised, paused for only a second. "Never been there." It was the truth—not even when Rose Woods had lived at one end of it and John Mitchell at the other. Only the sound of Nixon's voice had ever penetrated the circular buildings of the complex, pieces in a shell game that he'd foolishly played and long ago lost.

27

DECEMBER 7, 1986

"*Oooh*, great *medal*," said Merv to Yehudi Menuhin, one of the six honorees who were dining with a thousand other people, prior to the evening's gala entertainment, in the Kennedy Center's Grand Foyer. The artists already had been fêted during an afternoon reception at the White House and they now awaited the arrival of the president and Mrs. Reagan, who would lead them up the staircase, in full view of the diners, to the presidential box.

A slow-moving wave of applause indicated gradual notice of the first couple. Ray Charles's assistant explained to the singer what was happening and turned him to face the approaching Reagans. Antony Tudor, another of the honorees, looked displeased, as if all this could have been better choreographed.

Nancy smiled and nodded and left the waving to her husband. Her attention was seized for a moment by the enormous bust of John F. Kennedy, which appeared to be made of still-moist clay that awaited smoothing by its sculptor. The bust's feeling of incompletion gave her a sense that even Kennedy's place in history—let alone Ronnie's—remained precarious, an unsettled fact, no matter that his name was on this building and his widow's was carved into one of the interior walls.

The first lady's shiny gold gown brushed against a table near the foot of the stairs. She leaned over and gave Merv a quick peck on the cheek, then blew a kiss to Jerry Zipkin, a bit further away, so that her best pal and walker in New York wouldn't be jealous, though Jerry being Jerry, he'd soon find something else to get annoyed and a little ugly about.

"Kitty's here," said Merv, pointing to a nearby table. Mrs. Hart waved to the first lady and caused Nancy to wonder who the square-jawed blonde next to her might be. Realizing it was Pamela Harriman, Nancy guessed that there was some show-business connection to one or two of the nominees—maybe the Cronyns—through her marriage to Leland Hayward. She smiled, sort of, in Mrs. Harriman's direction.

"Shall we?" said the president, offering his arm not to his wife but to the evening's unquestioned center of attention, Bette Davis. The first lady climbed the stairs behind them, between Tudor and his boyfriend; Hume Cronyn and Jessica Tandy followed. The applause swelled and finally thundered.

"I feel that I should be hearing Max Steiner's *music*!" Miss Davis cried into Reagan's good ear. She referred to the theme that had played when she mounted the stairs in the last scene of *Dark Victory*.

"Oh, that would be wonderful," said Reagan.

Miss Davis looked put out that no one had thought of it. But she courteously changed the subject. "To think that you *both* could have been in *Eve* with me!" she exclaimed to the president and his wife as they reached the carpeted area outside the box.

Nancy cheerfully groaned, recalling the bitterness of her disappointment in losing out to Celeste Holm.

"Maybe it's not too late for us all to get cast in the same picture," the president replied. "Lew Wasserman's down there somewhere!"

Miss Davis thought to herself that Wasserman had never done all that well pushing Reagan's career. "Well, you can't get *anywhere* without a good script," she said, hoping it sounded vaguely polite.

Nancy agreed, silently wishing there was still some scenario being developed in Rewrite that would save the political day.

"Well," said Miss Davis to the president, as if they were in the Warners cafeteria instead of above a thousand applauding guests, "*I* wanted the part in your *Kings Row* that went to Betty Field. I would have been *great* as Claude Rains's crazy daughter!"

"You know, my mother was an actress," the first lady informed her.

"I'd rather *be* a daughter than *have* one!" Miss Davis replied. "Daughters don't *need* a serpent's tooth. They just need to get a book contract!"

Nancy smiled, pretending not to have this sort of betrayal in common with the star. The only silver lining in the current, engulfing disaster? Her estrangement from Patti meant less than ever to her.

The honorees did some last waving to the crowd below, as if to say: See you in a few minutes. Nancy could spot Glenn Close, Baryshnikov, Lena Horne. And there was Kitty, fluttering her arm with genuine *isn't-this-wonderful* enthusiasm. Next to her, Mrs. Harriman expended only a polite smile that said, *No, not really.*

Turning around, Nancy touched her press secretary's assistant on the arm. The girl leaned in to hear whatever order was coming, and the first lady delivered it before she could second-guess the wisdom of the small inspiration she'd just had. "Have someone bring Mrs. Hart and Mrs. Harriman up here at intermission. Just the two of them."

The lounge that led into the box wasn't much bigger than a college dorm room. It had just space enough for everyone to stand and chatter for a couple of minutes before going out to take their seats. The president went over to a little locked refrigerator that held champagne splits and said, "I'll let you in on the combination so that you'll remember it when we come back here. It's three-four-five-two—the date of our anniversary."

"How sweet," said Bette Davis.

As the house lights went down, with everyone seated at the rim of the balcony, Nancy delved into her worries. The dark would conceal her cogitation, and when the lights in the opera house came back up she would remember no more of what she'd been watching than if it had been a movie at Camp David.

They had still been up there this morning when, in a moment of weakness, ten minutes before boarding the helicopter, she had called Joan Quigley, who'd warned her that Uranus, the planet that had caused Watergate (she'd never mentioned that before!) was now fully in league with Saturn in its operations against Ronnie. Uranus was "a throne-toppler," said Joan, using this term for the first time, while warning that there wasn't just impeachment to worry about but new threats to Ronnie's safety as well. The conversation was so dire and painful that Nancy had wondered whether Joan wasn't deliberately trying to hurt her, trying to darken an already black picture for an ungrateful client who had lately been neglecting her. It was all so different from the halcyon days of '84, when Joan would point out inspiring facts like how Lincoln and FDR were Ronnie's fellow Aquarians. All she could offer today was a slew of dates in January and February on which Ronnie should not just avoid the press but take care not to step out of the White House. Nancy had written them down before imagining what it would be like to approach her dream chief of staff, Bob Strauss, with them. Then she'd thrown them all away.

A few chairs away, her hand clutching the balcony's red-velvet rim, Bette Davis watched some dancers perform a Tudor ballet. She paid the proceedings even less attention than the first lady was giving them. The script for this entire event was absurd! After each of the six artists received homage from below, they were all just supposed to stand up here in the box like cuckoos in a clock. It didn't matter that they'd saved her segment for next to closing; she wanted to be onstage *saying* something, not remaining here mute with Little Ronnie's rainbow ribbon around her neck.

She thought about the president's toasts at this afternoon's reception. Had Tandy really been *heart-stopping*, as he'd claimed, playing Blanche DuBois? Her own Southern accent in *Jezebel* had been more authentic, she was sure; more pleasing to the ear. Right now her own ears were scarcely being penetrated by the onstage rendition of "Georgia on My Mind." She was again hearing Steiner's music, once more ascending the staircase in *Dark Victory*. How she'd had to *fight*, and then fight some more, to keep them from softening the ending—from putting in a last scene in which dead Judith's horse manages to win the big race! The debate over that had gone on for days, with everyone on set—George Brent, Goulding, Geraldine—getting into the act. She now remembered asking Little Ronnie Reagan what *he* thought. Well, forget just having the horse win; Ronnie wanted Judith to recover and live!

He was, she realized, curiously like the Hollywood Communists he would spend so many years fighting: he believed that pictures should give the audience not what they wanted—that was the studio-executive view—but what they *needed*, some idealized view of a world toward which they should work and aspire. For the film-business reds, who'd always bored her, that was a workers' paradise; for Ronnie it was a nice small town with some straight-up white steeples. But it amounted to the same thing: both he and the Communists thought that films existed for the people who went to see them. This moderately intelligent boy had wanted to lose himself in something bigger, some higher purpose, whereas she knew the screen had been created simply as something for her to crash through; it was the ring of fire through which the circus lion leapt to fulfill *itself*, no one else.

———

Pamela Harriman felt bloody well annoyed as the elevator carrying her and Kitty and one of Nancy Reagan's flunkies rose to the tier of boxes. To be *sent for* by this woman, when she hadn't even been on the guest list for this afternoon's reception! It only worsened the unpleasant feeling she'd had about attending tonight's event with Kitty. Carter Brown might be able to escort her—a major potential donor—to museum events, or be at her side touting the city's virtues to the DNC; but his being here tonight would have looked a bit personal and premature. And while she was happy to have Kitty as her guest on N Street, showing up with her as a dinner companion felt a trifle Sapphic.

There was nothing at all grand, Pamela thought, about the box's anteroom, where the tightly packed honorees now stood drinking more water than champagne, as if keeping themselves fit for additional display. During her years with Leland, Pamela had always hated the sweaty calisthenics of "backstage," and at this moment her feelings toward the presidential box were scarcely less hostile than the ones John Wilkes Booth must have brought to Ford's Theatre.

Tudor seemed to find her vaguely familiar; he nodded from a few feet away. Had they met, Pamela wondered, at some long-ago benefit, perhaps in the baleful company of Princess Margaret?

Kitty was kissing Jessica Tandy—"I'm so thrilled for you!"—and earning for her trouble a scornful look from Bette Davis.

"Hello, Miss Davis, I'm Kitty Carlisle."

"Of course you are," said the actress, who turned her attention to Ray Charles, shouting, "How are you finding all of this?" apparently convinced that he was deaf as well as blind.

The first lady caught sight of Mrs. Hart and came right over. "I couldn't stand the thought of not getting to say hello once I saw you down there."

Even Kitty guessed that the real purpose of this summons involved only Pamela, and she quickly presented Mrs. Harriman to Mrs. Reagan.

"Hello," said Nancy, extending a hand less bejeweled than Pamela's own.

"A pleasure," said Mrs. Harriman.

Nancy glanced over at Ronnie, a few inaccessible feet away, talking to Yehudi Menuhin about all the violinist's concerts for troops during the war.

"I'm sorry about this chaos!" said the first lady, who added, with a sheepish look, "I suppose I should say congratulations."

Pamela flinched, imagining this to be in reference to the *Vanity Fair* piece, which would have arrived last week on all the glass coffee tables of Nancy's vulgar friends.

"He put up a hard fight," said the first lady, pointing to her husband, "but in the end a lot of our candidates were no match for you."

Realizing what Mrs. Reagan was actually talking about, Pamela felt, for a moment, flattered. But she quickly put herself back on the defensive: the first lady was only attempting the same strategy of appeasement that she herself had begun employing with Hitchens.

"Well, thank you," she finally replied. "We all want the same thing ultimately—a better America."

"Oh, absolutely," said Kitty, who looked as pleased as Vigdís Finnbogadóttir would have, had Reagan and Gorbachev reached an agreement in Reykjavik.

"You know," said Nancy, "Bob Strauss is a good friend, and I've been really grateful for his advice about how to deal with the present . . . commotion."

It was the mildest word she could come up with. She gave her fragile laugh, and the fragility only excited Mrs. Harriman's aggression, her innate need to vanquish any female within the same perimeter. Even so, Pamela was feeling envy, too: for all the fakery in Mrs. Reagan's saying that her husband was too occupied to join them, there had been love and mother-henning in the look she'd shot his way. It had made Pamela recall her own pampering of Ave, made her realize that, however much she might be enjoying her new svelte and spotlit independence, she rather missed him.

"What was Bob's advice?" she asked Mrs. Reagan, with a hard look. "Was it sound?"

"It was," said Nancy, answering the second question and ignoring the first. "I'd love to have it on a regular basis! In fact, I'd love being able to persuade him to join the administration with all his wonderful talents. There are precedents, of course, for that kind of bipartisanship."

"Oh, yes," said Mrs. Hart. "Remember how Doug Dillon went into Jack Kennedy's cabinet?"

Pamela met the first lady's revelation with a stare. What position, exactly, was she talking about for Bob? Chief of staff, as likely as not, since it was Don Regan's head everyone was after. If this awful woman could make that happen, Bob would be running Reagan's every moment. People would be so taken by the novelty of it that interest in the Iran scandal would be cut by half!

"And how did Bob respond to that suggestion?" Mrs. Harriman asked.

"He didn't really say yes or no, but I was grateful for his obvious feeling that whatever differences we have should be settled without bringing down the whole presidency."

Kitty could feel a terrible tension between the two women; she suddenly thought of the opera-house chandelier that fell and crashed in the old Lon Chaney film.

When Mrs. Harriman didn't respond, the first lady continued: "What I really hope is that we can all go on talking frankly but civilly, as friends who want to keep the country strong and united." She realized that she was rambling, something she never let herself do, and she ordered herself to reel the chatter back in, to try instead for some small, realistic gain. "I'm wondering if you'd consider joining me and Kay for one of our 'ladies' lunches' sometime soon." She pronounced the phrase self-mockingly, to show that even she had acquired a pinch of the era's obligatory feminism.

"Oh, that sounds marvelous," said Mrs. Hart.

"We usually go to Le Pavillon," Nancy added.

"Well," said Mrs. Harriman, "we should be getting back to our seats. I wouldn't want to be late for the tribute to Bette Davis."

Nancy's eyes widened, as if trying to measure the extent of the rebuff. Her face reddened the way it had that afternoon a year or so ago when a college boy deliberately went off-script at a Just Say No event and told her, in front of two hundred others, that he enjoyed snorting cocaine and saw no reason to quit doing it.

"Thanks for coming up," she finally replied to Mrs. Harriman. "This was a treat."

"The same for me," said Pamela, who offered another handshake instead of a kiss. Nancy turned to greet the Cronyns as Mrs. Harriman went out the door ahead of Kitty, who tried to pretend that things had gone well. "You're right," she said, "we'd better take our places. If there was one thing Moss hated—and I'm sure Leland was the same—it was people who came back late from intermi—"

"We're not going back into the theater, Kitty. We're going next door. Come with me."

Next door, it turned out, meant the Watergate East, where Pamela could expect to find Bob Strauss if he wasn't himself in the vast audience.

Kitty was nonplussed. But what could she do? She was Pamela's house-guest, after all, and their driver would still be waiting for them an hour from now. It took the women just two minutes to cross F Street and arrive at the Watergate lobby in their evening gowns. Kitty was for a moment reminded of how she used to appear before *To Tell the Truth*'s studio audience in a fur stole and long white gloves.

Strauss let them up the moment he heard Pamela's distinctive voice through the doorman's phone. His wife was, in fact, at the gala next door, but he had had enough showbiz for a while, having thrown a luncheon for Lew Wasserman yesterday at the F Street Club. Pamela herself had put in a momentary appearance, but only to check on one of her senators-elect. Her absorption by politics exceeded any she'd experienced from the entertainment industry during her time with Leland, and she was baffled by the degree to which candidates and office-holders always seemed star-struck when meeting the most ordinary television "personality."

Strauss, in his courtly fashion, settled the two women on a couch in the study from which all his Christmas cards had finally gone out. He handed Mrs. Harriman her drink. "So, Pammy, what's got your knickers in a twist?" Urgency and annoyance were all over her face, but he laughed at having managed to fetch up the right Britishism.

"I want to know if you're planning to take Donald Regan's job."

Strauss laughed again. He hadn't even leaked the Thursday meeting yet. "Who's been tellin' you that?"

"Nancy Reagan. Not quite telling, but broadly suggesting."

"She's a feistier broad than I thought!"

"You can *not* entertain such an idea. We have the blade in; it's time to turn it."

Mrs. Hart winced. Strauss ignored her and looked, evenly, at Mrs. Harriman. "Darlin', that's not the way we do things."

"Maybe that's why we've lost the White House four times out of the last five."

"And we'll lose it again if we overplay our hand. You need to relax a bit. If there's more to this Nicaragua-and-Iran thing, the drip-drip-drip will wash the Republicans away."

No one knew what to call it. As soon as the papers tried one coinage—Iranscam, Iranagua—they dropped it for another that didn't sound quite right either.

"More *to* this?" cried Pamela. "You don't think there's enough *already*?"

Strauss tried to soothe her. "Give stuff a chance to come out. You know, I talked to my old pal John Connally this afternoon."

Connally, Pamela knew, was more than an old pal. He and Strauss went all the way back to law school, and Bob had been rewarded with a seat on the Texas Banking Commission after helping to elect Connally governor.

Pamela groaned. "Was he giving you advice on how to change from Democrat to Republican?" She wondered if, stopping short of Connally's full conversion, Strauss had concluded that the best chance of attaining his heart's desire—a big ambassadorship, the same as she longed for—lay with a grateful Republican president rather than one who might still come from the Democratic Party he'd once chaired.

Strauss ignored her provocation. "Connally was telling me he went to say goodbye to an old friend today—a deathbed visit, really. A fella named Katz, or Cox; I can't remember. But this fella, who used to do work for John, got to talkin', and John says you would've thought he was taking truth serum with the rest of his medications. It seems the same guys raising money and running weapons to Nicaragua have also been *hiding* money with this fella—who talked to Connally like he was proud of it. Makes you wonder exactly where that money comes from and where it's going, doesn't it? John sure wonders."

He didn't have to say that Connally was enough acquainted with illegal fund-raising to have once handled some campaign cash with rubber gloves.

Pamela, interested but not mollified, made a jotting inside the little notebook she took from her purse.

"Let that kind of stuff come out," Strauss again advised her. "If you go after Reagan too hard, on your own, they'll come after *you*. They'll start wonderin', on the Sunday shows and in Meese's office, if you maybe violated PAC rules by talking certain *strategic* details with some of the fellas you funded, whether it was Cranston or Bob Graham. Now, *I* know you wouldn't do such a thing, but that won't stop them from *suggestin'* it. Like I say, don't overplay your hand."

Pamela watched him rest his drink on an end table that was less convenient for the purpose than the coffee table right in front of him. He had set down the glass, she noticed, on the latest issue of *Vanity Fair*. And only when he saw that she'd taken this in, did Strauss turn his attention to Mrs. Hart. "It's just ages since I've seen you, Miss Kitty-Kat."

28

DECEMBER 18, 1986

PROFLIGATE, Hitchens wrote on a napkin. Perhaps *that* was the right name for the interlocking scandals. He took out his notebook to work up a definition for this coinage that he might put into his next piece: *After boring us for years about "big government" and the need for "less government," they have landed us with a big-spending invisible government.*

Patsy Cline, brought back from the musical dead by a recent movie, sang "Crazy" through the speakers here at Afterwords, the Kramerbooks café. Hitchens looked toward the magazine section near the register to see a stack of the latest *Vanity Fair* that purchasers had satisfyingly diminished by half. He had spent the morning trying to get an apparatchik at the Soviet embassy's nearby chancellery to give him a mockable quote about the workings of party justice now that Sakharov's release from "internal exile" in Gorky was believed to be imminent.

The café's TV was showing an instance of liberation already accomplished. Irina Ratushinskaya, two months out of prison, had arrived at Heathrow—for medical treatment in England, her husband explained. Her heart had been damaged by her stay in the gulag. Nonetheless, she was retaining her Soviet citizenship, intent on returning someday to a democratized Russia whose birth pangs Mr. Gorbachev still couldn't decide whether to induce or stop. CNN split the screen to show another airport arrival, this one in Wisconsin, where Eugene Hasenfus, the captured supply kicker, had just returned home, courtesy of Daniel Ortega.

Why, Hitchens wondered with a trace of irritation, was this filthily corrupt administration receiving such Christmas presents from the worldwide Communist conspiracy rather than another lump of coal to swell its stocking? Why, at least at moments, did it seem to have its foreign enemies nervous, when domestically the regime appeared to be on the run? He wondered if all the effort that Reagan's nasty lieutenants put into figuring out his nullity—and perhaps projecting something *onto* it—didn't give his government a peculiar centripetal energy. Did this grinning, infirm film star, himself so entropic and gaseous, actually keep accruing might and gravity, a sort of unconscious creativity, from all the cogitation by the courtiers in his orbit? Did their various hypotheses about the president's nature somehow supply him with consequentiality, a kind of superreality—whereas by himself he lacked any reality at all?

These large thoughts gave way to personal concerns when, as arranged, Kelly Proctor, on her lunch break from Hill & Knowlton, brightly entered the bookstore café.

"Hey, you," she said, kissing Hitchens's cheek and sitting down.

For a moment it seemed a shame that his goal for this luncheon was valedictory.

"So," he said, taking note of her expression, "I take it the bloom has not gone off the rose? 'Job-wise,' that is?" he added in flat-voweled Americanese.

"Loving it!" Kelly proclaimed. "But I'm starved. What's the drill here? Does somebody come by, or do you go to the counter?"

Hitchens pointed out a waiter, and while Kelly flagged him down he reached into his pocket for his key to her place—which she had given him with such premature exuberance. She frowned, slightly, when it appeared on the table.

"I know this must be a disappointment," said Hitchens.

"Huh?" she asked, with an absence of surprise. "It's a *little* bit of a disappointment, 'cause so long as you had it I didn't have to think about giving it to this guy I'm working with and sort of seeing. He's adorable, but a little *too* temporary for a key, I think."

"I see," said Hitchens. "I'm sorry I proved so temporary myself, but I do believe—"

"*Ça ne fait rien,*" said Kelly, smiling. "See? You're not the only one with these foreign phrases. Listen, I think we had a *great* time. And did you see how many magazines we sold?"

"How charming that you've given yourself half the byline," said Hitchens, who felt such relief at not having to endure a scene from her—there were enough of those at home these days—that he almost succumbed to the temptation to make a bit of a scene himself, to stage a little quarrel between his id and superego about the wisdom of so easily giving up this big blond available American girl.

"So you'll never guess who I heard from," said Kelly.

"Who would that be?"

"Not 'whom'?" asked Kelly, her face momentarily clouded by doubt.

"No, my dear. It's a subject, not an object. At least in my question."

"Okay, whichever; I'll never get that straight," she said, stopping to order her chicken salad before continuing. "You know, better grammar was the one permanent thing I was hoping to get out of this relationship. But anyway, I heard from Pammy herself."

"Is she threatening you?"

"She was nice as pie! Called me last week at my desk. Asked me how I was 'getting on.' Then started talking about *you*."

"Indeed," said Hitchens, curious whether Mrs. Harriman had already abandoned her strategy of rapprochement for something more complicated, now that he'd shown himself less than eager to explore that tributary of the Iran scandal she'd mentioned. *Iranaground?* he wondered for a moment. No, that wouldn't stick either.

Kelly corrected herself: "She didn't really *talk* about you. Just sort of left a message for you—and made sure I got it right. She says you should find a man named Katz or Cox who once worked for John Connally 'in connection with what we recently discussed in a friendly fashion.' That's the phrase I wrote down, since it was so fucking la-di-da."

Hitchens inked Katz and Cox into his notebook and underlined the second name, twice.

"You don't look pleased *or* pissed," Kelly observed, as she picked up the key from the table and put it into her purse.

Hitchens did feel more interest in this tip than he had in the less specific one Mrs. Harriman provided on Thanksgiving. He also felt a degree of annoyance that she seemed to be getting ahead of him on a story he ought to be making his own. He nodded thanks to Kelly while he put away his notebook and purred with a kind of for-old-times'-sake seductiveness: "How could she ever have let you go?"

"I let *myself* go, remember?"

While Kelly began munching the overly tricked-out fowl plunked down by the waiter, Hitchens watched someone buy yet another copy of *Vanity Fair*. The check from Tina Brown, his largest ever, had arrived yesterday, and with that as a cushion he knew he could now, if he wanted, afford to go after this Iran story (*Contra-Mullah?*) for mere *Nation* money. A pattern for his life, the modus vivendi he'd envisioned, seemed to be emerging in fact. Outside, the sun blazed down upon Dupont Circle. Here it was December, and one scarcely needed a coat, whereas back in England, Ms. Ratushinskaya would be getting her first kiss of freedom from the misty muck of skies gone dark by 3:45 p.m.

No, he thought, pulling the bill to his side of the table. Home was no longer over there; it was here, in the Moronic Inferno, as Martin liked to call it via Bellow and Wyndham—or was it Sinclair—Lewis? A minute later, out on the sidewalk and into the sunlight, flooded with relief over having finally *decided*, he turned with protective nostalgia toward Ms. Proctor, his shiny escort into the Magic Kingdom. "Don't be too free with that key, darling."

Kelly gave him a big smile and bigger kiss. "Oh, *please!*" She was off to catch the Metro to Hill & Knowlton, where she'd no doubt be representing characters even worse than Spitz Channell and John Connally. Hitchens waved, and went back inside to the take-out portion of the café. He looked at the pastries, thinking of his next errand.

"What do you recommend for a dying man?" he asked the boy behind the counter.

———

"This is *so* 1984," said Neal Grover, discarding a surgical mask and latex gloves after completing his patient visit inside the AIDS ward of Georgetown University Hospital.

Hitchens, who had just arrived, was perplexed by the Orwell reference; he couldn't recall such medical items being in the novel.

"Not the book," said Grover, detecting his puzzlement. "The actual *year*. Two years ago."

"Ah, yes," said Hitchens, recalling the time of Ron's landslide, before anyone was fully sure the AIDS virus didn't travel by air or casual touch. Despite epidemiological advance, the nurse now handed him a pair of gloves and a mask. "These are for Mr. Dolan's protection," she explained. "Against *us*. He's battling enough problems already."

Hitchens took note of various warnings posted on the walls. Nothing so festive as *on me, not in me*. But he hesitated to don the mask; he still wanted to speak to Grover, who hadn't finished gathering his things. "Talked to the Durenberger committee?" he asked.

"No. Should I be insulted? All they seemed to want from me were any documents that Ollie or Spitz might have generated or seen."

"Perhaps they're saving you for the new Congress," Hitchens replied, as if bucking up a wait-listed college applicant.

"What brings you here?" asked Grover.

Hitchens had learned from Little the other day that Dolan was reaching the end. Perhaps he was hoping to hear some deathbed revelation—or recantation? A full denunciation of Falwell and the Moral Majority, beyond the disapproval that Terry had hinted at in recent times? On a page of his notebook, several days ago, Hitchens had written: *a gay coterie among RR's bizarre network of lucre, guns, and contras.* This all seemed the extension of a peculiar, somewhat sordid tradition on the right: the well-oiled, sword-swishing Mishima; all that Wagnerian towel-snapping among the SS boys before the Röhm Purge. How had the squeakily sincere Mr. Little come to gain a place on Roy Cohn's track team? This continued to interest him more than whether Paula Hawkins had gotten illegal funds from the Ayatollah, an acquisition little more vicious than the legal contributions she'd no doubt also obtained from Archer Daniels Midland. But where to publish a musing upon the modern Homintern? Perhaps Tina and Navasky could fight over it.

"I'm really just here to say goodbye," Hitchens explained to Grover, surprised to realize that this was, in the main, true. Three rather tumultuous months had passed since the night of Mommy's big drug speech and his own chat with Dolan at Annie's; why *not* come to say goodbye? The human duty to do so was surely greater when one knew that every dying man was crossing into nothingness, not paradise.

"Hey, Chris," said Dolan, hollow-eyed, in a hoarse whisper, grating Hitchens's ears with the detested diminutive. Was it too much to ask that he get this right before entering the void?

"Don't try to speak," Hitchens replied. He reached for the button to raise the bed after he noticed Dolan's agonized effort to sit up.

Once elevated, the patient smiled and pointed to a copy of *Vanity Fair*. "I got a kick out of that! You really gave it to her, didn't you?"

"I suppose so."

"I couldn't follow all of it," Dolan added with some embarrassment. He tapped his head and fluttered his hand to indicate fogginess.

Hitchens opened the small package of vanilla cookies from the bookstore café. "I'm told that these are so blandly inoffensive they can be tolerated by anyone." He brought one of them to Dolan's mouth; the patient strained to bite down, but most of the cookie crumbled onto the pale-blue bedsheets.

"Take a rest," advised Hitchens.

Grateful that he wasn't being asked to do any political jousting, Dolan smiled and pointed weakly to a chair.

"Yes," said Hitchens. "I'll stay for a bit. I don't expect we'll be interrupted by a visit from Senator Helms."

As Dolan dozed, Hitchens picked up *Vanity Fair*, its pages as smooth as the latex gloves he finally hadn't bothered with, the patient clearly being past any utility they might have. Opening the magazine, he turned directly to "Pamela: Virtue Rewarded," preferring the excitements of his own prose to any that might be provided by a photo spread of Melanie Griffith. He looked up from his reading only when he heard a voice.

"Oh! Somebody's in dreamland."

Hitchens recognized Little's diversion, the lavender preppy who'd interrupted drinks last month. As soon as Nicholas Carrollton recognized him, too, the young man frowned. "Sorry," he said, lest his expression be taken for rudeness. "It's just who you're making me think of."

"I didn't mean to trigger bad memories."

"They're *great* memories! That's the problem!"

"You're Dolan's 'buddy,' as I recall."

"Yeah. He's not doing so hot." The young man, so silly on the surface, began crying tears from some substantial place inside. Hitchens offered him a cloth handkerchief.

"How old-fashioned," said Nick, sniffling. "And gall-*ant*."

"How is Mr. Little?"

"You've probably seen him since I have."

"Well, I have spoken to him about—" He nodded toward Terry Dolan, who seemed nearly inanimate. "I've not actually seen him since he gave his bit of testimony in the Hart Building."

Nick looked as if he might cry again. "That was the last time *I* talked to him. Or I should say *he* talked to *me*. He told me I was supposed to grow up, go see Spitz about the mo—" Halted by a small surge of caution, he decided not to finish the sentence.

Hitchens made ready to go. "Say goodbye to Dolan for me." When he got to the door, he added, "I believe I'm going to speak to Mr. Little this afternoon. Anything I should tell him?"

Nick handed Hitchens back his handkerchief, though he was looking as if he might need it yet again. "Just 'hi,' I guess?"

———

Half-factual updates and brand-new rumors were being whispered up and down the receiving line, both ahead of and behind Anne Macmurray and Anders Little, who shuffled forward with the others, from the Red Room to the Blue, past the madrone wreaths and Mother Goose–themed decorations. One person claimed that the CIA director, operated on today for a brain tumor, was already dead; another asserted that a taping system had been discovered in the Situation Room and that this Nixonian touch would soon yield evidence that explained everything. A woman just in front of Anders noted that a special prosecutor, an old Eisenhower-era judge from Texas, would at last be appointed tomorrow; the man, named Walsh, could be counted on to move with dispatch.

"He's supposed to have worked for *Dewey*," Anders told Anne. The emphasis was meant to indicate how venerable the appointee was; Anders realized his faux pas only when Anne said, "Careful, buster."

This was the only light moment of their evening. Both could feel themselves at the edge of a steep drop: Peter's closer-than-ever death; Anders's career peril and maybe even legal ruin. For the moment, he remained in sufficiently good standing to have stayed on the invitation list for this last of the season's Christmas parties, which over the past two weeks had brought perhaps two thousand guests, from newspaper stringers to Air Force generals, into the White House. Tonight was dedicated to senior staff, but the cabinet members and agency heads swam alongside a miscellaneous group of last-minute additions filling places for which people had sent regrets. Anders had so far seen only one other person from the NSC: he already knew that the first lady's social staff had decided to dilute and disperse that group's now-toxic personnel over the two-week range of Yuletide gatherings.

Anne had expected Mrs. Reagan to be in red, but the first lady's gown was white, and glittering. She was a little snow queen, feet away from the Blue Room's Christmas tree and its gingerbread rendition of the Little Old Woman Who Lived in a Shoe. Nancy's face, Anne could tell, had already been expertly, modestly lifted, but even so it was visibly lined and careworn. The makeup, however expensive, appeared slightly cracked, as if from strain. Reagan himself, by contrast, looked more real than she had anticipated. The cheeks were naturally ruddy, not rouged, and the hair had a shine to it rather than the flatness of the dye everyone suspected.

"Mr. Anders Little and Ms. Anne Macmurray," the Marine announced with surprising volume.

The two of them stepped forward, Anne first. The president and first lady said "Merry Christmas" in unison, perhaps a trick they'd learned to speed things along, one more technique to be added to all the assembly-line social graces Ronald Reagan had acquired before ever running for office—at movie premieres and war-bond rallies and General Electric plants. Knowing that concision was the only gift she could give her hosts,

Anne said, "It's a pleasure to be here," moving leftwards to shake the president's hand as she spoke the words, and relinquishing the first lady to Anders.

"Merry Christmas, Mrs. Reagan, Mr. President," he said. "I'm with the NSC. It was a privilege to travel with you to Iceland."

"Oh, yes," said Reagan, pretending to remember him. Anne watched Nancy; the initials "NSC" clearly weren't music to her ears. She could also see the first lady trying to figure out whether this woman with Mr. Little was his mother. Surprisingly, Anders continued speaking: "I even did a bit of notetaking during your last session with the general secretary."

"We had quite an exchange!" said the president.

Anne noticed a spark of impatience in Nancy's eye. Guests might be entitled to one sentence of self-introduction—but two? And the failure at Reykjavik wasn't really party talk.

"You fellows at the NSC have had a rough month," said the president. "Don't let it spoil Christmas for you." He winked at Anders. Anne was touched by the decency of this, as if Reagan had brought the NSC low instead of the other way around. If the words of comfort were rote and phony, they were no more so than Christmas itself, and no less welcome. She and Anders snapped into position for the photo—on the count of three; then the insurance shot—and were soon on their way to the East Room. Anders gently propelled her by the arm; she could feel the trembling in the hand that cupped her elbow.

All the guests who'd been through the line were being asked to take seats, so that once the president and first lady finished shaking hands, everyone could watch a short show by Doug Henning, the long-haired Canadian magician. With no children present and no Christmas theme, the twenty minutes of illusion seemed an almost punitive entertainment for the audience, who wanted only to begin eating and resume gossiping. When Henning was through, he presented the Reagans with two magic wands; one to be waved for world peace, he said, the other to banish illegal drugs.

Anders's nerves were still on edge when he and Anne stood in the

State Dining Room's buffet line. Neither said anything as they made plates of bay scallops and roast turkey. On either side of them and across the long table, complaint and rumor continued humming:

"*Deaver ought to come back as chief of staff. It really is too bad about his problems.*"

"*This whole thing is overblown. Did you hear Meese today? What they thought was ten million dollars was probably only four.*"

"*I'll bet it's still more fun here than at the Bushes'!*"

The vice president, whose own Christmas party was taking place later tonight up at the Naval Observatory, was widely believed to be in a worse position than anyone else, given his ties to Max Gomez and the greater likelihood that he, rather than Ronald Reagan, would have had some hands-on knowledge of the arms movements. If the Democrats fell short of impeaching Reagan, they could still make unthinkable the idea of electing his vice president to succeed him.

Anne and Anders took their plates and cider cups to a spot by the wall that put them within earshot of Maureen Reagan and Frank Fahrenkopf and a few others from the Republican National Committee. "It's just like the president suggested," one of them was saying to Ronald Reagan's daughter. "If they really wanted to get the truth out fast, they'd give immunity to North and Poindexter."

"And that," said Maureen, "is exactly what the Democrats *don't* want! Not when they can drag this out through '87 and into '88."

The man who had teed up this response nodded flatteringly, as if Maureen were expressing an insight no one else had attained.

Not realizing that this woman was the president's daughter, Anne had let her focus drift to a young man on the other side of the group. He had just popped a cookie into his mouth as if it were a single kernel of popcorn. Once she recognized who he was, Anne decided that she should alert Anders.

His eyes and Nick Carrollton's met at the same moment, and after a second's hesitation the young man tried to disappear into the cluster around Maureen. But his unceremonious "Hi!" to the president's daughter produced a burst of displeasure. "Are you *proud* of yourself?" she asked him.

He didn't understand.

"That videotape the first lady made for the Hawkins campaign. You were involved in that, weren't you?"

"Yes, but . . ."

"Well, you should have taken better care of it, and not let it get tangled up in some stupid scheme to embarrass Pamela Whatshername. Do you think, with all the troubles we have right now, that we need to be reading about dirty tricks, from our own side, in *Vanity Fair*? We don't! We don't need another little Donald Segretti making things worse!"

Nick was too young to remember this peripheral Watergate prankster, but he tried to think as fast as he could: Terry had wanted to show him something in *Vanity Fair* this afternoon but been too out of it to make himself clear. Nick could also remember messengering that Jimmy Buffett tape to somebody, and thinking from the attached note that it was somehow tied up with the footage they'd shot of Mrs. Reagan. But there was no time now to figure all this out, let alone explain. Maureen was already walking away from him, moving her entourage back toward the crab cakes.

Finally, after noticing Anders, Nick found a place to put down his cider cup and left the room.

"Anders," Anne finally said, "you need to tell me—"

"It's just what it looks like."

"Romantic troubles? The end of an affair?"

How, he wondered, could she phrase it so casually when he was so ashamed to be living it?

"Can we walk?" he asked.

Out in the hall there was no sign of Nick. They moved past the red-jacketed Marine violinists and down the staircase to the first floor, where Anders excused himself and went into the men's room: he would be sick if he didn't splash his face with cold water. He left Anne in a small room near the library, a space that drew visitors in with its portrait of Jacqueline Kennedy. A few minutes later he found her standing two pictures away from that one, in front of Pat Nixon's quietly shattered expression.

"This is what politics does to people," she told Anders.

"From what I can tell, he's become a better husband than he used to be."

"I'm not just talking about the Nixons. I'm talking about you. I don't know anything about that boy, but I know you should be working someplace where you're as free to run *after* him as away from him."

After getting their coats, they walked out into the mild night and, though they'd seen enough Christmas trees inside, decided to make a circuit past the giant one on the Ellipse.

"I'll probably be looking for a job after New Year's," said Anders. Frank Carlucci, the new national security advisor, was determined to remake the NSC. The innocent would be going, along with the truly guilty and the inadvertently guilty. "Hitchens called me this afternoon. He's telling me to quit, to become a source for this article he's writing. A chance to 'reinvent' myself, he says. I can leave my job; give a fair account of my views through him; present myself as some odd type that—"

"I don't think you're odd at all."

After a pause, Anders said, "His name is Nick."

"I remember," said Anne.

"He's in the same sort of mess Peter's in. There's money parked with him, too. And there are probably more of them. Hitchens seems on his way to figuring it out."

"Peter's not going to know he's in any trouble," said Anne.

"Why?"

"Because he's going to be dead. I'm leaving for Dallas tomorrow morning—I'm going down for the end. We'll be the only ones to feel the shame of whatever foolishness—"

"But you'll come back, won't you?"

"When it's over. And then I'll think about things. What exactly am I accomplishing at WAND? About as much as one could with that *magician's* wand. I don't know."

He gave no thought to saying I told you so, to making her admit that it had always been more complicated than she believed. He took hold of her tightly and buried his face against her shoulder, getting a scratch from a Christmas pin that had been on her coat since last year in Owosso.

"You're wrong about everything," he whispered. "And you're still the only person who ever makes sense to me."

Anne stroked the back of his short haircut. He couldn't seem to get hold of himself; he kept murmuring, *"I'm sorry, I'm sorry."*

"For what?" she asked.

"I don't know."

They completed their round of the huge lawn and crossed Seventeenth Street. A homeless man lying against an office building reached up and asked for help. Anne gave him two White House macaroons that she'd intended to bring to Texas as novelties for her children. Anders noticed the gesture and began to cry again. As they walked away, she took his arm and tried to lighten things by saying, "I was going to give him a dollar, but I knew you'd say 'he'll only spend it on drugs.'"

"Let's get a cab," said Anders.

"Let's get two," she responded.

"Why?"

"Because you're going to go see Nick and help him. I'll call you from Dallas."

29

DECEMBER 28, 1986

John Hinckley accepted an extra piece of pumpkin pie and displayed what his parents took to be an encouraging, if intermittent, interest in the football game on TV. With one quarter to go, the Redskins led the Rams; Hinckley himself had three hours left on the pass granted him by the hospital's Forensic Review Board. It had allowed him to enjoy Sunday dinner here in Reston, Virginia, at a house maintained by Prison Fellowship Ministries. Gordon Loux, the man Chuck Colson had picked to run the organization, sat on a couch with Hinckley. Elsewhere in the room, Mrs. Loux and the assassin's mother quietly showed each other family photos.

That Washington was beating Los Angeles seemed meaningful to Hinckley. It was a coded signal that the president, at his California hotel since yesterday, had been routed, whereas John Warnock Hinckley, Jr., was now out and about in the Greater Washington area. Reagan had run from him to the tower of the Century Plaza like a treed squirrel.

The only damper on Hinckley's day came from the fact that his furlough from St. Elizabeths, unlike Reagan's trip to California, had not been announced to the press. Until some reporter tipped to it, or he contrived a way to leak the news himself, the world would not know that he had legally gone over the hospital's walls. No one—not Jodie or Ted Bundy or even Leslie—knew that he was here, but once back at the Howard Pavilion he would find a way to get the word out. His mother must have shot two rolls of film this afternoon but had not noticed how he had managed to place today's newspaper with its large recognizable headline—SAKHAROV WEARIED BY EXILE YEARS—in at least three of the pictures. Placed beside him on the arm of an upholstered sofa near a noninstitutional knotty-pine wall, the newspaper would prove that he had been out of St. Elizabeths on this date—the way it worked in videos that Middle East hostages were forced to make.

He had done everything correctly all morning and afternoon, right down to saying grace. Whenever he looked at his father, he imagined him as Judge Parker, to whom future petitions for releases longer than this one would have to go. If he had not made much conversation, he had taken pains to make it appear that he was listening to everyone else; he had said yes and no in response to questions, and avoided expounding upon hidden connections that the others wouldn't grasp in any case.

"John," said Jack Hinckley to his son, once the Redskins had put away the Rams, "what do you say we do some walking around outside?"

The younger Hinckley got up without saying anything. Mr. and Mrs. Loux, as well as his mother, did the same. The five of them were soon descending from the porch of this nineteenth-century dwelling that had become the showpiece of Colson's prison ministry. Mr. Loux pointed out to Jack Hinckley the spot where the organization's new offices were being constructed, explaining that they had been lucky to acquire the land just before the announcement that a new road to Dulles airport would go right by here.

"Did you hear that, John?" asked Jack Hinckley, as if his son were routinely interested in the same sort of things that had made the father a successful executive. When Loux noticed the older man looking disappointed by his son's lack of engagement, he tried to buck him up with an illustration of how all things are possible if you have faith: "You know, Jack, our accountant here is actually a convicted embezzler." He said it with a laugh, but nodded to show that it was the truth. "We all need to keep believing in miracles."

Two Secret Service agents walked ten paces, and then five, behind the younger Hinckley. As the gap narrowed, an assistant to the Howard Pavilion's Dr. Patterson reminded them, somewhat peremptorily, that the Forensic Review Board decision allowed them to *watch* the patient but not to *accompany* him.

One of the agents pointed to a stone wall that looked as if it might have been running along the property since Confederate times. "You know those 'intrusive thoughts' your reports always worry about 'the patient' having?"

"Yes."

"I'm having one of them now."

"Oh?"

"It involves picking you up and slamming your ass against those rocks. Happy fucking New Year," he added, while further narrowing the gap between himself and John Hinckley.

———

The president was telling everyone he so liked the horse blanket Nancy got him for Christmas that he'd brought it along to California, even though they'd only be at the Century Plaza and the Annenbergs' this trip. The schedulers had told him there wasn't time for a single night at the ranch.

The Reagans had gotten to the hotel yesterday and would leave it tomorrow, and even here his aides had the president working. With the blanket slung over the back of his chair, he leaned into the microphone on his desk to begin recording a New Year's greeting that the Voice of America would beam into the Soviet Union:

. . . let us remember that respect for those rights, for the freedom and dignity of individuals, is also the bedrock on which any true and enduring peace between our countries must be built.

There had once been plans for him to give the greeting over Soviet state television, but the bad feelings since Reykjavik had scuttled that. So Charlie Wick, the family friend who headed the United States Information Agency, had come up with the VOA idea instead.

Halfway through his text, the president saw that he had an audience at the open door: Maureen and Ron and Doria. He smiled at them in midsentence, never losing the thread or cadence of what he was saying.

"You're now his favorite person, you know," Maureen whispered to her sister-in-law.

"How's that?"

"You got *him* to go to midnight Mass this week." She poked her atheistic little half brother in the ribs.

The horseplay derived from shared nervousness, and when their expressions once again became grave, all three could see the president noticing the change. The smile on his own face faded into apprehension.

"He's scenting an ambush," Maureen whispered.

"Worse than that," responded Ron. "He's worried that something's wrong with Mom."

They were attempting what Just Say No called an intervention; this afternoon might be their last chance to perform it. Tomorrow the president would head for Sunnylands, the vast Annenberg estate in Rancho Mirage. Right now he was talking about the long-suffering Russian soul:

Let us in this season of hope hear the voice of this soul that encompasses so many peoples and traditions. Let us hear the voice of all humanity's soul—the voice that speaks through Leo Tolstoy and through William Faulkner, through the martyrs, the poets, and the saints.

"Did he ever consider that the Russian soul *likes* being oppressed?" Ron whispered.

Doria Reagan patted her husband and Maureen on the arm. "You know what?" she murmured. "I think this will go better if I leave it to you two."

Reagan finished up, and his two children entered the room while the Signal Corps unplugged the recording equipment. The president looked hopefully over Ron's shoulder to see if Nancy might be with them after all. But the first lady, who knew about this planned exercise in persuasion, had arranged to be out for a late lunch with her friend Harriet Deutsch.

Maureen pointed to her father's text. "It's a shame this has to be smuggled in over the VOA's frequency. You should be able to do it live on Russian TV."

"Well," said her father. "Things haven't been so good since Iceland. They got even worse when George Shultz was in Vienna."

"Yes," argued Maureen, "but the Soviets are now taking advantage of your weakness here at home."

Despite two months of catastrophic political news, the president appeared surprised that someone would think he was in trouble. "Well," he said, forcing a twinkle, "you know I always preferred radio to TV."

"And taped to 'live,'" Ron reminded her.

The president beamed. He knew that Ron was referring to the long-ago days when announcer Dutch Reagan would reconstruct those Chicago Cubs games over WHO in Iowa. Skipper was about to go into the routine he'd been taught by his father as a little boy. The president played along, pretending to be "Curly" handing him a piece of teletype from which to improvise. Ron took over and imitated his dad, as if it were twenty years ago at the house in Pacific Palisades: "It's a called strike breaking over the inside corner, making it two strikes on the batter." The president smiled, eager for nostalgia to be the only purpose of this meeting with his children. But Maureen tugged him back toward the current unpleasantness. "I'm worried, Dad. We need to talk."

"Is it about your mother?" he asked, as if Jane Wyman didn't exist.

Maureen and Ron assured him that Nancy was fine. "It's Iran and the Contras," his eldest child explained.

"Mermie," said the president, with a sort of scolding forbearance, "we're on vacation."

Ron pointed to the presidential seal on a paperweight. "Come on, Dad. You don't really *get* a vacation."

"You need to stop the drift," said Maureen. "You need someone new to take charge."

"You're talking about Don Regan."

"Yes," Ron replied.

"This is really your mother speaking," said the president through pursed lips.

It was strange to hear Nancy invoked as a source of exasperation rather than wisdom and goodness. Maureen and Ron looked at each other, stymied.

"I'm not going to fire Don," said their father.

"Why not?" asked Ron.

"What's he done wrong?" the president countered.

"He's the chief of staff!" exclaimed Maureen. "And he can't report to you on what people have been doing because it seems that no one bothers reporting to *him*!"

Trying to lower the temperature, Reagan gave his daughter a half-smile. "I can't fire a man with whom I'll be ringing in the New Year on Wednesday night."

"Don Regan?" asked Maureen.

"I don't think so, Dad," said Ron.

"I know that the Annenbergs invited him," the president protested. "Don was tickled about it."

"He sent 'regrets,' " Maureen explained.

Her father looked a bit stricken.

"Regrets, he's had a few," sang Ron, hoping to keep things light.

Reagan shook his head and said, once more, "Your mother."

"You're kind of scaring us, Dad," said his son. "That doesn't sound like you."

Maureen decided that a radical change of subject might give her father the necessary shock: "Dad, why did you ask me to pray for you the day you went to Iceland?"

"Did I?" asked the president. "Well, I had lots to accomplish over there."

"But you'd never asked me to do that before, even when a lot was on the line."

The president swiveled ninety degrees in his chair. His children looked at each other and then followed his line of sight. He was regarding the nuclear football, the briefcase with the launch codes, on the other side of the room.

"Dad," said Maureen, frustration now filling her voice, "we're wondering if you know how bad everything is, how much trouble you're in. Things are *worse* than they were at Thanksgiving. And they were terrible then."

"Oh, I don't think so," said the president. "We've got John Tower's commission working hard. We'll find out what happened."

"We need a *strategy*," Maureen said.

"Well, I suggested giving immunity—"

"You need to try something else. The Senate shifts to the Democrats a week from now."

Ron made another suggestion: "You need to 'change the conversation,' as they say. Maybe with some big new initiative?"

"Your mother wants a Democrat to run the White House!" The president's tone contained some of his previous exasperation, but also a measure of his customary marveling over all that Nancy said or did. He then tried some subject-changing of his own. "Take a look at this. They brought it to me this morning." He showed his children a Christmas card from Nicholas Ruwe, the ambassador to Iceland, which featured a photo of Ronald Reagan strolling with Vigdís Finnbogadóttir. "She's a nice gal," said the president, pointing to his Icelandic counterpart.

"That giant fur collar!" exclaimed Ron, laughing and shaking his head. "You look like you just won the Preakness."

A young man whom Maureen recognized as one of Don Regan's mice entered the office. She glared at him as if he'd stowed away on the plane from Washington. "*Excuse* me?"

"Now, Mermie," said the president.

"I'm sorry, sir. And I'm sorry, Mrs. Revell. The speechwriting office wants the president to sign off on the *Voyager* citation." Before leaving for Sunnylands tomorrow the president would confer medals on the designer and crew of the experimental plane that had just flown nonstop around the world. Reagan now looked at the text as if to indicate it might require quite a bit of tinkering—maybe enough that Mermie and Ron would have to leave him alone? But his two children merely moved to the side of the room; they would wait.

"Know why he likes this *Voyager* stuff so much?" Ron whispered. "It reminds him of his boyhood. It's aviation, not space."

Maureen agreed. "I know it's supposed to give people a lift after *Challenger*, but it feels so antique and creepy—all about landing a plane before you run out of fuel."

"*Dad* is the one out of gas, isn't he? He really seems paralyzed."

Don Regan's mouse scurried away, and the president's children returned to his desk.

"Dad, you can't do *nothing*," Maureen asserted. "You can't let things remain static."

"This whole Iran thing is just a bunch of 'static,'" the president protested.

Ron sided with his sister. "No, Dad, it's not static. It's a thousand volts coming right at you."

Reagan displayed the same frozen expression they'd seen him wear on Christmas Eve. Then, suddenly, he asked: "Did you hear that?"

Maureen and Ron both said they heard nothing. It seemed to them there wasn't a sound on the whole glass-enclosed, bulletproof thirty-second floor.

"It sounds like a grandfather clock, ticking," the president explained.

But there was no such timepiece in the room.

———

The December issue of *Vanity Fair* had been banished from Pamela's house in Barbados, but atop a table in the entrance hallway she had set *Fortune*'s September 15 number up on a little easel. The magazine's lead story on Ronald Reagan's "management philosophy" was now the occasion for barks of irony from every Democrat entering the premises. *Surround yourself with the best people you can find*, read the cover line. *Delegate authority and don't interfere.*

Pamela reclined under some mango trees on a terrace by the pool. She had come here straight from Dulles after returning on the Concorde from nine days at Claridge's. David Mortimer, Ave's grandson via his first wife, snoozed on some nearby piece of patio furniture next to a wife of his own. Pamela had been doing her best to keep the family peace, but the heirs were beginning to convey the feeling that they should have gotten rather more from Averell Harriman's will. Still, the trusts that she administered were producing more income than anyone had expected, thanks mostly to the booming stock market. (Like most Democrats, Pamela had long since stopped using the word "Reaganomics.")

David was handsome and always cordial. And why shouldn't he be? Pamela had been very generous in assigning the range of dates on which he and his wife might use the Sun Valley house between now and the coming of spring. Moreover, she had invited David to come along with her to China in a few months for what would be her most serious foreign-policy trip yet. Even so, there seemed to be trouble ahead.

She returned her attention to some of the paperwork on a breakfast tray that spanned the width of her chaise longue. She had begun trying to take more of an interest in the House of Representatives, instinct telling her that she would be able to boss around the mousey incoming majority leader, Tom Foley. She was writing him a note, and wondering if she shouldn't perhaps ask him to come down. Not right now, but maybe at Eastertime. Over the next couple of weeks things would be quite crowded here. It wasn't just the Mortimers. Dick Helms and his wife were coming for New Year's; she'd put them in the little cottage where Ave had been more comfortable toward the end, in close proximity to his nurse. It now occurred to her that the Helms she really ought to be inviting was Jesse! Suppose the Senate should shift *back*, and he was chairing Foreign Relations when a Democratic president finally rewarded her with a post requiring confirmation? It was not so unlikely a thought, and she looked out over the pool to ponder it.

She reached for the *Post*, under which she'd been hiding a Dominick Dunne novel. There was Sakharov on the front page, blinking his way back into the light beside his physically wrecked wife. Terrible as what they'd endured might be, the story could not hold her. Perhaps Ave, with his long Soviet experience, might have had something interesting to say about this release, though he had never really adapted to the present day's premium on the crisp sound bite.

What *should* the Democrats be saying about this turn of events? Taking credit for it, perhaps? Hadn't the party's small Scoop Jackson wing been the political faction to make human-rights violations a real issue? Yes, she thought, but all that involved Moynihan, so there would be no pleasure in pointing it out. Maybe one of her new senators could make a remark about how the U.S.S.R. was opening up while Ronald Reagan would be filling American jails with low-level drug offenders? No, that didn't quite track. This really was one of those times she needed Arthur to tell her what her position was.

The butler now brought a white phone to the terrace, and David's wife looked as if she might be hoping it was for her—a distraction from the routine that she seemed to find boring after only twenty-four hours. But it was Kitty.

"Too early to wish you a Happy New Year?" asked the always-buoyant voice from New York.

"Of course not, dear. How are you?"

"Just fine," said Kitty. "I *love* Manhattan at Christmastime! I take the subway instead of cabs—so much quicker getting around. People are *wonderfully* nice when they recognize you."

"I'll have to try it."

"Now, speaking of trying," said Kitty. "Did you ever read what I left for you at N Street?"

Pamela grimaced. "Oh, you mean the Dr. Aston business."

"Yes, Pam." Kitty was a great believer in all forms of uplift, and had been trying to talk her friend into the plastic surgery that Pamela kept hemming and hawing about. She'd gone so far as to get Dr. Aston's office to prepare a customized, reassuring memorandum about what the operation involved and what splendid benefits would result.

Despite the memo's soothing tones, Pamela had actually been horrified by its descriptions. Not wanting the young Mortimers to hear any of this, she lowered her voice. "Yes, I read it."

"And?" asked Kitty.

"It sounds awful!"

"Well, it *is*, but only for a week or so. And then you're fifteen years younger and full of punch!"

"Kitty, they cut the muscles *under* the face."

"Well, yes, but—"

"Shouldn't a face-lift, of all things, be more . . . superficial?"

"I see your point, but—"

"I can't think about it now."

"Well," said Kitty, "you've taken the first step. You're a brave girl to read what he sent, and I'll call you again on New Year's Day."

After replacing the receiver, Pamela looked out at a boat idling not far beyond the edge of the dock. A well-built young man was standing on its deck doing things with ropes and sails. Watching him, she formed the sudden, firm conviction that, however green he still might be, Al Gore—not the ever-agonizing Mario Cuomo—was her man for '88, the one most likely to have her sitting here two Christmases from now with news of her ambassadorial nomination. At that point the N Street house would be filled with briefing books not for "issues evenings" but to bone her up on whatever important country had been laid at her feet. France? Yes. Or perhaps even the Soviet Union? Whichever it was, she should get first pick, well ahead of Bob Strauss.

Bob had called her in London, making sure things were all right between them. He'd also made an argument for why Reagan should *not* be impeached, whatever the investigations turned up. His ouster would make Bush the incumbent, like LBJ in '64, he reminded her, and the voters would not want to remove him for a third president in the space of what might, by the time impeachment was done, be less than a year. And that would keep the Democrats out of the White House until '92. Did she really want to risk having her reward postponed to a point when she would be too old to enjoy it?

Nonetheless, Pamela remained committed to apocalypse. And she wondered now whether that treacherous girl who'd gone to Hill & Knowlton had gotten anywhere with Mr. Hitchens. If she inspired him to land a body blow against Reagan's congressional cronies, Pamela would take her to Paris, or Moscow, and put her on the embassy payroll.

———

Terry Dolan, who helped provide Ronald Reagan with a Republican Senate when he entered the White House in 1981, died from congestive heart failure today in Washington, D.C. He was thirty-six years old. As chairman of the National Conservative Political Action Committee, Dolan marshaled significant financial resources and ideological energy on behalf of Republican candidates during the first half of the decade, until intramural battles with fellow conservatives like Paul Weyrich—and the rise of liberal counterparts like Pamela Harriman's Democrats for the 80s—diminished NCPAC's influence . . .

Anne had a vague notion that she'd heard of Terry Dolan, and yet, her nerves being what they currently were, she wished that the Dallas

NPR station, which she'd found the other day on Peter's expensive radio, would take a break from the news and supply a half-minute of that dulcimer music, or whatever it was, that public radio used for clearing the listener's mental palate. The "intramural battles" the newscaster had just referenced now seemed as silly to her as the dust-ups between Helen's lieutenants at WAND.

Politics fulfills man's essential and permanent function as a social being, as a part of God's creation.

Anne could still quote this line, which she'd heard Frances Perkins, FDR's secretary of labor, speak over the radio from the Democratic convention in 1948. Its gravity and optimism had so impressed her that she copied it onto a card that she taped to the cash register in Leo Abner's Owosso bookshop. She still wanted to believe the words but suspected she never would again. Peter's political ambitions, once conventional and lately exotic, had delivered mostly comeuppance and delusion to his life, just as Anders's own hard-edged idealism now seemed to be bringing him low. *Think globally, act locally* was one of WAND's many catchphrases. Well, Anne had more or less decided to leave the globe to others. She'd begun to sense not only her own local futility but also the likelihood that Reagan, and even Gorbachev, for all that they were officially in charge of the globe, might just be making it up as they went along.

A fine hospice nurse, a Mexican woman, was at this moment in the bedroom with Peter. Marita seemed to Anne a softer translation of the starchy, capable Irish housemaids she remembered from growing up in Darien. The woman treated her as if she were Peter's current wife, not his ex. Out of natural considerateness? Because Ralph and Susan had suggested this was appropriate? Maybe even because Peter himself had shown Anne such deference when she got here more than a week ago, while he was still lucid and even conversational.

Anne had been surprised to see that her status extended to several documents her son had set out for her to read. There were three different powers of attorney, and she was listed on every one of them, the equal of her children—very much by Peter's wish, Ralph had assured her.

His pain was terrible. Sometimes the medications overrode it and sometimes they didn't; for the moment everything was quiet.

She had always known, and told him, even before the wedding, that they would never reach their twentieth anniversary together. But he was still too young to be *dying;* they hadn't even gotten to what would have been their fortieth, though lots of couples they had known were now routinely passing that mark. Marita and her husband, Anne had learned, were coming up on thirty, though the nurse scarcely looked old enough for it to be possible.

Anne thought she heard her coming out of the bedroom. "Marita, is that you?"

"Yes, Anne. I'm going to get some dinner. He's quiet now."

"Would you like me to cook something for you here?"

"No, no, it's all right. I need the air." She was already getting her coat and hat, but once she had them on she came back into the living room. "I don't think it will be very long," she said.

Anne nodded. She knew this was Marita's gentle way of urging her to get back in there, to return to the deathbed—which she didn't want to do. She hesitated even when Marita had left, going instead into Peter's office to call Anders, as she'd promised to do when he phoned her, briefly, from North Carolina on Christmas Day.

Once he was on the line she heard crying. Again? It turned out to be Nick Carrollton, a foot or two away from the receiver. "A friend of his died today," Anders explained.

"Oh, I'm sorry."

"How's it going *there?*"

"Very close to the end—maybe even tonight. The nurse has a lot of experience and good instincts."

"Anne, I know a few details now that I didn't know the last time we talked about Peter and the money—that night at the White House. Does he have a safe-deposit box in Dallas?"

"I can look."

"When is your son coming back? Can he get into it?"

"I can probably get into it myself. I seem to have been given every possible legal power. For Peter that's a form of affection."

"You should be able to find the money—the Channell money parked with Peter—in a safe-deposit box. That's where he would have been instructed to put it, and it'll be cash." He paused before adding, "It's the same with Nick."

"What am I supposed to do with it?"

"Go to the bank and get it as soon as you can. Then bring it back to Washington with you."

Was this maneuver supposed to save Peter's reputation? Ensure that the *Argus-Press* back in Owosso, the town he left so long ago, ran a respectful obituary rather than some scandalous wire story, what would be that day's dose of Iran news? She agreed, almost absently, to do what Anders asked, and she promised that she would call again once Peter had "passed"—Marita's word.

Still postponing her return to the bedroom, she stopped in Peter's kitchen and regarded the array of amber-colored prescription containers lined up on the counter. She looked forward to sweeping them—a little army of valiant but defeated pawns—into the trash once Peter was gone. *Passed:* she liked the word. It suggested that there was a next phase to things, which she didn't believe in, but then again didn't *dis*believe so strenuously as Christopher Hitchens did. She decided she would try the verb out on him if they ever met again.

Standing against the kitchen counter, squeezing one of the drawer handles, she gathered her courage. Then she yanked open the drawer and went rummaging for the Truman button she'd found there last October. She put it on before walking to the bedroom and turning the doorknob.

She lay down beside him. His body felt cold, as if the chess game between the cancerous cells and the healthy ones had already ended. She placed her arm across his chest, the way she always had during their early years in the marital bed, and she felt an absurd 1940s-ish fear that Marita would return earlier than expected and "catch" them this way.

Within minutes her dread subsided; Peter remained so quiet that she nearly fell asleep watching the outdated digital clock. Each minute, printed on a tiny square, dropped down like an eyelid. When Peter finally did begin to stir, and moan, she felt frightened, and wished Marita would come back quickly. She tried soothing Peter with a gentle petting of his shoulders, hoping he knew who was doing it, suspecting he had no idea she was there.

She glanced over at the wire-mesh wastebasket, half-filled with tissues that she and Marita had used to mop sweat from his forehead all yesterday and today. The sight of the balled paper threw her back absurdly, yet again, to the fall of '48, to a crowded high school football field in Owosso, where one Friday night she had tried to teach Peter to fold and staple crepe-paper flowers. They were for one of the floats being built for the big Dewey parade. The hometown boy would be at its head, leading them all to a permanent spot on the American map. She and Peter got into one of their sparrings that night: she was going to marry Jack, she told him, and he'd just have to accept that. No, he'd insisted, he and she were going places, together. She had come to Owosso to write *The Time Being,* her small-town novel, just as he'd picked the town off a wall map at the state Republican headquarters—one that marked it as having an open seat in the state senate. They would be leaving Owosso before she knew it; she loved him, he explained, because he represented risk. *I'm the only person within a hundred yards of you who's likely to fall on his face in the next ten years.*

She could now feel the letting-go, though there was no sign of the death rattle one always heard about. She kissed her husband's once-golden hair and held him, falling all the way back into that long-ago, upside-down autumn. Her own life had proved an upset; but had she won or lost?

30

DECEMBER 31, 1986

Nixon finished his grapefruit juice along with the *L.A. Times*'s obituary for Harold Macmillan—a more formidable character, he thought, than the mustachioed fop Americans used to imagine—if they even paid attention to overseas news!

The former president was up early this New Year's Eve morning, happy to be in one of the guest "cottages" on Walter Annenberg's desert estate, rather than a bedroom suite inside the enormous main house. He had more privacy this way and was just as lavishly cared for.

Annenberg had been the most loyal of friends, resigning the British ambassadorship Nixon had given him as soon as Nixon had to resign himself. In the years since there'd been many visits here to Sunnylands, and the treatment was always "Mr. President" all the way. Whenever he thinks of the tapes being released—with those stupid, compulsive remarks about the Jews; his own goddamned idea of locker-room toughness, he supposes—it's the thought of Walter hearing them that makes him cringe.

Looking out the cottage window, across the golf-course fairway, he could see a couple of white ducks resting on one of the eleven lakes. Annenberg has told him that once in a while they'll be chased by coyotes. Christ, what a place. It brought to mind the old joke about what God would do if he had the money, but why would God force himself to keep living in the Middle East? Nixon knew that Lee and Walter didn't come here in the summer, but really, why did anyone come to the desert at all?

He decided to put on his windbreaker and go for a walk before the sun got too high in the sky and burnt the patches of bare scalp on both sides of his square widow's peak. Finding a path through some olive trees, he spotted Reagan's helicopter, its blades motionless, resting near the edge of the estate. The current president had been here for two days. Nixon himself had gotten in only last night and had yet to see him. Too frail and too little interested to make the trip, Pat had assured him that she'd be fine in Jersey with visits from the girls and the grandchildren; he should go and enjoy himself and meet with some of the Nixon library people while he was out in California. Christ, even now they hadn't broken ground for that thing—a Potemkin Village that would be devoid of his papers, which were *still* held hostage back east! It was unclear whether it would even rise before Reagan got *his* library.

Nixon knew he'd be bored here today, but nothing bad would happen; there'd be no nervous moments of the sort he'd experienced even at that party for Jeane Kirkpatrick. And there was, he supposed, a chance he'd get a moment to knock some sense into Reagan over the Iran-Contras business.

On the breakfast tray they'd sent around a list of the day's activities and golf foursomes. He saw that Reagan's included Shultz and French Smith, his old attorney general. Nixon had given up the game ages ago. When he was on his way up, it had always seemed like some compulsory cocktail party. For all the high spirits he deployed on the course, he'd felt like a caddy to Ike and his rich friends. Even so, Pat was right: a couple of days out here would do him good. But living here would be death. The names of the surrounding towns—Rancho Mirage, Cathedral City—made the place sound like some rich man's afterlife that had been assembled in outer space, the celestial impression only increased by the wind turbines outside Palm Springs, hundreds of them by now, soon to supply all the electricity. He wondered if the EPA—an agency the kids no doubt think Johnson founded—had a hand in them.

Up ahead he saw a small woman in a straw hat. Her hair didn't look blond, so it wasn't Lee Annenberg, and he hoped it wasn't one of tonight's dinner guests, some CEO's wife he would be expected to recognize. Then he saw two men walking behind the woman and realized it was Nancy herself. She waved first—neither of them really wanted to see the other—and he waved back. Once they reached the same spot he accepted a peck on the cheek and offered her his arm.

"We're so disappointed that Pat's not here," said the first lady.

Pat, he remembered, had once described Nancy as a Fabergé egg that talks. "She sends her love," he said.

"I think these are so wonderful," remarked Nancy, pointing to the olive trees. "Just look how clean the ground beneath them is—no gooey mess. Lee told me it's a special pesticide that keeps them from bearing fruit. So you get the pretty trees without all the olive muck."

Christ, it sounded like Agent Orange. "Have you started to think about a house?" asked Nixon. "For when you both come back to California?"

Nancy appeared startled, ready to say, *What's the rush?* "Maybe Bel Air, or Pacific Palisades," she answered. "Not Beverly Hills."

"It's hard to know where's right. We thought we'd be in San Clemente for the rest of our days. Then I got stir-crazy and we went to New York, which didn't work for Pat. Of course our circumstances were a little different. The retirement was rather sudden!"

"I worry that ours may be the same!"

Nixon could see her immediately regretting the little burst of candor. Her facial expression now pretended it was a joke, but her tone had betrayed her.

"I know you've talked to Ronnie a couple of times," she said.

Nixon smiled, slyly. "And I know you've talked to Bob Strauss."

"Oh," said Nancy. "He's told you?"

"Yes."

"What do you think of my idea?"

"It's not a bad one at all. But it'll fall short because it's too clever. What's needed is something simple and sweeping. If you give them a sword," he explained, quoting his famous line to David Frost, "you've got to fall on it yourself. That's the only way of pulling it out and surviving."

She knew that he was recommending an abject televised apology. "Please talk to him later," she entreated. "Face-to-face may be more effective than the phone."

"Or I could send him another fax!"

It was Nixon's turn to wish he hadn't said something. But she just looked at him with those huge eyes; he could see she didn't know what he was referring to.

She came to a halt, and the agents behind them stopped as well. She patted his arm. "You know, Ronnie always hoped to make you ambassador to China. He says that you accomplish more on your private trips over there than Winston Lord does for us officially."

"Well, I'm touched to hear that. But it was never in the cards." Nixon paused. "You know, what Ron needs to think about is not just where he wants to live but what he wants to *do* once it's over. In '89, I mean," he hastened to add.

"Yes," Nancy answered, with a sigh that acknowledged how much there was to survive between now and then. Nixon could see that in and of itself the question about postpresidential activity didn't really engage her. There'd always been, for all their ambition, a strange laziness to her and Reagan.

They walked in the direction of the pool, toward its terrace's circular white awnings, which rose on long poles, like lorgnettes positioned to shield individual sunbathers.

"Well," Nancy now told him, "I promised Lee I would check on my rose." All the first ladies and female British royals had one bred in their honor here. There was a whole little garden of them.

"And I should turn back," he replied.

Each was relieved to be veering off from the other.

"See you at lunch?" Nancy asked.

The idea appealed to him no more than golf. Dinner, with all the money men and showbiz waxworks, would be plenty.

Nixon flashed her his don't-blink-or-you'll-miss-it smile. "Let's say cocktails instead. I'll keep to myself for lunch. I'm looking forward to just some cottage cheese—in my cottage!"

———

The Arlington branch of the Riggs National Bank, which held the checking account of Mr. Nicholas Carrollton ($416.50 in available funds), remained open until noon on New Year's Eve. The branch also housed a safe-deposit box in that name, and at eleven a.m. Nick went to the bank with Anders Little and removed an envelope from the long, flat metal container that he'd seen only once, some months ago, when Spitz Channell helped him fill out the paperwork required to obtain it.

Once they returned to the car, Anders counted the money without removing his leather gloves, which were thin enough not to interfere with his flicking of the bills. The cash amounted to just under forty-five grand.

"And you never touched any of this, right?" he asked Nick one more time.

"No. When I made that joke to you about having a great cash flow, it was just 'cause, like, I knew the money was *there*? I still don't know exactly *why* it's been there, or what you and I are going to do with it."

Anders put the bills back into their envelope. "Did Terry Dolan have any favorite charities?" he asked.

"I don't know."

"What about the organization that helped him?"

Twenty minutes later the two of them were parked outside the offices of the Whitman-Walker AIDS clinic in Adams Morgan—on the corner of Belmont Road, as it happened. Anders could look through the driver's window and toward Channell's apartment. Nick, wearing a knitted cap and a scarf that covered his mouth, went inside and put the envelope, now marked DONATION/FROM AN ANONYMOUS FRIEND, on the desk of a receptionist who'd gotten up for a quick break.

"Wow," he said to Anders after returning to the car. "I don't suppose I could take a tax deduction for that? *Kidding!*"

Anders wasn't surprised to find himself laughing. Since Sunday night, after talking to Anne, he had felt a lightening of the spirit, a sort of pleasant limpness, as if a fever were breaking. This morning at six-thirty, when Nick had brought him his running shoes—holding them by the laces with his teeth, in imitation of a faithful dog—Anders had, to his own and Nick's disbelief, rolled over and said, "I'm sleeping in. Why don't you do the same?"

Neither had to go into work today, and once the money was gotten rid of, Anders drove back to Arlington and dropped Nick at his own place.

"You still haven't told me," Nick said, as agreeably as he could.

The uncertainty involved whether they would see in the New Year together by going out to a bar that Nick had suggested.

"What time should I pick you up?" asked Anders.

Nick brightened hugely. "That's so great! Say eleven?"

Anders looked at him skeptically.

"It's going to be a *long* night. Take a disco nap!"

Anders didn't know what the term meant, but once Nick was out of the car he realized he was feeling anticipation about the evening ahead, instead of the postcoital remorse he usually felt when Nick left his presence.

After parking in his own building's garage, he found Hitchens waiting for him in the lobby.

"Happy New Year," said the writer, putting out a cigarette.

"I thought you'd be in England, bothering me from across the ocean."

"No, not until Friday. And then just for a week. May I send you collect faxes whilst I'm there? Assuming your new boss, Mr. Carlucci, will accept the charges."

"I'm not sure he'll be my boss come Friday."

"He's cleaning house that fast?"

"How do you know I won't clear out on my own—and accept your proposition?"

Hitchens looked at Anders's wristwatch. "Why don't we go upstairs and toast the just-arrived Australian New Year? Unless"—he hesitated for a moment—"someone's sleeping up there?"

"No, he's at his place," said Anders, amazed at how easily he imparted the information, instead of using whatever evasion he would have only weeks ago. "You're not done grilling him?"

Hitchens had called Nick on the twentieth, two days after running into him at the hospital. The writer had already figured out a good deal from that encounter—*He told me I was supposed to grow up, go see Spitz about the mo*—and a little more face-to-face conversation with the unwary young man had allowed him to puzzle out much of the rest. He'd closed in on details like the safe-deposit boxes, something Little hadn't known about himself until he visited Nick after the White House party.

Throughout November Anders had deliberately not pressed Nick for particulars. If he was going to know too much, he had wanted the knowledge to come from somebody besides this boy whose ongoing existence he had so much trouble admitting.

"So does he get to keep a sort of commission?" Hitchens asked as the elevator rose to Anders's apartment. "On the Khomeini contributions?"

"There's no commission and there's no money."

"Where's it gone?"

"It's out performing good works," said Anders.

"South of the border?"

"No, just across the river."

Hitchens smiled. Eager to fence and deduce, he took out his pad.

"You're an optimist," said Anders, pointing to the notebook and telling himself to be careful. Once inside, he let Hitchens fix his own drink, the usual Johnnie Walker and Perrier.

"I'll think about using ice if I ever become a citizen," Hitchens informed his host. He noticed that the apartment was less orderly than when he'd been here last. He pushed aside some Christmas boxes, presents from Anders's nieces and nephews in Mooresville, before sitting down.

"So what would you like me to confess?" Anders asked, pointing again to the pad.

"What a nice boy like you is doing in a place like this." He gestured vaguely toward the capital across the river.

"You mean nice *girl*?" Anders asked.

"No," Hitchens said, evenly, meeting Anders's gaze, indicating that man-to-man respect, even affection, would obtain during any interviews they had.

"Sorry," said Anders, who looked down at his bottle of light beer with an expression that seemed to say: *Give me time. I'm adjusting to all this.*

"Where's Dolan's funeral going to be?" asked Hitchens.

"St. Matthew's, I think."

"Ah, where they said farewell to Joe McCarthy."

"And Jack Kennedy," Anders pointed out.

"Why don't we put in a joint appearance?"

"You think being there is going to help you understand this—what was the word you used?"

"Homintern."

Anders laughed scornfully.

"I'm quite willing to be persuaded that there's nothing to it," said Hitchens. "Convince me of homosexuality's irrelevance here."

"In my case it *is* irrelevant."

"Then talk to me about other phases of your apostasy. Moderate young Democrat comes under the spell of La Kirkpatrick, then embraces anti-Communism by any means necessary."

"I didn't leave the Democratic Party; the Democratic Party left me."

"Has a familiar ring."

"I'm quoting Ronald Reagan."

"I know that, dear boy. I'll even concede to you that he had a point—one that was all to the credit, however minimally, of the Democratic Party."

"Why do you want my views if you're just going to pummel them? You only want me to come to you like some straw man you can set on fire."

"Not in the least. I'm fascinated by your possible authenticity, by the fact that you may truly believe what you espouse."

"You know what?" said Anders. "I do believe it. I think Reagan may yet end the Cold War, on our terms."

"No more bipolar world."

"That's right."

"Wait until you see the sectarian one that'll replace it."

Anders waved his hand to dismiss the possibility.

"Anyway," said Hitchens, "we were talking about you."

Anders looked back down at his beer. "There's half a world to be freed before I can have *my* freedom. And I don't think I—"

"You mean your sort?"

"Yeah, my *sort*. They, we, might at least think of going to the back of the line, behind the half of the world that's actually enslaved. Poland means more to me than, what is it, Stonewall. God, have you ever heard a homosexual talk about the glories of Castro and Cuba? I have. All the left-wing ones, and that's ninety percent of them, will go on and on about that. Universal health care, literacy programs, blah blah blah. Well, boys, go down there and give José a big kiss on the dance floor; the two of you can then share a cell in a detention camp. The left-wingers, not me, are the ones with the contradiction. Who's kidding who?"

"Whom."

"Fuck off."

"This is going to be a wonderful piece. You sound almost *alive*, Little."

As Hitchens refilled his own drink, the bell rang. "Always a surprise here, isn't there?"

Anders got up and opened the door. "You were going to let me pick you up at the airport!" he exclaimed.

Hitchens watched him embrace Anne Macmurray, whom the doorman now knew well enough to let up without announcement.

"I had a couple errands that were better done on my own. Oh, hello," she said to Hitchens, wondering if Nick Carrollton was here, too, replicating the full cast from the Saturday night Mrs. Thatcher had been in town.

Peter had been cremated yesterday, and this morning Anne had boarded the first flight from DFW to National, carrying the money she'd retrieved from the safe-deposit box. When she first counted it, she'd been astonished at how much was there, a bit under fifty thousand dollars, but on reflection she'd felt surprised it wasn't more, given the source and the things it was involved with. Straight from the plane, she'd gone to the WAND office to clean out her desk; she'd fax a letter of resignation tomorrow. Roaming over Capitol Hill, she had entered St. Peter's Catholic Church and, on a whim, put ten thousand dollars into the poor box. She was stopped from inserting even more by a strange feeling of extravagance, which she now supposed also came over people performing acts of charity—if that's what this really was. She still feared that one day she'd have to account for the money, no matter that Anders's clear intention was to keep anyone from ever knowing where it had come from and where it had gone.

Hitchens watched Anders pour her a glass of white wine and pondered whether the gesture looked connubial or filial. E. M. Forster and Mom back in Weybridge? Once she sat, he said to Anne, "I'm sorry for your loss."

She thanked him, still unsure of how he'd learned whatever he knew about Peter and the parked money.

Nor was Hitchens sure he should tell her. A couple of days ago he had gone to work in earnest on Mrs. Harriman's tip, calling Cox's apartment once he got hold of a phone number. A Spanish-sounding nurse answered and told him that the occupant had "passed," making it seem as if Cox had just wandered by her or succeeded at his O-levels. How insistently to press the more-or-less widow, now that he was in her presence, remained a question.

He didn't need to worry about the matter for long.

"Christopher," Anne said, "in the Hart Building you asked me if it was better for you or the FBI to have Peter's secrets."

"Anne," said Anders, cautioning her.

"I thought, instinctively, that the answer was you. And I think I was right."

Hitchens replied, "I've been trying to get Mr. Little to entrust me with *his* secrets, as well as his beliefs."

Anne turned to Anders. "Have you made a decision?" She could see from his face that he was ready to go over the edge and say yes, so she pushed him, handing Hitchens the envelope with the rest of the money. The writer made a quick, silent inspection of it. "I did always imagine it was Mr. Cox and not 'Mr. Katz,'" he finally said.

Anders and Anne looked at each other. There was no point in asking exactly what he meant; the point was *he knew.*

"Okay," said Anders, "you want me for your article?"

"Madly."

"Two conditions. You don't mention Peter Cox or Nick Carrollton. Not in that article or any other you write."

"Done."

"That was two names but one condition."

Hitchens smiled. "Liberation is making you quicker, Little. What's the second?"

"*You* get rid of this money—as you see fit."

Hitchens contemplated the four crisp stacks of bills. "I have a thought," he said at last. He turned to whisper it to Anne, who was soon laughing for the first time in weeks.

"Are you going to tell me?" asked Anders.

Hitchens explained: "A small remnant of the Greenham Common women"—the antinuclear protesters so despised by Mrs. Thatcher— "have settled in for a long winter. I know just whom this can be given to, so that the *pasionarias* can be fed and clothed in their vigil against American missiles."

Anders appeared ready to explode, until he looked at Anne, whose expression seemed to say *We're beyond all that now.* He then looked back toward Hitchens, realizing, with a sort of exasperated wonder, that he, too, trusted him more than the FBI.

"There's not much you can do, Little. You're caught between two fires. That's the terrible thing about having principles."

"I think you just complimented me," said Anders.

"I did."

31

DECEMBER 31, 1986–JANUARY 1, 1987

Nancy didn't like the way she looked. In the mirror, getting ready, she'd seen a sort of burnt matchstick in a long red gown. But the dread could only be dealt with by throwing herself into the evening. As the forty-five-minute cocktail hour got under way and the men posed in front of the fireplace for official-looking pictures (Walter was nothing if not an archivist of his own life), she played off her own bossy image, supervising the photographer, fussing and flirting with each group she rearranged around Ronnie.

While some of this went on, Annenberg pointed to the painting above the mantel. "As most of you know, that's van Gogh's *Pink Roses*. If you want to see his *White Roses*, you've got to go to Pamela Harriman's house in Washington—but I suspect that invitations there have been pretty scarce for this crowd!"

Nancy looked toward the other paintings, lots of Postimpressionists that hung on the room's pale-green wooden partitions—simple, almost rustic planks that didn't go quite to the ceiling. Ted Graber had been in on designing the house back in the sixties and had explained to her that the truncation was designed to keep this enormous modern space feeling like a single room. She understood the theory, but the planks always reminded her of the "walls" for an interior set that had been built upon a soundstage. She half expected to see a boom mic above the edge of the wood.

Ronnie was pointing to one of the madrone wreaths, which he'd just noticed. "Ted Graber told us about those!" he informed Lee and Walter and everyone listening. "We feel right at home!"

Nixon had walked over from his cottage to the main house—it was good for the phlebitis—wearing his black-tie rig and arriving at the front driveway twenty minutes into cocktails. He passed the fountain, some sort of Mexican column, then entered the huge single-story premises. A waiter greeted him with a tray of drinks near a little indoor pool surrounding a Rodin. The former president noted the bandstand set up on one side of the prodigious living room, and he hung back from the picture-taking, which was properly Reagan's show.

Taking his drink, he went off alone to Walter's "Room of Memory," a little self-created museum to the owner and his wife. Annenberg's new Medal of Freedom was conspicuously displayed near a wall with nothing but framed Christmas greetings, year after year, from the Queen Mother.

Suddenly, across the room, Nixon saw Pat, her black-and-white image inside a little silver frame. In the picture she was talking to Lee and Walter, and he could tell from the tight curl of her hair that the photo dated from the vice-presidential years, when Walter was still making his climb.

On another wall, higher up than the Queen Mother and the rest of the royal family, you could see Walter's ancestors, humble Jews photographed or painted into oval frames, all of them looking too shy to speak while they presided over their descendant's unlikely domain. Walter's whole life had been spent redeeming his old man, who'd gone to prison on a tax rap, and for all that he was bent on overcoming the disgrace, he had never done anything to hide it, either, a thought that made Nixon feel ashamed. This morning he'd pushed away half a lemon on the plate beside the tea they'd brought him; it was his own know-it-all father—the failed lemon ranch, the crazy nostrums, the temper—that he was shoving aside.

Unlike Walter, Nixon had never been much interested in curating his own past. The goddamned tapes had been meant to prove a point, that he, not Henry, had crafted the big ideas in foreign policy. When he'd written *Six Crises*, the first of his autobiographies, it was less to preserve his experience of those half-dozen calamities than to make sure he'd have a chance at another six, and six more after that. Even this make-believe library of his that was aborning in Yorba Linda: there are times when he finds it hard to sustain interest in the thing.

He didn't want to head into the clatter of cocktails any sooner than he had to. So he asked one of the waiters the best way to slip off outside for a moment by himself. He'd also had too much of the past; too much decay and dying. He'd called Anders Little this afternoon from his cottage— Walter could afford the long-distance charges!—and learned that Connally's man Cox, that odd character who'd looked so bad at the party for Jeane, had just checked out. He should write a condolence note to the wife—or was it the ex-wife? He forgot what Little had told him.

He made his way along a pebbled path, guided by the memory of an earlier visit to the garden Nancy had pointed at this morning. And sure enough, there it was, Pat's flower, a few rows back, with her name on a white card. *My wild Irish rose!*

———

Inside the house, the tight ship of the party was sailing through the last minutes of cocktails before the dinner bell was rung precisely at nine. Annenberg showed Northrop's Thomas Jones a big jade water buffalo, a tabletop sculpture from China. "It took two first-class plane tickets to get it over here!" Nearby, Kirk Douglas told Lee Annenberg, not for the first time, about an encounter he'd had early in his career with her uncle, Harry Cohn, at Columbia Pictures. Caspar Weinberger, not far from the water buffalo, eyed some Chinese figures from the same dynasty that had produced those now-famous terra-cotta soldiers. He looked around for Nixon, his former and favorite boss, but didn't see him.

Once dinner began there were ten people seated at each of nine round tables. The only married couple permitted to occupy the same one were Jimmy and Gloria Stewart, since without her by his side he would get even more tongue-tied than usual. Jerry Zipkin, out from New York as a treat for Nancy, was less than pleased to be across from the Stewarts; the actor was such a straight arrow—worse than Reagan himself—that Zipkin would have to keep his claws retracted. Right now he could see Gloria experiencing a sudden surprise at being so close to the ground, the way everyone did the moment they sat down here. Would it be too bitchy for Jimmy's taste to mention what Ted Graber had once told Nancy? Namely, that all the furniture in the house had been designed to cut guests down to the owners' size (five-seven and five-four)?

Lee Annenberg wore a gold dress with white appliqués—very Palm Springs. Nancy watched her stand up for the most formal moment of the evening, the introduction of Ronnie, who would make the predinner toast. Lee said simply, "The president of the United States."

Towering over her with his raised champagne flute, Ronnie began: "Looking out at so many familiar and, yes, beloved faces, I'm struck by how much I've depended on all of you throughout the years. Jimmy," he said, pointing his glass in Stewart's direction, "I don't suppose you could join the new minority in the Senate next week and reenact that famous *Mr. Smith* filibuster from time to time, whenever I need you on an issue?"

Everyone laughed, and then the president made his little tribute to the Annenbergs: "You know, back in Washington we live over the store, but the only Being who lives above this house is God, up there in the pure desert sky. Maybe that's why we all feel such peace and contentment every time we come here. They say that people who live in glass houses shouldn't throw stones. Well, Lee and Walter have never flung out anything but their arms, to their country and their friends. Everyone here will have a wonderful year in 1987, because it will have *started* here, with them."

"Hear, hear," said everyone, raising their glasses.

Nancy had given him a little help with the toast—she herself said that last line to Lee every year—but she now worried that Ronnie seemed so flat. He hadn't added any little zingers of his own to the bit about Jimmy; nothing about Walter's wealth or Kirk Douglas's dimple, the sort of stuff he usually put in.

The waiters set down glasses of Mondavi chenin blanc 1984. "Great *year*," said Merv, pointing to the label. Everyone knew he meant the president's reelection landslide, not the vintage.

"A better year than the one he just had!" cackled Malcolm Forbes.

Senator Laxalt, who believed the billionaire to be as full of hot air as the balloons he piloted, turned his head away.

As the *suprêmes de volaille* arrived at the tables, Eva Gabor, on the other side of Walter Annenberg from Nancy, asked him, "Is zee library all done?" They had not seen each other since Betsy Bloomingdale's dinner back in August. Charmed by her accent, and the *Green Acres* guilelessness of the question, Annenberg chuckled. "Well, it's not exactly like raising a barn. But it's going well." Nancy, who would have preferred almost any other topic, saw him looking in Nixon's direction and wondered if he was thinking about the kind of political catastrophe that puts an end to donations.

The eating was quick and sparing, as if to consume too much of the beautifully presented food would be to insult it. By the time the ice cream soufflé came around with the petit fours, people had already begun table-hopping, and Tony Rose's band could be heard warming up in the living room. Nancy made her way over to George Shultz and asked, as brightly as she could, "Save me a dance? I told Helena I'll get her one with Kirk Douglas if she'll relinquish you."

"Happy New Year, my dear," the secretary replied, with a kiss that felt consoling.

"Do you think we're going to get past this?" Nancy asked him.

The question was wistful, self-indulgent, and unanswerable. The only person to whom it might reasonably be addressed was Joan Quigley. What now made asking it even worse was the moment of hesitation she saw George exhibit before he answered "Of course." His sympathetic, canine eyes betrayed uncertainty. She kissed him back and then turned her attention to Nixon, halfway across the room, urging him with a tilt of her head to go talk to Ronnie.

There was already a line of people waiting to have a word with the president, who'd yet to get up from his seat beside Lee. Nixon didn't relish the situation, but knew he'd better make his move before the dancing reached full swing and the music claimed all of Reagan's available hearing. Everyone allowed him to go to the head of the line, with courteous cries of "Another president!" and "Happy New Year, sir!"

"I got to take a stroll with the first lady this morning," said Nixon, once he reached Reagan.

"She told me," said the president.

"She's got great political instincts—same as Pat," said Nixon.

Unexpectedly, the remark produced a frown from the sitting president. Nixon offered a bit of elaboration to the two CEO wives listening in: "Pat told me not to run for governor out here in '62, and she was right. I was lucky to carry Palm Springs!" He was sweating, trying too hard with the least hostile audience one could assemble. But it seemed impossible to engage Reagan himself. Nixon would say that the president's mood was off, but he wasn't sure that Reagan even *had* moods. He decided against asking for a private word tomorrow morning, let alone tonight.

Soon enough everyone, even the current president, had moved to the living room's vast pink marble floor. Charlie Wick, a frustrated musician, borrowed one instrument after another from members of the band, taking a turn on each, even while the fellows were in the middle of a number. Between two old Glenn Miller songs, Bob Hope grabbed the microphone and said, "It's great to see the president. I haven't had the chance to thank him for backing off that agreement in Iceland. If he and Gorbachev had signed it, they'd have put me out of business. And if I can't go entertain soldiers, I lose my last chance to sneak off with Morgan Fairchild!"

Reagan leaned down to Lee Annenberg, still beside him, and asked if she could repeat the joke. Dolores Hope playfully pushed her husband away from the mic and by prearrangement with the band began singing "Why Can't You Behave?" When she finished, Tony Rose had his boys go into a Duke Ellington number, which prompted Nixon—still in the effortfully upbeat mode the CEO wives had induced—to take Eva Gabor out onto the dance floor. Amidst applause, he told her, "You know, I'm the man who brought dancing to Whittier College."

"Really?" she asked, uncomprehendingly.

Nixon just smiled, not having the patience to go into the whole Quaker business.

Betsy Bloomingdale, looking on from the edge of the room with Nancy, leaned over and said to the first lady, "Charlie Wick tells me there's a surprise coming."

"I hate surprises!" said Nancy, who did. At lunchtime she'd learned from one of her agents about Hinckley's day out, which had added, however irrationally, to her sense of danger and besiegement.

"But maybe you'll like this one," said Betsy, who squeezed her friend's hand and noted how exhausted she was. "You know, I don't care how many hours I get with you on the phone. We haven't *sat* together since that dinner for the library. How long ago was that? August?"

"Oh, don't mention the library!" cried Nancy, in a kind of mock-mock-horror—pretending that her real fear was actually fake.

She kissed Bets and began moving dutifully from one cluster of guests to the next, acting as if this were all a respite from the White House rather than an extension of the same ordeal. When Tony Rose, who'd probably seen the Gershwin show, cued the band to play "Love Is Here to Stay," she and Ronnie got out on the floor and everyone else cleared off to watch.

She felt no hint of relief until twelve o'clock neared and she knew it would soon be over: one could usually hear most of the limo drivers turning over their motors before the band got through "Auld Lang Syne." As everyone counted off the seconds to midnight, she held her husband's hand and whispered longingly to Merv, on her other side, "How about you buy this place from Walter and then lease one of the cottages to me and Ronnie?"

"I don't think I could do a deal that big in only two years," said Merv, almost seriously.

Well, at least he thought they had that long left in Washington!

We two have paddled in the stream,
From morning sun till dine;
But seas between us broad have roared
Since auld lang syne.

Something was different from other years. Walter was commandeering the bandleader's microphone.

"If Charlie Wick can put down his clarinet, I'm going to let him offer you tonight's *pièce de résistance*."

"Ladies and gentlemen," said Wick, boyishly eager to oblige, "if you'll all go into the Game Room and take seats, we have a very special audio presentation that will be the perfect way for you to see in—or, I should say, *hear* in—this New Year of 1987."

The president shrugged his shoulders in a *don't-ask-me* gesture, and the first couple marched off in what became a conga line with everybody else. The backgammon tables had been cleared from the Game Room, where many of the guests had at one time or another watched films, but it felt strange to be assembled like an old-time studio audience at a radio station. On the screen there was only a still picture of Ronald Reagan.

Wick's voice came through speakers while he remained out of sight in the projection room. "You've all seen that familiar wall map near where you're sitting, the one that Frank Sinatra gave to Walter and Lee. Hey, come to think of it: where *are* Frank and Barbara tonight?" The guests laughed but wondered where this was going. "That's the map that moves, the one that shows you which parts of the world are experiencing sunlight and which are in the dark. Well, ladies and gentlemen, right now it is ten fifteen a.m. in Moscow, and this is the Voice of America."

After dimming the lights, Charlie pressed a button for the live radio feed. In a few seconds they were all hearing Ronald Reagan's voice, the way a handful of Soviets were now hearing it, too, as it alternated with the voice of a Russian translator.

I had hoped to address you by way of television, and to have General Secretary Gorbachev address the American people on United States television, as was done last year. Unfortunately, your government officials declined our offer to have such an exchange of greetings. I regret that we were not able to take advantage of the opportunity to build mutual trust . . . So I come to you tonight over the Voice of America. This season, in and around the New Year, is a season of love and hope; a time for reflection; a time of expectation . . .

Everyone remained quiet, even during the translations. Nancy watched her husband exhibit an abashed contentment. The tape, already created and stored away, was now doing its job.

After our Reykjavik meeting, both sides took time to reflect on what had been accomplished and on ways to move forward again . . .

Nancy looked at Shultz and then at Dick Nixon, who had taken out a pen and pad in order to make notes.

Whenever there's a restoration of human rights to a man like Andrei Sakharov, or a woman like Yelena Bonner, as happened recently, it helps strengthen the foundations for trust and cooperation between our countries . . .

Exile—prison! It was her greatest fear, and not unthinkable. She remembered Ronnie telling her a dozen years ago that Nixon, facing the possibility of it, was consoling himself with the fact that throughout history some statesmen had done their best writing—manifestos and so forth—from jail. She had put her hands over her ears when he said it.

And now, over the radio, Ronnie was talking about the Russian soul, sounding like a soothing, forgiving god, one who had made an appearance and would soon retreat into the heavens:

So, once again, on behalf of the American people, let me wish you all a happy, healthy, and prosperous new year. Thank you. God bless you, and good night.

More than a few people, Walter included, were crying. "I can't think of a more fitting way to welcome in 1987," he said, as the lights came up and Sinatra's wall map moved a millimeter further from light to darkness and darkness to light. The band resumed playing in the distance.

The president and Nancy were the first to stand, and Nixon took a good, curious look at them. All the life seemed drained from her face. He watched the president say good night to people he'd known for decades, doing it with the kind of detachment one might bring to a rope line of strangers at an airport campaign stop. His expression was blankly grave when he reached Nixon.

"Dick, I never thanked you for that fax."

Had he deliberately not done that in their phone calls since Reykjavik? Had he simply forgotten until this moment?

"Well, I'm always happy to help. And my advice is usually worth just about what it costs."

"Happy New Year, Dick."

Had the fax convinced him? Confirmed his own thinking? Bought him a little cover in disagreements with Shultz and Nitze? Did Reagan even remember?

Along with Nancy, he was gone.

The William French Smiths were staying in the Pink Suite, on one side of the Game Room, while she and Ronnie, as always, had the Yellow, with its blond-wood furniture, golden quilt, and jar of pale-yellow jellybeans.

Ronnie took off his black tie and then removed her earrings, an old jokey ritual they had, as if the task demanded more mechanical aptitude than she possessed.

"Happy New Year," he said with a kiss. "And I'm sorry about before."

He was referring to an argument they'd had in this room right after lunch. She'd been on him about Don Regan—*I was right about Al Haig, right about Stockman and Jim Watt; why shouldn't I be right about Don?*—and he'd said, "Honey, please get off my back." He'd uttered the words in what anyone but the two of them would have regarded as the sweetest way imaginable, on the order of a plea to be allowed another half hour of golf. Even so, she'd heard that phrase only twice in the past thirty-five years—when she wanted him to break up Ron's affair with an older woman, and tried to speed up his decision on whether to run in '76. She was still spinning from hearing it today. Those words were one of the main reasons she'd hated tonight, been irritated by everyone here from Lee to Jerry.

Ronnie went into the bathroom. She knew she should use these minutes to call Ron and Maureen and wish them a Happy New Year; they'd done their best the other day. But that could wait until morning. Her head would come off if she didn't get a few minutes by herself.

She stepped through the sliding glass door and into the cactus garden, waving to the agent to indicate that everything was fine. She was just going to stroll past the corner of the house and get a breath of air.

She looked for what everyone called "the peacock sculpture," a spray of wires that had always reminded her not so much of that bird's tail as a weeping willow. There was something calming, a sort of floating suspension, to the filaments. But as she stood before the piece of art, she continued to fixate on all that was coming—the hearings; the revelations; the instant memoirs written to curry favor with the prosecution and the press. And the ridicule! *What didn't the president know, and when did he forget it?*

Suppose Ronnie *did* apologize and get rid of Don. Suppose something could shake him free from this mystical torpor that had come over him since Reykjavik. Could the great ocean liner of the presidency come off the sandbar and begin to sail again, until Saturn and Uranus had finally finished their murderous dance?

Before it was over, one way or the other, her mother would be dead.

She looked up at the stars in the desert sky and knew they meant nothing. Astrology was no more real than religion or a script. That she pretended to believe it wasn't a weakness; it was a sign of will and self-discipline, an ability to pull the wool over her own eyes if that's what it took to feel better and get through.

Her heart sped up when she heard the last of the limousines pulling away. She looked over to the cottages and lakes before turning around on the path that would lead her back to the cactus garden. Within seconds she was at the sliding door to the Yellow Suite, which was now bathed in only the glow of a night-light. Ronnie, lying in bed in his boxy, old-fashioned pajamas, had already fallen asleep. She went to slide the door and discovered that it had locked itself.

She didn't want to make a fuss with the agent. In a moment Ronnie would stir, get up, and let her in. So right now she just looked at her husband in the night-light's glimmer and felt flooded with a love for him she hadn't experienced in weeks. He had always been *her* script, to read and study and revise. As she gazed at him, sleeping peacefully and floating toward ruin, she struggled once again to pierce the mystery of the last two months. Was he fearful, and manfully hiding it? Blindly faithful that everything would work out? Possessed of a factual certainty—*I know something you don't know*—that it was going to? He seemed to feel that everyone's desire for him to act was a kind of imposition, an unreasonable demand from people who didn't know that his work in the presidency was done, that he had completed whatever he was supposed to do and that nothing more could be asked of him.

Her moment in the rehab facility with Mike came back to her now—

that feeling she'd had of being dragged by a current when she asked him: *How did you understand Ronnie?* She had seen from the look on his face that Mike was protecting her, but realized only now why he hadn't answered. If he had—had admitted that he didn't really understand Ronald Reagan—she would have had to ask the same question of herself, and her answer would have been the same as his.

No. Still looking through the glass, she shook her head: it couldn't be. Not when Ronnie had told people, time and again, forever, *And then along came Nancy Davis and saved my soul.* The letters, the endearments, the Truluv canoe that was tied up beside Lake Lucky, at the ranch, even at this moment—all were evidence, proof, of the closeness they had, the closeness that had been their own sort of space shield against others, even their own children, deflecting and pulverizing them when they flew too near. It was real.

The desert stars twinkled implacably. She heard a coyote in the distance. She kept her fingers on the handle of the door that would not yield. Her breath fogged the glass as she whispered *I love you.*

Which she did.

But she didn't know who he was, and she never had.

AUGUST 12, 1996

668 St. Cloud Road, Los Angeles, California

A woman in a white uniform comes in and sets down a glass of what he thinks is called cranberry juice.

"Why, thank you," he says, never having lost his manners.

He doesn't lift the glass to drink, and he can see her following his gaze, trying to pinpoint whatever he is looking at. This happens whenever she is in here, and his instincts tell him that she has been told to do it.

"*Cattle Queen of Montana*," she says, slowly and clearly, pointing to the framed poster he's looking at. "Yes!" she adds, with a wide smile. "You were once in the movies!" She points to the poster with more insistence when his eyes start to wander from it. "Barbara Stanwyck," she says, meaninglessly, in the Spanish accent she shares with the men who tend the pool outside the house. Sometimes, until he hears the accent, he thinks that she is Miss Darby, back in Illinois, preparing the fifth grade for a test.

"That's a *Remington*," she says, pointing now to a bronze cowboy and horse that sit atop a long table covered with important things, treasures. "And that's *you*," she adds, pointing to the small marble head of a man beside the cowboy.

"Dick Nixon is dead," he tells her.

"That's right!" she replies, excited, as if he's imparted something fresh and extraordinary. "Two years ago. And there he is," she adds, indicating one framed picture amidst many others. Encouraged, the way Miss Darby is when they get things right, she points to another photograph. "The Statue of Liberty. On the Fourth of July," she says.

More pictures: "Mr. O'Neill. Mrs. Thatcher." He moves his eyes from one to the next.

She picks up a giant card that has been here for some time but not so long as the photographs and the bronze cowboy. "You're eighty-five years old," she says. "This birthday card was signed by all the congressmen, the senators, the ambassadors." She points to several swirls of ink. "Mr. Crowe in London. Mrs. Harriman in Paris."

This time, once his gaze shifts, her enthusiasm fades. She smiles, as if accepting defeat, and begins to straighten things up without saying anything more.

He knows that there is a whole building full of these pictures and objects. You can find it where the mountains begin, not a very long ride from here—and not where they first said they would build it, far to the north. The last time they took him to it he thought he was going to the ranch, thought he was going to ride his horse. Everyone at the building seemed stunned to see him arrive; they all waved and applauded as he got out of the car. He wanted to stay outside in the sun, but they made him go inside and look at all the pictures and all the things that were carefully arranged and labeled. He can recognize letters and numbers, one at a time, but cannot put them together, and he soon grew tired of half-recognizing things, of being on the verge of saying their names, of almost recalling whatever event went with them. And then he had become frightened, looking at the headless woman standing inside a glass box in a long red dress. He understood, after a minute, that this wasn't a real woman, and wasn't really *her*, but not before he'd begun, just for a moment, to cry.

When they were back in the car, everyone remained cheerful, the way everyone always does, but on the way home, when they thought he was dozing, he heard her say to the man in the seat in front of them: *That's it. No more. Not here; not even to the ranch. And, above all, not to the convention. Tell them no. Not for so much as a wave. If Bob Dole wants* me *to speak, I will.*

He had displeased them—without meaning to. He wanted to apologize but didn't have the words.

"You want to watch?" asks the woman in the uniform, the woman who is in this room with him now. She points to the box.

To be polite, he says yes. The colors, once they're switched on, produce pictures that move.

"Oh, right in time!" the woman in the uniform exclaims. "Look who it is! Talking to the delegates! Look how pretty!"

People are cheering for the woman inside the box. It is *her*, the woman who sleeps next to him at night and winds his watch in the mornings. He looks at the timepiece often because her attention to it means it's important.

He remembers a big room with a desk, not this room but one with curved walls where he used to work, a room with a great green lawn beyond the window. It was down at the end of the big house where he believes they both, he and she, may have lived.

He looks at the box. It's showing a man and woman he recognizes as Jerry and Betty, but he can't remember a thing about them besides their names. They, too, are listening to the woman who sleeps beside him. She is talking to a crowd inside a great hall:

Thank you for the life you gave us. A life that we never thought we'd have. It was interesting. It was challenging. It was fascinating. It was sometimes frightening. There were times that the sun forgot to shine, but those days have dimmed in comparison to the accomplishments that now glow brightly . . .

The woman who is really in the room, the woman who speaks with an accent, is getting ready to leave. He can sometimes still understand things, figure matters out, and he believes that she feels he should have privacy while he watches *her*, the woman on the *screen*, a word that has just come back to him.

"Good night, Mr. President."

He recognizes this as a second name for himself but doesn't know what it signifies.

And now he is alone.

We've learned, as too many other families have learned, of the terrible pain and loneliness that must be endured as each day brings another reminder of this very long goodbye.

His mind moves abruptly from one thing to another; he is aware that he doesn't think the same way as the other people who come in and out of this room. For a moment he isn't hearing the box at all, but his attention comes alive once more when she, the woman whose red dress it was, begins to talk of a shining city on a hill.

He believes that she has made a mistake. If he looks out the window here, he can see the lights of a city, some of them just coming on, but it is not on a hill; it is stretched out below. Sometimes when he looks down into it, at this hour of the day, he imagines a particular white house in its midst, not the large one where he thinks he and the woman lived, but a different white house, much smaller and made of wood, which he remembers being in a cold place up above the sea.

He has already lost the name for cranberry juice—the words always come and go so fast—but he finally picks up the glass that was placed beside him. He sips from it carefully, but when he puts it down a small red stain spreads over the napkin underneath it. The shape and color of the stain make him remember the head of a man whose name he has forgotten. This is an urgent memory, one that makes him see the small white house, inside of which he and the man once sat together. He knows the memory will not last, but it stays long enough for him to hear his own voice. *Ten years from now I'll be a very old man . . .*

Is he an old man? He does not know. For a few seconds he sees himself wearing an old coat and can even feel a fur collar around his neck, but a moment later these things are gone, along with the small white house and the man who'd been inside it with him.

Soon the fellow who gets him ready for bed will be here. He'll turn off the box, its moving pictures, its sounds. Right now they are cheering for her, the way he believes they once cheered for him. Is that Mermie standing there beside her—waving? He isn't sure, but he blows her a kiss; and when she's no longer visible he gets up from the chair he is in to see if he can find her picture among all the ones in silver frames.

By the time he reaches the long table he has forgotten her name, forgotten what he was looking for. But he begins to touch and examine some of the pictures and souvenirs, all of them laid out so carefully, everything recently dusted. There are medals and ribbons and small statues—and his lifeguard's whistle, all shined up! He knows that these things are beautiful, clever. They have been brought to him as gifts, and he has sensed the happiness in the givers. Picture after picture, object after object, all of them infused with good feeling, except for the one thing just past the end of the table, the one object that always displeases and perplexes him: a jagged block of concrete, ripped from something immense, smeared with paint and pocked by hammers, bearing the numbers 1961–1989 and placed on a wooden stand all its own. Whatever it may be, this object, too, has been brought here to make him happy, but it is something cruel, different from everything else in the room, and often, when he stands before it, he feels an impulse to knock it down.

ACKNOWLEDGMENTS

My editor, Dan Frank, has lent this project the same insightful support and enthusiasm he has given to eight other books we've worked on over more than two decades. My gratitude to him really can't be measured. Thanks, too, to my agent, the matchless Andrew Wylie, and his associate Kristina Moore.

I couldn't have done without Ed Cohen, Altie Karper, Thomas Giannettino, and Betsy Sallee during editing and production.

In Washington, Jeffrey M. Flannery and Dr. James Hutson of the Library of Congress assisted me in using the papers of Pamela Harriman and Donald T. Regan.

Dr. Steven H. Hochman of the Carter Center in Atlanta provided me with useful information about former president Carter's travel and activities in 1986, and Lisa Nickerson Bucklin of Father Martin's Ashley, the drug-addiction treatment center, cleared up a vexing point.

At the Reagan Library in Simi Valley, California, I was helped by archivists Kelly D. Barton and Steve Branch, and by docent Bob Dirks. Thanks to the Reagan Foundation's Barbara Garonzik and to Genevieve McSweeney Ryan, my friend for the thirty-five years since she was my student. I've more than once, while writing this book, recalled a conversation I had with Genny on the steps of the Vassar College library in 1980, during which I asked her what she intended to do that summer. She told me she would be working for Ronald Reagan's presidential campaign, and with my unerring talent for prognostication, I told her that he was too old to get elected.

I appreciate the cooperation I received from Daniel Katz and Paul Cunningham at the U.S. embassy in Reykjavik—and am grateful to Jillian Bonnardeaux for helping me establish contact with them. Special thanks to Anna Kristinsdóttir, chief of protocol in the Reykjavik mayor's office, for the room-by-room tour of Hofdi House. Thorir "Toti" Ingvarsson also shared memories of the '86 summit.

My visit to the Annenberg Retreat at Sunnylands, in Rancho Mirage, California, was set in motion by Michael Singer, and made fruitful by Frank Lopez and Daniel Modlin, the excellent archivists there.

Christina Bellantoni and Jim Corbley of WETA in Washington made it possible for me to view a tape of the Gershwin performance held at the White House and described, with some liberties, in chapter 19. This is perhaps as good a place as any to repeat what I said in a note to a previous novel: "I have operated along the always sliding scale of historical fiction. The text contains deviations from fact that some readers will regard as unpardonable and others will deem unworthy of notice. But this remains a work of fiction, not history."

Jim Lehrer and Frank Sesno shared with me their memories of covering Ronald Reagan during his presidency. I've also benefited from conversation with Evan Thomas and a sharp-eyed reading of the manuscript by Dr. James Graham Wilson at the U.S. Department of State. The friendship of Tom Duesterberg and Susan Cooper and, above all, John McConnell has aided this book at many different turns.

I'm very grateful for the support of Peg Barratt during her time as dean of the George Washington University's Columbian College of Arts and Sciences. Also at GW, Faye Moskowitz is a constant source of wisdom and friendship.

Dozens of histories, biographies, memoirs, and diaries played a part in my research. I'm especially indebted to Sally Bedell Smith's life of Pamela Harriman, *Reflected Glory* (1996), and to *Hitch-22* (2010), the memoirs of my beloved friend Christopher Hitchens. As the months and years of writing this book went by, the idea of fictionalizing Hitch felt less strange than consoling. If he was wrong about the afterlife, and can see this, I beg his forgiveness.

Nothing in my own life would be possible without Bill Bodenschatz, whom I met six days after Ronald Reagan finished his presidency.

Washington, D.C.
April 3, 2015

Thomas Mallon is the author of nine novels, including *Henry and Clara*, *Dewey Defeats Truman*, *Fellow Travelers*, and *Watergate*. He is a frequent contributor to *The New Yorker*, *The New York Times Book Review*, and *The Atlantic*, and he was the recipient of the American Academy of Arts and Letters' Vursell prize for prose style. He has been the literary editor of *GQ* and the deputy chairman of the National Endowment for the Humanities. He lives in Washington, D.C., and teaches at the George Washington University.

A NOTE ON THE TYPE

This book was set in Janson, a typeface long thought to have been made by the Dutchman Anton Janson. However, it has been conclusively demonstrated that these types are actually the work of Nicholas Kis (1650–1702), a Hungarian, who most probably learned his trade from the master Dutch typefounder Dirk Voskens.

Composed by North Market Street Graphics, Lancaster, Pennsylvania

Printed and bound by Berryville Graphics, Berryville, Virginia

Designed by M. Kristen Bearse